GOLD OF OUR FATHERS

Also by the author

The Inspector Darko Dawson Mysteries
Wife of the Gods
Children of the Street
Murder at Cape Three Points

Death At The Voyager Hotel
Kamila

GOLD OF OUR FATHERS

Kwei Quartey

Published by
Soho Press, Inc.
853 Broadway
New York, NY 10003

Library of Congress Cataloging-in-Publication Data

Quartey, Kwei.
Gold of our fathers / Kwei Quartey.

ISBN 978-1-61695-630-1
eISBN 978-1-61695-631-8
I. Title.
PS3617.U37G65 2016
813'.6—dc23   2015028758

Map of Ghana: © Rainer Lesniewski/Shutterstock

GOLD OF OUR FATHERS

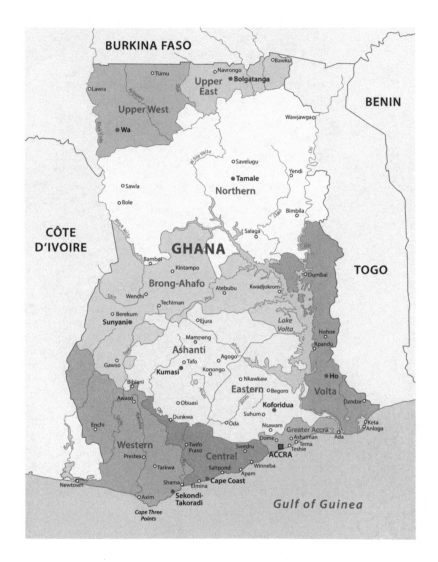

GHANA

CAST OF CHARACTERS

Adwoa: female resident of Dunkwa.

Armah, Daniel: retired policeman, Darko Dawson's mentor.

Asase: officer assisting Darko Dawson.

Bediako, Frank: commander, Ghana Armed Forces Northern Command, Kumasi.

Brave: one of the workers at the Aniamoa dredging site.

Chikata, Philip: inspector, Darko Dawson's junior partner at CID Accra Central Headquarters.

Dawson, Christine: Darko Dawson's wife.

Dawson, Darko: detective chief inspector, Criminal Investigations Department in Accra, Ghana.

Dzamesi, Prosper: director-general, Criminal Investigations Department.

Dzigbodi, Gbedema, Kwame, and Kweku: Kudzo Gablah's fellow mine workers.

Ekaw: Kudzo Gablah's friend.

Gablah, Kudzo: alluvial mine worker who discovered the dead body.

Gifty: Christine Dawson's mother; Darko Dawson's mother-in-law.

Granger, Chuck: American owner of gold mines next to the Lieu site.

Helmsley, Akua: environmental reporter for *The Guardian* (UK).

Huang, Leonard: Chinese miner/merchant frequently acting as interpreter for Darko Dawson.

Kobby: a constable in Dunkwa.

Kwapong, Phyllis, MD: forensic pathologist.

Lartey, Theophilus: assistant commissioner of police (ACP); Inspector Chikata's uncle.

Liu, Bao: Chinese illegal alluvial miner and murder victim.

Liu, Lian: Bao's wife.

Liu, Wei: Bao's younger brother.

Manu, Deborah: deputy commissioner of police, regional commander, Ghana Police Service, Ashanti Region.

Nkrumah: pathology technician.

Obeng, Augustus: detective sergeant; Darko Dawson's junior partner at Obuasi Divisional Headquarters.

Okoh, Amos: brother of Yaw Okoh.

Okoh, Yaw: worker in a local mine, murder suspect.

Longdon, Ata: assistant commissioner of police, commander, Obuasi Divisional Headquarters.

Queenie: flirtatious Dunkwa resident, a.k.a. Smoothie.

Sackie: inspector, Dunkwa Police Station supervisor.

Samuels, Joshua: freelance photographer for Akua Helmsley.

Tanbry, Beko: American gold investor.

Thompson, Tommy: director of Precious Minerals Marketing Company (PMMC).

AUTHOR NOTES

• Police jurisdictions: For purposes of the story, the police station at Dunkwa is depicted as being under Kumasi Regional Headquarters in the Ashanti Region. In fact, Dunkwa is in the Central Region on its border with the Ashanti Region. Therefore, its head office is actually at Cape Coast Regional Headquarters.

• Opposite to Europe and the USA, June to August is the coolest season in Ghana due to rainfall during those months.

• Ghanaian languages such as Ga, Twi, Ewe, and Fante are distinct, not "dialects" of each other.

PROLOGUE

DARK GRAVEL, THE GRAY-AND-BLACK color of an aging man's beard, renders the most gold. One has to dig beyond the water table to reach the coveted ore. As far as Kudzo Gablah's eye could see, machine-excavated pits and craters disfigured the once lush landscape. Mounds of tawny soil surrounded each scooped-out depression, as if a giant hand had reached inside the earth and turned it inside out.

Short-handled shovel in hand, Kudzo stood in the middle of one of the craters, his old ill-fitting Wellington boots sinking into the soft earth. At the top of the pit, which was more than twice Kudzo's height of five-eleven, his four fellow *galamsey* workers joked and jostled with each other, and even though he had yelled at them that they might as well begin work while waiting for the boss to arrive, they were slow to start. At only twenty-four years old, Kudzo was the most experienced and the most senior mine worker, the others barely out of their teens.

He planted his first stab deep into the gravel, enjoying the crisp sound of earth giving way to the sharp blade. He and the other guys would be digging all day. It would be especially grueling without the aid of the hydraulic excavator, which had broken down two days ago. Their Chinese boss, Bao Liu, had said he would come in early this morning to attempt a repair of the vehicle, but he was nowhere to be seen. It was almost 6:30 now, and that was odd because when Mr. Liu said he was going to arrive early, he meant *early*. Perhaps he or his wife had fallen ill.

Kudzo looked up to see Wei Liu carefully making his way toward them over a narrow muddy crest at the top of one of the pits. About thirty-five, he was Bao's younger brother, but the two were as unlike as a yam tuber and a thin stalk of sugar cane. Wei was stout, while his older brother was hard and wiry. Bao yelled a lot and insulted people, whereas Wei was quiet and sullen. They knew some English and a little bit of Twi. Between those two languages, they managed to communicate with the Ghanaian workers. Sometimes Kudzo and his friends made fun of the Chinese brothers' accents and mimicked the sound of Chinese as they perceived it. Kudzo didn't like Wei, much less his older brother.

"Where Bao?" Wei asked Kudzo abruptly, without even a "good morning."

"Please, I don't know," Kudzo said, thinking, *Shouldn't you know better than me where your brother is?* "Maybe he went somewhere." More specifically, Kudzo was thinking Bao might have gone into the bush to relieve himself, the way everyone did around the mines. "Didn't he call you?"

"Yeah," Wei said. "Four twenty this morning."

Looking worried, Wei left to examine the excavator. Something was jammed in the hydraulic arm attached to the bucket—the huge, clawed scooper shaped like a cupped hand. As far as Kudzo knew, Bao and Wei were supposed to have tried to repair it early this morning, and Bao's truck was parked in the usual spot.

Kudzo's companions picked up their shovels and slid down into the pit beside him. Before long, they would be smeared with mud as they worked. The warmth of the morning hinted at the heat that would begin to peak before noon. As fit as the young workers were, they still found the ten working hours physically and mentally punishing. Not everyone could do it. Dropping out after a few weeks was common, especially for city boys. Unable to handle the pace and intensity, they often packed up and left. Sprains and injuries happened all the time, and two drowning incidents had occurred during the last rainy season. All this pain and exertion for what? Sometimes only a few specks of gold after all the ore had been washed at the end of the day. But every once in a while, a dazzling amount of the glittering yellow metal was found, and then it all seemed worth it again.

The boys coordinated smoothly with each other. Kudzo shoveled soft, clayey gravel rapidly into a wide shallow pan, which Gbedema snatched from between his feet and lifted onto Dzigbodi's head. On his way to the sluice box where Kweku washed the gravel, Dzigbodi would pass Kwame going in the opposite direction to pick up his new load from Kudzo. Throughout the day, they would rotate positions. It was like a dance.

At intervals, they chattered noisily with one another to break the grinding monotony, sometimes making crude jokes at each other's expense, and at other times shouting encouragement when one of them flagged. They depended on each other to keep going. Occasionally an argument might break out, but it was seldom more than fleeting.

Kudzo glanced up to see Wei on his phone again—not talking, just calling, but then he put it away when apparently no one answered. He was probably trying to get hold of his brother again. *Where was Bao?*

At the top of the pit on the side where they were working, the earth was a light brown with an orange tinge, in contrast to the gray-and-black beneath it—as if someone had recently dumped soil taken from a different area. Kudzo was sure it had not been that way the day before, and he remarked on it to his friends. They concurred with him but there was no time to give it that much thought, and they soon forgot about Kudzo's observation.

He might have put the light-colored soil out of his mind had some of it not caved in as the darker gravel was dug away from underneath. Kudzo didn't want this kind of earth because it was usually poor in gold, so he began pushing it aside with his shovel. The blade struck something dull, relatively soft and immovable. He hit it a couple more times to dislodge it, but it didn't budge.

Now Kudzo saw a dark spot in the light soil. Frowning, he cleared some of the earth away.

"What are you doing?" Kwame shouted in Twi, annoyed at Kudzo's break in the rhythm.

"Something is here," Kudzo returned. "I don't know what it is."

Kwame joined his partner to help clear away the soil from around the object. The other two boys, curious, came over to watch. Kudzo felt a shiver travel down his back. Something about the object made him uneasy.

Wei, who was on his phone again and had seen them cease work, walked quickly in their direction. "Hey!" he yelled. "What you doing?"

Dzigbodi pointed at what Kudzo and Kwame were unearthing. Wei jumped down into the pit to get a closer look. "Dig more," he instructed them, as if he were contributing anything new to what they were already doing.

As they saw what it was, Kudzo gave an exclamation of shock. Kwame tried to stand up, but slipped in the mud instead. It was clear now. The object was a human head. Wei grabbed a shovel and began to help scoop the soil away. As the eyes and nose came into view, he let out a cry. Kwame scrabbled out of the pit in fear, but Kudzo wrenched himself out of his paralysis and used his shovel to help Wei pull earth away from the head. Now one shoulder was visible. Wei was weeping and babbling hysterically in Chinese. Kudzo already knew the truth, but it had a dreamlike quality. The dead man buried deep in gold ore was Bao Liu, Wei's brother.

ACCRA
JULY

CHAPTER ONE

"Now that you're chief inspector," Christine said to Dawson, "does that mean they won't send you to different parts of the country as often as they used to?"

On a late Saturday afternoon at the Mmofra Park, Darko Dawson and his wife, Christine, were sitting in the shade of a neem tree watching their sons, Sly and Hosiah, playing with a group of kids.

Dawson grunted. "Not necessarily. One of our deputy commissioners, which is a very high rank, got moved up all the way up to Bolgatanga."

Bolgatanga was a town in the very north of Ghana, some 460 miles away from Accra.

"I hope that happens to Theophilus Lartey," Christine commented dryly.

Dawson laughed at her entrenched dislike of the man who had been Dawson's boss for several years. She considered Lartey a domineering bully, particularly when it came to sending Dawson off to other parts of the country far from Accra, which was home to the family. For his part, Dawson had always resisted leaving his wife and sons behind for extended periods, only to go down in defeat after a stern warning from Lartey about insubordination and a threat of being fired.

During the last round of promotions two months ago, Lartey had been elevated from chief superintendent to assistant commissioner of police. Dawson had been promoted from detective inspector to chief inspector at the Criminal Investigations Department (CID) in Accra, Ghana. Dawson had mixed feelings about his imminent separation from Lartey. In the first place, although the man could be cantankerous, Dawson was accustomed to him, and he could always depend on Lartey to stand behind his junior officers—barring any malfeasance, of course. As grumpy as he could be, he was scrupulously honest. Dawson's assistant on all his criminal cases, Detective Sergeant—now Inspector— Philip Chikata, also happened to be Lartey's adored nephew. In the early days, that had worked against Dawson, but he had now mastered how to get what he wanted from Lartey through Chikata, and it had proved to be a powerful tool.

Dawson stole a glance at his wife, pretty in form-fitting jeans and a sleeveless Ghanaian print top. Her hair, cinnamon-colored and elaborately braided in the latest style, was gathered behind her neck in a loose bundle. She was never poorly turned out, and Dawson took a secret delight in showing her off.

He felt relaxed with her in this park, *Mmofra,* meaning "children" in Fante, which provided a safe space for children's play and out-of-classroom learning with exposure to Ghanaian culture in a natural setting. A portion of the grounds was dotted with drought-resistant shrubs and *cassava* plants, but the rest was uncultivated and waiting for landscaping when funds came in.

Hosiah and Sly were engaged in a game of treasure hunt. The two competing teams, with the help of an adult chaperone, had to consult their table of Adinkra symbols to figure out each clue and how to proceed to the next station. Dawson, no stranger to clues himself, liked the idea of that game with its Ghanaian twist.

Not all the kids were participating in the game. Sitting in chairs carved from tree trunks, one group was poring over children's books, and yet another was on the swings, watched over by a volunteer. A boy and a girl of about seven were playing the traditional board game of *oware* carved into a recycled log and mounted on a wooden pedestal.

Christine had volunteered herself a few times here after she had discovered the place. Before she'd known about it, she had lamented the lack of a functional playground in Accra. This was one of them, along with the new eco-park at the edge of the city.

Hosiah and Sly came running up, treasure hunt over and the team of the older brother, ten-year-old Sly, triumphant. Hosiah was slightly crestfallen.

"It's okay," Dawson said, pulling him close and hugging him. "Next time you'll beat them."

Hosiah was sweating and Dawson wiped his forehead with a washcloth he had handy. At age eight, Hosiah looked just like his father, with a large contribution from Christine to his deep, expressive eyes. But the incandescent smile that could light up a room and melt even a murderer's heart was all Hosiah's own. Skinny and loose-limbed, Hosiah had had a growth spurt over the last twelve months after cardiac surgery to correct a congenital defect. Sly's physique contrasted with that of his younger brother's. He was already showing the beginnings of teenage muscularity, as is common in boys who have lived on the streets, as Sly had done. Adopted at age eight by Dawson and Christine, it was clear he was not related by birth. Hailing from Northern Ghana, his face was more angular than anyone's in Dawson's family, wide cheekbones tapering sharply to his chin, and his lips were thinner.

He affectionately put his arm around his younger brother's shoulders. "Come on, let's go to the swings. I'll push you."

They ran off together as their parents looked on fondly. Dawson loved to see them together, and he was happy with the way things were going, especially for Hosiah. Because he could now fully participate in sports, he had a lot more friends both in school and out, and he was more outgoing than before. A year ago, before the cardiac surgery that saved him, his condition had worsened, and he had become short of breath with even the slightest exertion. Thank God for the surgeons at Korle Bu, the largest tertiary hospital in the country, who performed Hosiah's expensive surgery on a largely charitable basis.

Sly too was doing well. Many of his rough edges had smoothed out. Fights at school were a problem in the beginning, but his adoptive parents had worked patiently with him to curb his feral instincts. But Sly's fierce protection of his younger brother had been unwavering: anyone attempting to bully Hosiah paid dearly.

So, much contributed to Dawson's feeling of contentment: the lifting of the worries over his beloved boy, his promotion and subsequent uptick—very slight, but better than nothing—in his salary, and Christine's recent promotion to an assistant headmistress at her school.

He glanced at his phone. "Shall we go?" he asked Christine.

She nodded. "I think so."

Dawson walked over to the swings and joined Sly and Hosiah for a few minutes before calling time. Then it was back to the car with Hosiah riding atop his dad's shoulders. Dawson felt remarkably happy, but he should have known that nothing good lasts long. Or more accurately, he did know. He had simply forgotten.

CHAPTER TWO

MONDAY MORNING DAWSON MADE his way to work on his Honda motorcycle. It was the fastest way to deal with Accra's choked traffic. It was also dangerous. Survival on a motorcycle required a certain level of aggression and without question, catlike reflexes. At Kwame Nkrumah Circle, the new overpass was open, but for all its complexity, Dawson wasn't sure whether it helped or worsened the chaos.

Oh, Ghana, he thought, shaking his head. *Why can we never get it right the first time?* With his surgical mask on to filter out some of the vehicle exhaust fumes, Dawson wound through cars and *tro-tros* like a snake evading capture. In Accra's traffic tangle, the margins for vehicles and pedestrians alike were razor thin.

The congestion cleared somewhat once Dawson got onto Ring Road Central, and there was only one more logjam to tackle at the Ako Adjei Interchange before he got to the Criminal Investigations Department Central Headquarters on Ring Road East. Civilian vehicles were no longer allowed in what used to be parking spaces around the building, and even official police vehicles entering were checked underneath with long-handled inspection mirrors. Terrorism wasn't an improbability for Ghana anymore. Often, it engulfed parts of Nigeria only two countries away to the east. One could not be too careful.

Other things had changed too. In the previously empty space

between CID and the Ghana Police Headquarters, a separate
entity, the public relations building, had been completed. The
new structure would have press conference and media rooms with
Wi-Fi for reporters to file their stories in a comfortable atmosphere. Evidently the Ghana Police Service (GPS) had decided
it was better to win friends and influence people than to make
enemies. The seven-story CID building, which had been around
for decades, was itself undergoing piecemeal improvements as
well. It had a new sun-yellow coat of paint.

Dawson parked the Honda outside the rear wall of the CID
premises and walked around to the front entrance, where the sentry, a sergeant, saluted him and deferentially waved him through.

Dawson went up the narrow stairway to the fourth floor detectives' room. Apart from the four large tables and a bunch of
scattered chairs, the room was quite bare, with no adornments on
the beige walls. This time of the year was the coolest, and a light,
refreshing breeze came through the now modern tinted sliding
panes that had finally replaced the old-fashioned louvers.

This room was always noisy—a microcosm of Accra itself.
Officers of every rank from lance corporal up to chief inspector,
Dawson's new title, sat writing reports or stood around perched
against the tables talking, arguing, and laughing. *Don't people have
anything to do?* Dawson wondered. He caught a snatch of a debate
among four officers on the veracity of a bizarre news item about a
woman accused of bestiality, and a more reasoned but just as vocif-
erous discussion around the economic mess Ghana suddenly found
itself in. In spite of offshore oil now flowing, the cost of living had
shot up. That meant everything: fuel, transportation, food, and
lodging. Like so many other Ghanaians, Dawson and Christine
had been experiencing the economic pinch with a sinking feeling
that Ghana was sliding backward.

In the midst of the racket in the room, two male officers were
interviewing a handcuffed male suspect while other officers stood
around watching. CID didn't have private interrogation rooms.
One used whatever space one could find.

Dawson's junior partner in the Homicide Division of the Crime Unit, Inspector Philip Chikata, was in the middle of another heated discussion with a fellow officer over which soccer team was most likely to win the next Africa Cup.

"Morning, boss," Chikata said, as Dawson pulled up a chair and sat opposite him.

"Morning, Philip."

Dawson shook hands and snapped fingers with Chikata's companion, a corporal who was back from spending two weeks on duty in the mayhem of the charge office on the ground floor.

"How are you?" Dawson greeted him in Twi. "How was charge?"

"Fine, sir," the corporal said. "But I'm glad to be back."

"What do you think?" Chikata asked Dawson. "Ghana will beat Egypt in the next round, *anaa* am I lying?"

Dawson shook his head. "You know I don't talk sports or politics at work."

"Please, excuse me, sir," the corporal said, standing up. "I have court this morning."

"Later," Dawson said to him, turning back to Chikata to ask him about a cold homicide case they were working on. *Cold as the corpse itself.* No new leads had materialized over the weekend with Chikata's investigations.

"What should we do next?" he asked Dawson.

"Let's wait for the DNA report."

Chikata sucked his teeth. "This DNA lab. So slow. It's been four weeks now."

"It's not so much the slowness," Dawson said. "It's the backlog."

Chikata conceded the point. Ridiculously handsome and powerfully built, he was sporting a neat regulation mustache these days.

Dawson turned his head toward a loud bang, unmistakably the impact of flesh on flesh. The handcuffed suspect, who could not have been more than twenty-three or so, was reeling from an open-handed slap delivered to his right cheek by a detective sergeant. "Please, I beg you, no—"

"No, what?" The sergeant hit him again. "How do you think your victim felt when you were assaulting him, eh?"

"What's going on over there?" Dawson asked Chikata

"Armed robber," he answered. "They caught him red-handed attacking an elderly man."

The kid was crying and some of the officers began to laugh and derisively call him *kwasea*, a word for "idiot." Yet another officer whacked him on the back of the head, making the boy shriek and attempt to get away.

"Where are you going?" the sergeant asked, pushing him back into the chair. He raised his palm up again, and the suspect cowered and began pleading again.

Dawson glanced around and saw that for the moment, no one in the room was senior to him in rank. "Jess," he said, quietly.

"Yes, sir," the sergeant said, turning.

Dawson transmitted the message with his eyes. *It's enough.* "Have you completed the paperwork on the suspect?"

"Almost, sir."

"Okay, then proceed."

The sergeant took his seat and the other officers dispersed. It would have been poor form to chastise an officer in front of a prisoner, but Dawson hadn't wanted the beatings to continue. Vigilante justice was common in Ghana, *But as police officers, let's be at least a little above it,* he thought. There was one hopeful sign these days: compared to fifteen years ago when Dawson had joined the force, the quality of new police recruits had improved, with many of them holding bachelor's degrees. Perhaps their approach would be more intellectual and less physical.

"Chief Superintendent Oppong is in, by the way," Chikata said, referring to the man who had taken over from Theo Lartey. Dawson detected an over-casual inflection in the inspector's tone. He was going to miss the uncle who had always been like a father to him, but he was being brave about it.

It was perhaps this separation from Lartey that was prompting Chikata to stray in other directions, which concerned Dawson a good deal because he did not want to lose his partner. Chikata had developed an interest in the Panthers Unit, an elite strike force based at CID Central Headquarters. Trained in the use of firearms and tactical maneuvers, the Panthers' officers were the very best: fit, fast, and fierce. Chikata was all that, and that's why Dawson feared he would one day be snatched away.

"You've met the chief super?" Dawson asked.

"Yes," Chikata said, without much enthusiasm. "This morning. He told me to ask you to go up to his office when you get in."

"I will," Dawson said. "What is he like?"

Chikata shrugged. "He's okay."

Dawson smiled slightly at the tepid endorsement. "All right," he said, standing. "I'll go now."

He went one flight up to the chief superintendent's office. He couldn't count the number of times over the years that he had made this trek to face Theophilus Lartey, almost invariably a firing squad experience. It felt strange to be going to someone new. The brass nameplate on the solid door now read CHIEF SUPERINTEN-DENT JOSEPH OPPONG. Dawson knocked and heard the faint "come in" from the other side. As he entered, Dawson immediately took account of the scrupulous tidiness of Oppong's desk, a transforma-tion from Lartey's chaos. The man in the leather executive chair was different too. He was tall and bone thin, whereas Lartey had been diminutive.

Oppong looked up over a pair of half spectacles. He was prob-ably in his midfifties, but his hair was a premature and shocking white. He wore an impeccable dark suit and tie.

In a condensed form of a salute for non-uniformed officers, Dawson put his hands at his side and braced.

"Good morning, Dawson," Oppong said neutrally. He gestured at the chair on the other side of the desk. "Have a seat."

Dawson sat. He didn't know Oppong at all, since the chief superintendent had been stationed outside Accra at different divisional headquarters of the GPS for at least a decade. Dawson's first impression was that he was methodical and quiet—another contrast to Lartey. Anticipating a lecture about what was expected of him, Dawson waited while the chief super flipped the pages of a large notebook in front of him.

"I've just been reading through the hand-over notes from my predecessor, now Assistant Commissioner Lartey," Oppong said, looking over his glasses again. "I have reviewed your file. You've shown good work—apart from some growing pains in the beginning."

That comment, delivered in a voice that sounded to Dawson like a 60-hertz electrical hum, could have been a wry joke, but Oppong cracked not even to trace of a smile. He was referring, no doubt, to Dawson's anger management difficulties years ago—an explosive temper that had slowly settled down since.

Oppong was studying a sheet of paper headed with the GPS insignia. "Were you made aware of your impending transfer to Obuasi?"

Dawson's eyebrows shot up. "Transfer to Obuasi, sir? What transfer?"

Oppong read from the document. "Following the untimely death of Chief Inspector Pascal Addae, supervising crime officer at Obuasi Divisional Headquarters, his post is to be filled for a period of at least one year by Chief Inspector Darko Dawson of CID Headquarters, Accra."

One *year?* Dawson fell back in his chair, dumbfounded. Oppong looked up at him. "Evidently this comes to you as a surprise."

"No one told me," Dawson said, hearing his voice sharpen. "Was this a decision by ACP Lartey?"

"I don't know whose decision it was," Oppong said kindly. "All I know is that the notification is signed by him. Since he is my senior officer, it is my duty to implement it, not to question it."

Dawson was furious. This was a dirty trick by Lartey—a parting shot, a last laugh even as he left his post. He *knew* all about Dawson's family, the trials of Hosiah's surgery and nursing him back to emotional and physical health, and yet he had still done this.

"Dawson?"

He startled back to the moment. "Yes, sir."

"You need to get to Obuasi as quickly as possible," Oppong said. "Seeing as how you are taken by surprise by this development, I will give you a grace period of two weeks, so that you can get your affairs together. Are you planning to move with your family?"

Dawson's impressions of the chief superintendent changed. Seemingly aloof at first, Oppong appeared to have the heart that Lartey did not.

"I'm not sure, sir," Dawson said despondently. "I don't know. What happened to Chief Inspector Addae?"

"I think it was some kind of stroke," Oppong said.

Dawson felt guilty that he wasn't feeling as much sympathy as he should have. "Who will take my place here at headquarters?"

"Chikata will report directly to me on any cases."

Dawson nodded. At least that would be good. Chikata could gain added experience and prestige that way.

"Well," Oppong said, folding his long fingers in front of him. "That's all for now."

"Thank you, sir."

Dawson didn't remember getting up and leaving the room. He was in a daze.

CHAPTER THREE

THE QUIET MYOHAUNG STREET at the rear of the CID premises, named after a place in Myanmar in recognition of Ghana's contribution to the WWII defeat of the Japanese in Burma, was often Dawson's place to think and brood. He thrust his hands in his pockets and walked in the shade of the trees that lined the street, passing embassy residences and expensive gated communities.

So much to think about. He tried to clear his head and work through it methodically. *Obuasi.* About 160 miles away in the southern part of the Ashanti Region, it was one of the major gold-mining towns in Ghana and home to the huge multinational AngloGold Ashanti. Dawson thought the population might be around a couple hundred thousand people. It and other areas in the region had been in the news of late because of illegal gold mining by not just hundreds, but *thousands* of Chinese who had flooded into Ghana from a certain region of China—Dawson couldn't remember the name at the moment—and succeeded in laying waste large tracts of fertile land as they dug feverishly for alluvial gold.

Dawson couldn't possibly be away from Christine, Sly, and Hosiah for that long, could he? No, they would have to come with him to Obuasi. But that meant finding the boys new schools and Christine a new job. He winced at that. Christine had *just* been promoted to assistant headmistress. How could she be so prematurely uprooted now from a post that was providing her experience and prestige, and bringing in a little more income? Maybe the family *should* stay in Accra and Dawson could visit from Obuasi as often as possible? But he knew what that meant in reality. When a case becomes very busy, there is barely time to get away. He would be missing his family for intolerable weeks on end.

A new worry struck him. Over the last year, Hosiah had gained social confidence and overcome the physical and emotional consequences of his long illness. With new activities in which he could take part, he was enjoying life to the fullest. In particular, he had become best friends with one boy in his class called Seth. Sometimes it seemed that Seth was at the Dawsons' home more than his own. Wrenching Hosiah away was going to be tough on both boys.

Sly was more adaptable to change than his younger brother because of his past street life. Dawson wasn't worried about him, and in fact, Sly would be of great moral support for Hosiah.

In the evening after the children had gone to sleep, Dawson would talk it over with Christine. He turned back toward CID, his stomach churning with anxiety.

AS SOON AS Dawson walked back into the office, Chikata saw that something was wrong. The two men had known each other long enough to intuitively sense each other's moods.

"What happened, boss?" Chikata asked him. "Chief super gave you a tough time?"

Dawson slumped into a chair beside Chikata. "Your uncle has posted me to Obuasi. For one year."

Chikata's jaw went slack. "*What?*"

Dawson despondently rested his forehead against his fist. "Oppong just told me. The transfer is in your uncle's hand-over notes."

Chikata shook his head. "I don't believe it." He picked up his phone from the table. "I will call him right now."

Dawson put a gentle restraining hand on Chikata's. "No, don't do it. There's no point."

"How no point, boss?"

"Forget it, Chikata."

"I'm sure this isn't my uncle's doing," he insisted. "I should call him to reverse the decision."

Dawson hesitated, torn. He didn't like to use his junior officer as a tool, but it was tempting. If he *could* get the decision reversed . . .

"Okay," he said finally.

Chikata made the call, and left a message when his uncle didn't pick up. There wasn't any point dwelling on the matter further, so the two men moved on to other things. After discussing both the cold cases and others, Chikata left for training with the Panthers Unit, and Dawson was alone for the rest of the morning.

JUST BEFORE LUNCH, Dawson's phone rang. It was from ACP Lartey, who got straight to the point.

"The decision came down just yesterday," he told Dawson. "I did not have time to call you this morning. No, it was not me who thought up the plan of sending you to Obuasi. It came from higher up than me. Sorry, Dawson, but that's how it is. Unfortunately, when you are as good at your work as you are, you come to people's minds very quickly."

Half praise, half blame, Dawson thought ironically, like honey sprinkled with quinine.

"The Obuasi office needs you, Dawson," Lartey added. "Don't let them down."

And as he always did, Lartey ended the call quickly and abruptly, leaving Dawson feeling not much better.

AT THE END of the day, Dawson wanted badly to talk to Christine about the situation confronting him, yet he was dreading it at the same time. How would she react? In the past, his postings to different parts of the country had not sat well with her.

Darko fought evening peak traffic for an hour before finally reaching his neighborhood of Kaneshie. He pulled into the small yard of their once cream-colored bungalow with olive trim. It needed a fresh coat of paint. Inside, Christine was helping the boys with homework, which they interrupted to give Dawson an animated account of all that had happened in school that day. Dawson had to keep track of all the characters—good and bad—in their school. He pushed aside the events of his own day to pay close attention to theirs, giving no indication that anything was amiss. Hosiah in particular was apt to pick up negative signals.

It was later on when the boys were in bed and Christine and Darko were cleaning up in the kitchen—she washing the dishes and he sweeping up the floor—that he broached the subject. He leaned the broom against the counter.

"Christine," he said. "Something has come up at work."

She looked up, searched his face for a moment, and then shook the excess water off her hands. "I can almost predict. They want to transfer you, right?"

He nodded, glad in a way that she had guessed correctly.

"I knew I shouldn't have asked you anything about transfers on Saturday when we were at the park," she said regretfully, wiping her hands on a towel. "I put *juju* on us."

She sat at the table, as though she thought it best to be sitting down as he delivered the brunt of the bad news. "Where is it this time?"

"Obuasi."

"Oh," she said, cocking her head. "Well, I guess it could be worse. You could be going to Bolgatanga."

"It's not the distance," Dawson said moodily. "It's the duration."

"How do you mean?"

"I could be there for up to a year."

She pulled back as if someone had tried to jab her in the face. "A *year!*"

Dawson winced. "Yes," he said, not meeting her eyes. The timer was ticking down to the explosion.

"So you're going to be away for a year," she said flatly.

"Well . . . basically, yes."

"A year is a long time."

"Yes, it is. I was thinking . . . what do you think of the idea that all of us move to Obuasi—or Kumasi?"

She opened her mouth to say something, then shut it as she began to consider that as an option. Dawson felt encouraged that she hadn't immediately rejected the whole idea, and pushed on. "I mean, for the boys, I don't know the school situation in Obuasi, but there'll be something good for them in Kumasi, so maybe we could stay there. It's only about one hour drive north of Obuasi."

She was pondering. "And Mama has a place in Kumasi," she said.

Dawson stiffened inwardly. He had not even thought of that, and it should have occurred to him long before now. Dawson and his mother-in-law, Gifty, did not get along. To him, she would not be an asset in this already tricky situation. He couldn't say that to Christine, though, and his face grew hot as he realized she was scrutinizing him, waiting for a response that was clearly taking too long to materialize.

"Dark," she said reproachfully. "My mother's not going to ruin everything."

"Did I say that?" he protested.

"You were thinking it."

"Not at all," he denied, lying badly. "But do you think she can really accommodate us?"

"Why not? I don't think she has a tenant in the guesthouse right now."

Gifty lived in Accra, but she was a proud Ashanti woman. Kumasi was her hometown and she had a lot of family in that city as well as some property. Gifty, who was quite well off, used the guesthouse from time to time as either a rental or a place for family members to stay, or both, perhaps.

Dawson had never been able to shake the feeling that his mother-in-law condescended to him. Before Christine had met him, she had been dating a doctor whom Gifty highly fancied as her future son-in-law. A policeman was a big step down in Gifty's eyes, and Dawson was convinced that she had never gotten over her daughter's change of mind.

All this mutual resentment between Dawson and his mother-in-law had come to a head years ago when Gifty had decided she would take the troubling problem of Hosiah's heart disease into her own hands. Acting without the permission of the boy's parents, she took him to a traditional healer—with disastrous consequences. That had sealed Dawson's discomfort with Gifty.

"I'll call her to ask if she can accommodate us," Christine said, bringing him back to the present.

Dawson was surprised at the way she was taking this. "So you would actually consider moving to Kumasi for a year?" he asked in surprise. "In the past, you were fit to be tied whenever I had to go somewhere on assignment. What's changed?"

She leaned back, contemplating. "I still don't like it, but ever since your promotion, I've been thinking differently and realizing maybe this is the price we have to pay for your moving up in the force. It was different when it looked like you were stuck at the same rank and getting nowhere. So I've decided to have a positive outlook on it. Within reason, of course."

"But what about your job here?" Dawson asked. "You don't want to leave that, surely?"

"I can get a leave of absence and then find a job in Kumasi." She thought it over for a moment. "But for the kids' sake, we have to secure some good schools up there before we do move. Maybe I should go up for a few days and see what I find. Hopefully we can get them in for the start of the school year in September."

Dawson agreed. As a schoolteacher, Christine was the ideal person to look into this.

"What about relocation expenses?" Christine asked. "Has the Ghana Police Service gotten any better at paying for that?"

Dawson shook his head in annoyance. "No. They're supposed to, but it never happens in practice."

Christine sighed. "This is not a family-friendly organization," she observed.

"You're right," Dawson said, gazing at her in admiration. "You know something?"

"What?"

"You have no idea how relieved I am at the way you're taking this. It's wonderful. I love you, woman."

He dived across the table and planted a fat kiss on her lips. She began to giggle as he awkwardly slid onto her side of the table and pulled her onto the floor on top of him in a heap.

"Darko!" she exclaimed. "What are you *doing?*"

"Making love to you," he said, nuzzling her neck in her ticklish spot.

Convulsing with laugher, she wriggled out of his clutches.

"You're terrible," she said, staggering to her feet.

Flat on the floor, he extended his right hand to her. "Help me up."

"Oh, no," she said, knowingly. "You think I'm that stupid? You'll just pull me right down again."

He watched her as she left the kitchen. "Hey, where are you going?" he called out in protest.

"To bed," she said. "Good night."

"I'm still coming to get you," he said, getting up.

She shrieked as she saw him coming and raced to the bedroom to lock him out.

OBUASI, ASHANTI REGION

AUGUST

CHAPTER FOUR

SIX A.M. ON A Thursday morning, Dawson got out of bed bleary-eyed and weary for his first day at work. Leaving Accra the day before had been chaotic and delayed as Dawson had scrambled to tie up all the loose ends at CID Central. *There's always more than you think to do.* He had taken the last-scheduled VIP bus, the most comfortable intercity service available, from Accra to Obuasi via Mankessim, getting into his hotel at almost midnight. Miners' Lodge was the cheapest place that Dawson had found with the help of Google Maps, and it was on the same street as Obuasi Divisional Headquarters, meaning he could skimp on transportation costs.

In the dead of night, the surroundings had not meant very much to Dawson, but he began to get his bearings in the light of day as he dropped his key off at the front desk and stepped out onto Obuasi High Street—the main thoroughfare of the city. It ran east to west flanked on either side by neighborhoods like Wawasi, where Dawson's hotel was, and Tutuka, the location of the police station to which he was about to report.

Dawson glanced at the gray sky, wondering if it would clear. Heavy rain earlier on, and now the drizzly remnants, made High Street slick and glistening. The morning was cool, so the walk of less than one mile to the station, even at a slight incline, would be pleasant. He took mental snapshots of the town. Ordinary, clean, and quietly paced. Open-fronted, canopied stores with corrugated metal roofs, sidewalks better constructed than many in Accra. On Dawson's side of the street, a group of navy-and-white uniformed girls hurried to school while on the other, a young woman walked by a fast-food kiosk called David & Goliath, a wide tray of pots and pans balanced easily on her head. She moved nimbly aside without having to steady the tray with her hands as a passing car splashed muddy water in her direction. She was unfazed.

Dawson skirted a row of kids' bicycles for sale on the pavement and made a mental note of the Cool Cuts Barbershop—he would soon need his fade refreshed. Behind the pavement was a small Airtel mobile phone station underneath a wide red-and-white umbrella, right beside a vendor of cheap knockoff Coach and Michael Kors bags from China, and a secondhand TV and appliances shop next door to that.

The sign ahead on the right said OBUASI DIVISIONAL POLICE HEADQUARTERS. Dawson remembered seeing the building on the way in last night, but in the darkness he had not appreciated how small and unlike a headquarters it was. It could have been a largish two-story house or a store. The basic yellow-and-blue GPS color scheme was there, but several shades of faded, chipped paint did not quite do the job. The upstairs windows were barred with hideous metal burglarproofing, which led Dawson to believe that the building had indeed once been a retail outlet or home. On the upstairs balcony, a policeman and two civilians leaned against the balustrade and placidly watched the goings-on below.

Half a dozen cars or so were parked in front, including a black Tata SUV belonging to the GPS. Several people were standing around waiting their turn to report their issues to the charge office behind blue double doors that looked more like the entrance to a warehouse. Citizens and uniformed policemen walked in and out. Dawson approached the charge office, but paused to one side for a moment to get an idea of how the officers were conducting themselves.

A buxom female lance corporal behind the high counter stifled a yawn of utter boredom as the two people in front of her—one a skinny, shifty-eyed young guy and the other an older, wizened man with a deeply lined face—argued vociferously about what seemed to be a circular dispute over a plot of land.

The lance corporal couldn't take any more. "Okay, okay," she bellowed. "Go and wait outside. I will call you."

The two men left, barely skipping a beat in their argument.

"Stupid people," the lance corporal muttered.

The male sergeant next to her grinned as she sighed heavily and looked despondently down at the daily diary open in front of her. It was the large recording book into which every event during each shift at the station was recorded, even the weather. "I don't feel like writing any report down," she said. "Waste of time."

Dawson stepped up to the desk and took note of the lance corporal's nameplate. "Even if you think it's a waste of time, Dodu," he said, "you are still obligated to write a report."

She looked up at Dawson, eyes blazing. "And who are you?"

"I am a well-informed citizen."

"*Eh?* You say you are what? An informed citizen." Dodu sucked her teeth and began to laugh. "You are funny. My friend, who are you, and what do you want?"

"I am your chief crime officer," Dawson said.

Dodu and the sergeant looked at each other and went into hysterics. Dawson smiled and waited patiently for the hilarity to run its course, and then took out his ID badge and showed it to them. The grin disappeared from the lance corporal's face as if Dawson had ripped it off. Dodu leapt to her feet, almost falling over her capsized stool as she staggered back and began to salute. "Sir, please, sir. I'm sorry, sir, I didn't know—"

Her colleague was standing to rigid attention as if turned to stone, but Dawson could see he was shaking slightly. As a sergeant and the more senior of the two, he was the more accountable, and was supposed to be setting an example of correct conduct.

"Do you know the motto of the Ghana Police Service?" Dawson asked him.

He swallowed hard. "Yes, sir."

"What is it?"

"'To Protect and Serve with Honor,' sir."

"And is that what you were doing just now with me?"

"No, sir. I beg you, sir."

"Sit down, both of you," Dawson said.

Mortified, they took their seats, hardly daring to breathe. Dawson went behind the desk counter and stood at one end. "Give me the diary, please."

"Oh, yes, sir," Dodu said, jumping up again and hastening to bring it to him.

Regardless of rank, high or low, one had to sign in for duty in the diary when visiting or taking on a new position at a divisional or regional headquarters. Dawson glanced at his phone and wrote in the time. He noticed that between midnight and 6 A.M., no entry in the diary had been made, suggesting that absolutely nothing had taken place during that time, which didn't seem likely. More likely, someone on duty had been lazy.

"Where is the crime office?" Dawson asked, once he had signed in.

Dodu respectfully offered to show him, and he followed her outside to the left, passing the entrance to a small CID office where detectives sat to do their work. Above the second door was a small sign, CRIME OFFICER.

"Please, it is here, sir," Dodu said, opening up the locked door and standing aside so Dawson could get in. "Thank you very much, sir. You are welcome to Obuasi."

"Thank you, Lance Corporal."

She left him and he stepped inside to switch on the light. *Ewurade*, he thought. *Look at this place.* The musty room was about sixteen square feet. The desk was buried underneath stacks of paper and folders. A dust-coated computer monitor—the old type with a protruding cathode ray rear end—had been moved to the floor to make room for more junk. The folder-laden shelf on the wall near the desk was tilting dangerously, and Dawson decided that was the first item he should attend to before something snapped and sent the shelf's contents flying. As he carefully removed the documents, he heard a movement behind him and turned.

The man at the door was potbellied with a melon-sized head and a jagged smile.

"Good morning, sir."

"Good morning," Dawson said. "You are?"

"Detective Sergeant Augustus Obeng, sir," he said, bracing briefly. "Oh, please, let me help you, sir."

He rushed forward to relieve Dawson of the weighty stack of papers, which he dropped onto the first available space he found on the seat of an old armchair.

Dawson shook hands and snapped fingers with Obeng. Dawson had been told that he would be his most direct assistant—equivalent to Chikata, but not even close in physical comparison.

"My condolences for the loss of Chief Inspector Addae," Darko told him.

"Thank you, sir. It was a big shock."

Dawson sensed pain in Obeng's voice. "I understand he had a stroke?"

"That day," the sergeant explained, "he was having a terrible headache. We took him to Obuasi Hospital and they said his blood pressure was very high. But before they could give him some medicine, he collapsed dead right in front of us and they said he had bleeding inside his brain."

Dawson visualized and felt the intensity of what must have been a catastrophic scene. "I'm sorry."

"Yes, sir."

"Is the commander in?" Dawson asked.

"Yes, please. I can take you to see him."

Dawson followed Obeng up one flight of stairs. Compared to the constant buzz at CID headquarters in Accra, this place was as quiet as an empty church. The top veranda had a nice view of Obuasi High Street. The drizzle had stopped and it looked as if the sun planned to come out.

A corporal was on guard in the anteroom of the commander's

office. He knocked on the dark blue door and put his head in to announce the visitors.

"Please, you can enter," he said, stepping aside to let Dawson through, but Obeng stayed out.

Assistant Commissioner of Police, Commander Ata Longdon, was tall, imposing, and hefty—too much sitting at a desk all day long. *A thin Commander Longdon is in there somewhere,* Dawson thought. He himself had always been thin, and though he was six feet tall, people sometimes underestimated his physical strength— a bad mistake for anyone who challenged him. But he had tamed his violent streak, or perhaps it had sputtered out under the pressures of parenthood.

Longdon looked up as Dawson entered and his face brightened—not a smile exactly, but something approaching it.

"Good afternoon, sir," Dawson greeted him.

"How are you, Chief Inspector Dawson?" Longdon said. "Have a seat. Thank you for coming from Central to assist us here in Obuasi. Pascal Addae's death has shocked us greatly."

"Yes," Dawson said with sympathy.

"I think you have already visited the crime office downstairs?"

"Yes, sir. I have." Dawson wanted to put this delicately. "Seems like there's some work to be done."

"Yes, that is true." Longdon was unconsciously drumming three fingers on his desk. "Months ago, I ordered Pascal and Sergeant Obeng to embark on a reorganization of the office, but then Pascal began to get sick. He didn't know that he had very high blood pressure and kidney failure until it was too late. I appealed to Central for some assistance because Pascal was absent so often and the junior detectives were without guidance, but they delayed in taking action. I tried to fill in for him, but, well . . ."

Looking both bitter and sad, the commander was silent for a while, and Dawson said nothing. He was getting a picture of a divisional headquarters reeling from the tragic death of one of its own, and as a result suffering from low morale and disorganization.

"So," Longdon resumed, recovering, "I will be depending on

you to get the office back in shape. I have directed Sergeant Obeng to be at your service. You will also supervise the other detectives on their active cases."

"Very good, sir."

"Any problems, don't hesitate to come to me."

"Thank you, sir."

"That's all for now. I will have Sergeant Obeng take you around the division.

IT WAS NOTHING much to see. The impression Dawson had formed that the building had not originally been built to house a police headquarters turned out to be correct.

"Before," Obeng explained as they went downstairs, "it was a house belonging to a certain businessman who donated it to the Ghana Police."

Nice of him, Dawson thought, wondering if the businessman could now build them a fresh and modern facility.

"But Ghana Police is building a new place for us," Obeng said, as if reading Dawson's mind.

The charge office, CID room, and Dawson's office-to-be occupied the front of the building. At one end of the dim rear corridor was the court office, which faced the CID room. Dawson put his head in and found a couple of lawyers with three officers preparing a case for court.

In the tailoring room, a tailor at his sewing machine repairing a police uniform looked up absently at them and smiled. "Morning, sir."

Next in the hallway, Obeng opened the door to the exhibit room. Dawson let out a low whistle. Items from machetes to stolen trinkets were thrown chaotically one on top of the other, mixed in with a jumble of dusty folders and manila envelopes from old cold cases.

"We have to work on this," Dawson said, although he admitted privately to himself that even the exhibit room at Central was a disaster.

The jail was at the other end of the gloomy passage lit by a

lonesome curly fluorescent bulb in the ceiling. An eight-by-six-
foot cell, it was designed to detain a maximum of ten prisoners.
By Dawson's count, it contained seventeen at the moment. The
powerful odor of unwashed bodies was supplemented by the stink
from the rudimentary latrine. The prisoners regarded Dawson with
a mixture of curiosity and hope. Could this be someone coming to
rescue them from jail?

Dawson hated to disappoint them, but no. "Okay," he said.
"Thank you, Obeng." He tried to sound upbeat, but in fact he was
feeling profoundly depressed by the entire picture. The place felt
fragmented and at a low ebb.

Returning to his office with Obeng, Dawson took a look at the
documents the sergeant had been trying to sort out. Cold cases,
interrogation transcriptions, documents, fingerprint records,
DNA data here and there. It was a mountain of material, and in
Dawson's opinion, some of it would eventually need archiving
in off-site storage. But what portion? He took a deep breath and
blew it out through his cheeks, feeling daunted.

"Okay," he said. "We'll take a closer look at everything tomorrow."

"Yes, sir, thank you, sir," Obeng said enthusiastically.

Dawson sensed that the sergeant was grateful for his arrival,
as though he had been overburdened without the guidance of a
senior officer. He smiled at Obeng, studying him for a moment
and noticing a few untidy stains on the sergeant's light green shirt,
which stretched to bursting point over the rotund belly. He wasn't
slovenly, but he didn't have far to go. Troubled in some way? A
chaotic home life?

"Everything okay with you?" Dawson asked.

"Oh, yes, please, sir," Obeng answered quickly.

His voice changed slightly, and Dawson's left palm tingled
for a second. He had synesthesia, where vocal qualities were
experienced as a sensation in his hands, the left one in particular. Sometimes it meant an untruth was being told, and Dawson
sensed that all was not well with Obeng. Whether it was, or would
be, affecting his work, Dawson would no doubt find out.

CHAPTER FIVE

DAWSON SLEPT BADLY THAT night. The skeletal mattress was lumpy and smelled stale. He was almost glad to rise early and freshen up for the day. The bathroom was dingy, with mold growing in the grout of the shower stall. While the cool water trickled anemically over him, he kept his slippers on, not wanting to pick up some kind of infection on his feet.

He could not wait to be out of this hotel when Gifty's Kumasi house was ready. As planned, Christine had traveled from Accra to take a look at the house her mother had offered them and to secure a school for the boys. She had been successful with the latter, but the lodgings had been in bad shape. Whoever was supposed to have been maintaining the property had been doing a terrible job and lying about it.

Embarrassed, Gifty had scrambled to find a foreman to get the place back in decent shape. It would take another two weeks, or so he had said. Dawson had been tempted to suggest to Christine that they simply look for accommodations elsewhere, but he knew what that would get him: a whole lot of trouble. He could hear his mother-in-law launching her high-pitched complaint, *What, my house is not good enough for you?* Besides, rents in Ghana had become exorbitant, some landlords demanding not one, but two years in advance. Dawson could not afford that.

Dressed and groomed, he felt much better as he left the hotel

for the walk to the station. It was a little past six and he was eager
to get a head start on the paper mess in the office.

At 6:18, with HQ within sight, Dawson's phone rang. It was
Obeng.

"Good morning, sir. Please, I have received a call from Dunkwa
Police Station, sir. They say someone found a dead body at one of
the *galamsey* sites."

The town of Dunkwa was about forty kilometers southwest of
Obuasi.

"Please, I am going to Dunkwa Police Station now," Obeng
continued.

"Have they secured the area in question?" Dawson asked.

"Well, they say they have a constable there."

"Then wait for me at the Dunkwa station. I'll join you there."

Dawson felt excitement as he sprinted the rest of the way to
HQ. A *murder—barely a day after I arrived here.* He was hoping the
station vehicle was available, but it was not. Commander Longdon had it—a meeting in Kumasi, the desk sergeant said.

Realizing his expectations of transportation in an official
police vehicle had been a little optimistic, Dawson flagged down
a taxi, bargained the fare, and hopped in. For police officers
everywhere in Ghana, especially in smaller municipalities, getting to a crime scene was always by a mishmash of means. Often,
the detective took a taxi, or the family of the victim gave him
or her a ride. Every once in a while, an actual police vehicle was
available to transport an officer to the scene, but more likely
than not, it was in use by the commander of the unit. *Use* was a
loose term that included anything from legit police business to
a shopping spree for the commander's wife. As they left Obuasi,
Dawson noticed a slate-gray hill towering above the outskirts
of the town. "What is that mountain?" he asked the taxi driver,
pointing.

"Be from digging the deep mines."

Oh! Dawson thought in shock. It was an entirely man-made
elevation.

"It be one of the AngloGold Ashanti mine," the taxi driver explained further.

They drove along Obuasi High Street, which turned to Gold-finger West Road before a roundabout with a gold-colored statue of a worker drilling in a mine shaft.

"The old AGA office dey there," the taxi driver said, pointing to a dilapidated AngloGold Ashanti sign to the right, in front of an equally run-down building with a rusty corrugated metal roof.

Leaving Obuasi, the taxi driver, whose name was Kofi, passed through Anyinam, a township that housed the mine workers in green, almost lush surroundings. The distinction between the workers' quarters and the houses belonging to management was obvious to Dawson.

Turning his attention away for a minute as the residential setting thinned out and was superseded by bush on the open road, Dawson looked forward to meeting up with the most admired and influential man in his life—not his father, but a father *figure*. Daniel Armah, who lived in Kumasi, was Dawson's mentor. He was the man who, as a CID detective some twenty-five years ago, had done his utmost to find out how and why Darko's mother had mysteriously disappeared when Darko was a mere ten years old. Armah had not succeeded in his quest, but the care and dogged-ness he had shown had inspired Darko.

Through his teen years and into early adulthood as Dawson began training as an officer in the Ghana Police Service, the two men had remained steadfast friends. Reaching back into the long years of his experience as a detective, Armah always had wisdom and insight to share whenever Dawson discussed a case with him. Armah held a special place in Dawson's heart. He had taught Darko about determination and tenacity of purpose, and provided to him the role model and father figure that Darko's own father was not.

Dawson tried Armah's number several times. It rang, but no one picked up.

• • •

DUNKWA, ANOTHER MINING town, was one-fifth the size of Obuasi. It stood practically on the banks of the Ofin River, hence its full name, Dunkwa-on-Ofin. Dawson had never been there, but he knew it was one of the major destinations of thousands of illegal Chinese miners flocking into Ghana to get at its gold. Dawson wasn't exactly sure how the whole phenomenon had even started, but a lot of them had subsequently been kicked out of the country, while many remained on the run or in hiding. Dawson thought of it in a funny way: thousands of Chinese people concealed in Ashanti forests like hidden colonies of ants waiting for the anteaters to lose interest and wander away. And then they'd come right back. He didn't know every detail of how the Chinese came back so successfully, but he knew the general mechanism: bribery and corruption. It got you everywhere in Ghana.

The road into Dunkwa was appalling. Unpaved and deeply rutted, vehicles swerved around the worst of the potholes and depressions in a kind of strange dance. Deep puddles of rainwater from the previous night and mud as thick as corn dough made the going very difficult. Only SUVs could proceed at a reasonable speed. The rest, like Dawson's taxi, had to slow to a crawl at times.

Finally, at the crest of a hill, they saw the town ahead of them, and to the left, a segment of the Ofin River along with a large tract of land scoured bare and churned into hills and valleys of grayish-yellow soil.

Kofi looked over for a second and followed Dawson's gaze, then back to the roadway shaking his head. "These China people," he said in disgust. "Look what they have done to the land with their excavators."

Look what we've let them do, Dawson thought.

DUNKWA WAS NOTHING spectacular by way of buildings or roads, and Dawson had not expected it to be. In most of the lower half of Ghana, certain fairly similar characteristics could be anticipated in towns of a certain size. It was only as one traveled into the arid north that architecture radically changed.

Dawson saw square brick homes with the standard corrugated tin roofs, unpaved streets and houses in random arrangement. Worn away at the sides to a strip in the middle, the main road through town was flanked on the sides by wide trash-strewn gutters, and then by chop bars, small vegetable stands. But then he had to admit that Dunkwa had a little twist to its otherwise unsurprising appearance: gold-buying stores. Lots of them.

"Ofin Gold Trading Company," Dawson read out from one of the signs.

"Many places here to buy and sell gold," Kofi said, in Twi this time. He turned off the main road and proceeded slowly through a narrow lane between several small buildings. He pointed. "See the line on the houses? That's when the town flooded."

Dawson at first didn't understand what Kofi meant, but then he saw a faint brown border at the base of each building, the watermark of a notorious flooding of Dunkwa last year when torrents swelled the Ofin River beyond its banks.

"The police station is just here," Kofi said, making a final left turn and pulling to a stop in front of the small building painted GPS-signature yellow and blue, or sometimes white and blue.

"Wait for me here, Kofi," Dawson told him. "We will go somewhere else after this."

"Yes, please."

Obeng was waiting on the front verandah with a uniformed officer, whom he introduced as Inspector Sackie, a lanky man of about forty with a scar across his top lip.

"Good morning, sir," he said to Dawson deferentially.

"Morning, Inspector."

"Please, shall I give you a report first?"

"Let's not waste precious time. You can tell me on the way there."

CHAPTER SIX

THE MINING SITE WAS farther out than Dawson had expected. As they traveled more and more deeply into the bush along a laterite road whose red dust tarnished the vegetation alongside it, his sense of direction told him they must have been diverging from the course of the Ofin to meet it at some farther point along its course.

"This road," Inspector Sackie said, "the Chinese built it."

So they have been good for something, Dawson thought. If they had not constructed it, there might have been no road at all.

But the good roadwork came to an end as Kofi reached a point where a long, deep puddle obliterated the road's surface. Only a 4x4 could get through that. Dawson and the two other men got out, skirted the border of the puddle to avoid sinking into the muddy thigh-deep water, and continued to their destination on foot.

"What is that noise?" Dawson asked, becoming aware of a monotonous drone in the distance somewhere to their right.

"Excavators," Sackie said.

As they walked, the noise grew louder, and over a small rise, the source became evident—a vast area below them ploughed up in a fashion similar to what Dawson had just seen close to Dunkwa. To the right, four excavators were clawing up soil from the sides of deep pits and transferring them to the side. His instincts about the Ofin River had been correct. It had reappeared in the distance, making a wide *U* with the convex side toward them.

Ahead and to the left of more gouged-out pits, Dawson saw a stationary excavator, its claw bucket resting on the ground like an exhausted animal, and not far away from that, a crowd of people was staring at and discussing a deep, wide cavity in the mudbank. Yellow cordon tape had been strung up using the shafts of four shovels, but one of the shovels had toppled over and people had crossed into the would-be restricted area. *Presumably that is the crime scene? Where is the body, and where is the constable who has supposedly secured the scene?*

Dawson, Obeng, and Sackie half slid, half walked down the muddy incline, and all eyes turned to them.

"What are you doing here?" Sackie demanded of the crowd in Twi.

"Please, the body was here," a young man volunteered.

"Where is it now?" Dawson asked.

"Please, they have taken it."

"Taken it where?"

"To the Chinaman's house."

Dawson didn't understand. "What Chinaman's house? Where?"

A teenager pointed behind them and the men turned.

Now they saw a second gathering of people crowded around a wooded shack behind two mountains of excavated land.

"Is the constable there too?" Dawson asked.

The crowd chorused assent.

"Okay, let's go and see what's going on," Dawson said, bemused. "But Obeng, I need you to clear everybody out of here."

Dawson and Sackie walked toward the shack, leaving Obeng to secure the area and keep it that way. Dawson wondered why the backup from the Dunkwa station was so poor. Why had only one constable been sent when clearly there needed to be at least two of them? As if reading Dawson's mind, Sackie said, "Sorry, sir. I wanted to send another officer to assist, but we don't have enough men."

Dawson nodded. He wasn't happy, but he understood the difficulty. It was often the case that the rural police stations were understaffed.

About twenty people milled about the front of the poorly constructed wood structure, which had only a dirty curtain as the door. As Dawson and Sackie approached, a constable in dark blue uniform came out of the shack sweating and looking shaken. Obviously stressed, he yelled at everyone to get away from the door. They backed up but stubbornly stood around to watch. A crowd could be as obstinate and unmoving as an oil tanker in a swamp.

"Morning, sir," the constable said separately to Sackie and Dawson.

His badge read KOBBY. He was lean and tall, and very boyish in the face.

Dawson had become aware of a sobbing sound coming from the shack. "What is going on in there?"

"The brother of the Chinese man who died," Kobby explained with frustration. "When the body was found this morning by the *galamsey* boys, he told them to help him bring the body here because he didn't want all those people staring at his brother."

They moved the body from the crime scene. Dawson's heart sank. It was a forensic nightmare.

"And then they helped him bring the body here and the brother washed the mud off," Kobby added.

The blood in Dawson head drained, leaving him cold. *He washed the mud off?*

"And now he won't release the body," Kobby said.

"What do you mean he won't release the body?" Dawson asked.

"He says he wants to take it back with him to China."

Eventually, sure, Dawson thought, *but not right now.* "All right. Let's go inside."

The angled wooden slats of the dwelling let some air in, but it was still warm and stifling, and it smelled awful. Dawson could detect decaying flesh, urine, fuel, and stale food. In the middle of the dirt floor, the victim's brother was weeping and mouthing words in Chinese as he cradled the corpse, shaking it every few seconds as if trying to wake it from sleep.

A chill went down Dawson's spine. Covered in clumps of soil, the dead man was clothed except for his shoes. His back was arched concavely. His legs pulled up backward to meet his wrists behind him. His head strained upward with his eyes open and mouth agape, as if he had been in a desperate struggle to escape this terrible, anatomically impossible pose. Moving a little closer, Dawson saw that the ankles and wrists were free of ligatures, but ligature marks were present. The man was no longer tied up. He had gone into rigor in that position. Dawson spotted two slashed, knotted lengths of rope on the ground beside the corpse. Trying to reconstruct events in his mind, he imagined that after the dead man had been discovered, his brother had hastily cut the ligatures away in an effort to "release" the corpse, only to find that the body was fixed the way it had been found.

Dawson's eyes shifted around the room: food-caked tin plates and pots and pans stacked in one corner, plastic gallon containers in another, and soiled clothes in a third next to a pump-action shotgun—the weapon of choice among miners.

Kobby was looking at the scene with revulsion.

"Do you know the Chinese man's name?" Dawson whispered to him.

"Which one, sir?"

"Both, I suppose."

"Please, I don't know the name of the dead one," Kobby said, "but the people outside say the brother's name is Wei."

"Does he speak English?"

"A little bit."

Dawson went closer to Wei and kneeled down. "Mr. Wei, my name is Detective Chief Inspector Dawson."

Wei was a chunky man. He pulled back from Dawson as if he'd been threatened and began shouting. Perhaps he *did* think Dawson was threatening him. In a moment of confusion, Dawson realized that the Chinese man was speaking in Twi. It was bad, but it *was* Twi.

"Get away from me!" Wei said. "Look at my brother!"

"Mr. Wei—"

"They kill him!" he said, switching to broken English. "They kill him!"

"*Who?*" Dawson asked urgently. "Who killed him?"

"*Galamsey! Galamsey!*"

"Which ones? Who?"

Wei didn't answer, his crying trailing off abruptly, and only his lower lip trembling as he looked down at his brother. "Oh, Bao. Oh, Bao."

Bao had been thin, but putrefaction was beginning to bloat him. Tropical weather never treats corpses kindly. Dawson would need to talk to Wei a lot more very soon, but he was too distraught to get any useful answers out of him at the moment. For now, he needed to get the man away from his dead brother Bao.

Dawson stood up again and spoke quietly to Inspector Sackie. "Is a crime scene unit available?"

He looked skeptical. "There is one in Kumasi, but they have to cover so many places in the region. We can call them, but usually they cannot arrive for twelve hours or more."

That didn't surprise Dawson, as bad as it seemed. CSUs were hard to come by in smaller towns and villages. Dawson made a decision. Forget the CSU. He could not allow the corpse to stay here for several hours.

"Let's get the body to Komfo Anokye morgue as soon as possible," he said.

Komfo Anokye Teaching Hospital, often called KATH, was Kumasi's largest.

"We can get a four-by-four to transport it there," Sackie said, taking out his phone to make a call.

"Thank you," Dawson said, studying Wei for a moment and trying to decide the best way to handle this. He returned to the Chinese man's side. "We are going to take care of your brother, okay, sir?"

"*Wha'?*"

"We are going to take him to the hospital for autopsy." Dawson realized he was speaking louder. How ridiculous.

Wei shook his head, and Dawson wasn't sure that he really understood. Getting to his feet, he touched Wei's arm softly and indicated that he should follow his lead.

"Come on, my friend. Let's go now."

He stayed stubbornly where he was. Kobby came to Dawson's aid by grasping Wei firmly under one arm and urging him to get to his feet. Abruptly, Wei exploded, lunged at the constable, and took a swing. Kobby sidestepped and deflected the blow, which put the Chinese man off-balance and sent him to the ground in a graceless heap. Dawson, Sackie, and Kobby moved in to cuff him.

"I don't know what your problem is, my friend," Dawson said, "but you are under arrest for assaulting a police officer. I wish I knew how to say that in your language."

Then, Dawson reflected, Wei could even be the culprit. Who knows? All that babbling in Chinese might have been his confession: *I killed my brother.*

"Take him outside to sit down," Dawson instructed, breathing heavily. *What a way to start the day.*

Kobby escorted Wei out as the Chinese man kept shouting something they didn't understand. Now Dawson and Inspector Sackie were alone with the dead body. No police photographer meant Dawson had to improvise. He took his phone out, backed up, and took a long shot of the corpse and the interior of the shack before moving in. He photographed the ground around the body, including a white plastic bucket containing dirty water and a rag that Wei must have been using to wash his brother's body, the two lengths of rope on, and a close-up of the knots. It might help determining left- or right-handedness of the killer, but not necessarily.

Dawson looked up at Sackie. "Do you have any specimen bags?"

The inspector shook his head. "No, sir, but I can send someone to get some from the town. Plastic, or paper?"

"Both plastic and paper, please."

"Yes, sir."

Sackie went outside, leaving Dawson by himself with the

corpse. Dawson saw deep bloody gashes in the top of the scalp and
wondered what had inflicted them. Perhaps a machete, probably
the most common murder weapon in Ghana. Was that what killed
this man?

Dawson picked up a twig and gently lifted the pile of rags and
old clothes in case a machete was concealed underneath, but he
found nothing. He looked up at the ceiling. Sometimes, people
slipped weapons between the beams. Nothing there either.

He didn't see blood spatter anywhere. If the man had not
been bleeding when he was discovered, the wounds might
have been inflicted postmortem, but Dawson still had to return to
the original crime scene to look for signs of blood before he came
to that conclusion. He took a look at the shotgun, examining it
for bloodstains without success. He had been thinking that maybe
someone hit the Chinese guy on the top of his head with the barrel
or stock of the weapon.

He photographed Bao's head wounds from different angles,
both with and without the flash. When he moved his attention
to the man's face, Dawson recoiled. It was a picture of fright, as
if he had died screaming. Perhaps in pain as the machete blows
were delivered.

Or perhaps he was shrieking in terror as he was tied. *Could be
two assailants*, Dawson reflected, because it was tricky to tie up
someone who was struggling—especially in this bizarre position—
and Dawson was pretty certain that, if his temper was anything
like his brother's, Wei was fighting at the time of death.

No marks on his belly, which was an odd, mottled grayish-yellow
color. At the sides of his trunk closest to the ground, the purplish-
red coloration of pooled blood—lividity—suggested the position he
had been in after death: on his belly. To confirm, Dawson turned
the body, which rolled in one piece, like an artless statue. Yes,
there was the blanched, oval section on Bao's abdomen, where
his weight had prevented blood from pooling.

Dawson took photos of all of this, because the lividity would
change with time, and if it took a while to get the body to the

morgue, which he suspected it would, the corpse would deteriorate in all sorts of other ways.

Sackie returned as Dawson was taking pictures of the ligature marks on Wei's wrists and ankles.

"Someone is bringing the bags for you, sir," Sackie said.

"Thank you. How is the victim's brother doing?"

"He's just sitting there saying nothing."

"Tell Obeng to escort him back to the taxi and wait for us. I'm going to look at the other site. When the bags arrive, I want these ligatures collected, all the clothes, the pots and pans, the shotgun, and the bucket. Please don't throw the water out. There could be traces of blood in it."

"Yes, sir."

Dawson walked back to take a look at the site's lone excavator resting high on the crest of the collection of pits. It was sullen yellow in color and caked with mud. The long boom attached to the hydraulic arm and the intimidating claw bucket bore the manufacturer's name—XCMG. Chinese make, Dawson supposed. He turned to look around, the slight elevation affording him a better view. Several hundred meters away in the dry, unforgiving laterite where only the hardiest plants grew, two Toyota pickups were parked at an angle to each other. Dawson assumed that they belonged to the Chinese brothers.

He took a walk down to look the trucks over. They were similar, although different models. One of them, dull charcoal in color, looked like it had taken quite a beating on bad roads. The other, clearly a newer pickup, was metallic red. Dawson tried the doors, but both were locked. The inside of the charcoal vehicle was full of trash and discarded food cans. The red one was decent. Dawson looked closely at the truck beds for any signs—especially bloodstains—that the vehicle had transported Bao's body from another location. He couldn't find anything, but whichever pickup belonged to the victim would have to go to the Motor Traffic Unit (MTU) at Regional Headquarters in Kumasi for further examination.

Returning to the site where the body had been dug out, Dawson saw a man and woman alighting from a silver-gray Toyota Prado at the edge of the site, where the crowd had now thinned out to just a half dozen or so. The man had a TV camera on his shoulder. Dawson made short work of the space between him and them.

"There's no filming allowed," he called out as he approached them. "This is a fresh crime scene we are still investigating. Please put the camera away."

The man hesitated and didn't quite obey.

"And who might you be?" the woman asked.

"Detective Chief Inspector Darko Dawson. And you are?"

"Good morning, Chief Inspector. Akua Helmsley. Environmental reporter for *The Guardian* newspaper. I'm doing a documentary on illegal gold mining in Ghana."

She had a British accent. Her skin was fair and flawless. She was tall for a woman—just a couple of inches shorter than Dawson. She gestured to the man behind her. "That's my cameraman, Joshua Samuels."

"Please, Mr. Samuels," Dawson said, "put the camera back in the vehicle."

Sullenly, Samuels put the camera down in the front passenger seat.

"What are you doing here?" Dawson asked Helmsley.

She seemed to smile somewhat as she considered him, as if a little amused. He didn't let it bother him.

A light breeze lifted her flowing black hair slightly off her shoulders. "You've got a dead Chinese man, I understand, Chief Inspector," she said. "Do you know who he is?"

"The investigation is only in its preliminary stages," Dawson said. "I know almost nothing about him."

"He was buried in that mound of mud over there?" she asked, pointing.

"Yes. How did you know?"

"Your Sergeant Obeng told me," she said, flashing a smile. She was almost too pretty to be surrounded by this wrecked landscape. "I met him back at the taxi where he's holding the suspect."

Evidently, Obeng had let her charm information out of him. How annoying.

"Definitely homicide, I suppose?" she said.

"Nothing is definite yet," he countered. Her knowing tone was getting on his nerves. "We have to get the body to the mortuary for a full autopsy."

"Ah," she said. "Are you aware just how backed up they are with bodies at the KATH mortuary?"

"Yes, of course," he said, matching her self-assuredness. "All hospital mortuaries in Ghana are backed up."

She smiled again, her eyes shrewd and dazzling. "I like 'detective chief inspector' on you. It suits you well. You say we can't film the crime scene. What about still photos?"

"You can take photos of the surrounding area"—he pointed in all directions—"but not the crime scene itself."

"But it's so common in Ghana even to see photos of murdered victims right on the front page of a newspaper," she pointed out.

That was true. "Yes, and I hate that," Dawson said. "Bad police work."

"I'm impressed," she said. "Nice to meet someone who knows best practice. I've been back and forth to the Ashanti Region from England regularly over the past year, but I've never met you. Are you new around here?"

"I was transferred here from CID Central in Accra—arrived only yesterday. What is your documentary about?"

"It's an in-depth look at all aspects of the gold mining industry in Ghana, but particularly the phenomenon of the mass influx of Chinese illegals."

Dawson saw his opportunity. "Maybe you can explain how this Chinese invasion happened, Miss Helmsley, because I don't understand it well."

"Okay," she said, propping a foot on a fallen, decaying tree trunk. Her jeans were a snug fit, and Dawson noticed the fine curve of her hamstring muscles. "Quick tutorial. Ready? The people of Shanglin County in China's Guangxi Province have had a gold-mining tradition for centuries. Basically, they mined their own land dry as a bone, so they began looking elsewhere in China to get their gold. But the Chinese government said, 'Oh no you don't. We're not giving out licenses to small fries like you. Go somewhere else.'"

"And so they heard that Ghana was the second highest gold producer in Africa and came running here?" Dawson asked sardonically.

"More or less," she said. "Stories circulated in China about miners coming to Ghana for gold and returning home as millionaires. Much of it could have been urban legend, but they called the thousands of Shanglin miners flocking to Ghana the 'Shanglin Gang.'"

"And all of them are illegal?"

"Yes, because it's illegal for foreigners to engage in *galamsey*, or small-scale surface mining—whatever your term of preference. But who cares, right? Visa brokers in Ghana can get on-arrival visas for incoming Chinese workers by bribing officials in the Ghana Immigration Service. There's also a trafficking system involving Togo and other countries."

Dawson shook his head slowly, feeling a stab of anger over the depth of the corruption involved. "All the trouble they go through must be worth its weight in gold," he commented.

"Nice one, Chief Inspector," Helmsley said. "It's true. Even though western mining companies like AngloGold with its massive deep mining sites produce more than seventy percent of Ghana's gold and the *galamsey* contribute less than thirty, the Chinese illegals do well. And so do a lot of other people. The landowner and the local chiefs get paid by the Chinese, and unemployed Ghanaian kids hanging around the villages get to do some work and earn some money."

"No wonder the illegal Chinese guys get to stay," Dawson murmured, understanding the picture more completely now. He gestured to the ravaged landscape. "They are useful to us at the expense of mother Ghana."

"Yes," Helmsley agreed. "Just the way it's been since at least the fifteenth century." She and Dawson held glances for a moment. "I think we'll take our leave now, Chief Inspector . . . Oh, just one thing. I'd like to exchange numbers if possible. I may need to get in touch with you on another occasion."

She could be useful to the case, he thought as they traded their contact information. *Very useful*. There was also something exciting about her, like a bright strand of gold in a length of fabric one can't resist touching.

CHAPTER SEVEN

IT HAD TAKEN THREE hours for Bao Liu's corpse to be picked up and transported to the mortuary at KATH. Wei was in custody at the Dunkwa Police Station, at first loudly protesting and then falling silent and brooding.

Dawson's search of the site where Bao had been discovered had turned up no traces of blood, and besides, the area had been trampled with a thousand footprints of meddling onlookers. None of the *galamsey* boys who had reportedly found the body were around to be questioned, and no one knew where they were—or no one admitted to it.

Dawson and Obeng went into town to look for a Chinese interpreter to help question Wei. They split up and began popping into gold-selling and -buying stores on either side of the street. Dawson first tried the shop he'd seen earlier—Ofin Gold Trading Company. In a small room, he found an impeccably turned out Ghanaian in a white linen shirt sitting at his desk weighing a lump of gold on a digital scale. The Chinese man who had brought it in waited anxiously for the verdict: the weight, the trading price, and how much cash he was going to get.

"Fourteen point one six grams," the Ghanaian man said. "Which is almost half an ounce, or twenty blades."

Dawson had never heard of a "blade," but obviously forty blades equaled an ounce.

"Four hundred dollars," the Ghanaian man said.

"*Eh?*" the Chinese man said, looking put out.

"Four hundred."

"You pay me six hundred dollar."

The Ghanaian smiled. "Six! I don't think so, my friend. The gold is not pure. Sorry."

The Chinese man looked at the buyer and back to the gold, undecided. "No," he said finally, shaking his head. "Today you no good."

He took his gold nugget back and left. The Ghanaian man shrugged and laughed. "He won't get a better price anywhere else," he said to Dawson, as if he had been in on the conversation from the start.

"How much is gold going for at the moment?" Dawson asked.

"Almost thirteen hundred dollars per ounce," the man replied. "Are you buying or selling?"

"Neither." He showed his badge. "Detective Chief Inspector Dawson, CID."

"George Danquah," the man said, rising to shake hands. He was clean-shaven, neat, and was wearing a subtle fragrance. "Please, have a seat."

Dawson took the stool on the other side of the table. "I'm investigating the death of a Chinese man at a mining site."

"Is Bao Liu the dead man you are speaking of?"

"Yes. You knew him?"

"Like I know the other Chinese miners," Danquah said with something of a smirk. "They come and they go. I do business with them, but I have no interest in them personally."

"What was Mr. Liu like?"

George pulled a face, as if he had smelled something bad. "Unpleasant, always losing his temper, shouting, calling people stupid." Raising his voice, he launched into a singsong, mocking imitation of Chinese, which Dawson admitted sounded quite authentic. It probably wouldn't to a Chinese speaker, of course.

"But for sure," George added, "he knew how to mine for gold and he brought me good material."

"Do you know anyone who might have wanted to kill him?" Dawson asked.

"Not specifically. I do know that he wasn't consistent about paying his *galamsey* boys at the end of the day. So they might have resented him for that. I'm just speculating."

"Explain that—paying the boys at the end of the day."

George nodded. "The miners wash the gold ore they dig up all day long, and any gold that falls out is mixed with mercury to form an amalgam. After that, they burn the mercury off and the gold is left behind."

"And that's what they bring to you?"

"Or we go to the site and pay them on the spot," George said. "Whichever way, it's something of a gentleman's agreement that you as a boss make sure you pay your boys for the day's yield."

"Did you go to his site often?"

"Often enough."

"What about last night?"

"No. I have not been there in a while, and I'm not sure when he was last here. Wait, let me ask my wife . . . Efua!"

Said Efua appeared. She was solid and endowed in several areas. Dawson thought of a baobab tree.

"That Mr. Liu, the Chinaman," George said to her, speaking in Twi, "did he come in this week?"

She shook her head. "No. The week before."

"Thank you." George turned back to Dawson. "There you have it, Mr. Dawson. Or what was it—Inspector, *anaa?*"

Dawson waved it away. "It doesn't matter. 'Mister' is okay. One other thing: Mr. Liu's brother, Wei—do you know anything about him?"

George turned the corners of his lips down. "He was always in the background, very quiet the one or two times I saw him here in the shop—always looking at his phone. So no, I don't know much about him."

"We have him at the police station and we need to ask him

some questions. Do you know a Chinese person who can help us with that?"

George thought for a moment. "There's this one guy named Mr. Leonard Huang who has a hardware store in the Sofo Line area of Kumasi. I trust him. He's been here for years and speaks quite good English. The only problem might be that he won't want to come down here all the way from Kumasi." He picked up his mobile from the table. "Let me see if I can get him for you."

While George was dialing, Dawson looked around the store. A number of plaques and framed documents on the wall made it evident that the store and its business were licensed and certified by the PMMC—Precious Minerals Marketing Company, the government's trader in gold, diamonds, and precious stones.

George had apparently gotten through to Leonard and from this side of the conversation, it seemed to Dawson that George was having a tough time persuading him to act as a translator.

"Oh, no, no, Leonard," he was saying in reassuring tones. "You won't get involved at all. You will be a neutral translator for Inspector Dawson to help him obtain some information. Can you do it for me, please?" George looked over at Dawson after a moment's pause in the negotiations. "He will do it. What time?"

"As soon as possible."

"Leonard—how quickly can you be at the police station? One hour? Okay, that will be very good. Thank you very much, my friend." George ended the call and smiled at Dawson. "Done. We are very lucky that he happens to be in Dunkwa right now."

"I appreciate it, Mr. Danquah."

"No problem. He was trying to get out of it by saying he speaks a different kind of Chinese from Mr. Liu, but I know that's not true. He's forgotten I've seen the two of them conversing before."

"There's more than one kind of Chinese?" Dawson asked, feeling ignorant.

George shrugged. "So I'm told. Mandarin and, em . . . another one I forget." He called out again. "Efua, what are those different China languages? Mandarin and what again?"

"Cantonese," she supplied.

"Yeah, that's the one." George winked at Dawson. "That woman is a walking encyclopedia. That's why I married her."

Busty and brainy, Dawson thought. "One other thing, Mr. Danquah, what is your view of the illegal Chinese miners?"

"Ah," he sighed, leaning back again. "This is complicated." He snatched a piece of scratch paper and drew two circles on it. "The Chinese are here in this circle, and we the Ghanaians are here in the other. Where the circles intersect is where we trade in some fashion, or work together and so on. Other times, it is a clash of cultures. Did you hear about the shooting at Aniamoa several months ago?"

"No," Dawson said.

"A gang of Ghanaian boys waylaid some Chinese guys who were walking to a mining site, and the boys demanded gold from them. The Chinese said they didn't have any and the boys should go away, which they did. But then, they returned with some macho men to beat up the Chinese people at their mining camp and presumably steal some stuff. One of the macho men was armed, but so were the Chinese. The two groups exchanged gunfire and one Chinese and two Ghanaians were shot dead."

"It sounds like it was a critical scene," Dawson said.

"But wait," Danquah said, holding up a finger, "that wasn't all. When the police arrived to investigate, one stupid Chinese man started firing his weapon and wounded a sergeant. You see, Inspector, some of these Chinese are criminals—no good, worthless, low-life people in their own country. Now, I don't deny that we have the same good-for-nothings here in Ghana. I'm saying, please, China, keep your offenders and convicts in your own country." Danquah shook his head grimly. "It's just too bad. You see all this destruction of land around us and the pollution of the rivers? *They* have done this to us."

"But Ghanaians are engaging in the same illegal mining, aren't they?" Dawson said.

"Oh, yes!" Danquah exclaimed spiritedly. "We Ghanaians, the

fools that we are, are in bed with these people. Why? Because we see a little money waving in our faces and we want to grab it at once without thinking of the consequences. And me who has been in the gold business for so long, I don't like what these foreigners are doing to the country, but I have a wife and kids to support. I would be a fool to turn them away at the door. You know, it's like taking bitter medicine."

"So what do you think is going to happen?" Dawson asked, feeling depressed.

Danquah shrugged. "Well, you see how the government is now chasing them out. Some of them are leaving voluntarily to go back to China because of these raids and so on, and their share of the gold has been diminishing. To be honest, some of them are in poverty. Some have money but are by no means rich. So, in the end most of them will leave, but by then they will have torn the Ashanti and other regions apart."

Dawson rose. "Mr. Danquah, I thank you very much for your help."

"You are welcome, sir. By the way, are you interested in buying or selling any gold today?"

"I don't have any gold," Dawson said, "and I certainly don't have any money."

CHAPTER EIGHT

MR. HUANG DID NOT show up at Dunkwa Police Station for another two hours. Dawson used that time to call Christine and the boys, who were now in the final third of the long vacation from June to September. Christine asked him how things were going.

"I have a homicide," he told her. "Happened only this morning."

"Goodness! They haven't even given you time to settle in."

"Exactly."

"Bad case?"

"Yes. A Chinese man who was tied up, bludgeoned with a machete, and then buried at a mining site."

"*Ewurade,*" she said, and he could almost hear her shudder. "Well, apart from all that gruesomeness, how are you doing?"

"I'm okay, but I want to get out of the hotel as soon as possible."

"Mama says the house will be ready by next week," she told him.

"Oh, good," he said, thinking, *I'll believe it when I see it.* No construction, repair or plumbing project was ever ready by the promised time.

"When do you think you'll be able to go to see the house?" she asked.

"I'll try this weekend."

"Okay. Hold on for Hosiah."

He spent a little while chatting to both boys, who missed him. They knew now about the move to Kumasi, and although Sly did not seem in the least worried about it, Hosiah was showing anxiety in his tone, and that worried Dawson.

MR. HUANG WAS a bespectacled fortyish man who was deeply sunburned, especially the bald patch at the crown of his flat head.

"Thank you very much for coming in to help me interpret, Mr. Huang," Dawson said, shaking hands. "I appreciate it very much."

"You welcome," he said nervously.

"It's just one or two things I need to ask Mr. Liu," Dawson said, sensing that Huang was anxious. "I understand that out of the two types of Chinese, both of you speak the same variety?"

A mixture of both amusement and annoyance passed over Huang's face for just an instant, but long enough for Dawson to notice.

"Did I say something wrong, Mr. Huang?"

"Oh, no, no problem," he said, but his eyes didn't meet Dawson's.

"Am I mistaken that there are two types of Chinese?" Dawson persisted, still certain he had blundered somewhere.

"Same like if I say there two type Ghanaian language!" Huang blurted, suddenly free of politeness. "Not make sense, right? China have many language!"

Dawson saw his point. "Yes, you are right," he said, feeling stupid for the second time today. "I apologize, sir."

Hastening to smile and now embarrassed himself, Huang waved the apology away. "'Sokay. No problem."

"Let's go to see Mr. Liu now, please."

WEI LIU HAD shrunk into a corner of the overcrowded Dunkwa jail cell, keeping himself and his eyes away from his Ghanaian cellmates. Just like the jail at Obuasi headquarters, this one contained far more prisoners than it was designed to hold. When Wei saw Mr. Huang, his face lit up. In a voice shaking with emotion, he called out to his countryman and threaded his way to the front through the clump of prisoners.

"Please explain that we are going to take him out for question-ing," Dawson said to Huang.

From either side of the jail bars, the two Chinese men had what seemed to Dawson a long and complicated exchange, and after a few minutes some of the Ghanaian prisoners began to giggle and do bad Chinese imitations.

Inspector Sackie, who was standing nearby, bellowed, "Heh! Shut up, all of you!"

The prisoners obeyed and Kobby opened the cell door to let Wei out, cuffing him as a precaution before taking him to the CID room. They had no guarantee that Wei was any less bad-tempered now than he had demonstrated just a few hours ago.

Most regional and divisional headquarters had a shared com-mon room for CID detectives to question suspects and write reports. Sackie, Obeng, and Dawson sat opposite Wei and Huang at two tables pushed together to make a single.

"Again, thank you for coming to help us," Dawson said to Huang. "Please explain to Mr. Liu that he is here for questioning regarding the death of his brother, Bao, and that he is also under arrest for assault and attempted battery of a police officer. Which is why he is handcuffed. I am going to read a caution statement to him, which you must translate to him the best that you can, and then I will ask him to sign it."

"Yes," Huang said.

It took several minutes to laboriously get through the caution preamble phrase by phrase. With some hesitation, Wei signed it after Dawson made sure he understood.

"He say he sorry for what he did," Huang said.

"Why did he do it?" Dawson asked.

"He say . . . he say he just feel so shock and so bad his brother die."

In a way, Dawson understood. He had seen all kinds of behavior exhibited by family of the deceased—catatonia, hysteria, fainting, fury.

Huang cleared his throat. "Mr. Liu, he wanna know if he is going to spend more time in jail."

"But of course," Dawson said. "He will be arraigned tomorrow, and then he will be remanded in prison custody."

Huang turned to Wei and another discussion followed. Wei was rubbing his hand repeatedly through his hair as if he was at the end of his rope.

Finally, lowering his voice, Huang said to Dawson, "Mr. Liu say he can give you a little something, is no problem."

"Look here," Dawson snapped, "Mr. Liu is in enough trouble already, and now he wants to bribe me?"

Wei stiffened when Huang translated that, and then seemed to droop completely. Dawson moved on. "Mr. Huang, I don't think I've asked you how you know Mr. Liu."

"I meet him one year ago. He come from his hometown in Shanglin—Guangxi Province. I meet Bao three year ago. He come buy 'quipment my store."

"Was Bao married?"

"Yes. His wife Stay Kumasi"

"Did he meet his wife in China or in Ghana?"

"China."

"Did they have children?"

"Daughter."

"I see," Dawson said. "Were Bao and Wei full brothers?" Dawson asked. "Same father, same mother?" He was thinking that a stepsibling situation might have hinted at conflict, although not necessarily. Huang checked with Wei, confirming that they had been full siblings.

Dawson sat back and contemplated Wei for a moment. "How was life in your town in China—in Shanglin County?"

Wei seemed uncertain or wary about the question, but after some hesitation, he said that life could be good for some, but not for others. When Bao left China, life had *not* been good for the Liu family. Like everyone else who left Shanglin for Ghana, the ultimate goal was to make a lot of money and return to the motherland rich.

"After Bao stay in Ghana two year, feel so lonely without Lian."

Huang continued. He beg her to come to him, and he tell Wei to come with her to protect her nothing bad happen."

So technically, Dawson thought, the Lius were members of the "Shanglin Gang" in the country illegally, as Helmsley had described. Dawson was interested to know more, but perhaps some other time. For now, he needed to get on with the investigation at hand. Obviously Bao Liu had not tied himself up like a contortionist and buried himself under a pile of dirt, and grief-stricken or not, Wei was a potential suspect.

Dawson took out his pocket notebook. He used a fresh one for each homicide case, and at home he had a carton with enough to last him for years, courtesy of his Takoradi cousin who owned a stationery store.

"How did Bao and Wei divide the duties once Wei arrived here from China?" Dawson asked.

"Wei do the day-to-day things," Huang replied. "Make sure everything work at site. Bao take care of the books—ordering, buying."

Bao was firmly in charge, Dawson thought. And why not? He had started the business and his brother came along after that. "Where did Bao live?"

"Kumasi. Wei too."

"In the same residence?"

"When Wei first come, they live together, but then Wei say he want to stay another place, so he moved."

Dawson wondered if there had been arguments between the two brothers. "Has Bao's wife been informed of the death?"

Huang asked Wei, who shook his head.

"He hasn't had time call her yet," Huang explained.

"Okay, we'll take care of informing her as soon as possible."

Huang translated, and Wei nodded.

"When was the last time he saw Bao?" Dawson asked.

The Chinese men conferred, after which Huang turned back to Dawson. "Yesterday morning," he said, "he go to Bao house in Kumasi, tell Bao for two days now, something wrong with the excavator hydraulic"—Huang stumbled over the word—"arm, not working and need new part. So Wei and Bao went into the town to look for the part."

"They find the part to buy, and so by the afternoon, Wei go back to the mining site in Dunkwa to try and fix the arm with one of the *galamsey* boys, but it take long and start to get dark, and still the arm have trouble. So he call Bao and say he gonna continue very early next morning before the work start, because you know, without excavator, lose time, lose *money*. And he ask Bao if he can come in the morning too so he can help, and Bao say, yes, okay, he will go to the mining site at four o'clock in the morning."

With Dawson's new and growing comprehension of alluvial mining, he recognized the importance of getting the excavator repaired. He didn't know how much gold ore those huge machines could dig up in a day, but it was certainly thousands of times more than a human could. The Lius had already lost two days or more of excavation, and they were anxious to reverse the trend, even if it meant fixing the machine by flashlight.

Dawson jotted down:

Bao & Wei: plan to meet 4 a.m. Friday.

"Okay, what happened next?"

"So, Wei say too late to go back to Kumasi—too far," Huang went on, "so rather he stay with some friend, one Chinese man who live in Dunkwa, so it won't take him long to go the mine site in the morning."

That stood to reason, Dawson thought. It was at least a two-hour drive back to Kumasi, prolonged mostly by the atrocious Dunkwa–Obuasi segment. If Wei was to get back to the mine by four in the morning, he would have to leave Kumasi at about 2 A.M.

"So," Huang said, "he stay with that friend and suppose to wake up three thirty, but he so tired he forget to set phone alarm and not hear Bao trying to call him four twenty this morning. It was his friend who knock on the door of his room at six o'clock to wake him up and ask him if he not going to the mine."

Alarm not set for 0330, woke up 6

Thinking about the panicky feeling that must have gripped Wei as he realized he had badly overslept, Dawson glanced up. The Chinese man held his head in his hands, the stark implications of his phone alarm lapse evidently not lost on him. If only he had joined his brother at the appointed time, he might have thwarted the plans of Bao's killer—or killers.

"He arrive mining place at about six twenty-five," Huang continued. "By that time, he see Bao pickup there already, and he ask the *galamsey* boys where Bao, and they say haven't seen him. So he call Bao phone and don't get no answer. He call another time, and another time."

"What about between four and six? Did Wei receive any calls from Bao?"

"Only one, at four twenty, and then nothing after that."

"Can he show me the call log on his phone to prove that?"

Huang asked Wei, and to Dawson's relief, he agreed. The business of police investigation of personal phone data had become complicated in Ghana. One clever lawyer had won a case on a technicality that the investigating officer had examined all the accused phone's SMS messages without asking permission. If Wei agreed to show them a limited amount of information, Dawson thought they would be okay. "Please bring him his phone from the confiscated belongings," he asked Obeng, then turned back to Huang. "What time did the *galamsey* workers get to the site?"

"They usually get there about five forty-five."

This is good, Dawson thought. It set the time of death between 4:20 and 5:45 in the morning.

Obeng got back with the smartphone, an LG with a Chinese keyboard, and Dawson asked Wei to bring up the call log. It confirmed Bao's call at the time Wei had stated.

"So, the two pickup trucks I saw parked at the site belong to Wei and his brother?" Dawson asked Mr. Huang.

He nodded. "Yes."

"Which one is Bao's?"

"The red one."

"Thank you," Dawson said. "After Wei got to the mining site, what happened next?"

Huang listened to the next part of the narration from Wei.

"While Wei try call his brother," Huang translated, "one of the *galamsey* boy say he hit something inside the soil while digging. After that, Wei come, and he help the boys dig. Then they can see it somebody head, and they see it's Bao. Take 'bout thirty minute get whole body out, and they put it on the ground. By that time, many people come to watch, and Wei say, no, he don't want people to look at his brother like that. And so he carry Bao to the shack and try to wash the body."

"Why did he try to wash the body?" Dawson asked.

Huang asked Wei this, and he didn't seem to understand the point of the question.

"Because body dirty and is his brother," Huang said simply.

Undoing, Dawson thought—trying to reverse the unpleasantness of the way his brother had been found. "Did he see any blood anywhere on Bao's body or head?"

Huang asked Wei, who shook his head. "No."

That was important too. "But who would want to kill Bao like that?" Dawson asked.

"Maybe some of the *galamsey* boys," Huang said. "Two people from the village, while they were standing near that place where they were digging to free Bao, Wei say he hear them say, 'These *galamsey* boys, now they kill the boss.' Wei ask them, 'What you say? Why you say that?' But they turn away and go."

"Why would the *galamsey* boys want to kill Bao?" Dawson asked.

"They hate him because sometime he don't pay them at the end of every day," Huang said. "Sometime he wait next day, so they think he cheat them. But he never cheat them. And they hated Wei too, so that's why they want him to see his dead brother's body inside the ground."

Dawson supposed that in an environment where the mine workers' pay was so low, withholding the day's wages might motivate a killing, but the signature here was so full of anger and intent to torture that Dawson didn't find it credible. It could be Wei was trying to shift blame. Dawson's hunch was that he had *not* killed Bao, but Dawson wasn't ready to completely dispel the notion yet.

"The man with whom Wei stayed overnight," he said to Huang, "will he be able to confirm that Wei was there all night until morning when he says he woke up?"

This time, the discussion between the two was long and complicated and Dawson truly wished he understood Chinese— whichever type they were speaking.

"Okay," Huang said, turning to Dawson and evidently preparing to launch into a long explanation, "this how it is. In the man's house—his name is Feng—he has two room, so he let Wei sleep in one, but tell him close door because Wei snore very loud, and he disturb. So maybe you ask Feng. He tell you if he hear Wei snoring during the night."

"How did he know about the snoring?" Dawson asked. "Had Wei stayed at Mr. Feng's home before?"

"Yes, many time," Huang answered.

Snore alibi, Dawson thought. *That might be a first.* "Okay, then you will take us to this Mr. Feng so we can talk to him. One more thing: Where is Bao's phone? Did Wei locate it anywhere?"

The answer to that was no. Wei's opinion was that whoever had killed Bao had also taken his phone, and he suspected the *galamsey* boys, who had scattered without a trace, were the responsible party. Dawson admitted that their disappearance was troublesome, but Wei's imagined scenario didn't quite fit the picture. There was still a lot that didn't make sense.

Dawson stood up. "Let's go to Mr. Feng's house."

CHAPTER NINE

HUANG DID NOT KNOW where Feng lived, so Wei would have to travel with the group to show them the route. As Dawson, Obeng, Mr. Huang, and the handcuffed prisoner walked out of the station toward Huang's SUV, Akua Helmsley and her cameraman Samuels were waiting outside in the shade of a mango tree bearing early fruit.

"Chief Inspector," she said. "We meet again."

"And I'm sure not for the last time," he said, barely slowing his pace as he walked by, but she kept up with him.

"Progress?" she asked.

"Not much."

"Is Wei Liu your prime suspect in the murder?"

"No."

"Why is he still in handcuffs then?"

He looked at her. "Actually for a different offense."

"For being an illegal miner?"

Dawson shook his head. "The legal status of miners isn't my concern, Miss Helmsley."

Obeng got in the backseat of the SUV with Wei.

"So, no prime suspect so far," Helmsley said. "Where are you going now?"

"To make some inquiries," Dawson said unhelpfully as he got into the front passenger seat.

"I'll check back with you in a couple of days," Helmsley said "Is that okay?"

"Yes," Dawson replied, not certain he meant it.

DAWSON, OBENG, WEI, and Mr. Huang picked their way through the thick weeds and shrubs that hampered the walk up to Feng's house, which was literally in the bush off an unpaved road. Two Chinese men, one in his late twenties and the other in his midforties, were loading the back of a mud-caked red Toyota pickup. They turned as Dawson and Huang approached.

"Nǐ hǎo," Huang greeted them.

They responded, and Huang introduced Dawson and explained the purpose of the visit. The older man was Feng, the younger was a friend who was helping him transport some new water pumps to a mining site around a village called Aniamoa. As Huang spoke, Feng was nodding. He had high, tight cheekbones and sharp wrinkles like starbursts at the corners of his eyes from squinting. He put a cigarette between his lips, lit it with a match, and said something.

Huang turned to Dawson. "He say, yah, it's true Wei stay here last night, because he have to get up early and not want to go all the way back to Kumasi."

"Does Feng know what time Wei went to bed?"

Huang conferred again. "He doesn't remember exactly. About eleven o'clock, Wei went into his room to sleep."

"Does the room have a door?"

Feng confirmed that.

"You want me to ask him if you look inside the house?" Huang asked Dawson.

Ten points for excellence, Huang, Dawson thought. "If Mr. Feng has no objection, I would appreciate it."

Feng considered the request for a second and then said yes.

It was a small brick house that had never received a second coat of paint. Inside, it reeked of cigarettes and was rudimentary—a battered settee, a table, and two plastic chairs in the sitting room; a hot plate in the kitchenette on the far right with a couple plates, pots, and pans; and two buckets filled with water no doubt from the borehole Dawson had noticed outside. The toilet took up minimal space in the far left corner.

Feng indicated the "bedroom" in which Wei had spent the night. It was nothing more than an eight-by-six space with a mosquito-netted window and a thin foam mattress on the concrete floor. Most importantly, though, the room had a door.

"Did Wei shut the door when he went to sleep?" Dawson asked.

Feng said yes. Whenever Wei stayed there, he shut his door to minimize the disturbance his snoring might cause.

Dawson looked across to the other bedroom, which was considerably larger. Clothes were strewn across the bed and on the floor. He had no interest in seeing anything more than that, nor did he need to. "And did Feng also shut his door when he went to bed?" he asked Huang.

Feng replied that he had.

"Could he hear Wei snoring during the night?" Dawson asked. He waited while the two men discussed this.

"Feng say he hear it little bit," Huang said, "but when he wake up go to toilet, he hear it well."

Dawson perked up. "What time was that?"

"Not look at the time, but he say he usually get up one time at night to piss around three o'clock."

Dawson nodded. "And the next time Feng woke up was when?"

"Six o'clock," Huang said. "He see Wei door still close and hear Wei still snore, and so he knock and open it and say, 'Hey, man, what you doing? You not go to the mine!' And Wei jump up and look at his phone and start to shout, and run out of the house to his truck."

Dawson was satisfied. "Okay," he said to Huang. "Thank you. How do you say that in Chinese?"

"*Xièxiè.*"

Dawson looked at Feng. "*Xièxiè.*"

Feng smiled and gave an appreciative, phlegmy laugh.

•   •   •

THEY TOOK WEI back to the Dunkwa station and locked him up. Dawson, cognizant of how much of Huang's time he had taken up, asked him to please bear with him for just a little longer, and Huang graciously agreed.

Dawson took Kobby aside. "I have been telling the Chinese man that we will be prosecuting him for the assault, but I don't think it's worth it, the way our courts and remand prisons are already clogged. So, unless you insist that we proceed, I intend to have the charges dropped and release him. Are you okay with that?"

"Yes, sir," Kobby said, nodding. "What he did is not worth so much *palava*. Thank you, boss."

Getting started on the paperwork, Dawson decided he would carry out what the GPS sometimes did for offences it decided to overlook. Before release, Wei would be asked to sign a warning letter that said if he ever were to repeat such behavior, he would be prosecuted to the full extent of the law. That was about as far as Dawson wanted to go.

CHAPTER TEN

FREED FROM JAIL, WEI had the task, along with the police, of notifying Bao's wife that her husband had been murdered, but everyone including Wei agreed that the burdensome duty shouldn't be done over the phone. Besides, for Dawson, it was always helpful to witness the reaction of the family member receiving the bad news, because those closest to the victim were so often involved in his or her murder.

Huang drove back to the mining site so that Wei could retrieve his pickup. Dawson thought about Bao's vehicle. It shouldn't be left alone for too much longer, as it was potentially a piece of evidence. "Does Wei have a spare key to Bao's truck?" Dawson asked Mr. Huang.

Wei took out a substantial bunch of keys from his pocket and looked through. He found one and tried it in the door of the red pickup. It opened up.

"Thank you," Dawson said, holding out his hand. "May I have it?"

Wei handed it over and Dawson gave it to Obeng. "Drive it to Obuasi for now," he told the sergeant, "and then we'll transfer it to Kumasi HQ when they can take it." Dawson had no idea how packed Kumasi's MTU was, but if it was anything like Accra's, it would be jumbled and overflowing. Sometimes crime-related vehicles sat there for years.

With Dawson in the passenger seat, Wei took the lead to

Kumasi, followed by Mr. Huang, whom Dawson had persuaded to help with translation when they paid the fateful visit to Bao's wife. Wei drove like a maniac, even over the punishing Dunkwa-Obuasi portion of the journey. Dawson thought his internal organs were being rearranged. After a two-hour drive, they were back in Kumasi.

"Where do you live, Mr. Liu?" Dawson asked.

"Kwadaso Estate," Wei responded, looking at him with a smile. The Chinese man seemed friendlier now that he was free and the stress had abated somewhat.

Dawson had heard the name, but wasn't sure exactly where it was. At any rate, he thought he should know where Wei lived in case of an emergency. They were now on Melcom Road in the Ahodwo section of the city, passing The View Bar & Grill and a few hundred meters from that, a bed and breakfast called Four Villages Inn.

Wei turned right at J. Owusu Akyaw Street and pulled up to a black and gold metal gate three houses down on the right. He pumped his horn and a young watchman in a tattered pinkish T-shirt opened up and directed them to go through into the yard shaded with mango trees, where Wei picked a good spot to park behind a black late-model Kia SUV and a sleek silver Mercedes-Benz.

The front door was some kind of metal painted to vaguely resemble wood. The Ghanaian housemaid let Dawson and the two Chinese men into the air-conditioned house. She looked as if she never got enough to eat.

The sitting room was full of overstuffed shiny black imitation-leather sofas and chairs and black glossy tables with gold trim. In fact, gold seemed to be everywhere—a kind of assault on the senses. The dining area and kitchen were comparatively small, both with a lot of gleaming plastic and glass.

"Please, you can have a seat," the housemaid said softly. "I'm going to call her."

Wei and Huang sat on one sofa, but Dawson took a look at some framed family photographs on a black-lacquered sideboard.

One was a posed color portrait of a twenty-something man in a suit and tie and a woman with a frilly lilac blouse standing close together and smiling out at the camera—Bao and his wife, Dawson guessed, perhaps fifteen to twenty years ago. Another was an old sepia photograph of a large group of what Dawson imagined was extended family, with all the little ones in the front. It struck Dawson that no one was smiling in the photos. Everyone appeared stiff.

Dawson turned to Huang. "What is Bao's wife's name?"

"Lian," he replied.

"Does that mean something in Chinese?"

Huang thought about it for a moment. "Something like graceful flower."

As he said that, a woman appeared at the doorway leading farther into the house. She was tiny, girl-like, and pretty, with dark hair pulled back from her face to accentuate her defined cheekbones. She looked puzzled at the sight of the three men in her sitting room.

Wei stood up, appearing nervous. "Lian, *nǐ hǎo,*" he said, coming forward to clasp both her hands.

She seemed to sense his edginess and responded uneasily. "*Nǐ hǎo, nǐ hǎo,*" she replied, smiling uncertainly.

Wei began talking to her in Chinese, and even to Dawson's ears, it was clear how halting and tentative his speech was, as if he were trying to choose his words as carefully as he could. The more he spoke, the more Lian's face clouded over, and when Wei was done, she regarded him with an expression somewhere between incredulous and affronted. She took a step back, and for a moment Dawson thought she was about to retire to some internal chamber of the house, but instead she began to shout questions at Wei in a disturbing barking manner. He seemed to be trying to answer, but he never got very far, and after a while, overwhelmed by emotion, he covered his face with his hands and began to take deep, heaving breaths.

Lian staggered past him, looking confused, lost, and bewildered. Dawson watched as she swung around and shouted something else

unintelligible at Wei, and then bolted for the door. Wei caught
her before she got there, trying to hold her without hurting her as
she struggled, screaming.

My God, Dawson thought. Worse, much worse than he had
imagined, but then it often was.

Wei was trying to talk to her even as she was flailing. Then,
like a light switched off, the energy left her and she collapsed
into a ball on the floor sobbing in a strange braying fashion. The
housemaid, who had appeared in the sitting room in alarm, knelt
down by Lian, gently patting her back. After some moments,
Lian's crying lost strength, but quiet episodes were interrupted by
bursts of more grief.

"Can we help her to get up and sit down?" Dawson suggested.

Huang asked her, and she agreed. Wei assisted her to the sofa.

"Please," Dawson said to the maid, "can you bring her some
water?"

She hurried then to the kitchen and returned with a glass of
water. Lian took one sip and gave it back, staring ahead blankly
with swollen eyes.

"What was she saying when she first heard the news?" Dawson
asked Huang.

He shrugged. "Something like . . . not believe it. How Bao
dead?"

Dawson nodded. He'd seen the broadest range of emotions in
his time. This was only one of the many.

Lian sent Huang and Dawson a querying look. Wei said something to her, obviously in explanation.

"Tell her I'm very sorry for the death of her husband," Dawson
told Huang after he had explained to her.

Huang did that, and then she asked Wei a question. He sat in
the sofa closest to her chair and began what Dawson assumed was
an account of everything that had happened that morning.

"She want know why take so long you inform her," Huang said.

"Tell her I'm sorry for that," Dawson said. "It was because we
had to see to some police business first."

She nodded in acceptance and asked something else.

"She want know if anyone caught," Huang said, "and I told her no."

"Thank you," Dawson said. "Please ask her if she feels well enough for me to ask her some questions, or does she need some more time?"

Huang posed the question to her. "No, she okay, Mr. Dawson. You can go 'head."

"Did Bao sleep here last night?"

"She says yes."

"Excuse me for asking, but did she sleep in the same bed with him?"

"Yes."

"What time did he leave to go to work this morning?"

After a short discussion, Huang came back to Dawson. "He told her last night that he go to help Wei fix excavator four o'clock in the morning, and so he have to wake up two thirty. She set her alarm clock and wake him up, and he leave about ten minutes."

Kumasi to Dunkwa in under two hours, Dawson thought. Probably quite feasible that early, especially if Bao drove anything like his younger brother. "After she saw him for the last time," Dawson asked quietly, aware that this might trigger tears again, "did she speak to him again?"

He was right. When Huang asked Lian, her chin began to quiver and her face cracked, shredded again by grief. She shook her head.

"No," Huang said sadly. "She never speak to him again."

"I'm sorry," Dawson said. "I need to ask her something. Does she know of anyone who would want to kill Bao?"

A long discussion followed between the Lian and the Chinese males.

"She says she think Ghanaian *galamsey* men hate Bao, so maybe one of them do it."

"Anyone in particular?" Dawson thought he had discerned a name in Lian's long response. "She thinks Kudzo did it?"

Huang was astonished. "How you understand what she say?"

"I didn't," Dawson said. "I just heard the name Kudzo. Why does she think Kudzo did it?"

She shrugged in answer when Huang posed the question, and gave a sharp, short answer.

"She never trust them," Huang explained, avoiding Dawson's eye for some reason. "Always gave Bao trouble."

"That isn't all she said. Tell me all of it, Mr. Huang."

He was squirming. "She say she hate this country," he confessed. "She wish she never come here. She hate the black people, they lazy, all they want is money for no work. Thieves, make trouble all the time."

"Ah, I see," Dawson said.

"Sorry, sir," Huang said.

Dawson shrugged. "At least she's honest."

"Lian wanna know where Bao body," Huang said. "She want see him."

"By now it should be at the mortuary at Komfo Anokye Teaching Hospital," Dawson said. "If she feels prepared to go today, we can go there now."

"She says she wants to."

"Then let's go," Dawson said, "because today is Friday and there will only be a skeleton crew over the weekend."

CHAPTER ELEVEN

MR. HUANG'S SUV WAS much roomier than Wei's pickup, so with Dawson in the front passenger seat and Huang and Lian in the back, Wei drove ten kilometers north to KATH. On the way there, the weekend spectacle for which the Ashanti Region, Kumasi especially, was infamous was on full display. Starting every Thursday—sometimes earlier—Kumasi was thronged with funerals and their preparation. A sea of people filled the streets wearing traditional funeral outfits of the deepest blacks and brilliant reds from scarlet to maroon.

The deceased might have been nobody while he was alive, but now that he was dead, he'd be famous. The shack he lived in that none of his children offered to fix up despite his pleas for assistance would now become a palace for the funeral. Rich or poor, the family would try to put on a show to wow the "mourners," who might choose to attend based on how good the food promised to be, how expensive the alcoholic drinks would be, how many dance and drumming troupes would perform, and how fancy the coffin was. And the so-called mourners? How many yards of silky wax print fabric could you display, and what was the latest and most expensive in funeral fashion? How many gold bracelets could you fit on your wrists, how many rings on your fingers, and how much money could you contribute to the family bereavement fund for all to see?

Dawson turned away in some disgust, busying himself with his phone by texting Christine to ask how she was doing.

AT THE ENTRANCE, the KATH hospital sign, with the H in red, was perched on top of a kiosk of three ATMs, in case one forgot that cash would be needed for any kind of medical treatment. *Cash is still king.* The National Health Insurance Scheme was poorly funded, and services were not even close to free.

Mr. Huang found a parking spot and they walked the palm tree–lined path that skirted the parking lot and approached the newly painted white-and-bronze building. KATH had been around for a while and still had some of the old style louver windows. None of them knew where the mortuary was, but in Dawson's experience, a morgue was always to the rear of the main hospital building. Having it in front wasn't a particularly good omen.

Dawson asked directions from a passing nurse.

"That way," she said, pointing.

They crossed through a large waiting area and down a steep incline. Dawson stole a glance at Lian to see how she was holding up. Her jaw was rigid.

Lining each side of the walkway were clusters of men and women—mostly women—in black and red. Most of these people were waiting for the release of a relative's body. The buildings around which they loitered were old and worn, but at the bottom of the hill came something modern and spacious. Dawson opened the door for the other three and then followed them into a bright spotless lobby cooled to blissful temperatures. Offices lined the hallway in one direction, and down the other were an auditorium and a large comfortable waiting room. The mortuary was *here*? It seemed almost too beautiful.

"May I help you?" a woman asked from behind a half window in the reception office to the left.

"Good afternoon," Dawson said, moving closer. "Is the mortuary in this building?"

"No," she replied. "This is administration. The morgue is around the corner to the left."

Following her directions, Dawson and the others found the right place, and it conformed more to his general image of a mortuary. The inauspicious and unmarked entrance took them into a gloomy narrow hallway. A technician in khaki medical garb was walking down the corridor toward them. He knocked on a door and Dawson caught him just before he went in. The name on his breast pocket said NKRUMAH.

Dawson showed his ID.

Nkrumah, lanky with a bony face and shaved head, glanced at it. "Yes, please. How can I help you?"

"I'm working on the case of Bao Liu. Is the body here?"

Nkrumah sent a knowing glance at Dawson's companions. "The Chinese man. Yes, he's here. He just came. Please, one moment."

He turned and went back down the corridor the way he had come, disappearing through swinging double doors on the far left. Dawson caught the first whiff of formaldehyde and corpses emanating from there. "Mr. Huang," he said, turning to him. "You must warn Lian that Bao's body will not be nice to look at. He will seem very different from when he was alive."

Huang nodded. "Thank you, sir."

He spoke quietly to her, and she nodded.

"Is she okay?" Dawson asked.

"She's fine," Huang confirmed.

Minutes later, Nkrumah emerged and beckoned to them. Dawson and the Chinese trio walked down to join him, and the sickly, fetid smell of the mortuary room grew stronger. A large space with only three tables, the autopsy room had an open door on the far end to facilitate ventilation.

Lian drew in her breath sharply, pressing a kerchief to her nose. Wei tucked her arm into his to steady her. What she had seen was shocking: a corpse occupied each one of the tables, but six or seven of them were on the floor. *No one should see that,* Dawson thought. But the reality of most hospital mortuaries around the country was that capacity was inadequate. The bodies on the floor were up next for autopsies—or maybe they weren't—and there was nowhere to put them.

Bao Liu was not one of those corpses on the floor, and *thank God*, Dawson thought. Nkrumah took them into a smaller room where Bao's body lay on a table more modestly with a sheet covering him from the chest down. He had turned a mottled gray, an awful hue under the fluorescent lighting.

Dawson moved around to Lian's unsupported side just in time for what he had anticipated. After she had looked at Bao's face for a few moments, Lian collapsed like a sack of *cocoyams*. Dawson grabbed her on his side, as did Wei on his. Huang hurried to help.

"Let her rest her head on your lap," Dawson instructed him, as he and Wei let her down slowly to the floor.

Nkrumah, who had evidently seen this before, lifted Lian's feet up and seconds later she opened her eyes, looked up with a bewildered expression, and murmured something.

"What did she say?" Dawson asked Huang.

"She ask if it all a dream."

"Okay, let her rest there." He looked at Nkrumah. "Let's talk for a moment."

The two men stepped outside.

"When do you think the postmortem might be done?" Dawson asked.

Nkrumah angled his head, considering. "Please, maybe in about . . . three weeks?"

Dawson had feared as much. "Can we do better than that?"

"If only you want to talk to our physician on duty, Dr. Prempeh."

"Where is he?"

"He is in. I can take you to his office."

"Okay—after we check how the lady is doing."

They returned to the room to find Lian at least partially recovered. She was standing, leaning against Wei, and slowly he walked with her out of the room and the morgue, settling them on the two chairs in the hallway.

"I'll be back," Dawson told Huang. Nkrumah led him up the hall, knocked on a door marked DR. PREMPEH, and opened it. The room was full—Prempeh was at his desk addressing five other people, three standing, two sitting. He was in his early thirties with trendy glasses, a white shirt and checkered tie, and black slacks. He looked up at Nkrumah. "Yes?"

"Please, I have Detective Darko Dawson here regarding the Liu case."

"Oh, yeah, come in."

"It's okay," Dawson said hurriedly. The room was too crowded for comfort. "I'll wait outside."

Dawson thanked Mr. Nkrumah, and the tech went off about his duties. Dawson checked his phone messages to while away the minutes. Not too long after, the five people filed out. Two of them were women, one much older than the other, dressed in black; the men were in normal, rather tattered attire, and they appeared crestfallen. Dawson's guess was they were having a difficult time getting their relative's body released for funeral rites.

Prempeh's head popped around the door. "Still there? Oh, good. Come in. Sorry about that."

He and Dawson shook hands. "Please," Prempeh said, "do have a seat." He went back to his own and leaned back. "You said you're Inspector who?"

"Dawson. Darko Dawson."

"Okay, cool. How can I help?"

Dawson gave him a quick rundown of the case so far. "The problem is," he said, to the doctor, "Mr. Nkrumah is saying it will be about three weeks before we can get an autopsy on Bao Liu."

"Is that what he said?" Prempeh asked. "Ridiculous." He sprang up, jumped to the door, and yanked it open, poking his head around the frame and bellowing, "*Nkrumah!*"

"Sir!" a voice answered from the distance, and Dawson heard footsteps running down the corridor. "Yes, sir?"

"Why is it going to take three weeks to do the post on the Chinese man?"

"Please, we are very backlogged."

"We're *always* backlogged, so what's the difference? When is this alleged forensic expert coming from Accra to help us?"

"Please, I don't know. The director says he's working on it, please."

"Okay, okay. Go back to work."

"Yes, sir."

Prempeh, looking annoyed, pushed the door closed and flopped down in his chair again. "Do you know why it is going to take three weeks?" he asked Dawson fiercely. "Disorganization, that's all. Disorganization and inefficiency. All morning long I've been waiting for my cases to come up and they're not ready."

He looked up at a knock on the door, which opened to a woman and two men who slowly filed in and stood against the wall with hands crossed in front of them.

"Excuse me one moment, Mr. Dawson," Dr. Prempeh said. "Yes, how can I help you?"

The woman was dressed in deep red. The older man, about sixty, was in traditional swaddling black cloth that covered the left chest and shoulder with the right exposed. Dawson guessed the younger man was a son or nephew. He was about twenty-six in calf-length cargo shorts and a sleeveless T-shirt that looked like it hadn't been washed in several days.

Beginning with a salute of deference to the doctor and an imploring "*mepa wo kyew*," the older man launched into a complicated explanation in Twi as to why they had come. It appeared to Dawson that they had been given the incorrect information that their relative, who had suffered a premature and unsuspected death, would not need an autopsy. The man was appealing for the release of the body, repeating his plea multiple times.

The woman added to this by curtseying several times to the doctor while elaborately performing the traditional supplicant gesture of gently patting the palm of the left hand with the back of the right.

"What you have to do," Dr. Prempeh said with patience that surprised Dawson, "is go back to the one who told you no autopsy is needed, and tell him to write a letter to the mortuary director explaining why. Then the director will make the final decision."

They thanked him profusely and left. Prempeh looked at Dawson. "If I had said no, I won't release the body, they would blame me. Now I've tossed the ball back in the other guy's court. But honestly, they are never going to get the body released without the postmortem, and the trouble is they have no money to pay for it. It's sad, but there it is."

Dawson agreed—the sad, battered life of the poor and powerless in Ghana: wasting time and money traveling back and forth to no avail.

"On the other hand," Prempeh continued, "there should be no problem with this Chinese guy going to the top of the line. I'm assuming his folks have money." Prempeh leaned back. "Well, let me ask you this, Inspector. How important is this case to you?"

"How do you mean, Doctor?"

"I mean, realistically, this is not really a high-profile case to you, is it? Some illegal Chinese guy murdered? These *galamsey* people are murdering each other every week for some stupid reason— both the Ghanaians and the Chinese. You want to move fast on the case, or would you rather put this on low priority and get to something else?"

Dawson felt his blood chill a little. "Prostitute, bank executive, illegal gold miner—it's all the same to me. Murder is murder."

"Got it," Prempeh said, smiling. He leaned forward and unconsciously spun his pen in circles on the desk. "Here is what I will do for you. I could perform the post on this man, but you know, I'm not really a forensic pathologist, which is what you need here. There's a woman in Accra at Korle Bu—brand new Edinburgh graduate and first Ghanaian female forensic pathologist in the country—they say she's sharp as a tack. She was supposed to come up here and teach us some new stuff, but all the stupid bureaucracy has got in the way. Let me try and expedite it, and maybe we can get her up here to do the Chinese man as her first demonstration case in the posh facility in the new building—not here in this dump."

"I appreciate that very much," Dawson said, standing up. "I think you need to talk to the Chinese man's family to explain the situation."

"I will do that," Prempeh said. "Please show them in."

Dawson called the Chinese trio in but stayed out himself. Prempeh could handle it through Mr. Huang, and besides, Dawson did not want to be there if and when money changed hands. *See nothing, hear nothing, say nothing.*

LIAN WANTED TO return home, but did not want to be alone, so Wei offered to stay with her a while. But first he had to pick up his laptop. Mr. Huang said it was no problem to swing around to Wei's house. *Perfect,* Dawson thought. Wei directed Huang to take a right at Pine Avenue off Bantama Road, and then a left on West End Hospital Bypass. The streets of Kwadaso were somewhat serpentine with neat houses quite close together on either side. At length, Wei pointed out his house and told Huang to blow the horn at the gate. A few seconds later, a watchman pulled it open so that Huang could drive through.

Wei alighted and the other three waited for him. The house, a pinkish color, and the unpaved yard were clearly smaller than Lian's, but just like hers, the property was protected by an electric fence running along the top of the wall, which encircled the house and space around it.

It was stuffy in the car, so Dawson got out and casually looked around, making sure to exchange a few friendly words with the watchman sitting on a stool at his post near the gate. He said his name was David. A small, padlocked wooden shed stood behind him to the right. Dawson supposed it held tools for maintence work around the house, as well as, perhaps, a machete David might find handy if a burglar ever somehow wormed his way into the compound.

Wei came out with his laptop and a tangle of connecting wires. "We go now," he said to Dawson.

Yes, we go, Dawson thought. It had been a long day on his first case. Was it to be simple, solved in a matter of two days or so, or was it to be more complicated? He laughed to himself at the question. Having needed a Chinese interpreter already seemed an indication that complexity awaited.

CHAPTER TWELVE

THE GALAMSEY BOYS WHO had discovered Bao Liu's body were such an important element of the puzzle that it was vital Dawson locate at least one of them. He thought the chief of Dunkwa might be able to help, since chiefs often knew everything that was going on in their village or town.

On Saturday morning, hoping to make time and leave some of the day free to get to Gifty's guesthouse, Dawson engaged Kofi's taxi services and set out for Dunkwa at seven with Obeng. During the trip, Dawson found out a little bit about him. He was married with four children and was born and brought up in Aniamoa. He had managed to stay in primary school despite his father's attempts to keep him working on the farm, and then he had moved to Kumasi to live with an aunt while in secondary school.

As they got to Dunkwa, Dawson made one stop to buy an obligatory bottle of schnapps for the chief, whose name was Nana Akrofi. Showing up empty-handed was a no-no. His palace was at the top of an incline along a paved road eaten away at its edges and hugged by worn houses with corrugated tin roofs. At the road-side, an old man in a green shirt dozed off with his back against the wall of a building as he shared space with two other people on that typically Ghanaian item of furniture—the long wooden bench.

The color of the chief's brick house had been corrupted by accumulated layers of the ocher village dust, but the small veranda where a young man asked Dawson and Obeng to take a seat while he went into the house to get the chief was painted an uneven pink. They could smell palm nut soup cooking from somewhere in the back, and a baby was crying.

When Nana Akrofi emerged, he turned out to be younger than Dawson had imagined. He wasn't dressed in resplendent traditional garb either, but rather in a pair of tan khaki slacks and an orange T-shirt with RUTGERS UNIVERSITY written on the front in blue.

Akrofi shook hands with them, right to left, and then sat down in a white plastic chair. Times must be hard, Dawson thought, because the chief was without a linguist or spokesman. Or it could be this young guy was the "acting" chief and had dispensed with that old formality. Traditional life was changing.

Neither Dawson nor Obeng spoke out of turn. The chief had to start first, and with a fairly predictable script. After a pause in which he leaned forward slightly, he cleared his throat. "Eh-heh. Who are you?"

Dawson let Obeng speak first on their behalf. In this case, police hierarchy was subordinate to the sergeant's roots in the Ashanti Region. Speaking in Twi, he introduced himself, beginning with the deferential *"Mepa wo kyew,"* and then introduced Dawson. Then it was time to present the schnapps, which the chief gracefully accepted.

"So," he said, "what is your mission here today?"

"Please, Nana," Obeng continued, "a certain Chinese man died yesterday morning at one of the mines around Dunkwa and my boss here, Chief Inspector Dawson, and I are investigating what happened."

"Yes, I know about it," Akrofi said, looking directly at Dawson now. "If I can help you in your investigation, I will."

"Thank you, Nana," Dawson said. "The Chinese man's name is Bao Liu. He was the boss of some *galamsey* boys who found him buried in the soil yesterday morning. We need to talk to those boys, but they have all disappeared."

"Are they in trouble?" the chief asked.

"I don't think so," Dawson said truthfully, "but without

speaking with them, the investigation is incomplete because they are the first witnesses."

Akrofi appeared satisfied with that and nodded. "I know the one called Kudzo Gablah. He's from the Volta Region. I understand he left Dunkwa this morning and went to one of the mines at Aniamoa."

Dawson glanced at Obeng. That was the sergeant's home village. Connections like that were always good.

"*Mepa wo kyew*," Dawson said to the chief, "you say Kudzo went to Aniamoa. Is it because he was trying to avoid the police?"

Akrofi smiled slightly. "I don't know. Maybe you need to ask him."

Dawson nodded. "We will do so. Thank you, Nana."

"You are welcome."

It might have been the end to a short meeting, but Dawson was curious about other things, and now that he had given the chief his schnapps, he felt licensed to ask Akrofi if he had known Bao Liu or his brother Wei.

"I was not the chief here when Bao first came to Dunkwa three years ago," Akrofi replied, "but one time they came to pay their respects to me."

Dawson wondered if they had brought the chief some gold along with the schnapps. "Did you hear of any problems between the Lius and the farmers working in the area of the mine?" he asked.

Akrofi shook his head. "No problems at all."

But Dawson's left palm began to itch as if a caterpillar was walking across it, and he knew the chief wasn't being truthful. "*Mepa wo kyew*, Nana," he said, still very deferentially, "if you don't mind my asking, how have the Chinese people been received in Dunkwa?"

Akrofi reflectively rubbed his hands back and forth over the tops of his thighs.

"Well, you see," he began, "the China people have helped us a lot. They have provided the youth with employment where before there was no work. You know, these young guys don't want to work on the farms planting cocoa and all that. They want quick money. Cocoa is too slow. Look at how many years it takes for one cocoa tree to start bearing fruit. So this gold mining, it is very good for our boys. It keeps them out of trouble, prevents them from engaging in robbery and theft and all those things."

"*Medaase*, Nana," Dawson said, nodding to show acknowledgment of and respect for Akrofi's observations, but in fact he was slowly working up to the most troublesome aspect of the Chinese occupation.

"In addition," the chief continued, "they constructed two boreholes for us because the Ofin River has been polluted by AngloGold Ashanti mining. So we can now have a good water supply."

Interesting, Dawson thought. Akrofi was laying the blame for the river pollution at the feet of the multinational company, AngloGold Ashanti, rather than the small-scale miners. "I see. That's a good point." Now the tough question. "Please, Nana, what do you say about the farms that have been destroyed by the excavators? Maybe it's true that the young people get work on the mining sites, but at the same time, farmers who have spent all their lives planting crops have lost their livelihood. Is that not correct?"

Akrofi shook his head vigorously. "Please, Mr. Chief Inspector. First of all, don't believe everything that you hear about those excavated areas. It is not all farmland. Some of it isn't suitable for cocoa at all, because the soil is not good quality. And then, those farmers complaining are the same fools who sold their land to the Chinese. They are not supposed to do that without my permission, but still, some of them do. Then, when the money they took has run out, they come crying to me saying, 'Please, Nana, what should I do, Nana? The China people have destroyed my land.' You are rather the stupid one who allowed yourself to fall to the temptation of the money they offered you."

"In other words, Nana," Dawson said cautiously, getting close to the edge, "if a farmer did not want his land used for mining and the Chinese came to ask you permission to take that land, you would not allow it."

"Yes!" he answered fiercely. "Of course I would not allow it."

In his peripheral vision, Dawson saw Obeng averting his gaze, and he sensed that the sergeant knew or suspected that the chief's assertion wasn't altogether true.

"Look," the chief continued, "the only real problem with the excavators is that the Chinamen should backfill the pits once they have finished with the site."

"Why don't they?" Dawson asked.

"Because it costs money," Akrofi said simply. "It takes a lot of fuel and time. I was listening to the radio the other day and heard the Minister of Agriculture saying that they will come in and cover up all the abandoned pits and request the Center for Scientific and Industrial Research to plant and restore all these areas."

"Do you think that will happen?" Dawson asked.

The chief made a rude noise with his mouth. "It will never happen. These ministers are all liars. Spending the country's money on their Benzes and girlfriends."

Much truth to that, unfortunately.

"The Chinamen have built us roads that go far into the bush," Akrofi said. "If you wait for the government to do such a thing, you will wait until your hair turns gray. The Chinese even built a small school in one of the villages not far from here. So yes, they are good people. They have passion for the villagers. If I have a problem, I just go to them and they help me. The Chinese have been giving us money every two weeks to maintain the boreholes."

That surprised Dawson. He would not have expected that kind of generosity. Which made him think of something. "What about Bao Liu? Did he contribute to the boreholes?"

"Not as such," Akrofi said, "but I understand he planned to do so."

Could there have been any conflict in that area? Perhaps Bao had withheld funds from the chief, or had refused to bribe him for something? But as a motive for murder, it still seemed unlikely. *You know where your bread is buttered, even if the butter is a little long in coming.* Still, what was the chief withholding about conflict between Bao and the local farmers? Was he trying to gloss over the true situation, or was he shielding someone? Much as Dawson wanted to know that, confronting Nana Akrofi about it now would destroy any chances of questioning the chief in the future.

Dawson looked at Obeng, conveying that he had no more questions for the chief. Obeng nodded. He had none either. He and Dawson began the process of thanking the chief and wishing him the very best. He rose and again shook their hands, right to left.

Akrofi had an afterthought as Dawson and Obeng were about to leave. "When you go to look for that boy, Kudzo Gablah," he said, "just be ready. He will be afraid of you and he might try to escape before you find him."

CHAPTER THIRTEEN

.

GETTING TO ANIAMOA MEANT traveling thirty miles north-northwest from Dunkwa deep into the bush along unpaved red laterite. If Kudzo Gablah had indeed fled to Aniamoa, he obviously wanted to be as far away from Dunkwa as possible.

Dawson texted Christine, SORRY LOVE, CAN'T GET TO THE HOUSE TODAY—TOO MUCH GOING ON. WILL TRY TMRW. LUV U

She replied, OK, LU2

Whenever a rare SUV or truck appeared in the opposite direction, both vehicles squeezed over onto the verge to allow each other to pass. The dust, potholes and bumps made Dawson think wistfully of owning an SUV just for this purpose.

Obeng told Kofi where to stop and wait until their return. They would be walking the rest of the way because the road trailed off and the taxi would not be able to handle the terrain.

Like Dunkwa, Aniamoa had a number of small-scale mining sites dotted around the town. Obeng had a pretty good idea which one of them Kudzo was likely to have sought out as his new location.

The perishing afternoon heat seemed to make everything still as they walked, the brush softly crunching underfoot. A rhythmic chugging noise slowly became louder, different from the now-familiar excavator sound.

"*Ticki-ticki-ticki-ticki,*" Dawson said, imitating the sound. "What's that?"

"Dredging pump, sir," Obeng said. "This kind of mining is different from the one where they found the dead Chinaman."

After several hundred meters, they began a slight decline into a valley and the view opened up beyond a clump of trees to reveal a river below them. About ten young men were crowded on a barge secured to one bank. The *ticki-ticki* was from a filthy, smoking diesel pump, also on the barge.

Facing the barge was a smaller vessel with two boys on it. Together they used a long pole to stab and churn the riverbed, increasing the amount of gravel to the pump. The river was a murky, yellowish brown.

"You see how those boys are churning the riverbed?" Obeng said to Dawson, pointing. "That makes it easier for the pump to suck up mud and gravel. Then the gravel is washed and maybe they can get some small gold at the end of the day."

Dawson was trying to get a grasp of how much—or small—that amount of gold could be. "How much can the workers make?" he asked Obeng.

Obeng shrugged. "Most days just a few *cedis*. Sometimes nothing. Don't forget, the owner takes most of the profit. But what is sad, sir, is that the tiny amount these boys earn is more than they made in the hometowns they came from. So this is why they stay, doing this dangerous work."

It was a stark truth. Elsewhere in Ghana, street children eked out a meager living in urban centers like Accra, and they had similar stories: no work, and nothing to do in the villages they hailed from.

As Dawson watched the dredging, he reflected that he found this method of gold mining most intimidating because he could not swim and had an abiding fear of deep water. He spotted an eddy around the sandbar adjacent to the barge, which to him meant that a person could be swept away into the clutches of the wider river as it gathered strength and depth farther downstream.

One of the guys on the sandbar spotted Obeng, waved at him, and started his way toward them by plunging into the water between the bar and the bank. The level reached the top of his chest, even though he was quite tall, and Dawson could tell that the current was exerting a pull. He shuddered.

The depth of the river at the crossing point the man had chosen wasn't the only thing that caught Dawson's attention. The man had slipped off his shorts, left them at the sandbar and crossed the river stark naked, emerging completely exposed and in full view of his coworkers. He swept excess water off his body and sauntered to a clump of rocks to put on another pair of shorts waiting for him. Evidently this was the norm and *galamsey* boys were not in the least bit bashful. The man, in his early twenties, called out to Obeng with a familiarity that demonstrated that they knew each other, and walked in their direction with the same casual gait.

"Please, we can go down," Obeng said to Dawson.

From where they stood, the drop to river level was a few meters, and steep, so they had to jump, their feet imprinting the soft, squelchy loam. They covered the rest of the way to meet Obeng's friend, whose name was Brave. He was lean and muscled from hard physical work and rather fair colored with a broad, flat face. He and Obeng shook hands, snapped fingers, and traded a couple pleasantries, and then Obeng introduced him to Dawson.

"*Akwaaba*," Brave said in Twi.

But Dawson had guessed he was Ewe because Ewes loved names like "Marvelous," "Beauty," "Grace," and "Charity." He replied to Brave in Ewe.

Brave laughed, slapping palms with Dawson in delight. "Are you Ewe?"

"Half Ewe, half Fante."

"Oh, wonderful."

But to be fair to Obeng, who didn't speak Ewe, Dawson and Brave went back to Twi, the default Ghanaian language.

"You know Kudzo Gablah, right?" Obeng asked Brave.

He nodded. "Yes please. He's from Keta, my hometown."

"We're looking for him."

"Is that so? Please, isn't he working at Dunkwa?"

Obeng shook his head. "Nana Akrofi said he came to Aniamoa, so we thought maybe he was at this site."

"Oh, okay," Brave said. "He used to be with us, but no longer."

An older man came up to them who turned out to be the foreman.

"I have all my papers," the foreman said defensively in response to the detectives' inquiries about Kudzo. "This is a legal site, and I don't deal with troublesome boys like that Gablah. I told him a long time ago that I didn't want him working here."

"Relax," Dawson said with a smile. "It's not you we are investigating. Why did you not want Kudzo working with you?"

"Hot temper," the foreman said in English. "*Too* hot. He fought with me; he fought with all these guys." He gestured to his workers. "I don't know what is wrong with him."

"I see," Dawson said, wondering if this was going to be a short case. *Did Kudzo kill Bao in a fit of anger?*

"Please," the foreman said, switching back to Twi, "if you think he's around the Aniamoa area, then you should go into the town and ask."

"We will do that," Dawson said. "Thank you."

"You are welcome." The foreman turned away. Dawson could tell that he wanted as little as possible to do with this investigation.

Brave accompanied them part of the way back up out of the river depression, showing them a much easier path than the way they had come.

"So is your group of miners Ghanaian-operated?" Dawson asked Brave.

"Please, no. A certain Chinese man owns it."

"Sometimes you won't see any Chinese at the site," Obeng explained to Dawson. "The Ghanaian authorities have started to pay more attention to illegal mining so Chinese owners put a Ghanaian front man there so that people coming around won't become suspicious." He gave a hard ironic smile. "These China people aren't stupid at all."

Once Brave had bid them goodbye, Dawson asked Obeng a question that persisted in his mind. "I'm curious—is this site really legal the way the foreman said?"

Obeng laughed. "Don't mind him. No dredge mining is legal in Ghana. It is spoiling our rivers. Do you see how the water is colored that ugly brown?"

"Yes."

"That's not how it's supposed to be. That is all the pollutants making it like that. Now, imagine not just ten or twenty of these barges dredging, but hundreds and hundreds of them all along Ghana's rivers. How will our rivers survive, and the fish in the rivers, and the people who eat the fish and drink the water? And what can the government do? Nothing."

Obeng and Dawson fell silent as they returned to the taxi and considered the sheer magnitude of a problem that seemed to have grown larger than anyone could handle.

BACK IN THE taxi, they went on to Aniamoa. It was smaller than Dunkwa, a large village rather than a town. A group of boys was playing soccer in a dusty field devoid of grass and full of dips and rises that the boys negotiated as if it were second nature.

Since Aniamoa was where he grew up, Obeng knew a lot of people there, and as they alighted from the vehicle he was already calling out and waving to several. He and Dawson stopped by four men playing cards and asked them if they knew Kudzo Gablah. After some discussion, they decided they had seen him earlier on and pointed vaguely in one direction. Following that lead, Dawson and Obeng moved on. A skinny tan-colored dog resting under a tree watched them with interest and decided to follow them. Goats wandered about or stood placidly chewing whatever goats chew.

"I'll ask these women," Obeng said, indicating a young woman in front of a house pounding *fufuo* while her synchronized partner turned the glutinous mass in the mortar with the same rhythm.

"*Dabi*," she said, shaking her head without breaking her rhythm. "We don't know anyone by that name."

Something about the way she said that alerted Dawson. He looked around and spotted a young man appearing from behind the wall of the next house and then ducking quickly back when he saw the two detectives. Dawson touched Obeng on the shoulder and beckoned him to follow as he walked quickly toward the target house.

"I saw a guy just now," he told Obeng quietly. "I think it was him."

Dawson didn't know what Kudzo looked like, and he could be wrong, but he didn't think so. He signaled Obeng to circle round in one direction while he went the other. When he got to the back wall of the house, Dawson peeped around it and saw the young man on the lookout, his head craned the other way. Dawson stepped out quietly from behind the wall. "Kudzo Gablah?"

The man took off like a rocket and bolted for the bush at the outer perimeter of a row of houses, but Dawson was ready, and broke into a run just as soon as Kudzo did.

"*Stop!*" Dawson called out.

He was hoping Obeng would be coming around the corner at just the right moment. But it wasn't the sergeant who collided with Kudzo—it was the dog who had taken a liking to the two detectives. Its tail wagging as it looked back at Obeng, it didn't see the fleeing Kudzo in time to move out of his way. With a yelp, the dog tried to avoid Kudzo, but it was too late. Kudzo tripped and tumbled. The dog scuttled away, apparently unwounded except for his pride.

Kudzo was quick to get back on his feet, but he was smart enough to know that there was no escaping the two policemen.

"On the ground," Dawson commanded. "Get down now."

Kudzo obeyed, lying on his stomach and submitting to handcuffs. Dawson, breathing hard, kneeled beside him to rest a hand on his shoulder.

"Are you Kudzo Gablah?"

"Yes, please."

"I'm Chief Inspector Darko Dawson. You are under arrest."

"I beg you, don't beat me."

"No one is going to beat you. But you're still under arrest."

CHAPTER FOURTEEN

IT WAS LATE AFTERNOON by the time Kudzo had been processed into the Obuasi Police Station. Dawson was hungry and
tired but dismissed his flagging spirits. He was going to see this
through before he slept tonight. With Obeng in attendance, he
conducted the interview in the CID room. About twenty-four,
Kudzo was almost as tall as Dawson, but the intensity of the mining work had made him dense with muscle. His forehead was
creased with two lines, like a permanent question on his face.

Kudzo, like Brave, was an Ewe from Keta, in the Volta Region,
and Dawson's first question to Kudzo was whether he spoke Twi.
Not well, the young man answered. Obeng didn't speak Ewe, so
English would have to be the language of communication—for
this interview, at least.

"Why did you run away from us?" Dawson asked.

"Please, I haven't done anything," he said huskily.

"Then that should mean that you don't have to run, not so?"

"Yes, please."

But Dawson knew that the young man's instinct had told him
otherwise and led to his panicky attempt to flee. The police often
scapegoated poor people like him. "Do you know why we were
looking for you?"

Kudzo hesitated. "Please, because of the Chinese man?"

"Correct. We are not accusing you of anything. We only want
to know what happened. What time did you go to work yesterday?"

"Five forty-five."

"What did you do first?"

"I started digging the gravel."

"Apart from Mr. Bao and Mr. Wei Liu, how many people do you work with?"

"Please, three."

"Were they also digging?"

"Yes, please. First I started, then they also began."

"I see." Dawson was studying Kudzo, but the young man kept his eyes firmly directed toward the table.

"Mr. Bao Liu was your boss?"

"Yes, please."

"What about Mr. Wei? What did he do?"

"He was the manager. Usually, he is there every day, but Bao is there only on Tuesdays and Fridays."

"Mr. Wei arrived at what time yesterday morning?"

"Please, around six-thirty," Kudzo said. He seemed to be loosening up a little. "I thought Mr. Bao was there by then, because he told us he would come to fix the excavator early in the morning."

"So it was strange that he hadn't arrived."

"Yes, please."

"Okay, go on," Dawson prompted.

"I started to do my work, and Mr. Wei too, when he came to the site he asked me where Mr. Bao was and I said please I don't know."

"I see. And then what happened?"

"Please, when I was digging, then I hit something with my shovel, and I didn't know what it was. I hit it another time to try and move it."

The deep cuts in the dead man's skull. Rather than mortal wounds, they could have been from Kudzo's shovel.

"Then I saw it was somebody's head," Kudzo continued, "so me and my friends, we started to dig around it to get it out, and Mr. Wei too, he came to help and then he saw it was his brother."

Kudzo shuddered visibly, and Dawson had to agree that it was shudder inducing.

"Before you saw the body, did you notice anything different or strange?"

"Please, I saw the soil on top of the body is a different color."

"What does that mean, Kudzo?"

"That someone had poured another soil on top of the normal one—the one that was there the day before."

"In order to bury the body?"

"Yes."

"Where would someone get the new soil from?"

Kudzo seemed to be trying to hide some amusement. "Please, plenty soil is all around."

Dawson agreed inwardly he had put the question badly. "Okay, let's say it was you who wanted to bury the body. How would you do it?"

Kudzo swallowed and looked away uncomfortably.

"What's wrong?" Dawson asked.

"Please, nothing is wrong."

"Then answer my question. If you were to bury Mr. Bao Liu, how would you do it?"

"Instead of digging with a spade," Kudzo said softly, "I will use the excavator, to dig a hole, then put the body inside and drop the soil back on top."

"But your excavator was not working," Dawson pointed out.

The boy nodded. "But there are other excavators around there."

Dawson leaned back. This might be a lead. "You're talking about the four machines in the site next to yours?"

"Yes, please. That belongs to one American guy."

"You know him?"

Kudzo shook his head. "Please, I know his name only, but I never talk to him."

"His name is what?" Dawson asked.

"We call him Mr. Chuck."

"Okay." Dawson didn't know whether that was a first name or surname. "So, for example," he said, wanting to delve more into this, "if I use the excavator, how long will it take me to bury a body?"

Kudzo shrugged. "If you know how to operate it well, it will only take some five minutes. Plus the time to drive the excavator from where it is parked and back again. Maybe some twenty minutes."

The question was whether the murderer had been trying to hide the body or make it discoverable. Surely he—or was it they?—knew that the location chosen was an active digging site.

Dawson stared at Kudzo for a while until the boy became discomfited. "Do you know how to operate an excavator?"

Kudzo fidgeted.

"Who taught you how?" Dawson persisted without the answer.

"Mr. Wei."

Interesting, Dawson thought. "Did you drive the excavator over there to bury Mr. Bao after you tied him up like that? Did you help someone do it, or did you do it by yourself?"

Kudzo began to tremble. "No, please."

"He didn't pay you the day before, not so?"

Kudzo was startled. "Please, how did you know?"

Dawson dismissed the question. "And because of that you were angry with Mr. Bao and you wanted to kill him."

Kudzo withered. He shook his head sadly. "He pays me. Why should I kill him?"

"Then was it Mr. Wei who killed him and you helped Wei bury Bao with the excavator?"

Kudzo became tearful all of a sudden, and hastily wiped the moisture off his cheeks.

"Why are you crying?" Obeng abruptly chimed in, almost startling Dawson.

"Please, I don't know," Kudzo whispered.

"Because you killed the Chinese man, not so?" Obeng barked.

Kudzo shook his head dumbly, tears streaming, and Obeng snorted with contempt. Dawson didn't send any restraining signals to the sergeant. Sometimes, two contrasting interrogation styles could be effective.

"Did you notice any excavator tracks coming from Mr. Chuck's site over to your side?" Dawson asked Kudzo.

"No, please." He hesitated. "Please, when you are returning the excavator to the parking spot, you can go in reverse and drag the bucket of the excavator on the ground. That will clean the tracks."

Dawson was intrigued that Kudzo was suggesting how the crime could have been committed while denying he did it

"Where did you sleep Thursday night?" Dawson asked Kudzo.

"In Dunkwa. At the house of my mate's father."

"One of the mates who works with you at the mine?"

"No, please. A different one."

"Can he confirm you were at the house all night?"

"Yes, please. If you like, I can give you his number. His name is Ekaw."

Dawson appreciated that unexpected display of assertiveness. "Thank you."

Kudzo flashed the number to him; Dawson dialed it and put the phone on speaker. Ekaw answered promptly. Dawson explained who he was and why he was calling. Kudzo greeted his friend to confirm he was indeed there.

"Hold on one moment," Dawson said. He took the phone off speaker and left the room with it, shutting the door behind him. "Ekaw, I am now speaking to you in private. Kudzo cannot hear what we are saying. Did you sleep at your usual place Thursday night?"

"Yes, please." Ekaw's vocal timber was steady and resonant—a good radio voice, should he ever choose that career.

"Who was with you?"

"My friend Ibrahim and Kudzo and my family."

"Did Kudzo sleep there the whole night?"

"Yes, please."

"At any time, did you see or hear him leaving the house?"

"No, please."

"What time did you wake up, and what time did he wake up?"

"We wake at the same time. Five thirty."

"Is it possible for Kudzo to leave the house without your knowing?"

"Please, I don't think so," he said definitively. "With my mother and father and my brothers and sisters, there are ten of us in the house. Someone will ask him where he is going. On top of that, the door to the house makes a lot of noise when you open and close it."

"Okay." Dawson ended the call with thanks, put his head inside the door, and beckoned Obeng outside for a quick confab. He told the sergeant the results of the call. "What do you think?"

"Well, maybe he and this Ekaw are in it together," Obeng suggested.

"Maybe, but let's go back first to look at motive. Can we see any reason why Kudzo would kill Bao Liu? We've heard that Bao was sometimes tight with money and didn't always pay promptly, but is that good enough? I don't think so."

"In fact," Obeng said, cracking a smile, "I think that has happened to many of us."

"Amen to that," Dawson agreed. "I know you didn't have the benefit of hearing Ekaw answer my questions, but the way he did so satisfies me. I don't think he was lying about anything, and so I feel confident that Kudzo has established his alibi—at least for now. If something changes, we have his phone number and Ekaw's as well, and we'll track him down as needed."

"So, we should release him?" Obeng said.

"We have nothing to hold him on. But on his release, warn him to stay accessible to us."

"Yes, sir." Obeng appeared both doubtful and hesitant.

"Something wrong?" Dawson asked.

"Please, it's just that . . . these *galamsey* guys, they can't be trusted. It's so early in the investigation and as soon as we release him, he will bolt and we will never be able to get in touch with him again."

"What do you suggest, then?"

"Please, if we can hold him at least until tomorrow evening in case of any new developments in the next twenty-four hours."

Dawson nodded. He didn't see anything wrong with the sergeant's reasoning, and it was always good to go along with a junior officer's suggestion if it was a good one. "Okay, we'll do that. Thank you for thinking it through."

As Dawson returned to the room, he felt as if he were missing something. He searched for it in his brain and found it. The American miner.

"This Mr. Chuck you mentioned," he said to Kudzo, "the one with the mining site next to you, was everything peaceful between him and Bao?"

Kudzo clicked his tongue and shook his head. "Not at all. Terrible. They used to quarrel all the time. Bao always went to Mr. Chuck and tell him that he is trespassing on Bao's land; then Mr. Chuck say, 'Fock you, moddafocka, get outa here before I kill you.'"

That could be empty bluster, or it could be serious. At any rate, it was clear that Bao and Mr. Chuck did not get along. The question was whether Chuck had hated the Chinese man enough to kill him.

CHAPTER FIFTEEN

EARLY SUNDAY MORNING, DAWSON finally had a clear enough schedule to pay a visit to the Kumasi guesthouse he and his family would be occupying, God willing. Later on, in the afternoon, he would return to Obuasi to interview Kudzo one more time. He had no directions to Gifty's house, but he was to contact her Uncle Joe once he got into Kumasi. Uncle Joe owned a car rental business in the city.

Dawson took a packed *tro-tro* from Obuasi, arriving at the terminal Kumasi stop at Ketejia Market. Normally it was teeming with shoppers, vendors, head porters, and truck pushers, but this was early on a Sunday: everyone was getting ready for church—except Dawson, apparently. Enjoying the relative quiet of the morning, he called Joe. No one responded, but it was only seven o'clock, so Dawson decided to wait a little while and try again. He bought his choice of soft drink, a cold Guinness Malta on Asomfo Road and then, leaning against a storefront pillar, he watched smartly dressed churchgoers hurrying by, Bibles in hand. Dawson could hear hymns being sung from the red brick and white trim Presbyterian church up the street.

He thought about Kudzo Gablah and Wei Liu: two people worlds apart, both seeking gold fortune for themselves and family left behind, and both "misconducting" themselves—the Chinese man taking a swing at a police officer, and the Ghanaian running away from one. In the end, they could have saved themselves a lot of trouble because both were effectively off the suspect list—that is, if you could call it a list.

Dawson needed to find this Mr. Chuck, who, according to Kudzo, had threatened Bao's life while calling him derogatory names. If Chuck had no alibi, he merited further investigation. Land disputes, an infamous source of friction in Ghana, must be a thousand times more deadly where gold is involved.

His phone rang. It was Uncle Joe, who apologized that he wasn't going to be at the guesthouse, but the foreman was there. Joe had a squeaky voice that reminded Dawson of a cartoon character. Before ending the call, Dawson had an idea. "Please, Uncle Joe, I don't have any transportation here in Kumasi, and I have been using a taxi so far. Can I rent a small, cheap vehicle from you?"

"No need to rent," Joe said. "I have an old Toyota Corolla you can use. It's ten years old but still going strong."

"Thank you, sir. I appreciate it very much."

"No problem at all. I will have one of my drivers drop off the car at the guesthouse."

AFTER TORTUOUS DIRECTIONS that Uncle Joe modified several times during multiple back-and-forth phone calls, the taxi arrived at Gifty's guesthouse in the quiet, up-and-coming neighborhood of Patase, where new houses surrounded by high walls and electrified fences appeared to be sprouting about as fast as they were in Accra. Dawson paid the fare and rang the bell at the side of a black gate. A tubby man in his thirties opened up. He turned out to be the watchman. His name was Haruna, a Muslim—so no church for him.

"Good morning, sir," he said, after Dawson had introduced himself. "You are welcome. We are expecting you."

Dawson came in and gaped at the size of the residence. It was two stories and it must have had four bedrooms at least.

"This is where we're going to stay?" he asked Haruna, barely able to believe it.

"Oh, no," the watchman said apologetically. "Some tenants are already occupying it."

Dawson felt like a fool as he saw the small house they were approaching behind the mansion. He should have known it. Of *course* Gifty wasn't giving them a mansion.

"Is the foreman here?" he asked Haruna.

"Please, he have gone to church, and he say if you can wait for him small."

"Small" could mean anything. An hour, a day. It depended just where the man fell on the religious spectrum from casual church-goer to obsessive worshipper.

The guesthouse was tiny—smaller than Dawson's house in Accra. The stack of tiles in front of the guesthouse was both good news and bad: materials had arrived, but the work hadn't started.

The watchman unlocked the front door. The first room was the sitting room, with two battered, dusty chairs, a sinking sofa, some side tables, and an old-style, cathode-ray television. The air conditioner high up on the wall had wires poking ominously out of it. Dawson stepped—not that many steps—to the kitchen on the left. The space where the stove was meant to be was empty. The sink was caked with grime, and when Dawson tried the tap, he got nothing but a blast of air.

"*Ewurade,*" he muttered.

The watchman politely waited for Dawson as he continued his inspection of the house with growing dismay. In the bathroom, the mildewed shower stall was waiting for tiling—hence the stack outside—the new toilet wasn't installed, and the washbasin was cracked straight through the middle.

The smaller of the two bedrooms—and both were small—had a lopsided bed supported on one side by a couple of cement blocks. When Dawson put his hand in the middle of the mattress it sagged and released a puff of dust. He sneezed twice as he opened the louvers of the windows. As he had predicted, the mosquito netting was clogged with dirt.

Feeling angrier by the minute with the previous renters, the foreman, Gifty, and everyone in general, Darko stood helplessly in the middle of the floor and looked around. It was a spectacular disaster.

His jaw tense, he speed dialed Christine, and she answered on the second ring. "Hi, sweetie."

"This house is a mess, Christine," Dawson said hotly. "I mean, this is not fit for human habitation."

"Oh, dear. Is it that bad?"

"No, it's worse."

"Hold on. Mama is right here. Let me ask her about it."

Dawson groaned inwardly. Just his luck. He heard the back-and-forth exchange between the two women and then his wife came back on the line.

"Mama is going to call Mr. Nyarko. That's the name of the foreman. Are you there right now?"

"Yes. This Nyarko is supposed to be back soon, but I can't afford to stand around waiting for people, Christine. I'm working on the case and I don't have time for all this nonsense."

"I know, I know—"

"I mean, has your mother been monitoring the progress in the house or not?"

"She *has*," Christine said, her tone beginning to mirror his frustration. "She's been calling him all along, and he's been telling her things were progressing."

"Well, he's a liar," Dawson said sullenly. "No wonder he disappeared. He doesn't want to see me. He's probably run away with your mother's money."

"She hasn't paid him yet."

"How can she not have paid him yet?" Dawson said incredulously. "No wonder he hasn't finished the work! You know how it is with these guys: they do the jobs that pay the money up front."

"Dark," Christine said, sounding exasperated, "just . . . just go and solve your cases and let us take care of it, okay? Relax. We'll get it sorted out."

"We can't have the boys come to this mess," he went on, as if

she hadn't just tried to reassure him. "It's bad enough we're moving them out of their school and their neighborhood—"

"Dark, I get it, I get it. Go about your business. I'll call you this
evening."

Dawson ended the call in a high state of annoyance. Why, *why*
was it always the case that whenever and wherever his mother-in-
law was involved, things were guaranteed to go badly?

The watchman had tactfully gone outside, no doubt uncomfortable with Dawson's spirited exchange on the phone.

"This is my number," Dawson said to him, writing it down on a
sheet of paper in his pocket notebook and ripping it out. "Please
tell Mr. Nyarko to call me as soon as possible."

"Yes, please."

ONE OF UNCLE Joe's drivers came round with a dark blue Toyota Corolla. Dawson thanked him and got in, adjusting the seat
to accommodate his long legs. The odometer read 130,000 miles,
but except for a few rattles emanating from the rear somewhere,
the little car felt quite solid. It was going on eleven now. Dawson
wanted to get as much out of this Kumasi trip as possible, and he
thought of a way he could do it. He scrolled to Akua Helmsley's
name on his phone and called.

"Good morning, Chief Inspector Dawson," she answered cheer-
fully.

"Good morning, Miss Helmsley. I'm in Kumasi at the moment."

"Oh," she said with interest. "Anything I can help you with?"

"Do you know of an American man called Mr. Chuck?" he
asked. "I was told that he has a mining site adjacent to Bao Liu's."

"You mean Chuck Granger, from the beautiful state of Utah.
He was on this reality show last year called *Tropical Gold* on the
Explorer Channel, which is out of the UK—all about his adven-
tures in gold mining in Ghana."

Dawson frowned. "Really?" He'd never heard of this.

"Yes. After we—*The Guardian*, that is—ran a story on it,
the Ghana government got embarrassed because it gave the

appearance of sanctioning illegal mining right under their noses—not exactly the sort of thing that would look good on the Mines and Natural Resources Minister's CV."

"It isn't," Dawson agreed. "What happened next?"

"Well, the ministry made a big show of hunting the crew down, as they put it—which is a joke since it was common knowledge the crew were being put up by the Explorer Channel on the top floor of the Golden Tulip Hotel, where I'm staying myself. Then they made a big fuss of kicking them out of the country—Granger included—'in order to safeguard the interests of our dear motherland,' or some such nonsense. And guess what? A few months later Granger comes right back and continues his mining minus the cameras."

"Only in Ghana," Dawson said bitterly. He wanted to be more furious, but sometimes, righteous anger could be exhausting. "I suppose from the minister's point of view it was, 'How much is it worth to you to return, Mr. Granger?'"

"Exactly. Listen, Chief Inspector, since you're in Kumasi, why not swing by my hotel and I'll show you the *Tropical Gold* website plus all the information I've gathered on Granger. I'm down at the tennis courts. You can meet me there. Do you play, by any chance?"

"Tennis?"

She laughed. "Yes, Chief Inspector. Tennis."

"No. I don't go around in tennis circles."

"Nor do I, actually." She laughed again. "And I can't play either."

"I will see you as soon as possible, given traffic."

"I'll be waiting, Chief Inspector."

CHAPTER SIXTEEN

THE TENNIS COURTS WERE shaded and cool. Akua Helmsley was relaxing on the patio to one side in a reclining chair, wearing shorts that showed off her dangerously slim, smooth legs. Dawson firmly avoided looking, or even stealing a glance. She moved from the recliner to a table so that she could sit beside him with her iPad.

"All right," she said, waking it from sleep. "Let's look at Chuck Granger. Here's the official *Tropical Gold* page."

The page showed a bulky, redheaded American man in his early thirties with a five o'clock shadow and a fierce frown.

"'Property mogul Chuck Granger had it all,'" Akua read. "'At a mere twenty-eight years old, Granger was worth two million dollars. But so tied up in making the deal, so determined to make more and more money, he ignored the warning signs heralding the US housing crash that triggered the worldwide recession. Granger lost everything.'"

Dawson was following her reading, slightly distracted by the faint scent of her fragrance. "So he lost everything in the real estate crash," he said, "and decided the solution was to come to Ghana and mine for gold?"

"That's the premise of the program, yes."

Dawson sat back and laughed. "That's just foolishness."

"Not when it's watched by millions of viewers in the United Kingdom and the United States," she pointed out, leaning back in her chair and crossing her legs at the ankles.

Dawson's eyes very nearly strayed, but he remained resolute and held his gaze firmly on her face. "Only Ghanaians can lawfully engage in small-scale mining," he said, "but an American lands at Kotoka Airport with a film crew and proceeds to mine illegally under the full glare of cameras, and no one asks any questions." He shook his head in disbelief.

"But that attitude doesn't go far enough," she said, looking at him fully in the eyes. "I intend to find out exactly how and why that happened. Who gave these guys the green light, and who pocketed a tidy packet of dollars for it?"

Dawson felt moderate alarm stir within him. "Be careful how deep you dig, Miss Helmsley. Dangerous people high up want to keep things undercover."

"But I would never say that to you," she said. "I'm an investigator too—like you. Not a cop, but I have similar motivations. I *have* to go after these things and find out the truth. It's in my blood."

He felt he had expressed his sentiment poorly. "I just mean . . . well, pick your battles carefully. Even I drop police cases that aren't worth the trouble."

"Thank you for your concern, Chief Inspector." She turned back to her iPad. "Take a look at one of the *Tropical Gold* episodes—just to give you an idea of what they're like."

The scene showed Granger, a group of *galamsey* boys, and an engineer caught in a drenching downpour at a mining site. An excavator was perched at the edge of a pit, and the operator was attempting to move earth in the midst of rain and a burgeoning flood, which seemed unwise to Dawson. Gradually, as the camera pulled away, the sodden ground at the edge of the pit began to sink, and then collapse. A lot of yelling and running around followed, with the operator leaping from the excavator before it slid forward in the mud and ended up in the pit on its side.

Dawson was incredulous. "Is it real?" he asked, eyes glued to the screen.

"An equal number of people say it's fake as say it's real. Now, watch this."

She fast forwarded to the end of the episode and allowed the credits to roll up to a certain point, at which she froze the screen.

"Read what's at the very bottom, Chief Inspector, if you would."

"It says, 'Explorer Channel wishes to thank . . .'" Dawson blinked. "'. . . wishes to thank the Ministry of Tourism, Ghana.'" He exchanged an astonished glance with Helmsley.

"Exactly," she said, nodding. "They somehow got sanction and approval from the tourism minister to come to Ghana and tramp up and down digging up the landscape."

"Could be that Explorer lied about the true purpose of the visit?" Dawson suggested. "Maybe they told the ministry a half truth like, 'We'd like to film the beautiful forests of Ghana while highlighting the tragedy of environmental destruction at the hands of illegal gold miners.'"

"Wow," she said, looking at him with new admiration. "Beautifully put, Chief Inspector. You might have a career in journalism."

He grinned. "Thanks, but I'll stick to the police stuff."

"At any rate," Helmsley said, "you can see how addicting it could be to follow the weekly exploits of this, sorry to say, not very intelligent Chuck Granger."

"You've met him?"

"Oh, yes. Well, in a way. I went to interview him at his site and he yelled me off the property. Big, fat, ugly American."

Dawson almost laughed at the gusto with which she said it. "How well is he doing with the mining?"

"I don't have numbers, but I think he's making a killing. Sorry, bad choice of words."

Dawson smiled. "Maybe not. Do you think he would have a motive to kill Mr. Liu?"

"Oh, good gracious, no," she said with a flick of her head. "I don't think he gives a flying fig about the Lius. They could be dead or alive, so far as he's concerned."

Dawson didn't mention Kudzo's story of Granger calling Bao names and threatening his life.

A female waiter appeared and interrupted them to ask if they'd like anything to drink.

"I'll take a strawberry daiquiri," Akua said. "And Chief Inspector Dawson will take?"

"Just some bottled water, thank you."

"Still or carbonated?"

"Still, please."

The waiter left and Dawson turned back to Akua.

"Now, Chief Inspector," she said coyly, "let's do a fair trade, shall we?"

"Meaning?"

"I gave you some dirt on Chuck Granger. In return, talk to me a little about Mr. Bao Liu, as well as the young Ghanaian guy you arrested."

Dawson smiled ironically. "Seems like you know quite a bit already."

"But not enough. I need to do a little fact-checking. Can you oblige me?"

"I'll do what I can, but some things might have to be off the record."

"Understood. So, when we saw each other last outside the police station in Obuasi, you had Bao Liu's brother, Wei, in custody. You said it was not for suspicion of murder, but 'a different offense.' That different offense was?"

"We would have had him down at the station for questioning only, minus handcuffs, had he not taken a swing at one of my officers."

"Oh, dear," she said. "Bad move. Which officer was that? Can you name him?"

Dawson shook his head. "Leave him out of it, please."

"Very well. And when I saw Wei with you and the other officers, you were on your way where?"

"To confirm his alibi with a friend of his."

"And it checked out?"

"Yes. I can't give you the details, but they freed Wei from

suspicion, and as for the officer assault, we dropped the charge with a written warning that trying to hit a police officer can have severe consequences."

"I'll say," Helmsley said dryly. "Lucky you were there at the time, because otherwise Wei might have gotten his arse well and truly kicked."

"Maybe so. I don't know."

"Okay. And the Ghanaian gentleman?"

"Kudzo Gablah. He was one of the Lius' *galamsey* workers. Not a strong suspect, and the ventured motive that he killed Bao because the guy was often late paying the workers never struck me as being anything else but weak. And his alibi was solid as well."

"Who else do you have then, Chief Inspector?"

"No one."

"Oh."

She made a face of exaggerated disappointment, and he laughed. "Sorry."

The daiquiri and still water arrived. Helmsley took a sip of hers and murmured her approval. "Any idea when the autopsy on Bao will be done?" she asked.

Dawson shook his head.

"I would like to attend the autopsy with you," she said. "Is that possible?"

"You're asking the wrong person, I'm afraid. You'll have to consult the mortuary officials."

"I'll do that. How tough are the autopsies for you to watch?"

"It depends on the case," Dawson said. "The worst are those with advanced putrefaction, and floaters—dead bodies that have been in water for some time."

"I suppose you're used to them?"

"Never really get used to them—just my reaction to them."

"Yes, I see. Very insightful, Chief Inspector."

"Back to Chuck Granger. Do you know where he lives?"

"I know where he *used* to live, at least. Not sure if he's still there, but there's a bed-and-breakfast place in the Ahodwo area of Kumasi called Four Villages Inn. It's internationally famous."

"Oh, yes," Dawson said as he remembered passing it on the way to Lian's house.

"A Canadian man, Christopher Scott, and his Ghanaian wife own it. She's absolutely adorable, but he's something of a nutcase. Obsessed with short-term tourist visas."

Dawson shrugged. "I don't even know what those are."

"Nor do you need to," she said. "It affects him because he's in the hospitality industry. His hotel is quite unusual."

"You've stayed there before?"

"Yes."

Dawson imagined Four Villages would be expensive—for him, anyway, but he was certain Helmsley had money. She had an air about her. "Do you live in the UK?"

"About three-quarters of the year, and the rest in Accra, usually. You've heard of the Helmsley Company?"

"I can't say I have."

"Belongs to my father—men's and women's fashion clothing. You'll see the line in any mall in Accra or Kumasi."

Which is why I haven't seen it. Dawson didn't spend much time in malls. Christine and the boys, to some extent, but not him.

"Where did you go to school?" he asked.

"Primary school here in Ghana, secondary school and university in England."

He had guessed it. She had hot Ghanaian blood chilled by the frigid UK. "Do you speak any Ghanaian language?"

"My Twi isn't bad."

He nodded, but his mind was already moving onto something else. "Did your cameraman take pictures of the areas adjacent to the crime scene?"

"Yes, why?"

"I'm looking for tracks—excavator tire tracks—particularly leading from the crime scene area to Chuck Granger's site."

"All right. Well, let's check and see."

She had arranged all her laptop photos in logical, alphabetical order. She was exceptionally organized.

"What about this one?" she asked, stopping at a panorama that included Granger's excavators on the site. "I can crop out this area of the terrain between Granger's and Liu's site to make it larger."

She did that, and they both stared at the soil pattern in the photograph.

"See anything?" she asked.

"Not a thing."

"Are you thinking Granger was trespassing on Liu's site?"

"Maybe," he said, not mentioning Kudzo's observation that an excavator could have buried Bao Liu very quickly. He stood up. "I must get going now. Thank you for your help."

"Likewise, Chief Inspector Dawson. We have a video piece coming out on the *Guardian* website in the next few days. I'll send you the link."

"Thank you very much." As he left, he wanted to tell her, "Please be careful," but he thought he had expressed that enough. She had made her point: she was tough, and she didn't need to be told her job just because she was a woman.

CHAPTER SEVENTEEN

DAWSON GOT BACK TO Obuasi by just before two in the afternoon. In transit, he had tried to call Sergeant Obeng and was annoyed that the man did not pick up or return the call. It was true that network problems plagued telephone calls, but people used that excuse all too often.

When Dawson arrived at district headquarters, six or so civilians were playing the waiting game around the entrance to the charge office. The constable at the front desk straightened up as Dawson entered.

"Good afternoon, sir."

"Afternoon."

Behind the desk, a corporal was sitting in a chair dozing off. Dawson ripped a page out of his notebook, balled it up and lobbed it accurately at his head. He jerked awake and jumped up, almost losing his balance.

"Morning, massa," he stammered, mortified.

"It's afternoon, corporal," Dawson said. "Find something to do that doesn't involve sleeping on the job."

"Yes, sir."

"Who is in charge today?"

"Inspector Kwarteng, sir."

"Where is he?"

"Please, he has gone out."

Dawson frowned. "Gone out to where?"

The corporal was sheepish. "Please, I don't know."

"Have you noted his departure in the diary?"

"No, please."

Dawson was getting irritated. *Does anyone take any responsibility for anything around here?* "What about Detective Sergeant Obeng? Is he here? Or am I asking too much?"

"Please, I think he is in the back."

Dawson grunted, slipped to the rear of the charge office and turned right down the dim corridor toward the jail, but he stopped and reversed direction because he thought he heard someone crying out behind him. As he drew closer, he realized it was coming from inside the storeroom. He opened the door a crack, at first seeing only mops, brooms, and cleaning supplies.

"Why are you lying?" one voice said softly. It belonged to Sergeant Obeng. "Eh? You think I don't know what is a liar? Take your hands away from your head. I say, *put them down.*"

Dawson heard the sharp slap that followed and the corresponding yelp from the second person—Kudzo. Dawson opened the door fully. Startled, Obeng jumped and swung around, breathing heavily. The weapon in his hand was a wooden ruler which, as Dawson remembered all too well from his schooldays, could deliver quite a sting. Kudzo was cowering on the floor, holding his hands in front of his head in the classic defensive posture.

"What's going on?" Dawson said quietly.

"Please," Obeng stammered. "Please . . . I . . ."

"Wait for me at the charge office."

"Yes, sir." He squeezed past Dawson like a guilty dog.

Kudzo sat up partially with an imploring look. "Please, I beg you. Massa, I beg you."

"Stay right there," Dawson said, getting out his phone. He snapped one photo of Kudzo sitting there in distress, and then moved forward. "Lift up your face and look at me."

He was in tears, but his face appeared untouched.

"Don't move," Dawson said, and snapped another picture. "Now stand up and lift your shirt."

Kudzo did so. Dawson could see the welts. "Just as I thought. Is this where he was hitting you?"

"Yes, please. This side of my body. And on my head."

But deep black as Kudzo's skin was from hours in the sun, Dawson had difficulty making out the bruises in the dim light of the storeroom.

"Come with me," Dawson said.

He took Kudzo to the court office.

"Stand by the window," Dawson said.

The bruises were more visible now, though barely. Dawson took several photos. The results could have been a little more obvious, but it was the best he could do.

He put his head around the door and called for the constable to escort the suspect back to his cell in exchange for Obeng's return.

The sergeant came in with his head down, unable to meet Dawson's eyes.

"Have a seat," Dawson said.

"Yes, sir."

Dawson perched on the side of the table. "What were you trying to do?"

"Please, I wanted him to confess."

"That's how you get a suspect to confess?"

"No, sir."

"How long were you doing that this morning?"

Obeng cleared his throat. "When you came, it was just a few minutes, sir."

"Didn't anyone hear you and ask what you were doing?"

"Inspector Kwarteng has gone out, and only the corporal and constable are here."

Even if they had heard the commotion, Dawson thought, they would not have challenged their superior, Sergeant Obeng.

"The worst thing about this," Dawson said, "is that I promised the boy that no one was going to beat him, which is exactly what you have done. *Why?*"

Obeng was perspiring. Dawson caught an odor from him and

moved his face closer to the sergeant, sniffing the air around him. Obeng tensed up and held his breath.

"You've been drinking," Dawson said.

Obeng looked away without answering, rubbing the back of his head like an ashamed schoolboy in the headmaster's office.

"Until what time were you drinking last night?" Dawson pressed. "Until one or two in the morning? And then you slept and woke up and drank some more because you knew I wouldn't be in early."

Obeng stared at the floor morosely.

"How many people like Kudzo have you been mistreating?" Dawson asked. He suspected the sergeant wouldn't answer, and he was right. Nor did he need to. His silence alone was confirmation that this occasion had not been the first.

Dawson got up. "Okay. I will have to report this to Commander Longdon and you will probably come up before the disciplinary board in Kumasi in the very near future. For now you are dismissed for the weekend, pending Commander Longdon's decision on the next step. Clear? You may go home now."

DAWSON CALLED THE constable and corporal into the office to ask them if they had heard any commotion from the storeroom. The constable looked mystified and denied any knowledge of what had happened. The corporal on the other hand looked too studiously innocent, convincing Dawson that he was really guilty.

"You didn't hear any kind of noise or struggle?" he asked the corporal for the second time, phrased differently.

"Oh, no, not at all," he said.

His tone changed, and there was a slight tremor to his voice, which activated Dawson's synesthesia. He felt as if he had closed his left fist around a cactus stem. "I know you're lying. You don't want to get involved with any scandal."

The lance corporal looked down at his feet. "No, sir. Yes, sir."

"If you see something you know is wrong," Dawson said, "you report it. Understood? Bring Mr. Gablah back here and then get back to work."

Kudzo was subdued as he came in.

"Take a seat," Dawson told him in Ewe. "Tell me what happened from the very beginning."

"Please, he told the lance corporal to take me to him for questioning, then when I came to the room—"

"Which room? This one?"

"Yes, please."

"Go on."

"Then he asked me why I don't just confess that I killed Mr. Bao, and I told him, please, I haven't done anything. And he told me he will beat me if I don't confess, and I said no. So, then he took me to the store place and started to hit me."

"How long was he beating you?"

"Please, I don't know. Maybe ten or twenty minutes."

Dawson estimated that it was probably less.

"Did you Kill Mr. Bao?"

"Why should I?" Kudzo said more heatedly. "He was paying me, so why should I kill him? I never even had job before. Please, I came from Keta. When I was there, I couldn't get any work, and my father too, he wasn't working and my mother is sick and she needs an operation. A certain friend of mine was mining gold at Aniamoa and he asked me why I don't come and work with him there and then I can make some money to send home."

"Was that Brave?"

"Yes, please," Kudzo said, startled. "Please, how do you know?"

"We met him at the mining site. So you left Keta, your hometown, and what happened when you went to Aniamoa?"

"I started to work there, but one man, the foreman, he didn't like me, and he sacked me from there. That's why I came to Dunkwa to work."

"The foreman told me you have a hot temper. Is that true?"

"Me?" Kudzo said, pointing at himself incredulously. "No, please."

Dawson smiled slightly. "How did you come to work for Mr. Bao in particular?"

"I went to watch how they are mining at his site, and when he saw me standing there, he told one of the guys to go and call me, and then he asked me if I can do the work. I told him yes, I can do it."

"How is the mining job? Is it tough?"

"Wow!" Kudzo exclaimed, in an enthusiastic burst of limited English. "It is *tough*! When I started, I didn't even know. I thought because I did work on the farm in Volta Region that it would be easy for me." Kudzo shook his head slowly and ruefully. "When I was at Aniamoa with Brave, the first day, my hands started to bleed from using those poles to stir the riverbed. Some of the men started to laugh at me and told me, that's how it is."

"How did Mr. Bao treat you?"

"He liked to shout at people all the time. Sometimes he insulted us, saying we were lazy. But me, I didn't fear him, and that way he somehow respected me. Sometimes he asked me if I can go and catch some bush meat for him, like grass cutter or something like that. You know, these Chinese people, they will eat any focking meat."

"Any *what?*"

"Please, any focking meat, they like it."

"Oh, I see." Dawson let that odd observation go. "I want to ask you something."

"Yes, please."

"If you didn't kill Mr. Bao, who do you think did it?"

Kudzo's eyes darted away. "Please I don't have any idea about that."

His tone changed, and again triggered Dawson's synesthesia: a light, quick shock, like hitting one's funny bone. He leaned forward. "Kudzo, if you want to leave this place right now, you have to tell me the truth. If not, you will stay here another night."

Kudzo sighed and looked desperate and torn.

"I'm not going to tell anyone what you tell me," Dawson said, while thinking, *Why should he trust me when I've already broken my promise that no one would beat him?*

Kudzo was struggling, but the truth won. "Okay," he said finally, "a certain man in Dunkwa, his name is Amos Okoh. He and his father have a small farm near Bao Liu's *galamsey* site. Sometimes Amos's girlfriend goes to the farm to help Amos and his father. Mr. Bao too, he used to like Amos's girlfriend, so when she was passing to the farm, he used to try and talk to her, telling her he could give her plenty gold."

This is the kind of information I'm looking for, Dawson thought. "Go on."

"One day, Amos challenged Mr. Bao and warned him not to be looking at his girlfriend and talking to her. They had an argument. When Amos was leaving by the bridge, Mr. Bao started to shake the ropes and made the bridge swing so much that Amos fell inside the deep water."

Dawson visualized the catastrophe. "What happened?"

"Amos started to shout that he couldn't swim. Some workers tried to use a pole to pull him out, but they couldn't find one long enough. So Amos drowned. He died inside the water."

"Oh, my God," Dawson said, shocked.

"Some days passed, and then the body floated to the surface, and someone brought a canoe to go and pick it out of the water."

"Did the police arrest Mr. Bao?"

"No, please. They questioned him, and then they let him go. Somebody said he paid the police."

Dawson stiffened. "Did the family try to bring charges against Bao?"

Kudzo flipped up his palms and shrugged. "Please, what can they do? They are poor people. They can't do anything. But his younger brother—his name is Yaw—said something about it."

"What did he say?"

"He said he would kill Mr. Bao for what he did to Amos."

CHAPTER EIGHTEEN

AFTER HE WROTE HIS report about Obeng in painstaking long-hand, Dawson called Commander Longdon to tell him about it. Although he didn't answer, he called back about thirty minutes later. Dawson gave him a summary of events.

"You did the right thing, Dawson," Longdon said after listening to the account. "This is very disturbing and I'll get on it as soon as I get in on Monday."

"I gather that Sergeant Obeng has assaulted prisoners before, sir," Dawson said.

Slight pause. "Why do you say that?"

"The way he responded to my questions, I could tell."

"I see." Longdon heaved a heavy sigh. "Nothing like that has been reported to me."

Of course not, Dawson thought in annoyance. *Because no one reports anything to anyone around here—or in the GPS in general, for that matter.* It was a generalization, he realized, and not completely true. He had been in a state of irritation from the moment he had stepped foot in Gifty's guesthouse this morning.

"What about his drinking, sir?" Dawson asked.

"I know nothing about it."

It was possible, Dawson reasoned. Commanders had more inter-action with chief inspector rank and above, and less with the very low ranks. It was up to the chief inspectors to report problems like alcoholism to the commander. And it could be, too, that Obeng had successfully hidden his addiction until now.

"I'll attend to the matter on Monday," Longdon stated. "Do you have your report ready?"

"If one of the secretaries is available, I can have it typed early in the morning, sir."

"Yes. Please give it to my assistant, Lance Corporal Asante, and she'll do it."

"Thank you." He added quickly, "I have a request, sir."

"Yes, what is it?" he said, a slight edge of impatience creeping into his voice.

"I'm assuming that since Sergeant Obeng will be suspended, I won't have a partner to work on the case, so I would like to request that my normal partner, Inspector Philip Chikata from Central Headquarters, join me from Accra."

"What?" Longdon said, sounding incredulous. "Why from Accra? I have another sergeant in Obuasi we can replace Obeng with, and if that fails, we have officers at Kumasi Regional Headquarters, for example—which is much closer."

Dawson wasn't going to let it go quite that easily. "Working with someone I know and trust will expedite the case, sir."

"I won't agree to it, and Central won't either, Dawson."

"Please, sir, why won't you agree to it, sir?" he said, aware that if he wasn't challenging Longdon's wisdom and authority, he was dangerously close.

"Because that's the way it is," the commander snapped, plainly cross now.

He ended the call abruptly, leaving Dawson in an exceedingly bad mood. His mother-in-law, Obeng, Longdon, Obuasi, Kumasi . . . you name it, he was annoyed with him, her, or it. And if the commander thought he was going to forget about getting Chikata up here to Obuasi, he was very much mistaken.

At that moment, Dawson could have really used Chikata so

he could split the next important investigation steps: talking to Chuck Granger, and going to look for Yaw Okoh, the man who, according to Kudzo, had once threatened to kill Bao Liu in revenge for Liu's allegedly murdering Yaw's brother Amos by dumping him into a water-filled mining pit.

Which one should Dawson do first? He thought he would tackle Yaw today, and Granger early in the coming week.

His phone rang, and seeing it was his wife, he decided to make an effort to be nicer than he had been during the prickly last call.

"Hi, love," he said cheerily.

"Hi, sweetie," she said, more matter-of-factly. "Okay, I think we have this set up so things will go well from now on. Mama called Uncle Joe and put pressure on him. He promises to meet with the contractor at the house tonight, and then Mama will go up to Kumasi tomorrow to reinforce."

The plan had been for Christine and the boys to make the big move from Accra the following weekend. Knowing how things went where building contractors were concerned, Dawson could almost guarantee that the guesthouse would not be ready for his wife and kids. In any case, they would have to vacate the Accra house imminently to give way to the new set of renters who were waiting to get in with a one-year lease.

As much as he told himself to take a more positive outlook, Dawson remained relentlessly pessimistic as he got into the Corolla and headed to Dunkwa.

IT WAS LATER than Dawson had wanted it to be by the time they got there. The sun was making plans to retire for the day, and heavy rain clouds were moving in.

He had no idea where to look for Yaw Okoh, but he thought The Lord Is My Shepherd Chop Bar ahead was a good start. If Yaw wasn't there, someone might know where to find him. He pulled over and alighted.

The chop bar was bigger than Dawson had imagined, and hip-life music with the almost mandatory auto-tune vocals was blaring.

Men and women—mostly men—sat talking and drinking at bare wooden tables painted blue. In fact, everything was painted blue.

Dawson greeted a group of five guys at one table and, raising his voice above the music, asked if they knew Yaw Okoh.

"Which Yaw Okoh?"

Fair question. "The one whose brother Amos died," Dawson said promptly, because that was the most likely tidbit to get to the right person.

The men looked at each other knowingly.

"Yes, I know where he and his family live," one of them said.

Rather than get directions that were likely to be confusing or simply wrong, Dawson asked the man if he would please come with him to show him the way. He looked reluctant, but Dawson told him he would dash him enough money to buy another beer, which, if his pungent breath and heavy-lidded eyes were any testimony, he did not need. He nodded, drained his glass, and got up unsteadily to follow Dawson out to the car.

The drunkard gave him slurred instructions where to go, at one point nodding off to sleep, only to be jerked awake by Dawson barking, "Hey! *Chaley,* wake up!" When they got to the destination, the drunkard pointed to the putative house. Dawson gave him a couple *cedis,* and the intoxicated man lurched away somewhere—possibly to another drinking spot.

Dawson walked to the house. On the veranda, a woman around his age was doing an expensive hair weave on another woman whose bare shoulders were so soft and smooth Dawson could almost taste them.

"*Mema mo aha,*" Dawson greeted them, using the most courteous of forms for "good afternoon."

"*Yaa nua,*" they replied in kind.

"Is this the house of Yaw Okoh?"

"Yes." The hairstylist looked at him. "Who are you?"

"My name is Darko Dawson."

She finished one cycle of a weave. "Please wait here. I will call him to come."

"Thank you."

She went into the house, pausing to leave her slippers on the veranda before entering in her bare feet.

Smoothie looked at Dawson. "Darko. Are you from Accra?"

"Yes. How did you know?"

"The way you speak, I can tell you're not from here."

"Oh," he said, marveling at the clarity of her skin. "Is that bad?"

"No, not at all. I like it." She laughed, raking him from head to toe. "Dunkwa is boring. I like Accra men."

Something told Dawson she had claws he shouldn't get anywhere close to.

The hairstylist returned.

"Please," she said, shooting a knowing glance at Smoothie, who kept her gaze down, "Yaw is not in, but his father and mother are there. You can go inside."

"Thank you very much."

He took off his shoes before entering. Showing respect went a long way to getting answers. Light and ventilation were almost nonexistent inside the house. Mr. and Mrs. Okoh were seated on a haggard sofa in an otherwise bare sitting room. He greeted them and shook hands with the lady first. The man was dressed in traditional cloth slung over one shoulder, the woman in a more ordinary skirt and blouse. He smelled smoke on her and guessed that she had been cooking at a wood stove. She was small, in her late forties, and unlike Smoothie outside, had one of the worst cases of relaxer-fried hair Dawson had ever seen.

Mr. Okoh called out to someone to bring a chair, and a kid of about ten in a ragged shirt appeared like magic from nowhere with a rickety blue plastic one. *These must be all made in China,* Dawson thought with sudden insight into the ubiquity of the plastic chairs in Ghana.

"You say you are?" Mr. Okoh asked, squinting at him in the poor light.

"Darko Dawson. I am from Criminal Investigations Department,

Accra. I am looking into the death of the Chinese man Bao Liu. You have heard about it?"

Mr. Okoh sat up straight while his wife sent him an anxious look.

"Yes, please," the man said warily. "But we have nothing to do with it."

"Of course you do not, *Owura* Okoh," Dawson said respectfully. "But I understand that he—the Chinese man—caused the death of your son Amos."

Mr. Okoh looked away, his jaw clenching rhythmically. It was a long time before he spoke again. "Yes," he said simply.

Dawson nodded and waited another few moments. "Please, I want to find out what happened," he asked softly. "How did Mr. Liu cause your son's death?"

Mr. Okoh was looking down at his hands, which were twisting around each other. "Amos worked with me," he began. "We farmed corn, oil palm, and *cassava*. We used to have a big farm, but once those Chinese people came, they spoiled most of it with the excavators."

"Excuse me," Dawson interrupted as politely as he could, "how is it that they came and spoiled your land? Did you know that was going to happen?"

Okoh shook his head. "One day, they just arrived and started clearing all the trees away."

"Who gave them permission to do that?"

Okoh looked up. "The Chinese people come with their money and they pay the chief for land that they want."

It was the answer Dawson had feared, and could be the reason why Nana Akrofi had spoken so glowingly of the Chinese. "Did the chief tell you that they had paid him for the land?"

"No." Okoh practically snorted. "If you are living here in Dunkwa and you don't know that the Chinese people are paying the chief for land to look for gold, then something is wrong with you."

Theoretically, Dawson thought, the chief *could* sell off pieces of the land under his chiefdom, but he was also supposed to look after the well-being of his citizens. If what Mr. Okoh was saying was true, and unfortunately Dawson believed it was, then Nana Akrofi was a callous, greedy man who was looking out for himself alone, all too common a story in Ghana, Dawson felt.

"When they came and excavated almost all the farmland," Okoh continued, "we were left with only a small amount, and now, because the way is now blocked by the mining pits, we have to pass the pits first before going to the farm. During last rainy season, the rains were very heavy. It even flooded Dunkwa, and at one place, the dividing wall between two pits fell down and the pits came together."

Okoh was demonstrating with his hands, and Dawson got a good picture in his mind.

"So," Okoh went on, "because there was no more dividing wall to pass to the farm when the two pits became one, some of the Chinese people built a bridge from ropes so that you can walk across. The floor of the bridge, they made it with wood, and then the sides are of rope. That bridge . . ." Okoh stopped, shaking his head.

"It isn't strong?" Dawson prompted.

"Oh, it's very strong," he replied, "but when you are walking on it, you have to be careful because it bounces up and down and swings back and forth."

"I see."

"And one day, Amos's girlfriend Comfort was going to the farm, and that Chinese man Bao was there, and he started to talk to her. He knows how to speak Twi, so he told her she was beautiful, and he wanted to give her some gold, and she laughed and said okay. By that time, Amos was coming from the farm, and he saw Bao conversing with Comfort, and he became very angry and shouted at Bao, telling him to leave Comfort alone. Then Bao too, he told Amos to clear out from his land. *His land.*"

Dawson saw Mr. Okoh's anger rising like a wave gathering strength at sea.

"And Amos told Bao, what are you saying? You, a man from this faraway China coming here to steal the gold that has belonged to our fathers since time began, and now you are calling it *your* land? You are a fool!"

Even "fool" did not seem to carry the full weight of the fury that Amos must have been feeling at that moment.

"Who told you the story of what happened?" Dawson asked Okoh.

"Comfort, and many other people. Ask anyone who was there, Mr. Dawson. So many people were there, and they will tell you the same story."

Mrs. Okoh was looking directly at Dawson, nodding slowly. "*Ampa.*" It's true.

"Then Comfort told Amos not to mind Bao," Okoh continued, "and that he should come back to the house because the rain was coming again. Then she went on the bridge first to walk in front of him, because he always told her in case she stumbled. When they got to the end of the bridge, Bao started to hoot at Amos from the other side of the pit. He used bad words in Twi. You know, these Chinese people, when they come here, they learn the bad words in our language and use them against us."

"Please, *Owura* Okoh," Dawson said, "what did he say?"

"An insult about Amos's mother." Okoh shook his head. "I can't repeat it."

Dawson knew the one. It meant, *your mother's vagina.* It was the most odious offense of all—so abhorrent that its utterance could well result in one's being beaten to a pulp. Maybe Bao Liu didn't know how terrible an insult it was, but then maybe he did. Either way, Dawson was forming a picture of the Chinese man as a vulgar, malicious brute. Assuming *Owura* Okoh's account was true.

Mrs. Okoh's eyes had become swollen and red with grief, pain, and perhaps fury was there as well.

"Then Amos," Okoh said, his voice cracking, "he turned back and told Bao he was going to kill him for what he had said. Amos was holding a cutlass, and when Bao saw him coming back, he held the rope of the bridge and started to push and pull it to make it tip. And when it tipped, Amos . . . Amos . . ."

Okoh gulped for air, and Dawson felt his own chest twist inside like a wet towel being wrung out.

"Amos fell inside the pit," Okoh forged on. "The pit is very deep. The mud is thick. You can't even swim inside. He was shouting for help, but no one could help him. There was no rope to pull him, no pole that was long enough. One man, he tried to drive the excavator down to the water so that Amos could hold onto the bucket, but the excavator too, it was too heavy and was about to fall in the water."

Mrs. Okoh was sweeping away tears that were streaming down her face faster than the Ofin River, but she didn't make much noise—just desperate, glottal sounds, her mouth opening and closing like a fish out of water.

Dawson could say nothing for several minutes. The anguish of these two was unbearable. He thought of the unthinkable for a fleeting moment—Hosiah or Sly drowning in a deep pit of muddy water as treacherous as quicksand—and he shuddered.

"And that man," Mr. Okoh whispered, "that Chinese man Bao, when the police came to question him, he lied to them and told them Amos slipped. And he paid them to leave him alone."

Dawson's blood raced hot through his head. This was the kind of thing that made him crazy. "He paid whom?" he asked fiercely.

"I don't know," Okoh said with a shrug. "Do you think I was there? They don't do these things where everyone can see them, they do them hidden in some secret place."

Dawson nodded. He had hoped that Mr. Okoh would have details, but that was too much to expect. People with no influence are not privy to influential transactions.

"Mr. and Mrs. Okoh," Dawson said, "I am very sorry."

He stood up to shake their hands once more, this time in sympathy. He couldn't think of anything more to do. They smiled wanly at him, and he knew they appreciated the gesture, because in such affairs, gestures often mean more than material things.

Dawson sat down again and asked the Okohs to describe exactly where the tragedy had occurred. From what he gathered from their somewhat confused directions, the site was on the opposite side of the shack where Wei had carried his brother Bao.

Asking Mr. Okoh to establish his alibi might sound accusatory, Dawson knew, but it was a risk he had to take. "Please," he said respectfully, "early Friday morning when Bao Liu was killed, where were you?"

Okoh didn't appear to object to the question. "Maybe you don't know what life is like for us poor farmers, Mr. Dawson," he said. "We have to wake up very early every single morning to go to the farm. If the sun beats you there, you are too late."

"Do you and your wife normally go to farm together?" Dawson asked.

Okoh nodded. "Yes, and sometimes my nephew John—before he goes to school in the morning."

"The boy who brought the chair for me?" Dawson asked.

"Yes."

Dawson wanted to check the veracity of the alibi with John, but not in front of his uncle. He would find a way later.

"Please, Mr. and Mrs. Okoh," Dawson said, "if you will permit me, I want to ask you about Amos's younger brother, Yaw."

Now the man leaned back on the sofa, eyes to the ceiling, and said nothing.

"Mr. Dawson," the woman said softly, "he has not been the same since Amos's death. He loved his brother more than he loves me or his father."

"I would like to talk to him," Dawson said gently. "Is he around?"

She looked up as a shadow passed across the doorway, and there stood a sculpture of muscular perfection—a man of about twenty-eight, shirtless and constructed of granite and stone. He had a scar across his top lip that made it appear jagged. He looked at them, his expression as empty as a reservoir in a savanna drought, and then he turned and walked away.

"That is Yaw," Mrs. Okoh said softly and sadly.

"Will he speak to me?" Dawson asked.

She shook her head. "He cannot, Mr. Dawson."

He didn't understand what she meant. "He is not allowed to?"

"He cannot speak," she repeated, this time more emphatically. "He has been completely mute since Amos died two months ago."

CHAPTER NINETEEN

Dawson was puzzled. "Why has he not spoken?"

"His heart has been wounded," *Owura* Okoh said. "He loved his brother more than anyone."

Mrs. Okoh stood up, wringing her hands in a beseeching gesture. "Please, Mr. Dawson, talk to him. Tell him to unlock his tongue and forsake us no longer. Please."

Dawson stood up quickly. "I will be back."

Outside on the veranda, Smoothie was admiring her completed hairdo in a hand mirror.

"Did you see which way Yaw Okoh went?" Dawson asked them.

Smoothie made a face and rolled her eyes, but her hairdresser pointed to their left. Dawson ran in that direction, kicking up red dust as he looked right and left for a sign of Yaw. People stared at him in curiosity. Everyone could tell he wasn't from around there, and now they wondered what his excitement was about.

Getting closer to a fringe of the forest, Dawson stopped to address two young men sitting idly on a half-finished wall of an even less finished house.

"Did you see Yaw Okoh pass here?" he asked.

They looked at him languidly. "Who?"

"Yaw Okoh. Tall man, very strong?"

They shrugged and shook their heads, clearly not the slightest bit interested.

Dawson retraced his steps, looking for an alternative route that

Yaw might have taken. Although he seemed to have magically disappeared, it was simply more likely that he had gone another way and Dawson had rushed right by. Undoubtedly, Yaw knew the town inside out.

He walked back to the Okohs' house. It would have been nice to be returning with a somber but now vocal Yaw ready to sit down and once again talk to his parents, but nothing was ever that simple.

Dawson looked up at the darkening sky, and a mob of dark rain clouds glared back. A wind was beginning to kick up dust. Just a few hundred meters before the Okohs' house, Dawson saw John and four other boys about his age were trying to squeeze in as much soccer as possible ahead of the approaching downpour.

Dawson watched them for a minute, and then called out, "John!"

The boy turned and saw him, hesitated, and then trotted up.

"I like how you play," Dawson said, smiling. "You dribble very well."

He held up his palm, and John executed a solid high five. "Thank you, sir," he said, grinning broadly. "I'm a good striker too."

"Wow," Dawson said, impressed. "But you'll have to go inside soon because of the rain."

"Yes, please," John agreed.

Dawson slipped an arm lightly around the boy's shoulders. "You're growing very strong. You must work very hard."

"Yes, please."

"Do you ever go to the farm with your uncle?"

"Yes, please. I wake up early with him sometimes, and I help him for two hours and come back to the house and bathe myself. Then I go to school."

"Good boy," Dawson said, looking down at him. "Stay in school, okay?"

"Yes, please."

"John, do you know about that one Chinese man who was found dead a few days ago not far from your uncle's farm?"

"Yes, I heard about it," the boy said, nodding. "One of my friends was watching when they dug him out from the soil."

"At that time, where were you?"

"Please, I wasn't at the farm because I was having fever. I stayed in the house."

Interesting. "But your uncle went to farm that day?"

"Yes, please."

"Did you see or hear him leave the house?"

John wrinkled his nose. "I think so, but I don't remember so well, because the fever was making my head confused. My auntie was with me, and she said I didn't even know where I was until all the fever came out of my body. Anyway, I think he left the house the same time as usual."

"Which is what time?"

"Maybe . . ." John inclined his head. "Five o'clock? When we get to the farm, by that time it's starting to get light."

"I see. Thank you, John. You can get back to your match now."

"Thank you, sir. Bye." He skipped away, happy to return to the soccer game.

Dawson smiled after him. He was as straightforward as a preteen could be. Had he provided *Owura* Okoh his alibi? Not exactly. It was a conditional alibi, if such a thing existed.

Returning to the Okohs' house, Dawson walked slowly with his hands thrust in his pockets and his head down as he pondered. Okoh, as gentle a soul as he appeared to be, had a powerful motive to kill Bao Liu. If indeed the Chinese man had caused the death of Amos Okoh after having dishonored the family name with the most repugnant insult possible, what reason in the world was left *not* to kill the man?

But Dawson's mind vacillated like a pendulum over *Owura* Okoh as a suspect. Dawson's head said, *Altogether possible.* His heart said, *I can't see him committing the act of murder.* For the moment, the heart was winning the debate.

CHAPTER TWENTY

DAWSON WENT BRIEFLY BACK to the Okohs' to express his regrets that he had been unable to catch up with Yaw. He exchanged phone numbers with them and bade them goodbye for the time being. *Never leave without a phone number if one is available.* It was a fundamental rule.

Before he reached the Corolla, Dawson stopped in surprise. Fifty meters or so ahead of him, Akua Helmsley was interviewing a Dunkwa man while being filmed by Samuels. *This woman is always one step behind me,* he thought. *Or ahead.*

Dawson watched them as Helmsley finished up, thanked the man, and turned her attention to the video Samuels was playing back on what was obviously a very expensive camera. Dawson approached them.

"Chief Inspector," she said with equal surprise as she saw him.

"Miss Helmsley."

"Are you going to stop us from filming again?" she said with a teasing smile.

He smiled back. "This time I don't believe I have any right to."

"Then I'm very relieved. Come and have a look at this video I'm putting together for *The Guardian* to go out tonight."

The interview was about two minutes long. Akua explained to Dawson that she would be trimming it down and doing a voice-over in English to summarize what the resident had said in Twi. The gist was he feared what was going to happen when the rain arrived late that night. With about two continuous days of down-pour, flooding in Dunkwa was all but certain, and the last time that had happened it had been a disaster.

"I'll be back here covering it in the midst of the storm tomor-row, but I want to give the prelude this evening."

"Won't that be dangerous, Miss Helmsley? Why not stay safely in Kumasi until the worst is over and then come back?"

"That's for ordinary mortals and cowards." She laughed. "Per-haps they're one and the same. In any case, Dawson, I can assure you that Kumasi and Obuasi will have their share of the deluge, the only difference being that those towns don't sit on a river the way Dunkwa sits on the Ofin."

"It will break its banks, for sure," Dawson said, thinking of people being swept away in the swirling current: a terrifying image for him.

"And I intend to be here to cover it. Care to join me?" She said it almost teasingly, as if daring him.

"Thank you, but no. I have a lot of work I need to get done at Obuasi. The office is a mess." He realized too late that it sounded like a weak excuse.

"What brought you here today?" she asked.

"I came to talk to someone," Dawson replied. "Do you know anything about the case of Amos Okoh—said to have drowned in one of the mining pits after falling off a bridge?"

"It was probably one of the handful of tragic cases I heard about, but I didn't follow up on that one specifically. Why, does it have a bearing on the murder of Mr. Liu?"

"It might, yes."

She looked at him contemplatively. "But I sense you're not close to making an arrest."

"That's correct. I am not."

"You'll get it," she said confidently. "I have faith in you."

"Thank you very much."

"Where do you go from here?" she asked him.

"I want to take a look at the scene of Amos's drowning since I'm here." He glanced up at the sky. "Hopefully I can beat the rain."

"Is that your vehicle over there?" Akua said calculatingly.

She pointed at the Corolla and he said yes.

"Inspector," she said in half amusement, "the terrain is going to slice that little thing in two. Why not let us take you there in the four-by-four? In any case, I would like to see the place myself."

THEY CIRCUMNAVIGATED THE southernmost portion of Bao's mining area and approached from the north instead. Between here and the shack stretched another moonscape expanse of yellow-gray soil churned up by excavators. Solitary shrubs poked out of the barrenness here and there, and Dawson wondered what determined their individual hardiness and ability to survive in the midst of devastation.

Ahead, a deep pond with craggy sides stretched longer than it was wide. It was across the shorter dimension that a simple rope suspension bridge was constructed. Its narrow deck, made of wooden planks lashed together, arced down toward the water's surface and up again at the other side of the pond. At intervals, a vertical rope connected the planks with the upper rope that acted as a handrail.

"That must be the bridge the Okohs told me about," Dawson said, pointing.

He, Akua, and Samuels alighted and walked toward the giant water-filled pit. As they drew closer, Dawson was struck that the water wasn't the usual milky brown or yellow. Instead, it was blue.

"Why is it that color?" he asked Akua.

"Prussian blue," she said without hesitation. "Some of the cyanide that AngloGold Ashanti uses to extract gold from the ore leaches into the soil and combines with iron oxide. That produces ferrocyanide, which is a blue color."

"So that water contains cyanide?" Dawson asked, stunned.

"Yes."

"So if I drink it, I'm a dead man?"

"Actually no. Because the cyanide is tightly bound to the

iron, it's no longer toxic." She winked at him and smiled. "Still, I wouldn't try it if I were you."

"Don't worry," Dawson said dryly.

She gazed at the pond for a while, and then shook her head. "What a disaster." She looked around. "The whole thing is a disaster." Her voice shook a little, far different from the steady, professional tone she used in her video reports.

"How did you learn all this stuff?" Dawson asked with admiration.

She snorted. "The hard way. Sometimes people don't want to tell you anything at all."

Dawson approached the side of the pit where the rope bridge was lashed to two thick metal stakes implanted deeply into the soil two or three meters back from the edge. He had no interest in walking across the bridge, but he did want to see how it moved. He put one foot on the deck, depressed it a couple times, and generated a wave without too much effort. Then, standing to one side, Dawson pushed against the handrail until the bridge began to rock back and forth like a pendulum, the amplitude increasing with each shove.

Akua had been watching. "Looks quite precarious," she commented.

"It is," Dawson agreed. "I wouldn't get on that thing if you paid me."

But he could see how the bridge drastically cut down on the time it would take to walk around the pits to get from one side to the other. Time was money—or more precisely, gold.

He visualized what must have happened to Amos. His girlfriend, Comfort, came across the bridge from the other side of the pond. Bao was on this side and began to talk to her. Perhaps he was only being friendly, but that wasn't the way Amos saw it as he appeared on the scene. Amos's warnings to leave his girlfriend alone led to a shouting match, at the end of which Bao ordered Amos off "his" land. Were it not for Comfort pleading with Amos, he might have physically attacked Bao at that moment. Instead, he relented and went across the bridge to the other side with Comfort. But that wasn't the end of the matter because Bao began to taunt Amos, capping it off with the insult that tops all. Furious, Amos turned back menacingly, machete in hand.

Panicking—or not—Bao began to rock the bridge even as Amos approached. Perhaps the young man stopped to catch his balance, or he might have tried to keep moving forward despite the violent swaying motion. At any rate, to the horror of Comfort and everyone else looking on, Amos tumbled in.

It seemed strange that nothing had been at hand—no pole, no rope—to use as a rescue device, but from Dawson's years in the police force, he knew all about crowd paralysis—multiple onlookers apparently incapable of springing into action as a disaster unfolds before them, whether it is a drowning, beating, or a rape. So even if something had been available to pull Amos out of the water, precious and irretrievable seconds might have been lost. Now Amos was dead, and the murder of Bao that had followed was quite possibly in revenge for that death.

Akua joined Dawson as he walked around a portion of the pit's perimeter. The environment seemed alien and hostile to him.

He looked up at the sky as the first flitter of lightning showed, followed by a deep rumble of thunder. "We'd best be going."

BY THE TIME Dawson got back to his hotel, night had fallen and the rain had begun. He called Chikata.

"How far, boss?" the sergeant asked, slang for "How goes it?"

Dawson gave Chikata a brief rundown of the case and the grim discovery of an intoxicated Sergeant Obeng beating up a suspect.

"*Ewurade.* That's a shame. So, what's next?"

"I want you to come up from Accra and replace him, but Commander Longdon doesn't agree. He says he can find someone from either Obuasi or Kumasi, which I'm sure he can, but I don't care."

"Ah, massa." Chikata began to laugh. "You are really something. What do you want me to do?"

"I'm not asking you to do anything," Dawson said lightly.

"I'll work on it."

"Thank you, Chikata."

Dawson ended the call with the satisfaction that he had just launched a potent chain reaction. Chikata would be on the phone to his powerful Uncle Theo within minutes, and before long the heavy machinery would creak into action.

AT FIVE THIRTY on Monday morning, Dawson jerked awake to a fat plop of water in the middle of his forehead. He sat up quickly and looked at the ceiling. It was pouring outside and the roof was leaking. He jumped out of bed and fetched a bucket from the bathroom, putting it on top of the bed to catch the leak, only to discover another in one corner of the room. Disgusted, he pulled a T-shirt over his head and went outside to the front desk, where the receptionist was chewing gum and doing her nails.

"My roof is leaking," he said.

She looked up languidly with lashes so long they must have been weighing her lids down. "Mm-hm? Do you need a bucket?"

"No, I think maybe I need the roof to be fixed."

"Ah, okay. I will inform the manager."

I have no doubt you will. Returning to the room furious that he hadn't moved out before the storm, Dawson decided to pack up his things, check out and take his bags to the Obuasi office until he could find a better place to stay. His first phone call of the day was to Christine, who asked how he was doing. He complained about the rain and the leaking roof.

"How's the case?" she asked.

"Haven't got very far," he said gloomily.

"Something will break soon. What are you doing today?"

"Getting out of this rotten hotel first. I have to pack up my things before I have to swim out of here."

"Bye, sweetie."

"Oh, wait," he said hastily before she hung up. "I'm broke—can you mobile me a little cash?"

"Okay—I'll send what I can by MTN Money."

"Thanks, love. I appreciate it."

Dawson divided all his stuff between his small suitcase and

backpack, then went to the front desk, where he paid his bill with what seemed a painful amount of money when he considered that his paycheck was more than a week away. Miss Eyelashes wrote out his receipt in agonizingly slow longhand, and then Dawson was finally out of the place. The question was, where was he going to stay?

AS HE DROVE slowly along Obuasi High Street, Dawson couldn't help thinking about Akua Helmsley. By now, she would be fighting the elements in Dunkwa. He remembered her invitation to join her and felt uncomfortable about his quick refusal. True, it might not be police work exactly, but what would be wrong with joining her for the unique experience? And his excuse? Work in the office. Akua was going to brave the storm, and Dawson was going to tidy up the office.

He stopped at an MTN kiosk and picked up the cash Christine had sent him, and then he continued up the street toward divisional headquarters. He spotted a hotel called Coconut Grove on the right-hand side and pulled over. Soaking wet, he went into the dark lobby, which smelled musty and was lit by a couple of LED lanterns. No power, courtesy of the Electricity Corporation of Ghana.

Dawson asked what the room rates were. Not too bad, but he wanted to see the rooms before he took one. Now was a good time to spot leaks.

The receptionist dragged on a pair of slippers and showed him to the cheapest accommodations: a small room, tiny toilet, and shower. *At least there's air conditioning*, Dawson thought, looking at the unit on the wall. "Does that work?" he asked the receptionist.

"Yes," she said. "When the power comes on."

"You have no generator?"

"We have it," she said, "but it's not operating at the moment."

Wonderful. "Okay," Dawson said. "I'll take it. I'll bring my bags in later on when I return."

He paid a deposit at the front desk and went back outside into the rain.

Once inside the division office, he changed into the dry shirt he had brought with him, looked around the office, and vowed he was going to make a dent. He began by sorting old folders into two piles: more than two years old, and two years old or less. As he thumbed through them, Dawson frowned, noticing that some of Sergeant Obeng's reports were incomplete or slapdash. What in heaven's name had been going on at these headquarters?

He was a little over an hour into his work when he thought again of Akua. He slid his phone out, hesitated, and then called her. "Good Monday morning, Miss Helmsley."

"Good *wet* Monday morning, Chief Inspector."

"It is. You are in Dunkwa, I suppose?"

"I am. It's a disaster—environmentally and in all sorts of other ways."

"Are you safe?" he asked.

"Yes, thank you for asking. I have Samuels with me."

"I want join you," he said abruptly.

"What?" She almost gasped. "Really? Oh, wonderful!" She sounded happier than Dawson might have expected. "Do you have wellies?"

"Do I have what?"

"Wellingtons—rubber boots."

"I don't."

"You'll need some. There's cyanide and mercury and sulfuric acid and other nasty substances in the floodwater, all leached out of the runoff from the mines. Samuels has an extra pair of boots. What's your size?"

When he told her, she said she thought the Wellingtons should fit, more or less.

"I will leave in a few minutes," he told her. "Mind you, it might take me at least two hours."

"Not a problem," she responded. "We're going to be here for quite some time."

CHAPTER TWENTY-ONE

DAWSON WOULD NEVER MAKE it to Dunkwa in one piece in this weather. The road was flooded and impassable for a small vehicle. However, a solution did exist. In this part of the world, because of these very conditions, the *tro-tros* were old-style four-wheel-drive Land Rovers. True, they did not hold as many passengers as the usual *tro-tros*, but they were powerful and could withstand the punishing terrain, nasty weather, and treacherous mud.

Dawson drove to the Obuasi lorry park, locked the Corolla up, and joined the line for Dunkwa. Because the weather was so bad, it was less crowded than it might have been, but the queue was long enough in this misery that Dawson's torso was wet in no time, his feet were soaked, and the sodden ground squelched with mud that threatened to suck off his shoes every time he took a step.

The vehicle was packed to maximum capacity, and to get one extra person in, the driver's mate, who collected the fares and managed passenger entry and exit, rode perilously on the back of the Land Rover standing on the footrest. How he did that in this weather was beyond Dawson, who had ended up the man in the middle squashed between a corpulent woman and a bone-thin man.

On the Dunkwa road, the Land Rover dipped, swerved, and slithered around potholes and waded through deep puddles. *Our fate is in the hands of this driver,* Dawson thought, and the driver looked like he might have been twenty years old at the most.

The rain wasn't lessening. If anything, it was getting heavier. Every few minutes, a flash of lightning illuminated the sky, followed by a sharp crack of deafening thunder. When Dawson and the other passengers alighted at the Dunkwa *tro-tro* depot, water on the ground was ankle high. Crouching under his now almost useless umbrella, Dawson called Akua.

"Where are you?" she asked.

"At the *tro-tro* station."

"Okay, stay there, and we'll pick you up in the SUV. We're not far."

Dawson found an abandoned vegetable stand to shelter underneath, watching rivers of muddy rainwater flowing from the lorry park while pedestrians negotiated the least hazardous routes to tread while pulling up the hems of their trousers and skirts to avoid soaking them, but it was no use. A soaking was inevitable.

Dawson spotted Akua and Samuels approaching in the Prado. Dawson hopped into the backseat and heaved a sigh of relief to be out of the rain.

Akua smiled at him from the front passenger seat. "Weather couldn't get any nastier than this."

"Terrible," he agreed. "I'm an Accra man. We don't have rain like this."

"Some wellies and a raincoat in the back for you," she said. "Try them on."

"Thank you," Dawson said. To Samuels in the driver's seat, he said, "Morning, Mr. Samuels," although afternoon was close.

"Morning, sir."

The Wellingtons were a little tight, but they would do, and the raincoat was excellent.

Samuels turned off the main road at a snail's pace, engaging four-wheel drive as they dipped into muddy floodwater that grew progressively deeper.

"The river crested last night," Akua said. "Everyone is headed for higher ground."

Ahead of their vehicle, a stream of people waded through

thigh-deep water, some with their kids on their shoulders. A few random items like small pieces of furniture were floating free.

"The main road is at a higher elevation," Akua explained, "so that's where people are headed, and there's also a hill on the other side of town."

The Prado dipped even lower, making Dawson anxious that they might get stuck, but the vehicle handled it with barely a loss of traction and the water level dropped again as they came to the main road where people were standing under shelter on anything that would keep them above water level—stacked tables or chairs.

"Let's go up the hill," Akua said to Samuels, "and then we can take some shots of the Ofin River."

At the crest of the hill, much of the town had gathered to escape the floodwater, but it was still ankle-deep. Samuels pulled over and the three got out and trudged through the mud to a spot overlooking the Ofin. It was churning gray and brown as it rushed along swiftly, as if desperate to get to its destination, but at one silt-laden area, it had nowhere to go but up and over.

"We'll descend now, as close as possible to the riverbank," Akua said.

They slid down, holding on to vegetation to avoid slipping and tumbling. It was most hazardous for Samuels, as he had the expensive camera equipment. At one point, Akua did lose her footing and fell with a thud on her posterior. She cursed, and then began to laugh hysterically at the frank absurdity of the mission as rain pelted her in the face. "Oh, my God. Why do I even do this?"

Dawson, a little bit ahead of her, came back and stood over her smiling. "Maybe because you care about your work?"

"Ugh," she said. "There's caring, and then there's insanity."

Dawson extended a hand and she pulled herself up, still laughing. Samuels, a few meters away, asked her if she was okay.

"I'm good, Samuels. Come on. Let's keep going. I want to get to a good spot where I can do a piece with the river showing in the background."

Dawson admired her tenacity, and wondered if Christine would do anything like this. She would, but only for the most necessary of reasons—like to rescue a family member. He had a spontaneous vision of throwing his mother-in-law down this hill into the river, and had to suppress a laugh. *Not nice*. Still, it was funny.

"This should be a good spot, Akua," Samuels said, and for the first time Dawson wondered if there was anything between the two of them.

They spent some time setting up the scene and doing a couple run-throughs before the final take. Dawson's attention was drawn to the Ofin River. No mining sites were visible at this particular spot, and the vegetation on the banks was thick and green, but downstream, the telltale signs of a stripped landscape began. As Dawson stared at the area, he saw someone appear at the edge of the river on the same side. He wasn't difficult to recognize.

Yaw Okoh.

He was barefoot and shirtless, his taut, broad shoulders and V-shaped torso glistening wet. He had stopped to urinate in the bushes.

Dawson looked quickly back at Akua and Samuels. They were engrossed in their video production. Dawson began to make his way in Yaw's direction. The din of the rain, the noise of the river, and the episodic clap of thunder all combined to disguise any giveaway sound of Dawson moving in the bush.

Once Yaw had answered his call of nature, he continued walking downstream in the rain. Dawson tried to keep an eye on him while struggling with mud and vegetation, while Yaw seemed to move effortlessly. *I need to spend more time in the bush*, Dawson thought, annoyed at his clumsiness—not that his "wellies" were of any help.

As the river turned course slightly, it also narrowed, and to Dawson's surprise, Yaw approached the water and got close to the edge, studying the currents. *Impossible*, Dawson thought. Yaw could not possibly cross the river as swift and deep as it was, could he? But, yes, he took two steps into the water, gauging his landing spot on the other side and how strongly he needed to swim. Dawson moved quickly, half jumping, half sliding the remainder of the way to the river. One boot entered and he pulled it back sharply. Good thing it was a little too small, or he would have lost it.

"Yaw!" Dawson called out, but it wasn't loud enough. *"Yaw!"*

The muscleman turned his head, saw Dawson, and then deliberately continued his advance into the river.

Furiously, Dawson yelled out, *"Stop!"*

But as he got closer, Yaw had already waded into the river to neck height, launching himself across. Dawson stopped, his chest heaving as he watched Yaw making his way at a diagonal to the other bank. For Dawson, a man who could not swim to save his hide, it was incredible that one man could take on a river in a storm like this. Sure, it wasn't as wide as the grandest of Ghana's bodies of water—Volta, Pra, Ankobra—but it was still a significant river, especially in Dawson's eyes.

Yaw reached the other side and climbed up the bank as casually as if taking a stroll on a fine day, walked to the forest ahead of him, and disappeared without a word. Dawson's jaws were clenched. At first he had had sympathy for this man who had lost his brother, but now Yaw was being just plain evasive. That made Dawson all the more determined. *I will get to him and make him talk.*

RETURNING TO WHERE Akua and Samuels had been doing their report, Dawson found them wrapping up for the day. After she redid a couple of spots in the segment to perfect it, they packed up and Dawson joined them on the trudge up the hill. It was difficult to say whether going up or coming down was tougher.

"Where did you go?" Akua asked Dawson, breathing heavily.

"Just to take a look downstream," he said, his instincts telling him that it was not yet time to discuss Yaw Okoh with her.

In the shelter of the Prado, they heaved a sigh of relief and rested for a moment.

"Okay," Akua said to Dawson. "Let's get you back to Obuasi. Where are you staying?"

"Coconut Grove Hotel."

"You know it?" Akua asked Sammuels.

He nodded. "Yes."

As they made their careful way out of Obuasi, Akua removed a Samsung tablet from her bag, switched it on, and passed it back to Dawson. "I thought you might have a look at some of Mr. Samuels's photos of the different mining sites. We're going to put the best ones in an online gallery."

He looked through them, admiring the way she had sequenced some of the increased devastation at particular spots over several months—from forest to bleak, yellow-gray moonscape. Some of the photos showed *galamsey* workers toiling in groups at the edge of a river; in others they were panning for gold in solitude. There were also the large industrial operations with bulldozers and excavators, giant pits, and massive trommels washing tons of gravel by the hour. Dawson was struck by the tone of sadness conveyed by the way Samuels had shot the images.

"You are very talented, Mr. Samuels," Dawson said. "Congrats on these amazing photographs."

"Thank you, sir."

Dawson skimmed through more, stopping at an image of a Chinese worker operating a bulldozer as it mowed down a line of neatly planted cocoa trees as if they were nothing but insignificant twigs. The time stamp was from about three months ago.

In the next picture, also from three months ago, Samuels had captured an excavator in slow transit from one mining area to the next along a narrow, muddy path deep in the forest. He had shot it in sequence from wide angle to close. Here, the operator was not Chinese; he was Ghanaian. As the camera moved in, it showed him clearly. There was the scar across the lip and the infamous bare torso. Dawson's breath caught. *Yaw Okoh knows how to operate an excavator.* Three months ago, before his brother's death, perhaps he worked for a company or individual involved in small-scale mining.

It was a stunning revelation. The day was wet and gloomy, but suddenly Dawson saw it as clear and bright. What he had only yesterday considered unlikely had turned out to be entirely plausible.

CHAPTER TWENTY-TWO

DAWSON HAD HAD A good night's sleep at Coconut Grove with no surprise leaks but the hotel was still without power. For a few minutes as light crept to the sky, he lay in bed with his mind roaming. When would the family be up from Accra? When, if ever, would the guesthouse be inhabitable?

And this murder case. He felt there was a track he must follow, given yesterday's discovery that Yaw Okoh could operate an excavator. If that piece of heavy machinery was used to quickly bury Bao Liu, Yaw had the skills to do it, and he had a powerful motive as well. And so did his father. Could it have been a collaborative effort? In the overpowering of the Chinese man, two men would have been far more effective than one.

Dawson felt the sense of eagerness he always had whenever a potential lead appeared—like walking around without direction in the bush until a path suddenly appears that might well take you where you want to go. But he also knew that sacrificing any loose ends at the altar of a promising lead was foolhardy, and at the moment, the uninvestigated item was still Chuck Granger, the American whose mining concession was adjacent to the Lius' site.

According to Akua, Granger stayed—or had stayed—at the bed-and-breakfast called Four Villages Inn. It was time to pay a visit. Dawson swung his feet to the floor and headed for the shower. He hoped, at least, that water was flowing.

• • •

THE RAIN HAD diminished to on-and-off sprinkles, but that
didn't mean Kumasi traffic was any less chaotic than if the down-
pour had continued at full power. Flooding at various points of the
city was still very much in force, particularly at the roundabouts
where traffic came to a standstill and drivers lost their tempers with
each other. Trading insults in traffic was the Ghanaian way, but the
melodramatic displays were never as serious as they might seem.

Crawling forward by the inch toward the Ahodwo section of
the city, Dawson took the opportunity to call Daniel Armah, his
dear friend and mentor.

"How are you, Darko?" Armah said, his voice gentle and perhaps not quite as steady as when he was a younger man. By now,
he would be in his sixties, Dawson calculated.

"I'm fine, Daniel. So nice to hear your voice."

"I'm sorry it took a little while to get back to you. The wife and
I were in the Upper East Region, and reception wasn't very good
there."

"No problem at all," Dawson said, smiling. "I wanted to say
hello and find out when we can see each other again."

"Whenever you are free. My schedule is mostly flexible now
that I'm in semiretirement."

Dawson suggested he could come around with the family when
they came up to Kumasi.

"Excellent," Armah said. "I'll be glad to see you."

Whatever mood Dawson was in, it was always good to hear
Armah's voice.

AS HE NEARED Four Villages Inn, Dawson noticed several
Chinese establishments—hotels, restaurants. Outside a Chinese-
owned casino, a cluster of Chinese men and women smoked and
talked. Dawson wished he could get inside their heads. What did
they *really* think of Ghana and its people? Lian Liu had certainly
let her feelings be known, and Dawson supposed that the destruction of land carried out by the Chinese illegals was an indication
of just how much they didn't care. But over and over again in

history, it was much the same story. Just like the Portuguese, the Dutch, Germans, or British, the Chinese wanted what Ghana had, and Ghanaians were going to let them have it with few or no strings attached. *Why?*

Four Villages Inn was tucked into a lush, quiet corner away from the street, with tall eucalyptus trees flanking the outside wall of the compound. The uniformed watchman at the sentry box acknowledged Dawson as he pulled in.

"Good morning, sir," the watchman said, coming up as Dawson parked and got out of the Corolla.

"Good morning. I'm looking for Mr. Scott."

"Please, he is inside. You can knock on the door."

A generic brown-and-white dog barked fiercely at Dawson from the top of the steps leading up to the front veranda, but it took off with its tail tucked in as Dawson got closer.

The veranda was wide and festooned with hanging potted plants, and two sets of glass tables and cushioned wicker chairs were arranged at the opposite ends. It was far more like a home than a hotel. Dawson knocked on the solid mahogany door and waited, looking around at the beautifully laid-out garden to the right of the veranda.

The door swung open, and a petite Ghanaian woman in a smart outfit greeted Dawson, who introduced himself and asked to see Mr. Scott.

"Let me call him. Please have a seat."

Dawson chose the closest wicker chair and grinned at the dog, who had come back warily to eye him.

"Mr. Dawson, is it?"

He turned to find a white man in a Ghanaian-print shirt. His girth was generous, and his pale hair was thin and wispy at the top of his head.

Dawson stood to shake hands. "Yes, Detective Chief Inspector Darko Dawson, CID."

"Oh!" Scott exclaimed enthusiastically. "Whatever the crime is, I confess."

He burst into a hearty peal of laughter that seemed to rise from the depths of his abdomen, while his face colored pomegranate-red with mirth. "Have a seat, Mr. Dawson," he said, still smiling.

They both sat down, and Mr. Scott folded his fingers together over his jolly tummy.

"So how can I help you?" he said. He sounded American to Dawson, but Akua Helmsley had said he was Canadian.

"I'm investigating the death of a Chinese miner by name of Bao Liu."

"Ha!" Scott exclaimed. "I wish you the best of luck with that, Chief Inspector, but don't get your expectations up too high."

"Why do you say that?" Dawson asked with curiosity.

"No one's going to tell you anything useful," he said, chuckling. "Except me, maybe. Everyone's going to keep their mouths shut." He grew sober. "But yes, bad deal that murder, but"—he shrugged—"you reap what you sow."

"How do you mean?" Dawson asked, interested.

"Well," Scott said matter-of-factly, "if you run around trampling all over a country that doesn't belong to you, destroying people's farmland and their livelihood, then you're pretty much setting yourself up to be well and truly whacked, aren't you?"

"Whacked by whom?"

"Anyone!" he exclaimed. "The Ghanaian galamsey dispossessed by these Chinese marauders, the villagers and farmers whose land the Chinese guys steal—hey, if I was one of those cocoa farmers whose trees guys like Bao Liu bulldoze, I'd commit a couple of murders myself."

"You look quite serious about that."

"I am. Have you gone around to some of these mining sites, Chief Inspector?"

"I have."

"Then you know it's a goddamn shame," Scott said, his jaw hardening. "I've lived in Ghana for more than twenty years, and I've never seen so much destruction in so short a time. And what are the police and the government doing about it? Nothing, because everyone's palms are being greased—corrupt bunch of sycophants. They're about as disgusting as these Chinese plunderers themselves."

He certainly isn't shy with his opinions, Dawson thought. "You had a guest here called Chuck Granger, is that right?" he asked.

"Oh, yes," Scott said with a toss of his head. "I threw him out. Obnoxious American. As bad as the Chinese." He thought that crack was amusing too, so he rewarded it with his own laughter.

"What happened with Granger that you had to throw him out?" Dawson asked, smiling slightly.

"How about drunkenness, carousing into the wee hours of the morning with a bunch of women in his room, and disturbing my other guests? Is that good enough reason?"

"I would say so," Dawson said. "Interesting place you have here, Mr. Scott. Why is it called Four Villages Inn?"

"We have four rooms," Scott explained, "and each has the theme of an area in the Ashanti Region—for instance, one room has artifacts from the *kente* made at Bonwire."

"I see," Dawson said. "Very nice."

"Thank you. But back to Granger. What did you want to know about him?"

"Did you ever hear him discussing anything to do with his mining site?"

"Did I!" Scott exclaimed. "Ha! How could I not? He sometimes paced up and down right here on the veranda or inside the hallway talking on the phone in the loudest and most profane tones possible. 'Fuck this, fuck that. I need this piece of machinery right *now!*' And then he had this reality show filming crew swarming around, and that was a real pain in the ass—even though the Explorer Channel was paying me quite handsomely."

"I'm looking for names and connections, though," Dawson said, wanting Scott to focus. "Did you ever hear him threatening to do something to Bao Liu directly or indirectly?"

"Look," Scott said, "I don't remember him mentioning this fellow Bao Liu specifically, but Chuck hated the Chinese miners around his site because they were all illegal, and Chuck had had to move heaven and earth to get all his papers—or so he claimed, but that's another story in itself—and here were these Chinese miners all up in his face, sometimes walking onto his site with their pump-action shotguns and a bunch of Ghanaian thugs. So yeah, since Bao Liu was one of the miners next door to Chuck's site, so sure, I would say you need to go after Chuck, because he's a brute of a man who would kill someone and not think twice about it."

So there was motive, Dawson thought—at least according to Scott. "Do you know where Granger is staying at the moment?"

Scott shook his head. "Don't know, and don't care. He could be resting comfortably in Dante's Inferno as far as I'm concerned."

He laughed at that too, his belly jiggling with his glee. Dawson couldn't help joining in. Scott was certainly an interesting man.

Dawson stood up. "Thank you very much for your help, sir."

"You're most welcome. Anything else you think of, give me a call."

He took a card from his shirt pocket and handed it to Dawson.

"By the way," Dawson said, "just out of curiosity, how much is it per night to stay here?"

When Scott told him how much, Dawson almost laughed at how far out of his reach the price was.

DAWSON DECIDED TO return to Dunkwa in an attempt to find either Granger or Yaw Okoh—or both, if he was lucky, but he had driven barely two blocks when Gifty called him and asked him to meet her at the guesthouse, where she was waiting for the foreman. She didn't ask Dawson if he *could* meet her. It was more like a summons from a district court.

He gritted his teeth. "All right," he said. "I'll be there soon."

WHEN HE ARRIVED some twenty-five minutes later, Dawson found his mother-in-law in the living room berating a perspiring, sheepish-looking man who was wringing his hands and repeating at intervals, "Yes, please, madam."

Gifty turned as Dawson entered. "Darko! How nice to see you again!"

They embraced, only barely. She was wearing a fragrance that he admitted was subtle and alluring, and her general turnout was flawless. Still keeping her slim figure, she was dressed in a one-piece iridescent blue and pink wax-print with the prestigious Woodin label. Pink lipstick against her dark, soft skin set off the colors of her dress and made the entire picture very fetching. She was, as always, wearing one of her wigs. Not just any old wig—this was the kind that you had difficulty deciding if it was real hair or not.

She introduced Dawson to the gentleman. "This is Mr. Nyarko, the foreman."

Nyarko, who had taken the opportunity to mop his brow in the few seconds the heat had been taken off him, shook hands with Dawson. "Good morning, sir."

"Let's go to the kitchen," Gifty said.

There, she directed what needed to be done, and Dawson added a couple words here and there. Nyarko's basic reaction was, "Yes, I can do it, no problem, madam."

"Look, Mr. Nyarko," Gifty said after they'd gone through the whole house, "like I told you before, everything must be ready by Friday. If not, I won't be using you again. Am I clear?"

"Yes, madam," he said, nodding vigorously. "No problem, madam. Everything will be ready by all means."

Dawson didn't see it happening. It was too much to accomplish in four days. Outside again with Gifty, he said, "Mama, I think we need a plan B in case he doesn't finish."

"Oh, he will finish," Gifty said, pressing her lips primly together.

"I think he's making a promise he can't keep," Dawson said.

She smiled. "Darko, Darko. You can never stop doubting, eh? Always skeptical, never positive."

"I'm not doubting you, Mama; I'm doubting *him*."

"I will be here until the end of the week, don't you worry," she assured him. "I will make sure everything goes well."

"Okay, thank you very much."

"Because I know you're busy with all your, em, police stuff," she added. "What is it you're doing here in Kumasi again?"

As if she didn't know. "I'm working on a homicide case, Mama." *What else would I be doing?*

"Oh, yes—homicide. That's right. I remember now."

Don't let her get inside your head. "I have to leave now," he said abruptly.

"Oh, so soon?" Gifty said in fake concern. "I'll walk you out."

With Gifty following half a step behind, Dawson returned to the Corolla saying little as his mother-in-law talked about how much she was looking forward to seeing the boys again. Everything about her speech and her manner got on his nerves. How could Christine, a beautiful, loving soul, *possibly* be her daughter?

"We'll talk soon, Mama," he said as he got behind the wheel. He started up the car and sped away without a glance back. He wasn't going to let Gifty ruin his day.

DAWSON'S PLANNED TRIP to Dunkwa was scrapped again, this time with a call from Commander Longdon.

"Where are you right now?" he asked.

Dawson heard something grave in his tone. "I was on my way to Dunkwa, sir."

"I think you should come down to the division so we can discuss one or two things."

"Okay, sir. I'll be there as soon as possible."

Dawson was uneasy. The commander had sounded tense. A few minutes later, when he got a text from Chikata, Dawson thought he understood why.

LOOKS LIKE WILL B JOINING U. JUST 1 OR 2 THINGS MORE TO CONFIRM.

That must be what this is about, Dawson thought. Chikata's coming up to Kumasi ran counter to Longdon's recommendations for Obeng's replacement. Dawson had the uncomfortable sense he was in trouble, a feeling he knew all too well.

• • •

COMMANDER LONGDON WAS on the phone when Dawson entered the air-conditioned office, and he gestured to a chair for Dawson to sit down. After a couple minutes, Longdon hung up and began to jot something down in what Dawson guessed was an appointment book.

"I'll be right with you," Longdon said quietly, without looking up.

"Yes, sir."

The commander finished his notation, capped his pen, and leaned back. "All right, let's talk. How is your progress in the case?"

Dawson gave him a recap. Motives were appearing in different areas and among different people: mute muscleman Yaw Okoh might have wanted to avenge the alleged murder of his brother Amos by Bao Liu. But Dawson wasn't completely satisfied that Amos's *father* was eliminated as a suspect. The pain he felt over the loss of his son had been palpable when Dawson had spoken to him and his wife, and he had indicated that on the morning of Bao's death, he had risen between four and six in the morning.

"But would that give him enough time to commit the murder?" Longdon asked. "He has to walk to the mining site, kill Mr. Liu, and bury him under all that soil or gravel or whatever it is."

"It would be close," Dawson agreed, "but if he had the help of his son Yaw, and he woke up at, say, three instead of four—just using that as an example—he might be able to do it. Yaw would meet him at the site, and they would lie in wait."

"Ah, so you're proposing that Yaw and his father were in cahoots. That's a little too convenient, don't you think?"

Dawson didn't necessarily agree. Plots made between members of a family did occur.

"My point is this, sir," he said. "If Yaw murdered Mr. Bao, he could have done it all by himself, but if Mr. Okoh took part in the murder, then he had to have the help of Yaw. Why? Because Yaw knows how to operate an excavator."

Longdon rubbed his chin contemplatively. "Ah, I see. How do you know that?"

"Akua Helmsley has a clear picture her photographer snapped of him in an excavator."

The commander grunted. "That Helmsley woman. She has her hand in everything. Do we know to whom the excavator belonged?"

"The photo was taken around Dunkwa," Dawson said, "but so many companies have excavators all over the Ashanti Region. It could have belonged to anyone."

Longdon nodded. "In that case, a big priority is to find this Yaw."

Dawson appreciated his grasp of the case. "Yes, sir."

"You'll need some men to help in the search. I'll see what I can do."

"Thank you, sir." Dawson was relieved that this was going so well. Maybe he had imagined the tenseness in the commander's voice on the phone.

"What else?" Longdon asked.

"Well, there is one American guy, Chuck Granger, who has a mining site close to Bao Liu's."

"Is it that guy who was in that reality show, or whatever it's called?"

"Yes, on the Explorer Channel. Granger was living at Four Villages Inn, but when I went there today to meet Mr. Scott, the owner, Granger had already left."

"To where?"

"I don't know, but I'm going to find out."

"Did Scott shed any light on the man?"

Dawson nodded. He liked Longdon's logical progressions. "Scott says Granger hated Chinese illegals trespassing on his mining site, and they did that a lot, apparently—including Bao Liu and his brother, along with his Ghanaian assistants brandishing pump-action shotguns."

The commander appeared satisfied. "You have a lot to work with. Good job."

"Thank you, sir."

"I'll get you some manpower in the next couple of days to help you find Yaw Okoh."

"I appreciate that, sir."

Dawson was halfway standing to leave, but he should have known this had gone too well to be true.

"One other thing," Longdon said, his tone sharpening.

Here it comes, Dawson thought.

The commander folded his fingers in front of him. "I've received word from Central that Inspector Chikata is to join you sometime tomorrow, Wednesday."

Dawson's heart leapt. "Oh, wonderful. Thank you, sir."

"You are a good detective, Dawson, but your problem is that you are arrogant."

Dawson was shocked. "Arrogant, sir?"

"Yes," Longdon snapped. "You went over my head to get your man Chikata here, and I don't like that."

"Sir, I did not go over your head."

The commander wagged a finger at Dawson. "Don't start denying things, Chief Inspector. The best thing right now is to shut up before you get yourself into more trouble. I will let this one pass, but I will not tolerate this kind of insubordination again. Is that clear?"

"Yes, sir. But please, may I say one thing?"

"What is it?"

"The Chikata coming here is not a result of my going over your head. I can assure you of that."

Longdon took a deep sigh and shook his head. "It's the end of the discussion, Chief Inspector. You're dismissed."

ONCE HE HAD left the commander's office, Dawson reflected on the dressing down he had just received. *Am I really that arrogant?* He thought that was an unduly harsh opinion, one he'd heard on occasion from Assistant Commissioner of Police Lartey as well, but he wasn't going to worry about it. Right now all that mattered was that he was going to be working with Chikata again. The rest he didn't care about.

CHAPTER TWENTY-THREE

DAWSON CALLED DR. PREMPEH at Komfo Anokye Hospital. "Good afternoon, Doctor. Please, do you have any word on when the Bao Liu case will be done?"

"We are expecting Dr. Phyllis Kwapong very soon," he said. "I will let you know as soon as she arrives and I'll set up a date for the postmortem."

"Thank you very much, Doctor."

On ending the call, Dawson realized that Mr. Scott had just been trying to reach him, so he called him back.

"Chief Inspector," he said, "I found out from one of my contacts that Chuck Granger is staying with a friend in Asokwa, but he's at the Dunkwa mining site at the moment, so if you can get down there as quickly as possible, that would be ideal."

"I will—thank you for notifying me."

"Oh, and Chief Inspector? I would exercise caution with him, okay?"

THE SUN WAS out, blasting the earth through a freshly washed atmosphere, and the floodwaters at Dunkwa were receding. Just like the first time Dawson had come to Bao Liu's mining site in the taxi, he stopped the car at the point the route became impassable.

It was as hot as a plantain grill, but the soil was still as soft and mushy as fermenting *kenkey* dough. Dawson could see the excavators in the distance working on Granger's site, but before he reached it, he came to the Lius'. Wei was there, supervising a brand new crew of young Ghanaian guys in the digging, carrying, and washing of gravel, and lo and behold, the XCMG excavator was up and running again.

Dawson came up to Wei, who greeted him with an elaborate show of bowing and scraping. Dawson supposed he didn't want to chance spending any more time in jail and was being as deferential as he could just for that reason.

"*Nǐ hǎo*, Mr. Liu," Dawson greeted him against the drone of pumps and the noise of the excavator.

"Oh, *nǐ hǎo, nǐ hǎo*," Wei said, laughing. He seemed to like that.

"How is business?"

"Fine, sir," Wei said, beaming. "Everything is good."

Dawson was startled. Wei's answer had been fluent, but during the interview at the station when Mr. Huang had acted as interpreter, Dawson had been under the impression that Wei had little or no ability to speak English. Perhaps this short sentence just happened to come out right.

"Kudzo and your boys all left you?" he asked Wei.

"Eh?"

"Kudzo gone?"

"Oh." Wei shrugged and made a face indicating both regret and resignation.

"How is Lian?"

"Fine, sir."

"I would like to talk to her in the next few days when she's feeling a little better. Can I have her phone number from you?"

Dawson might have said that too fast, because Wei looked confused.

"Lian," Dawson repeated, then made the universal sign for talking on the phone.

"Ah," Wei said, laughing. He recited the number off by heart.

He pointed in the direction of Granger's site. "Mr. Granger over there—does he trouble you?"

"Trouble?"

"Yes."

"Oh, no trouble; no trouble," Wei said hastily, smiling.

He doesn't dare rock the boat he's in, Dawson thought. *He doesn't want any problems.* "Okay, thank you. Good luck. *Xièxiè.*"

As Dawson walked toward Granger's site, Dawson got a text from Chikata.

EVTHNG COOL BOSS. COMING THURS

Dawson texted back, WHERE U STAYING

FRIEND, Chikata returned.

OK

The timing was good, Dawson reflected, because he wanted Chikata to be there when he went looking for Yaw. For density of muscle combined with agility, Chikata was a very good match for Yaw. Dawson wondered if by "friend" his inspector meant a girlfriend, because that could well be the case.

Nearing Granger's concession, Dawson could see how much larger it was than Liu's, and how much more extensively dug up, what with four working CAT excavators. The peaks and valleys were severe, with several shades of soil—red, brown, gray, and the treasured black gravel. Here the mud was treacherous and deep, a little unnerving as Dawson walked along an undulating crest between two plunging pits full of milky-brown water. He thought of Amos falling into a pit like these, and then averted his eyes. Better to watch where he was planting his feet.

He had attracted attention from the workers on the site, and a Ghanaian guy built as solid as an SUV approached them holding a pump-action shotgun with the barrel resting against his right shoulder.

Not the friendliest person, Dawson thought. "Good morning, sir," he called out amiably, which is the way one should greet a man holding a firearm.

"Morning." Complete monotone.

"Chief Inspector Darko Dawson." He had his ID out and ready. He wouldn't show it to someone like Mr. Okoh or his wife, but to the likes of this guy, most certainly. The man looked at the badge, not really long enough to read it—if he *could* read, Dawson thought unkindly. "And your name, sir?"

"Godson." He flicked his narrow eyes up and down Dawson's frame, as if trying to size him up as a physical force.

"I'm looking for Mr. Granger," Dawson said. "Is he here?"

"Follow me."

Godson led the way, beyond the pits to a more shaded area at the fringe of the site where tree cover still existed. Dawson heard another droning sound of medium to high pitch as they proceeded farther, and then he spotted a large generator outside a cabin hidden by a thicket.

"Wait here," Godson said.

He knocked on the shack door, put his head in for a moment, and then looked back at Dawson. "You can come in."

Godson stood aside to let him pass. As he got in the door, the blast of cold air hit him. *Unbelievable*. In the middle of nowhere, this man had an air-conditioned shack. That was what the powerful generator was for, and Dawson guessed that the Explorer Channel had had the structure built. He saw now that it wasn't really a "shack" in that ragged sense. This was more like a comfortable, brightly lit office space with a desk, chairs, file cabinets, a settee, and not one but two air-conditioning units.

The man at the desk was standing with his arms folded. He was surely an example of how the popular Ghanaian phrase "red white man" came to be. Granger had reddish-blond hair and skin that looked like it was permanently pink and moist in the Ashanti heat and humidity. He was a *big* man the way only Americans were made—lots of bulk, but not necessarily more powerful pound for pound than someone like Yaw or Chikata, who were smaller than Granger overall.

He greeted Dawson with a near imperceptible upward flick of the head. His nose was crooked, as if broken several times in the boxing ring or in bar fights.

"Chuck Granger?" Dawson said.

"Yeah. Who're you again?"

Dawson still had his ID badge out. Granger looked at it considerably longer than Godson had, then indicated a seat for Dawson.

"I'm cool," Granger said to Godson, who nodded and left.

Granger sat not quite opposite Dawson. "What d'you need, Mr. Dawson?"

"I'm investigating the death of Mr. Bao Liu. The one whose mining site is next to yours."

Granger grunted. "Yeah, well, I dunno if I can help you. What d'you need to know?"

"Did you ever have any skirmishes with Mr. Liu?"

"The very first day I got here," Granger said, "he and his goons came onto my property and accused us of trespassing. I told them to fuck off, but up till the time of his death, he came sniffin' round here every few days like a jackal, trying to intimidate us."

"Did you ever exchange gunfire with Bao Liu or his people?"

"Well, someone came onto the property one night to collect soil samples," Granger said, "but we don't know if it was Liu's folks or not. Anyway, Godson fired warning shots and they took off."

"They collect soil samples to estimate how much gold you have on your site?" Dawson asked.

"Supposedly." Granger shrugged and his lip curled. "Stupid really, because you have to sample a whole lot more gravel than that."

"Where were you last Thursday night through Friday morning, Mr. Granger?" Dawson asked.

"In Accra," Granger said, with certainty. "I was there to see Tommy Thompson, director of PMMC."

"Why were you there to see him?"

"Site licensing issue," Granger said carelessly. "Not to bore you with the details, but I like to keep my nose clean and my records scrupulous, so I keep in close contact with Tommy."

It sounded good, but it wasn't enough for Dawson. "Do you have his phone number?"

"Sure." Granger picked up his phone. "Give me yours, Mr. Dawson, and I'll text you Tommy's info."

"Thank you."

While Granger was doing that, Dawson got a better look at the room. Framed photos of Granger and his family—wife and two pretty teen daughters—stood on his desk. He had a coffee maker on the other side of the room, and in one corner, a pump-action shotgun.

Such a lot of guns around here, Dawson thought.

"Can I give you a tip, Mr. Dawson?" Granger asked, leaning back with hands behind his head, elbows wide and knees apart.

"Of course."

"Look, I didn't like Mr. Liu, but I got better stuff to do than worry about a little piece o' shit like him. You looking for someone who could have killed him, you gotta look at folks who hated his guts."

"Tell me more."

"You heard about that one guy Liu dumped into a pit."

Dawson nodded.

"Yeah, I figured you'd know. Young guy, had a nice girlfriend, hardworkin' honest family, you know? And now Liu goes and kills the boy. Who do you think was really, *really* upset about that? His dad, his mom, and most especially his younger brother. From what I heard, those two boys were like this." Granger held up his hand with his index and middle finger intertwined. "Shit, if Liu did that to my brother? Hell to pay."

Dawson nodded. "Yaw has been mute since his brother's death."

"Mute, my ass." Granger snorted. "He's just getting away with murder. Can't interrogate him if he won't speak, right?"

Right. Dawson was interested in Granger's analysis, even if crudely offered. "It's been suggested that an excavator was used to bury Mr. Liu under layers of soil."

Granger shrugged. "Well, Yaw knows how to operate excavators. I've seen him myself. And he's damn good too."

"But Bao Liu's excavator was out of order that day."

"Hey, you can bring an excavator over from practically anywhere if you give yourself enough time, Inspector. I mean, they're all over the place."

"Including one of yours," Dawson pointed out. "And you're right next door to the Lius' mining site."

"What are you saying?"

"It's just an observation."

"If Yaw used one of our excavators, we would know, because the engine would have been warm when we got to work that morning—and it wasn't."

"How would you know? I thought you said you were in Accra."

"*I* was, yes," Granger said quickly. "But my guys would have reported something like that to me. I mean, I know you're trying to get something on me," Granger added, "and it's your job and all, but seriously, you're wasting your time. You need to concentrate on—what's his name?—Yaw. Don't be fooled by this 'I can't speak' crap. He's one smart, calculating dude, that guy."

Maybe Granger is right. Dawson stood up. "Thank you, sir."

"Yeah, anytime," he said, not sounding like he meant it.

As he prepared to leave, Dawson noticed three keys with the CAT logo hanging from hooks in a corkboard on the wall. A fourth hook was empty. "You always use Caterpillar excavators?" he asked Granger.

"Yeah, the real thing," he said, with a confident nod. "Not any of that cheap Chinese crap the Lius have."

"Your excavators are all at work now," Dawson observed. "So these are spare keys?"

"Yeah," Granger confirmed, looking slightly puzzled by the question.

"Where's the fourth key?" Dawson asked.

"One of the guys is using it." Granger sighed, sounding tired. "I dunno where the original went. It sucks the way you gotta keep your eye on every little thing around here. Anyway, don't wanna bore you with stuff you don't need to know."

"No problem," Dawson said. "Are you traveling back to the States anytime in the near future?"

"I don't plan to. Why?"

"Because I might need to talk to you again."

"No problem, man."

In fact, Dawson was certain he was going to meet up with Granger again. He just didn't know under what circumstances.

CHAPTER TWENTY-FOUR

WHEN DAWSON WAS DONE with Granger, he took the opportunity to drop in at the Okohs' home in the hope that they had seen Yaw recently or talked to him. As Dawson walked to the house, a young boy went by laughing as he pushed a little girl in a rickety homemade go-cart.

Dawson called out at the door.

"Yes?" someone replied from inside.

Dawson waited a moment, and a teenage girl came to the door wiping her hands on a towel. It looked like she had been washing clothes.

"Good afternoon. Are Mr. and Mrs. Okoh in?"

"No, please," she said. "They have gone to farm."

"Okay, thank you."

Dawson thought that although he didn't know exactly where the Okoh farm was, it couldn't be too far away from the bridge where Amos had met his end.

"*Ei!* Hello, Mister!"

Dawson turned at the female voice. It was Miss Smoothie emerging from between two crumbling brick houses. Her hair done to cornrow perfection, she sashayed up to Dawson with an exaggerated swing of the hips and slipped her arm into his.

"So you have come here again, eh?" she said, her tone dripping with honey.

"Yes."

She slipped her hand into his. "Darko, how are you? I'm Queenie."

Her fingers were playing with his and he gently withdrew them.

"Ah, Queenie! Can't you leave him alone?"

Dawson turned again. This time, it was Queenie's hairstylist, who had appeared out of nowhere and was walking up to them.

"Good morning, sir," she said, smiling. "Please, is she troubling you?"

Dawson smiled too. "No."

"You see?" Queenie said coyly. "I'm just talking to him." She looked Dawson over with approval. "Hm, Darko. Such a fine man from Accra. Do you have a wife?"

"Yes, I do."

Queenie pouted. "Where is she?"

"*Gyae, gyae!*" the hairstylist scolded her, using the Twi word for "stop it." To Dawson she said, "She has so many boyfriends already."

"Adwoa, you are telling lies!" Queenie dismissed her friend with a backward flap of her hand. "Don't mind her, Darko. It's not true. Did you come to Dunkwa to see me?"

"But did you invite me?" he challenged back.

Adwoa laughed gleefully. "Eh-heh, Queenie, what's your answer?"

"Maybe the two of you can help me," Dawson said, the idea striking him on the spot. "Do you know Yaw Okoh?"

Queenie looked away, pressing her lips together. The hairstylist looked at her and burst out laughing.

"What?" Dawson asked.

Queenie glared at her friend. "Don't say anything!"

Adwoa immediately turned to Dawson and spilled the beans. "She wanted to be his girlfriend but he won't even look at her."

"Adwoa!" Queenie protested, as her friend giggled convulsively at her expense.

"Do you know where I can find him?" Dawson asked, skipping the fun.

"He lives in the bush," Queenie volunteered.

"Do you know the place?"

She nodded, and Adwoa grinned. "She used to follow him there."

"No, I didn't," Queenie said, sulking.

"Can you take me?" Dawson asked, assuming her denial was an admission.

"Yes, we can go," Adwoa said, before Queenie even had a chance to speak up.

DAWSON AND THE two women tramped through the bush and ended up at the banks of the Ofin. A felled tree across a narrow segment of the river created a partial damming effect on the milky water, providing them a crossing to the other side. Dawson immediately named it Fallen Tree Bridge. As a result of the recent storm, most of the tree trunk was submerged.

They crossed. The foliage was thin for a while where tree clearing, probably illegal, had taken place, but it grew denser quickly. Queenie, who was wearing only slippers, picked her way more and more carefully. Dawson congratulated her on her sense of direction as they turned left and right, but he had some remembering of his own to do in case he needed to return by himself, and he had no doubt that he would. He was silently counting the number of rights and lefts, grouping them in his mind as sharp or gradual, while noting any landmarks along the way, like a clearing, or a felled tree.

"It's here," Queenie said finally.

They had arrived at a rudimentary shelter: a simple sheet of corrugated metal on four poles.

"He normally stays there at night," Queenie said, pointing.

"Hmm," Adwoa said teasingly. "And did you stay here with him too?"

"Oh, shut up," Queenie said crisply.

While the two women giggled and traded good-natured insults, Dawson went over to have a better look at the humble abode.

There was almost nothing there except a rolled-up mat, a soiled T-shirt, a pair of cargo shorts, and the type of small, old-fashioned charcoal stove that people rarely used nowadays.

"During the day," Dawson asked the two women, "where does he go?"

They shrugged. "People say they have seen him around. They say he drives excavators sometimes, or helps the *galamsey* dig for gold."

"Why won't he talk to anyone?" Dawson asked. When he saw Queenie wrinkle her nose, he added hastily, "I mean after Amos was killed."

"The Okohs are my friends, so I know something about what happened," Adwoa said, mixing her Twi with English. "It isn't that he doesn't talk to anyone; it is his family he won't speak to. Mr. Okoh wanted Yaw and Amos to work with him on his farm. Yaw said no, he wanted to learn how to operate an excavator with Amos, because they could make more money mining gold than they can make at the farm. Mr. Okoh didn't agree, and he tried to command the two boys to be with him. Yaw, his head is hard, and he walked away, but Amos, he was softer, and he agreed to go with his father to the farm.

"So then, while Amos was working with Mr. Okoh and Yaw was trying to get work as an excavator operator, a division came in the family. After Amos died, Yaw said to his father that if he hadn't forced Amos to work with him, this would have never happened. Then Mr. Okoh went to a fetish priest who put a curse on Yaw that he will never be able to speak again."

Oh, Dawson thought. This was a new wrinkle. "Did Yaw know Mr. Okoh was going to the fetish priest to place the curse?"

"Oh yes," Adwoa said, nodding vigorously. "The whole town knew about it."

Could it have been that Yaw's knowledge of the alleged curse had had such a profound psychological effect that it actually happened?

"Thank you, Adwoa," Dawson said with a smile. He always

appreciated a well-informed account. He walked around the perimeter of the clearing, poking around in the bushes with a stick and wondering half seriously whether he was conducting an illegal search without a warrant.

As they left, Dawson cast one last look at Yaw's shelter. He was rapidly planning what to do next.

CHAPTER TWENTY-FIVE

WHILE HE WAITED EAGERLY for Chikata's arrival, Dawson spent most of Wednesday morning cleaning up and rearranging the office. Then he met with some of the junior officers to review their cases and any difficulties they were having. Lack of resources to get things done—evaluation of crime scenes, for example—was a common refrain, but sometimes Dawson saw these obstacles as an excuse rather than a justified reason.

"This is Ghana," he told one officer. "Resources are scarce, so you work with what you have, or you devise a stopgap, but you don't just shrug your shoulders and forget about it. If you don't care about your work, you might as well do something else."

And to each and everyone, Dawson's stern warning concerned the daily diary. "There should be an entry practically every hour. I don't want to see an empty space from midnight to six in the morning. For all I know, it means you were sleeping. The government does not pay you to sleep."

By early afternoon, Dawson had not heard from Chikata and he became anxious. Finally, at two thirty, Chikata called. "I told them to reserve a jeep for me to go up to Kumasi," he said, sounding frustrated, "but one of the chief inspectors grabbed it. He'll see how much trouble he's in when he returns and gets called to Uncle's office."

Dawson smiled slightly, but actually, Chikata wasn't joking. The culpable chief inspector was about to face something worse than a firing squad.

"Sorry, boss," Chikata continued. "I can't make it there today, but I'll be in tomorrow morning. The driver and I will start out by five, so God willing we'll arrive around ten."

"Sure, no problem," Dawson said casually, to hide the heavy feeling of disappointment. "So we'll meet tomorrow, *inshallah.*"

After a couple of hours more of work, he locked up the office and left for the day. To entertain himself, he went to one of Kumasi's best and most crowded sports bars and devoured *fufuo* and piping hot groundnut soup while he watched Arsenal battle Manchester United in a fierce soccer match.

CLOSE TO HIS prediction, Chikata walked in the door at division headquarters around ten thirty Thursday morning. Dawson hugged him hard, surprising himself by just how glad he was to see his right-hand man. "How was the journey up?"

"It was okay, boss," Chikata said. "Traffic wasn't too bad."

He was wearing dark slacks and a blue pinstripe shirt that fit perfectly across his broad chest.

"Have a seat if you can find somewhere," Dawson said. "I've been trying to clear the place up. You should have seen it when I first arrived."

"Looks like a lot of work." Chikata sat. "I can take over if you tell me what to do."

"We'll go over it in detail tomorrow. Let me bring you up to speed on the case first."

"Okay. I'm listening."

Dawson started from the beginning: the discovery of the body in the gravel at the mine site.

"Do you think the killer was trying to hide the body or put it somewhere to be found?" Chikata asked. "It seems that if he was trying to hide it, then put it in the forest somewhere, or throw it in one of those pits. If he was trying to show it, then just leave it in the open."

Dawson nodded. "Or else burying him was the actual means of death."

"By suffocation?"

"Yes. But all this speculation may change when we finally get the autopsy done. I'm waiting to hear from a Dr. Phyllis Kwapong, a new forensic pathologist in Accra who should be coming up to Kumasi as soon as possible."

"Let's hope so. The results might even change the way we think about the case."

Dawson agreed. "So far," he continued, "a guy called Yaw Okoh is the prime suspect."

"Who is he?"

Dawson told Chikata about him.

"This so-called inability of Yaw's to talk," Chikata said, "did it happen directly after Amos's death?"

"Not directly," Dawson answered. "Yaw blamed his father partly for his brother's death. They quarreled about it and then Mr. Okoh went to a fetish priest, who people now believe struck Yaw with a curse."

"Which would be very convenient for Yaw if he was the killer," Chikata pointed out. "He could use that superstition to his advantage."

"Exactly," Dawson agreed, "or maybe he really did go into some kind of shock after Amos's death. Either way, he could be guilty."

"When I was a small boy," Chikata said, "we knew one woman who went blind after her husband's sudden death. People were saying she was possessed by evil spirits."

Dawson grunted. "So many tales like that in our society. I think it's a kind of psychological derangement or something like that. Bottom line, we need to bring this man in and somehow get him to talk." Something occurred to him. "Hey, you remember Allen Botswe, the criminal psychologist at the University of Ghana we consulted a couple of years back?"

"Yes, I do," Chikata said, nodding. "He would be the right person to ask. Meanwhile, though, when and how do we bring Yaw in? That's the part I'm interested in."

Dawson smiled. Chikata liked action. "Commander Longdon says he can give us a couple men to hunt for him. I wanted that to happen by the weekend, and look—it's already Thursday." Dawson felt some frustration. "We should go upstairs to see the commander shortly to find out what is going on with that."

"Do we have other suspects, boss?"

"Yaw's father too had a strong motive to kill Bao," Dawson said. "I can tell he loved Amos very much and his death has been very tough to take. If I were Mr. Okoh, I think I would want revenge for my son's murder."

"Did Mr. Okoh have opportunity to commit the crime?"

"Yes. He normally wakes up before dawn—let's say at five—but on that day he could easily have woken up earlier to get to Bao Liu's mining site on time. His ten-year-old nephew, who sometimes accompanies him to the farm, was suffering from a high fever, so he's not able to say for sure what time his uncle left the house. Mrs. Okoh was with him trying to make the fever go down, and she probably wasn't keeping exact track of time either, under those circumstances. We are talking about a difference of only an hour or so."

"Is it still worth questioning her?" Chikata asked.

"It would not hurt, and it will be easier now that you're here. You can engage the man while I talk to his wife."

Chikata nodded. "Okay, boss."

"Now," Dawson continued, "there's another person of interest—an American guy who has a mining site near Bao Liu's property. He hated the way Liu and his crew used to come over to his concession to try to intimidate him. If you talk to the guy you'll get the feeling he would have no compunction in getting rid of someone he doesn't like. He acts like he couldn't care less about the Chinese brothers near his mining concession, but I don't believe him. We need to confirm his alibi. He says that he was in Accra Thursday to Friday visiting with Tommy Thompson, the head of PMMC."

Before Dawson could continue, the doorway was darkened by

Longdon's shadow as he walked in. Both the inspector and chief inspector stood up in acknowledgment.

"Good morning, sir," Dawson said. "Inspector Chikata has just arrived."

"Very good," Longdon said, in a businesslike fashion. "Welcome."

The two shook hands, and Chikata offered him his chair.

The commander waved it away. "I'm not staying long. Just an update, Dawson, I will have two constables available to accompany you and Inspector Chikata when you go looking for the suspect Yaw Okoh."

"Thank you, sir."

"When are you planning to do it?"

"Tomorrow night."

"Night?" Longdon asked, raising his eyebrows.

"Yes, sir," Dawson said, "because the suspect's whereabouts during the day seems to vary, but it looks like he stays at one permanent location at night."

"All right, then." Longdon handed him a sheet of paper. "Here is the information on the two officers."

The Dunkwa officer was Kobby, and Dawson was happy about that because he liked the constable. The other officer's name was Asase.

"Thank you, sir," Dawson said.

"You're welcome. I won't be in the office tomorrow, but you may call me if needed for any emergencies."

With that, Longdon left and Dawson stared after him in some surprise.

"What's wrong?" Chikata said.

"He was more pleasant than I expected."

Chikata grinned slyly. "Because he knows he has to be if he doesn't want a report to go up the chain."

Dawson made a rueful face. "My junior officer is treated with respect. Me? I'm a bad boy."

Chikata started to giggle.

"Shut up," Dawson snapped. "Not funny."

"Sorry, sir," the inspector said, trying to straighten his face. It didn't last. Within seconds, he began to laugh again.

Dawson balled up a piece of paper and lobbed it at Chikata, who successfully dodged the missile. It was good to have him back.

CHAPTER TWENTY-SIX

DAWSON HAD CALLED KOBBY in Dunkwa to confirm the plan to apprehend Yaw Okoh, and the constable had sounded eager to go—almost thrilled. Now Dawson wanted to meet Asase, the other officer who would be joining the team. He was stationed at Manhyia Divisional Headquarters in Kumasi.

Chikata had arrived in a shiny black jeep with gleaming chrome wheels. The driver was a constable who would leave the vehicle behind and return to Accra with one of the couriers who transport valuable and confidential documents between the police departments of various cities.

On the way to Manhyia with Chikata, Dawson put in a call to Tommy Thompson, the director of PMMC, but he didn't answer and he didn't have voice mail. Dawson moved to the next item on his list.

Allen Botswe was a professor of criminal psychology at the University of Ghana, specializing in crime in sub-Saharan countries. He answered almost immediately and recognized Dawson's voice at once, which was good, considering that a year had passed since they had last spoken. Dawson told him about Yaw and his circumstances, and asked Dr. Botswe if it was conceivable that the death of Amos was so traumatic that Yaw could have become mute as a result.

"Almost anything is possible, really," Botswe said slowly. "This would be a kind of conversion disorder, that is a neurological symptom such as blindness or paralysis in response to a severely stressful event. It's a defense mechanism to cope with psychological trauma. I confess that although I've seen cases of blindness and paralysis, I haven't come across the inability to speak, but for instance, Yaw's muteness could be an attempt to neutralize the horrific thought of his brother's loud screams for help."

"But for months after the event?" Dawson asked skeptically.

"It could happen. There's really no time limit to an individual's response, but I agree with you that this gentleman could be using muteness as a subterfuge. I've never seen that. It's very interesting. Keep me posted."

"I will," Dawson said. He ended the call and gave Chikata an account of the conversation.

"So it's not *juju*, eh?" Chikata said as they pulled up to the station and parked. "It's this conversion reaction or whatever it's called?"

"Conversion, diversion, perversion," Dawson said as they alighted. "I don't care. I just want the guy to talk to us and tell us if he killed Bao Liu or not."

Manhyia Divisional HQ, painted an attractive pale peach with dark blue trim and comprising two separate buildings, was several times larger than Obuasi's division. Dawson and Chikata walked into the right-hand section station, and Dawson was startled by what he saw. Behind the counter doing paperwork was Sergeant Obeng in uniform. *Back at work already?*

Obeng saw him and jumped to his feet with a salute. "Morning, sir," he said crisply.

"Morning, Obeng," Dawson said, and he realized he must have betrayed his surprise in his voice. "I didn't know you were here now."

"Yes, sir. On desk duty, sir."

"I see. I'm looking for Constable Asase."

"Yes, massa," said the man at the far end of the counter, standing up straight. "Morning, sir." He was in his midtwenties, smallish in stature and impeccably dressed in shirt and tie and dark slacks. Dawson couldn't remember the last time he had worn a tie.

"Good morning," Dawson said. "I'm Chief Inspector Dawson, and this is Inspector Chikata. You'll be assisting us tomorrow in a police operation at Dunkwa. You're aware?"

"Yes, sir," Asase said coming forward. "Commander Longdon has informed me."

"Okay. Please be at the Obuasi Divisional Headquarters by four tomorrow afternoon, and we will proceed to Dunkwa from there."

"Yes, sir."

OUTSIDE, DAWSON WAS so lost in thought that at first he did not hear Chikata speaking.

"Boss?"

"Sorry, what did you say?"

"Something wrong?"

"It's Obeng," Dawson said, as they got back into the vehicle. "How is he back at work so soon? I expected this to go before the disciplinary board, but it seems Commander Longdon decided to deal with the matter himself."

"Maybe he's on official probation," Chikata suggested, "and that's why they want him at one of the main divisions so they can watch him better."

"Could be," Dawson said doubtfully. It still seemed odd, however. He pushed the matter aside for the moment. He wanted to stop over at the guesthouse to see how work was progressing. Its state of readiness—or lack thereof—was a looming issue. In two days, Christine, Sly, and Hosiah were to arrive in Kumasi.

THE DOOR TO the guesthouse was open, and Dawson and Chikata were greeted by the sounds of hammer and chisel. A heavily perspiring foreman Nyarko was at work installing the toilet, one worker was in the kitchen, and a third was working on the electric switches.

"Good morning, Mr. Nyarko," Dawson said, as Chikata wandered off to watch the electrician.

He looked up. "Oh, morning, sah!"

He rose with a bit of a grunt and offered his right wrist to Dawson rather than his dusty hand.

"So, how is it going?" Dawson asked.

"Everything is fine," the foreman said. "Only the plumbing is not good at all. We have to lay some new pipes. The ones here are the old style and they are also too narrow."

"That sounds like a lot to get done," Dawson said, even though he didn't want to be the perennial pessimist.

"Oh, it will be okay," Nyarko said reassuringly, in such a way that Dawson wasn't in the least bit reassured. "Please, what time will your family be coming?"

"Saturday morning," Dawson said keenly.

"Ah, okay. No problem."

"No problem?" Dawson echoed.

"No problem, sah."

"Okay, then I will call them to let them know that everything will be ready. Has Madame Gifty been here this morning?"

"No, please. She told me she will come at ten o'clock."

No matter that it's past that now. "All right," Dawson said. "Do you need anything? You have enough water to drink? You are sweating so much it looks like you have been in the shower."

Nyarko laughed. "Thank you, sah. We have plenty water to drink. Thank you very much."

As Dawson walked away with Chikata, he called Christine. "Nyarko says the place will be ready, but I don't see how."

"But Mama said—"

"I don't care what she said. I'm not taking the risk of you and the boys arriving here on Saturday with no place to stay. We'll just get our own temporary place in Kumasi somewhere."

"Like where?"

"I don't know, Christine," he said as he got back in the jeep, loathing the irritation in his own voice. "I have to think about it."

"Okay, then call me back."

"What's up?" Chikata asked as Dawson ended the call.

"You know anywhere my family can stay in Kumasi for a few days, in case this place isn't fixed up by Saturday?"

"Not exactly, but the friend I'm with should know. I'll ask him."

"Thanks," Dawson said, as he pulled into traffic. A funny thought struck him. "Maybe we should have asked some Chinese to fix up the house. They would have finished by now."

He and Chikata began to laugh, even though it was a bad joke, but after quieting down, the inspector sucked on his teeth. "The Chinese, they will finish the work quickly, but they'll give you some fucking shit equipment that will break in two weeks."

Dawson looked back at him. "What do you think of Chinese people?"

"I just don't trust them."

Dawson's phone rang. Akua was calling.

"Good morning, Chief Inspector. Are you in Kumasi by any chance?"

"As a matter of fact, on the way out."

"Could you possibly meet me at the hotel?"

"Sure. What's going on?"

"I have some information that might interest you."

THEY JOINED AKUA Helmsley beyond the pool by the tennis courts, which were empty of players for the moment. Dawson introduced Chikata to her, and then they got down to business. She appeared to Dawson more preoccupied than usual, and he noticed she glanced around a couple of times as though checking that no one was in the vicinity to eavesdrop. A light breeze was blowing, and the sky was a brilliant blue. Somehow Akua enhanced it.

"I've been in Accra the past four days looking into something," she said. "You know of the PMMC?"

Dawson nodded. "Precious Minerals Marketing Company. What's up with them?"

"A whistle-blower within the company got in touch with me

last week," she said. "I went to Accra to see if there was any truth in the claim the person was making."

Dawson was interested. "A whistle-blower?"

"Yes. Let's call him or her 'X-Factor,'" Helmsley said. "X-Factor is high up in PMMC and has integrity, so I'm inclined to believe the tip."

"And X-Factor says what?"

"That the PMMC knowingly buys gold from illegal Chinese and Ghanaian *galamsey* miners."

Dawson frowned. "What?"

"The figures the PMMC renders to the Ministry of Lands, Forestry and Mines for annual gold sales and revenue include illegally mined and traded gold."

"No way," Dawson said. "The PMMC is a trading company whose only shareholder is the government. They can't be sanctioning illegal gold."

"One would hope not," she said, "but let me ask you something. Why are so many *galamsey* sites operating with impunity all over the Ashanti Region? How can an illegal mine right outside of Dunkwa-on-Ofin, for example, operate in full view of everyone?"

"Because we can't keep up with the sheer number of these Chinese illegals flowing into the country," Dawson said. "They number in the tens of thousands. It's the military and police special forces like SWAT, which Inspector Chikata has been involved with recently, that are needed to eject these thousands of people. That takes a lot of resources, and then how do you make sure they don't come back?"

"Resources so scarce that the authorities can't even allocate contingency for effective, targeted raids?" Akua challenged.

"But raids *have* been done," Chikata put in.

"They're not genuine raids, Inspector Chikata," Akua said earnestly. "They're carried out just to prove to Ghanaians that the government is doing something. They catch a few Chinese scapegoats, photograph them for the papers, and then release them."

"So what are you saying?" Dawson asked.

"I'm saying that there's a consistent pattern of collusion with the police and other authorities and the Chinese illegals," she replied.

Dawson snorted. "Ghana Police Service is not even organized enough to get such an elaborate scheme going."

"But you admit that it's something we need to investigate, right?"

"We?" He smiled. "I don't know about you, but I'm investigating a murder, not a corruption scheme."

"But the murder might be related to the scheme," she pointed out.

She had Dawson's attention again. "Explain."

"To stay in business and not be harassed by the police and immigration officials, the miners have to sell their gold to the PMMC at below market price. It's a quid pro quo. But not everyone agrees to that and Bao Liu was one. For that, they could have disposed of him and put his more amenable brother in charge."

"You know for certain that Bao refused to play the game?"

"According to my source, yes."

"But they don't need to kill him for that," Dawson pointed out. "They could just kick him out of the country."

"And he'd come right back," she countered.

She has a point, Dawson conceded. Still, it seemed extreme to him to murder the fellow for that. After all, he wasn't the only gold miner around. The whole Ashanti Region was teeming with them. "What happened when you went to PMMC?" Dawson asked her.

"I got in to see Tommy Thompson, but as soon as I began interviewing him on the subject, he called security to escort me out."

"Really?" Dawson said, surprised. "Did you even get a denial out of him?"

"Of sorts. He said I was talking nonsense and then got security in. But if he thinks I'm done, he's very much mistaken. I have several other avenues, and I'm going to keep digging until I have the full story and all the names."

Digging was an unfortunate word. Dawson sat forward. "Akua, these people carry shotguns."

"I'm aware," she said.

"Okay," he said, trying to feel reassured. "Promise me something, however. If you are going into any situation that could be dangerous or risky, call me first."

"All right." But she responded so quickly, Dawson wasn't sure if she meant it.

CHAPTER TWENTY-SEVEN

AT JUST PAST SIX on Friday morning, as he was stepping out of the shower, Dawson's phone rang. It was an unknown number.

"Good morning, Mr. Dawson." It was a woman's voice, low, rich, and soft, like warm custard.

"Good morning, madam."

"This is Dr. Phyllis Kwapong."

Dawson dropped his towel. "*Yes*, Doctor!"

"It looks like we have a time slot to perform the autopsy on the Chinese gentleman."

Dawson wished he could dive into the phone and kiss the woman. "Oh, *thank* you, Doctor. I'm very grateful to you for this."

"You are very welcome," she said, a smile in her voice. "

"What time shall I meet you at the mortuary?"

"Nine. We may not get started till ten, but I want to be sure we're ready to go."

"All right. I'll be accompanied by my partner, Inspector Chikata."

"Thank you. Oh, by the way, we'll be doing the postmortem in the new building."

DAWSON AND CHIKATA arrived at KATH just before nine and reported to the new building for the sign-in procedures. No wandering around unauthorized in this facility. One of the office staff asked them to please wait for Dr. Prempeh, who would take them through. They sat down on comfortable chairs to the side.

"Nice place," Chikata murmured.

"It's a different world compared to the old mortuary."

Dr. Prempeh burst into the lobby. "Morning, gentlemen," he said briskly. "Ready?" He turned, and Dawson and Chikata jumped up to follow him. Walking faster than many people run, he led them down a wide, gleaming corridor to the changing room. "Dr. Kwapong is in already," he told them as they entered. "This will be a learning experience for me as well. I can learn from her expertise as a bona fide forensic pathologist."

Because very few autopsies, if any, had been done here, the familiar mortuary odor had not yet permeated the place, for which Dawson was grateful. They donned their gear and Prempeh gave them a look over and a thumbs-up, before proceeding through the double doors into the chilled mortuary chamber.

Four autopsy tables occupied the room, all well equipped with their own sink, water supply, overhead light, and scale. Nkrumah, the mortuary tech, was already busy with Bao Liu's pale body on the first table. Dr. Kwapong, a tall woman, at first had her back to them as she read the coroner's report on the side counter. When she turned to them, Dawson froze in place. She was in protective garb herself, but temporarily had her mask off. It was not so much that the doctor's facial features resembled his mother's as Dawson remembered them; it was her physique and carriage: the identical tallness and solidity, spine straight as a bamboo rod, and a slight royal lift of the chin.

"Detectives Dawson and Chikata," she said. "Good morning."

"Morning, Doctor," Chikata said.

She flashed a smile. She had dimples. "Which one is which?"

In a moment of confusion, Chikata automatically waited for Dawson as the senior officer to speak, but he was staring dumbstruck at Dr. Kwapong. He could feel Chikata glaring at him with a look that said, *What's wrong with you?*

"Oh, sorry," he said hastily. "That's Inspector Chikata. I'm Chief Inspector Dawson."

"Ah yes, okay." She was evaluating him, and he knew he must have been looking odd. "You know, if autopsies are not quite your cup of tea, you don't have to attend. I don't like resuscitating officers who have fainted."

"No, no, it's not that, Doctor," Dawson stammered, his embarrassment deepening. "I apologize."

"No worries," she said, appearing amused. "You weren't expecting a man, were you?"

"Not at all, Doctor," Dawson said. "I knew you weren't a man. I mean—"

"I'm teasing, Mr. Dawson," she said, chuckling. "Relax."

"Actually it's me who is the squeamish one," Chikata said, rescuing his boss. "When I start to get that sour taste in the back of my mouth, it means I have to go."

"Of course," Dr. Kwapong said knowingly. "A rule of nature is that the tendency to faint over medical procedures is directly proportional to muscular development."

The three men laughed at that, and the ice was broken. Dawson gave the doctor the police report, and she quickly read it over. Kwapong proceeded with the Y-incision, which she made very quick work of. Bao's pale, now almost greenish body was quite lean and did not have the thick layer of subcutaneous fat before Kwapong's scalpel got to the internal organs.

"I know you'll be interested in time of death," Kwapong said, moving to the right-hand side of the body. "In reviewing the details and just looking at the body preliminarily, I would say that it could be anytime within the twelve-hour period between six that Thursday evening to six Friday morning."

"That agrees with our estimate, Doctor," Dawson said crisply, trying to make up for his bumbling start. "We think he was killed between four twenty and five forty-five."

"Excellent, then," she said, surveying the corpse quickly from head to toe. "I'll tell you one thing for sure. He put up a mighty struggle. Look at all those avulsed fingernails."

Dawson saw what she meant. They were jagged, some of them

partially or completely ripped off the nail beds. He felt queasy at that.

"So a central question for you, I know," Kwapong said, "is the mechanism and cause of death here."

"Yes, Doctor," Dawson said. "Do you think it could be due to the gashes in his scalp? From say a machete?"

She bent forward to Bao's scalp, parting the gray hair for a better view. "I think they may be postmortem, actually."

Dawson had pleasurable brain shivers at the sound of her voice. "When the *galamsey* worker was digging," he informed her, "the blade of the shovel struck the scalp."

"I think that's what happened. We'll take a look inside the skull to see if there's a serious internal injury like a cerebral hemorrhage."

The tech put Bao's shoulders on the block, made an incision and in the scalp, pulled it back. Then he went to work with the skull saw, a noise that bit into Dawson's nerves like a fire ant. Meanwhile, Kwapong took a look into the chest and abdominal cavities. Dawson looked up at Chikata to see how he was doing, and he signaled he was okay so far.

The top of the skull was removed like a cap, and the two doctors examined it.

"Anything?" Kwapong asked Prempeh, gently testing him.

"No fractures that I can see."

"I agree."

She wrestled a few seconds with the brain, and it came free with a sucking noise.

"No hemorrhages or signs of trauma on the outside," Kwapong said, putting the brain down on a cutting board. "Would you section it, Dr. Prempeh?"

He sliced it with a large, sharp knife, and Dawson feared for how close it came to his fingers. "Nothing," he said.

Kwapong transferred her attention to Bao's neck. "No ligature marks, gentlemen. The hyoid bone and thyroid cartilage are intact. Very unlikely he was strangled. Which is not to say he didn't suffocate."

She picked up a scalpel and made a straight, sharp incision down the windpipe in one clean motion, and then spread the cartilage open. "Clumps and particles of soil in the trachea," she said grimly.

Dawson looked up at Dr. Kwapong and met her eyes. "So that means . . ."

"Correct, Chief Inspector," Kwapong said. "That means your victim here was buried alive."

CHAPTER TWENTY-EIGHT

"BURIED ALIVE," CHIKATA SAID, shaking his head before taking a swig from his bottle of water. "That is pure wickedness."

Dawson savored a sip of Malta that he had bought during a sudden and intense attack of craving for the rich drink. They were back at Obuasi headquarters to discuss the case.

"Wickedness, fury, sadism," Dawson said. "All those things. A desire not just to kill Bao, but to make sure he suffered in the process. To me it points to the people who had the most reason to hate Bao—Yaw Okoh and his father. So how could either one of them, or both, carry out this murder? You start."

"Yaw Okoh," Chikata began, "adores his brother Amos, whose death leaves a terrible void in his life. He wants to avenge Amos's death by killing Bao Liu. He knows that the Chinaman is going to be at the mining site that Friday morning around four to fix the excavator. Yaw waylays him there around four twenty-five or so, just after Bao has tried to call his brother, ties him up in that terrible position, and then with an excavator, he scoops up large piles of soil and dumps it on him."

"How did he know that the excavator was out of order," Dawson challenged, "and that Bao was going to come in at a certain time on that particular day to repair it?"

"He asked one of Bao's *galamsey* boys, who told him all about it," Chikata answered.

"Ah, how can Yaw have asked one of them when he has been mute since the death of his brother?"

"He's only *pretending* to be mute, though. It's a subterfuge, because the man is guilty."

"Okay, that's a good comeback, but where would he obtain the excavator?"

"He bribed Chuck Granger's guys to give him the key to one of the excavators so he could use it that night."

Dawson shook his head. "Too dangerous. He would be exposing himself."

"Okay," Chikata said without blinking, "then when one of the excavator operators was taking a break, Yaw stole the ignition key."

Dawson laughed. "That's stretching it a bit, but your point is good. We need to go back to Granger and also question his security guy, Godson."

"What about Mr. Okoh?" Chikata asked. "How would he be involved?"

Dawson picked up. "Mr. Okoh feels as much pain over the loss of his son as Yaw does, maybe even more. Amos was his favorite son. Okoh hates this Chinese man, the same one who drove the Okohs off their farm and reduced his plot of land to a pittance. And now the Chinaman has killed his son. To *not* avenge his son's death would be a dishonor to Mr. Okoh and his family."

Chikata nodded. "Okay, go on."

"He wants to kill Bao in a way that will cause maximum suffering, but he needs Yaw's help. Together they plot Bao's death, but they need the opportunity to carry out the deed. That's when Yaw goes to one of the Lius' *galamsey* workers and asks if he can let him know when Yaw is planning to come in early."

"Yes," Chikata said uncertainly.

"You don't look happy," Dawson observed.

"Yes, because we don't have a link between Yaw and Bao Liu's workers."

Dawson thought about that for a second. "We should question
Kudzo Gablah again. Maybe he has conveniently left out some
facts."

"Could Kudzo have helped Yaw?"

Dawson shook his head. "I've ruled him out. I just can't see him
doing it and he has an alibi. This is the way I see it. Watch."

He reached for a pencil and piece of paper and made a quick list.

ESTABLISHED ALIBI

1. Kudzo Gablah – with friends Ekaw & family overnight till
   0530 Fri`

2. Wei Liu – with friend Feng overnight till 0600 Fri`

NO ESTABLISHED ALIBI   MOTIVE

Yaw Okoh   Revenge for bro Amos's death
Thompson   Somehow profits from Bao's death?

SUSPICIOUS/QUESTIONABLE ALIBI   MOTIVE

1. Mr. Okoh: What time did he   Revenge for son Amos's death
   really wake up Friday morning?

2. Granger   Get rid of uncooperative Bao
                                   Mine more gold through Wei`

"Do you know who isn't on there but should be?" Chikata said,
after gazing at the diagram for a few moments.

"Who?"

"Bao Liu's wife. She has no alibi because the man who could
have vouched for her being at home while he was being murdered
is obviously quite dead."

"So well put," Dawson said dryly. "But what could be her motive? He is the money earner, and apart from him and Wei and perhaps one or two Chinese friends, Bao is her connection to her culture. Besides, this signature is that of a male."

Chikata tilted his head side to side as he considered it. "Okay. I think you are right on that one."

"So, our only loose ends now are Yaw, Granger, and Thompson."

Chikata looked bothered. "Boss, seriously, this thing Akua Helmsley has cooked up is not credible. The PMMC or Director Thompson having Bao Liu killed because he won't accept a low price for gold? Come on. Who is Bao Liu? He's small fish in a big sea. PMMC doesn't care about some little shit guy like him."

"I'm skeptical as well," Dawson said, "but we can't let something like that go when it's sitting right under our noses. There might be a wider picture to it. So here is what we need to do. Call Thompson and set up a meeting in Accra as soon as possible and then go down to meet him face to face. It shouldn't be anything confrontational, but you'll be watching for his reaction, body language, tone of voice, and so on."

"Yes."

"Let's try and get through some more of this mess," Dawson said, looking around the office, "and then it will be time to go down to Dunkwa so we can catch our man, Yaw Okoh."

CHAPTER TWENTY-NINE

BY FOUR THIRTY THAT Friday afternoon, Dawson and Chikata were at the Dunkwa Police Station with Constables Kobby and Asase. Dawson was glad to see they were both prompt. It was a good omen. For about thirty minutes, Dawson outlined the plan and answered any questions they had. They would split into pairs—Asase and Chikata, Dawson and Kobby—and leave Dunkwa by different routes fifteen minutes apart to avoid attracting attention. It was best that no one got wind of a police operation.

Dawson and Kobby left first, taking the route he had followed with Adwoa and Queenie to Fallen Tree Bridge. The sun was in the finishing stretch of its journey across the sky, but it was still hot and humid, and by the time the pair of them had reached the rendezvous, Dawson and Kobby had worked up a healthy sweat. They found some shade to wait for Asase and Chikata while keeping in touch with them by phone.

They arrived after twenty minutes.

"Ready?" Dawson said. "Let's go."

He led the three other men farther along to the riverbank and the bridge. Since the storm, the water level had dropped, exposing most of the large tree trunk.

"Nobody fall in," Dawson said over his shoulder. "Because I can't rescue you."

They laughed, and none of them had any trouble as they crossed.

It was a test of Dawson's sense of direction and his ability to remember the route Queenie had taken him. He quietly counted out the right and left twists and turns.

"It's somewhere here," he said, slowing down after they had trekked for several minutes. "At least it was. I hope he hasn't moved."

"Maybe there," Kobby said, pointing. "I see something white."

They moved in that direction and discovered that the constable was correct. In the slight clearing, Yaw had hung a shirt from the low bough of a tree. It had been washed and was still damp, a sign of its recentness and that Yaw would be back. The question was, would it be tonight?

Yaw's shelter spot was unchanged from when Dawson had seen it, except that he noticed an LED lantern that he did not recall from the first time. A hen, tied to one of the poles of the shelter, was pecking at the ground. It didn't know that it would soon be a meal.

Dawson and the other three discussed how they would position themselves to provide the best coverage if Yaw chose to flee, and then they went to their stations. It was just before six, and they settled into what might turn out to be a long wait.

AS IT TURNED out, it was just under forty minutes. Darkness had fallen. Dawson's phone buzzed with a message from Kobby, which meant that he had spotted the target, and then Dawson saw Yaw's bobbing flashlight as he approached the clearing. He walked to his shelter and put a sack of something down—some *cassava* perhaps—and proceeded to turn on the lantern.

Dawson moved quietly so he wouldn't give himself away prematurely. "Yaw Okoh."

Yaw whipped around and raised the lantern, which showed his musculature in relief. Dawson approached, his badge raised.

"Yaw, *maadwo*," Twi for "good evening." "I'm Chief Inspector Dawson, CID."

Yaw seemed frozen at the spot.

"Do not fear, and do not run," Dawson said. "You won't come to any harm."

He got closer and in the poor light he never actually saw Yaw move until it was almost too late. The tip of the machete he wielded swished past Dawson at chest level as he jumped back. He lost his balance, stumbled, and shouted out as he fell. Yaw dropped the lantern and bolted.

"He has a cutlass!" Dawson cried out. He saw a shadow pass across him like a blur, and then a thud in the darkness. Dawson's chest was heaving and his heart racing as he fumbled for the flashlight on his belt. *What was happening?* The beam found Yaw on his belly fighting to free himself from the steel grip of Chikata on top of him. It could have been a battle to the death between two men closely matched in physical power, but it was all over because Kobby and Asase were on each of his arms. Yaw had lost grip of the machete during the tackle.

Yaw stopped fighting them, and his hands came easily behind his back now. *If only you'd complied from the beginning,* Dawson thought furiously. All this struggle, and for what?

Barely able to speak for his gasping, Dawson kneeled and informed the prisoner why he was being arrested, putting in everything he could think of: evasion of a police officer, assault of a police officer, resisting arrest, and suspicion of murder of one Bao Liu.

Dawson stood up, feeling a little faint. He was pouring sweat as he retrieved the still-lit lantern Yaw had dropped. It cast a wider span of light than the more directed flashlights. Dawson returned to the captive as the other three policemen heaved him to his feet. Now he was being tiresomely passive-aggressive by acting like deadweight. Not a cooperative bone in the man.

Dawson realized that Chikata was staring at him with an expression of fright he had never seen in the inspector's face.

"Boss," he said. "You're bleeding."

"What?" Dawson looked down. His shirt was soaked not with sweat, but with blood. He touched his chest, and his hand came away crimson wet. He swayed, and as the world began to spin, he collapsed.

CHAPTER THIRTY

AT THE PACKED OBUASI Hospital, Dawson waited in the treatment area of the casualty department. Besides one or two flimsy curtains hanging at intervals, he had no privacy in the mix of crying infants; pregnant women in labor; people with cuts, breaks, and bruises; and malaria sufferers shaking with rigors on bare cots.

The young female doctor attending to Dawson advanced toward him with a syringe and what seemed to him a very long needle. His eyes went wide.

"What, are you afraid?" she asked.

"Yes," he said, cringing. "Can you wait a moment?"

"A moment for what?" the doctor asked.

"Don't move, sir," the assisting nurse said.

"Yes, I know, but . . ."

"But nothing," the doctor said. "I have to anesthetize you. The laceration is jagged, and I need to trim the edges in order stitch it up. Do you want me to do it without anesthesia?"

"Yes. I mean no, Doctor."

The nurse was not amused by Dawson's trepidation. "Stay still, Inspector," she said sharply.

"Ouch," he said, stiffening as the first burning jab of the needle went into the wound in his chest. In the excitement in the forest, he had not realized that the tip of Yaw's machete had caught him, gone through his shirt, and ripped his skin open over the left pectoral. A lot of blood, but nothing life threatening.

"Why are men such babies?" the doctor asked rhetorically as she made rapid work of infiltrating lidocaine into Dawson's cut as he winced. "Please stop moving, Chief Inspector. Aren't you a policeman who deals with dangerous criminals?"

"Yes, madam," he admitted.

"But you're scared of this little needle," she said. "I don't understand it."

The nurse handed her the suture needle in the needle holder, and the doctor began to stitch Dawson up with an ease that suggested she could have done it in her sleep.

"Okay," she said, dropping the needle and holder in the tray and snapping off her gloves. "All done."

"Oh," Dawson said, looking down at the masterpiece. "That wasn't so bad."

"Oh, but you're not done," the nurse said. "You need an anti-tetanus injection."

He looked up in terror. She had an even larger syringe with an even thicker needle.

BY SEVEN THE next morning, Dawson and Chikata were at Dunkwa Police Station, where Yaw was being held. Dawson felt the pressure of the day and its tug in more than one direction: he wanted first to interview Yaw and then to get to the guesthouse to welcome Christine and the boys. She had already called to say they would be on the road in another hour.

"How is the thing?" Chikata asked, tapping his chest to indicate Dawson's wound.

"It feels fine, thanks."

"Did it hurt when they sewed it?"

"Not at all," Dawson lied. He caught Chikata's amused, knowing look. "What's so funny?"

"Nothing, sir."

They had the use of a room to do the interrogation, and after Kobby had escorted Yaw in, Dawson and Chikata entered.

"*Maakye*, Mr. Yaw Okoh," Dawson greeted him as he and Chikata each took a seat opposite him.

Yaw's eyes flashed up at him for a second, and then looked away as if he simply couldn't be bothered. His mouth was unyielding, his jaw set as hard as a block of *onyina* wood. They had kept him handcuffed because he was potentially dangerous, and Kobby remained at the door as an extra precaution, even though Yaw was well aware that it was the inspector opposite him who had taken him down in a powerful tackle.

In English, Dawson recited the formal caution and the right to remain silent, which was ironic, because silence had been Yaw's MO all along. To be sure that the message would get through, Dawson had Chikata give the caution in Twi as well, since his translation was a little better than Dawson's.

"I'm not at all annoyed with you, Mr. Yaw," Dawson continued casually, the way he might with an old friend. "You put up a good fight, and I admire you for that. But now you are here with us, and it's time to talk."

In Twi, he ran through routine questions: name, place, and date of birth as recorded on the national voter ID they had confiscated along with his belongings at his forest, and the names of Yaw's relatives. The suspect's response to Dawson's every inquiry was dead silence. He stared at, and sometimes past, the two men with empty eyes.

How does he do it? Dawson wondered. *Or maybe he's completely mad.*

"Do you understand my questions?" he asked.

No response.

"I will assume your failure to reply indicates assent to my queries," Dawson said, jotting down, *no response from suspect so far, 0732.*

"Mr. Yaw," he went on, sticking to Twi, "approximately two months ago, your brother, Amos, came to his death at a mining site operated by a Chinese man, one Mr. Bao Liu. Amos fell off a bridge suspended over the water into a deep pit, and he was not able to save himself. Neither could he be saved by any who

were present at the scene. Is what I've said correct in your estimation?"

Yaw's expression registered nothing.

"Amos's girlfriend said he shouted for help many, many times,"
Dawson said, "but no help was forthcoming. I think I know what
pains you, Yaw. You could have saved your brother if only you had
been there."

Yaw's eyes shifted, and now Dawson saw fire in them. And
then the whites reddened, and shockingly, tears came. His nostrils
flared, his lips and chin quivered, but still he uttered not a sound.
Dawson was astonished. How did the man cry soundlessly? Was
he genuinely mute? One thing of which Dawson was certain—
attempting to bully him into responding was probably not going to
work. It was the opposite approach that showed the most promise.

"I'm sorry," Dawson said leaning forward slightly. "I am angry like
you are angry. I'm angry with Bao Liu for what he did to Amos."

Yaw's lids flickered, his eyes dry and clear again.

"I think you were justified in killing Mr. Bao," Dawson said.
"He deserved to die after what he did to your brother."

Dawson was putting himself in Yaw's position and imagining
a similar fate coming to his own beloved brother, Cairo. Would
he not feel murderous intent toward the culprit? He was certain he
would.

"And you," Dawson continued, "you are not to blame in any
part for Amos's death. If you were there, you would have saved
him, but you were not, and that is not your fault. Even if you had
decided to farm with him as your father had asked you, it does
not mean you would have been there that day at that time. You
might easily have been elsewhere. Only God knows what might
have been, and we cannot go back; we can only go forward. Do
you get me?"

Dawson hoped he saw a flicker of agreement in Yaw's face, but
it could well be his wishful imagination.

"Yaw, do you have anything to say?"

He remained silent and sullen, and Dawson's judgment told

him that the interrogation was over for now. He was not going to put himself in a position of weakness by begging Yaw to speak. He would keep him in custody for the forty-eight hours allowed and come back to him repeatedly in that time, chipping away bit by bit until the shell cracked.

CHAPTER THIRTY-ONE

LATER THAT MORNING, DAWSON arrived at the guesthouse before his family, but the news wasn't good. The bathroom and kitchen fixtures were in, but water was not flowing. Nyarko wasn't sure where the problem was, since the big house had water.

An annoyed and flustered Gifty was there standing over him and continuously asking what the problem was, while Nyarko ran around trying to come up with the solution. Dawson felt sorry for the man, but stayed out of it, already exhausted by the whole situation. He was resigned that nothing was within his control at this point.

Additionally, the beds for the boys' bedroom had not arrived and probably wouldn't until the following Monday. The furniture in the living room was serviceable and Dawson decided Hosiah could sleep on the sofa. For Sly, they would fashion a reasonably soft surface for him on the floor.

Christine and the boys were expected at about one, so Dawson hung around just outside the house by the bougainvillea sprawling over the wall of the front yard. He was impatient and anxious to see them, and by one-thirty when they hadn't shown, he called Christine, got no answer, and called again. On the third attempt he began to feel sick with fear that something terrible had happened.

Just as he was about to attempt calling for the fourth time, a taxi approached and Dawson recognized Christine in the front.

Thank God. He waved and the cab pulled over to the side. Dawson saw Hosiah's little head behind the rear window, and the taxi had barely stopped when the boy pushed the door open, scrambled out, and ran to leap into his father's arms. Dawson, ignoring the sharp jab from his stitched wound, hugged his son tight and kissed him.

"I missed you, Daddy."

Dawson was tearing up. "I missed you too."

Sly joined them and embraced his father around the waist. Dawson rubbed his wiry hair, and Sly smiled up at him.

"Hi, Daddy."

"How are you, Sly? How was the trip?"

"It was good."

"Okay, Champ, I've got to put you down. You're getting heavy."

Dawson joined Christine at the rear of the cab as the driver unloaded four bulging suitcases weighing down the boot. She smiled at him.

"Hi, love," he said, hugging her.

"Hi, sweetie."

"You're looking so beautiful. I missed you a lot."

She wore an orange chiffon sleeveless blouse that hugged her at the waist, and a pair of blue jeans.

"How was the trip?" he asked her.

"Exhausting," she answered. "Actually, the entire week has been exhausting."

"I can imagine," Dawson said, picking up a suitcase in either hand. "Good gracious. What is in these? Gold?"

"I wish it was," Christine said with a laugh, as she settled the bill with the cab driver.

"Should Hosiah and I bring in the other ones?" Sly asked.

"You could pull the one that has wheels, and Hosiah can push it."

"Okay."

The three men of the family lugged the suitcases into the courtyard toward the guesthouse. Gifty must have heard their voices, because she came running out jubilantly to welcome the boys with smothering kisses, which seemed to make Sly squirm, although Hosiah didn't mind. Hosiah didn't mind any number of kisses from anyone—at least for now. Dawson knew he was sure to grow out of it.

Making their initial survey, Sly and Hosiah scampered in and out of the rooms of the house. Dawson kept his distance somewhat from Christine and her mother as they inspected the progress, or lack thereof.

Mr. Nyarko hovered nervously. He had been working on a temporary solution to the water problem. At least until Monday, the next-door neighbors were willing to allow the Dawsons to fill two or three buckets of water a day from their backyard pipe for bathing and toilet flushing.

"But the kids have nowhere to sleep," Gifty said in distress.

"They'll be okay," Dawson said. "Hosiah can be on the couch, and we'll put down some padding for Sly on the floor."

"I see," she said, and Dawson could tell that Gifty didn't think that was a good idea. "Anyway, let's go to Uncle Joe's house now. He can't wait to see you all."

AT EIGHT O'CLOCK that evening, both Dawson and Christine were spent. They had passed some of the afternoon with Gifty and her brother, and she had pulled off a coup by suggesting the boys stay with them in Joe's house until the guesthouse was in order. This time, as tiresome as Gifty could be with her "divide and conquer" maneuverings with his children, Dawson appreciated the offer. In any case, the boys were already entranced by Uncle Joe's stunning high-definition, curved widescreen TV in a living room about as big as the entire guesthouse. Joe's car rental business was evidently flourishing.

After leaving the boys, Dawson and Christine had trekked to Ketejia Market to buy household supplies including the all-too-important buckets. Then it was back home to clear out the inevitable bits and pieces left behind by the workers. For now, all the Dawsons' clothes would have to be arranged on a makeshift countertop until they obtained some drawer chests and wardrobes. Their financial reserves were draining fast, and until Christine found a job, hers were in danger of being completely wiped out.

Both of them had had their rejuvenating bucket baths and were lying in a state of collapse on the unforgiving foam mattress of their narrow bed, Christine with her back to the wall and Dawson resting his head on her lap.

"It's a long time since my muscles have ached this much," she said weakly.

"Me too."

"It occurs to me that the kids have really gotten off lightly," Christine commented.

Darko snorted without much energy. "Spoiled, those children. When I was a kid, Cairo and I did all the cleaning up around the house, and if we didn't, Dad would cane us."

"Okay," she murmured, her eyes closed. "Go back to the Dark Ages then. I won't be joining you."

He grunted.

"And anyway," Christine said, with just enough energy to raise her head and open her eyes, "what do you mean they are spoiled? We spoil them. You and me."

"All right," he conceded.

"In fact, I think you're worse than me," she declared. "You love your children a bit too much."

He found that funny and began to laugh languidly.

"What's so amusing?" she asked, her eyes closed again.

"I'm not sure. It's just the way you said it."

She rubbed his head. "You need a haircut."

"I know. The boys do too."

"We'll have to find a good barber in Kumasi."

She slipped her hand inside his V-neck to rub his chest and he flinched.

"What's wrong?" she asked curiously, and at the same time she felt the small bandage on his chest. "What's this?" She snatched up his T-shirt. "My God, Dark, what happened?"

"It's nothing," he said, trying to tug his shirt back down.

"What do you mean, nothing?" she cried, pulling it right back up.

"It was a guy we were trying to arrest," Dawson said. "He swung at me with a machete."

"*Ewurade!*" She stared at him in disbelief. "I mean, he could have decapitated you!"

"I don't think so." Dawson thought about it for a moment, and then started to laugh again.

"I'm glad you think it's so amusing," Christine said in annoyance.

"Do you know how difficult it is to cut someone's head off?" Dawson said.

"You know what I mean," she said huffily. "Does it hurt? Who stitched it?"

"A doctor at Obuasi Hospital."

"And I suppose you were squirming like a baby, as usual."

"I don't know what you're talking about."

Christine made a noise with her mouth and they began to giggle with whatever strength they had left.

"Anyway, how is the case going?" she asked.

"If we're lucky, we'll be able to close it soon." He propped himself up. "I want your opinion on something."

Dawson told her about the Okohs, the tragedy of Amos, and finally, Yaw and his peculiar inability, or apparent inability, to utter a word after his brother's death. "What do you think?" he asked. "Fake or real?"

She thought about it for a moment. "Well, it's very difficult to not talk if you really can."

"So you think it's genuine?"

"I think he is talking to a chosen few and pretending to others."

"Oh, really? Interesting. Why do you say that?"

"I believe he really was in a state of shock when the brother died and lost his ability to speak. But now that's past and he's trying to punish his father. If his dad hadn't forced Yaw's brother to work on the farm, Amos would never have had the fatal encounter with the Chinese guy, and he'd still be alive today."

"Ah, I see," Dawson said, nodding. "I thought rather that it was guilt that was eating Yaw up and that he's punishing him*self*."

"He doesn't seem like the type," Christine said.

Dawson rolled on his back again and got comfortable against her. "You might have given me an idea."

She smiled. "Let me know if it works."

"I will."

They were quiet for a while.

"Christine?"

"Yes, love."

"Do you ever wish you got married to that doctor?"

She looked at him quizzically. "Nothing like that has ever entered my mind. What in the world made you ask that question, Dark?"

"Well, today it occurred to me, if you had been with that doctor, you probably would never be dealing with all this nonsense with the house and a place to stay and all that."

"No," she said. "This is our life. I love you and the boys, and whatever we have to go through together, so be it. No regrets, ever, ever."

"Okay," he said. "Good."

"Silly boy." She gave him a light but reproachful slap on his forehead. "Anyway, I heard he died."

"What?" Dawson lifted his head. "Who died?"

"The doctor. He died a couple months ago."

"Oh," Dawson said. "Poor guy. Wow, life is strange."

He thought about the ironies of existence for a while, and then realized that Christine had fallen asleep and was snoring with her head back and her mouth half open. *My wife*, he thought, shaking his head. *To this day, she refuses to accept that she snores.*

Dawson got up and gently repositioned her on her side of the bed. She rolled over and muttered something unintelligible.

He smiled. "Yes, my love. Whatever you say."

CHAPTER THIRTY-TWO

SUNDAY MORNING, CHRISTINE WENT to an eight o'clock church service with Gifty, Hosiah, and Uncle Joe's wife, while Sly, who was Muslim, stayed home with Joe. By then, Dawson and Chikata had already arrived at the Dunkwa Police Station. Dawson asked Constable Kobby to bring Yaw out to the interview room.

Dawson had hoped he would see a glimmer of light in his eyes, but none was there. Yaw was sullen and kept his eyes down to stare morosely at the table in the interview room. Dawson feared that he was now descending into deep depression, which would not help the circumstances.

Dawson had decided to have Chikata start the interview. Who knew? Perhaps Chikata could get a response out of Yaw.

"How are you this morning, Yaw?" Chikata asked after cautioning the suspect again. "Mr. Yaw," Chikata said a little more sharply. "I hope you have decided to talk to us today. Do you understand that if you don't say anything, we will send you back to your cell?"

Yaw seemed unmoved. Dawson thought about what Christine had said last night.

He leaned forward. "You have punished your father enough. He is suffering as much as you, and he doesn't need any more pain. I know you can talk. It's only that you don't want to talk to *him*. You know as well as anybody else that he didn't cause Amos's death. Did he send Amos onto the bridge? No. Please, take away some of his pain. Eh? Yaw, what do you say?"

Dawson saw no response whatsoever. He leaned back again. "You will go back to your cell now. Constable, escort the prisoner."

"What should we do next?" Chikata asked Dawson after Yaw had been taken out.

"I'm trying to shift the emphasis away from the murder itself," Dawson said, lost in thought. "If we can get past whatever is troubling him, I think the confession will come next. He has killed Bao in revenge, and now he's killing his father too—just in another way. I know something about that."

For a long time, Dawson had cut his ties with his father, Jacob, until he realized it wasn't worth hanging on to grudges over what he had suffered as a boy at his father's hand. What if the man should die without Dawson's ever speaking to him again? So, Dawson had broken his silence and returned to his side. And now, Jacob increasingly needed his sons' care, and had moved in with Cairo, Dawson's older brother.

"And you're sure Yaw is guilty?" Chikata asked.

Good question. "Ninety-five percent," Dawson said, and then reflected that the estimate might be a little high. "But we have twelve hours before we release him. I really don't know what's going to persuade him to start talking again."

HE AND CHIKATA returned to Obuasi and attacked the office again, separating old material that could be archived some-where—Dawson didn't know where yet—and cold cases that needed reviewing. After about twenty minutes, Chikata became absorbed by one of the docket files.

"What's so interesting?" Dawson asked, looking over his shoulder.

"It's a police report by Sergeant Obeng," he said. "I found it at the bottom of a pile of unsolved cases. An American guy called Beko Tanbry came to the Obuasi area about three months ago to buy some gold. After the transaction took place, he was on the way to Kumasi when he was stopped by two armed men who robbed him of the gold."

"No doubt a setup," Dawson said. "The robbers might have been in with the guys the American supposedly bought the gold from. Now the man has no money, and no gold either. Any other notes in the docket besides the report?"

Chikata shook his head. "Nothing. Empty. And the report is not even very detailed either. I wonder why the docket was so buried when it's not that old a case."

"It's a good question," Dawson said.

Chikata lowered his voice. "I really wonder if Commander Longdon has been keeping an eye on what's going on here."

Dawson grunted. "It doesn't seem so. I'm suspicious of the commander."

Chikata looked sharply at Dawson. "How so?"

"I think he's corrupt. Both Mr. Okoh and Chuck Granger independently stated that the Chinese miners pay off the police. Granger made reference to the commanders specifically." He and Chikata exchanged glances. "We don't have to pretend that our police service is not infiltrated with corruption like a poisoned cocoa tree."

Chikata nodded. "True. Is there any point in exposing Longdon if he is involved?"

"If it will help us solve this murder, yes," Dawson said.

Thirty minutes later, it was his turn to read a docket in puzzlement. "Another armed robbery—same situation," he said to Chikata. "This time, it was a man from the UK here to buy gold."

They read the report together. Like the first one, it was short in length and sparse in detail.

"This should have gone up to the commander of the division," Dawson said, "and then to the regional office and so on."

"If Obeng was drunk a lot of the time, that might explain the lapses," Chikata pointed out.

"I agree," Dawson said. "Let's see if we can find more cases."

In the next hour, they found nothing significant, so they put aside the two dockets in question, and then turned to another jumble of papers. Dawson stared at it for a moment, arms akimbo.

"Let's have something to eat before we deal with this," he said. He was feeling mentally tired from a combination of circumstances—the mess in the office, the lack of progress in the case, the back-and-forth between Obuasi, Dunkwa, and Kumasi, and not having any real quality time with his boys. It was getting under his skin.

At the David & Goliath chop bar, Dawson had *red-red*—fried plantain and black-eyed peas cooked to dripping succulence with palm oil and spices—while Chikata ate his favorite: *banku*—steamed, fermented corn with a tangy bite—and goat stew laced with hot pepper.

After all that, Dawson felt like taking a nap. That is, until his phone rang. Then everything changed. It was Constable Kobby at the Dunkwa Police Station.

"Good afternoon, sir."

"Yes, Kobby?"

"Please, can you come down to the station?"

Yaw wants to talk, Dawson thought. "What's going on?"

"Please, Mr. Okoh, Yaw's father, is here. He says he is here to confess to the murder of the Chinese man."

CHAPTER THIRTY-THREE

DAWSON AND CHIKATA HAD considered Mr. Okoh a plausible suspect, but this still came as a shock. Kobby had locked him in one of the back rooms of the station, one that would be no longer empty in another eighteen hours on a busy Monday. When Dawson and Chikata entered, Okoh was sitting at the table with his head in his hands. He looked up as the two detectives took their seats.

"*Agya* Okoh, *maaha*," Dawson greeted him respectfully in Twi. Suspect or not, he was still an elder, so Dawson had used the traditional term "father" to address him.

He replied in the traditional fashion. His shirt was threadbare, and he was sweating heavily.

"Mr. Okoh?" Dawson sat down next to him. "I understand you have something to tell us."

Mr. Okoh wrung his hands repeatedly and then cracked his knuckles. "Please," he said finally, "release my son. He has done nothing wrong. I am the one rather who killed the Chinese man to avenge Amos's death."

Dawson nodded. "I see. When did you kill the Chinese man?"

"Friday—one week and two days ago." Now he fixed his eyes on Dawson's face.

"Tell me what time."

"Around four o'clock in the morning. The mining site is on the way to my farm, so I know how to get there. I went and hid in the bushes to wait for the man."

"How did you know he was coming to the site so early in the morning?"

"One of the mining boys told me he would be coming to fix the excavator around that time."

His story isn't solid yet. "Which one of the mining boys?" Dawson asked.

"I don't want to make any trouble for him," Okoh said, "so I don't want to say."

Admirable, maybe—but not satisfactory. "Go on. You hid in the bushes and what after that?"

"He came and started to fix the excavator. After some minutes, I came behind him and killed him."

Not satisfactory at all. "*Owura* Okoh, exactly how did you kill him?"

"First, I tied him up. He was fighting me, but I made him stop. I brought his feet and hands together behind his back."

That was also information that Okoh could have gotten from one of the *galamsey* boys. "Was the Chinese man shouting for help?" Dawson asked.

"Yes, but I put a rag inside his mouth so he couldn't shout well."

A rag? That wasn't found at the crime scene, but . . . old pieces of cloth had been present in the shack where Wei had taken his brother to clean him up. Was it possible that one of those was a rag that had been stuffed in Bao's mouth? Wei could have removed it and tossed it away. Or it could have been dislodged when Bao was being pulled out of the mud. Something else struck Dawson. If the rag was severely soiled with mud, that could also explain the gravel in Bao's throat and windpipe. In any case, such a *specific* detail made Dawson begin to wonder. Was it possible that Mr. Okoh was their man?

"How did you kill the Chinese man?" Dawson asked him.

"I hit him on the head with my cutlass," he said, still watching Dawson closely. "Then he stopped moving, and then I buried him inside the earth."

The wounds to Bao's head were postmortem, Dr. Kwapong had said.

"How long did it take you to bury the body?" Dawson asked.

"I don't remember," Okoh said, his eyes shifting to his left. That was also not unreasonable. In the heat of such an act, one could easily lose track of time.

"All right," Dawson said "Thank you. Excuse us one moment, Mr. Okoh."

He and Chikata went outside, shut the door, and moved down the corridor out of earshot.

"What do you think?" Dawson asked him.

Chikata shook his head. "His confession is not strong."

"I agree. Also, did you notice how he fixed his eyes on me when he was speaking? Normally, when you talk to someone, you shift your gaze back and forth. When some people lie, they watch you carefully for a reaction."

"Yes," Chikata said, nodding slowly. "But still, there's something I wonder. Is it possible at all that Dr. Kwapong is wrong about the injuries to Bao's head—that they were postmortem?"

"I don't think so," Dawson said. "She considered it very carefully and she was very certain. So I trust her. *Owura* Okoh is not telling the truth."

"Why is he doing it?"

"He's afraid that he'll lose another son, this time to prison. He might think—or even *know*—that Yaw killed Bao, or he might not, but it doesn't matter. Either way, better Okoh be locked away than his son—that's the way he looks at it."

"So what do we do now?"

"You will go back to Mr. Okoh and respectfully tell him that we have no reason to believe that his account is genuine. Work on him until he confesses to not being a murderer. At the same time, I will work on Yaw."

YAW AVERTED HIS gaze as Dawson entered the room, which was much more confining than the one Mr. Okoh occupied.

Dawson sat and leaned on the table toward Yaw. "Good afternoon. Your father is here. He has come to tell us that he is the one who killed the Chinese man, not you, so you will be free to go as soon as Constable Kobby comes to release you. But your father will spend the rest of his life in prison. That's all I have to say."

Dawson got up and went to the door holding his breath and *hoping*.

"Wait, Mr. Dawson, please."

His heart missed a beat. He turned to find Yaw looking at him directly for the first time. "My father didn't kill the Chinaman," he said. "I did."

CHAPTER THIRTY-FOUR

ELOQUENT, YAW SPOKE IN both English and Twi, his voice husky and unexpectedly light, like the rustle of savanna grass in a soft breeze. It was more boyish than the heavy tone that Dawson had imagined he would have.

"Why have you chosen to break your silence?" Dawson asked him.

"I have forgiven my father," he said softly, "and now that I have forgiven him, I can't let him take the blame for me."

"Why were you mute for all these months?"

Yaw swallowed and stared down at the table for several moments, but the emptiness he had demonstrated before had been replaced with an expression of pain. "When I first learned of Amos's death," he said, "I felt like a part of my insides had been cut out—my heart, my throat. I couldn't talk anymore. I cried for two weeks, but it was inside—without sound. And after two weeks of sadness, I started to feel angry with the world, angry with that Chinese man, and angry with my father."

"Why were you angry with your father?" Dawson asked. "Because he made Amos work on the farm with him?"

"Yes," Yaw said, "because if he had not, Amos would not have been at that bridge for him to be drowned by the Chinese man. But not only that. Before Amos's death, my father had accepted money from Bao in exchange for some of the land we were farming, because the Chinese man wanted more space for his *galamsey* mining."

"Your father is suffering from the bad economy just like everyone else," Dawson pointed out. "People are just trying to survive."

"I know that, but how can you sell our ancestral lands to these foreigners for them to plunder our gold and spoil the forests? That is a terrible betrayal."

He might be a murderer, Dawson thought, *but he has principles.* "How did your father sell the piece of land when it is only the chief who is supposed to authorize a land sale?"

Yaw gave a dry, humorless laugh. "The chief gets plenty of money from those Chinese people. He lets them do whatever they want."

Dawson feared as much. *No end to this corruption.* It was everywhere, like creeping rot.

"The day I decided to avenge my brother's death by killing the Chinese man," Yaw continued, "I felt a great relief, as though there was no more struggle inside me. And my ability to speak returned. But still, I had anger toward my father, so I decided to keep silent and not talk to him. A story was going around that I had been cursed by a fetish priest, but it wasn't true."

Another blow to the *juju* hypothesis. "Describe to us what happened on the morning of the murder of Bao Liu," Dawson said.

Yaw cleared his throat and folded his lips between his teeth for a moment while collecting himself. "I heard that the Chinese man would come early in the morning to fix the excavator."

"How did you hear that?" Dawson interrupted quickly.

"One of the workers at Mr Granger's site told me, and they heard it from one of the boys at the Chinese man's site."

Plausible. "Go on," Dawson said.

"I wasn't sure of the time he will come, so I arrived there very early and waited for him. After about one hour, he came—at about something past four. He was carrying a lantern because it was still dark and he needed to see what he was doing while working on the excavator. I waited for him to start his work. It seems he was trying to call someone."

He knows that detail, Dawson thought, startled.

"I attacked him as soon as he turned his back to me," Yaw continued. "First, I gave him a blow on the back of the head to knock him out. Then I pulled the legs up behind and the arms also, so that they come together, and then I tied them."

"How many pieces of rope did you use to tie Bao?"

"Two."

Correct. "After that, what did you do?"

"He was still suffering from that blow I gave him, so he was only moving a little bit. I dragged him to where his *galamsey* boys used to dig, and I put him there. Then I went to Mr. Chuck's site and drove one of the excavators to where Bao was."

He's on the right track, but he's not there yet. "How could you drive it?" Dawson asked.

"At Mr. Chuck's site, one of the excavator operators, he sometimes used to leave the key in the ignition when he goes on his break around noontime. On that Wednesday, I hid in the bushes and waited for him to leave and then I went and stole the key."

That might account for Chuck Granger's missing CAT key, Dawson thought. "Continue."

"I drove it to the place where I was going to bury him. By that time, Mr. Bao had woken up and was trying to shout for help, but because of how I tied him, he wasn't able to breathe well, and he couldn't shout. I operated the excavator and took some soil into the loading bucket. Then I turned it and dropped the soil on him. I did it eight times until he was buried very well."

"Before you dropped the soil on him, did you strangle him?"

"Strangle him?" Yaw frowned slightly, as if puzzled. "Please, for what? He will try to breathe inside the soil and die like that."

Solid. But Dawson wanted to be completely sure. "In which direction was Mr. Bao's head facing when you buried him with the excavator?"

"If the pit is here," Yaw said, making a circle on the desk with his index finger, "then his head is here and his body is here."

He was correct and his account was accurate. "Why did you bury him alive?" Dawson asked. "Why not kill him on the spot?"

"Why?" Yaw asked indignantly. "He made my brother suffer by drowning. Shouldn't I make him suffer too?"

"Why bury him in the earth instead of drowning him in the pit water like Amos?"

"Because the gold he has stolen is in the earth, not in the water. What you have destroyed returns to make you suffer."

"What did you do after you buried him?"

"I reversed the excavator and dragged the bucket over the tracks to cover them."

Dawson threw a test at him. "Does the excavator have reversing lights?"

"Yes, and a reverse camera in the cab too."

He knows the excavator inside out.

Dawson, searching his brain for something more, looked at Chikata to see if he had any questions.

"Mr. Yaw," Chikata said, "after you buried Bao, where did you go?"

"By that time I was staying at the place in the forest where you found me. I took the Chinese man's lantern and went back there to sleep, and I slept well because a heavy load had been lifted from my shoulders."

Dawson gazed at Yaw Okoh. The man seemed to be truly at peace with himself, and ready for the charge of first-degree murder to be pronounced.

KUMASI, ASHANTI REGION

SEPTEMBER

CHAPTER THIRTY-FIVE

ON A SATURDAY AFTERNOON, Dawson and Christine sat with Daniel Armah and his wife, Mercy, while Hosiah and Sly spent time with the Armahs' grandchildren in the backyard.

The adults commiserated over the terrible state of the economy. In order to bring in some more income, Armah, who was mostly retired and had a head of gray hair, was considering going back to his private detective company. Prices of fuel, food, and lodging were soaring on an almost weekly basis.

After weeks of searching, Christine had found a part-time job at a school and was earning a little money at last—not enough, but better than nothing.

"How are the children doing in the new school?" Mercy asked. A gentle, bespectacled woman, she had an idiosyncratic stripe of gray like a lightning bolt on the left side of her pulled-back hair.

Dawson exchanged a glance with Christine.

"Hosiah's been having some adjustment difficulties at school," she said.

Dawson nodded. "He doesn't do as well with change as his older brother does. He missed the home environment in Accra as well as his schoolmates, and he had a brief period of behavior problems both at home and at school."

"Oh, sorry to hear that," Mercy said, looking concerned. "I hope he's straightening out now?"

"Yes, little by little," Dawson answered with a smile of relief, "but not without trying our patience."

The conversation drifted until the women were having one conversation, the men another.

"So you got your murderer," Armah said to Dawson. "Congrats on a job well done."

"Thank you. I owe thanks to Christine for that."

"Really? How so?"

"She pointed out to me that Yaw Okoh might be trying to punish his father psychologically for forcing Yaw's brother Amos to go to farm with him."

"A great husband-wife collaboration," Armah said.

Dawson's phone rang and he stepped out to take it. It was Akua Helmsley. She had reported two stories about Bao's murder. Dawson had found her accounts to be factual and fair.

"Chief Inspector," she said, after exchanging pleasantries, "I wanted to do a profile on you and how you solved the mystery of the Chinese man's murder. Would that be possible?"

"Well, yes, I suppose so," Dawson said doubtfully. He had never had a profile done, at least not in depth.

"If Mr. Samuels could have one or two photos of you in a couple different settings, then I'll do the actual interview. It will just be about your background, what made you want to become a detective, your inspirations, and so on."

Dawson told Helmsley that Commander Longdon would need to authorize an engagement like this.

"Of course," she said at once. "I understand. When will you know?"

"I can ask him on Monday."

"Thank you."

"I don't feel quite comfortable about the photographs," Dawson added, after a moment's thought.

"All right then. That isn't a problem." She paused. "There's something else. We have another set of photographs that you're not aware of, and they might be useful for you to have a look at. Also, I'd like you to indicate which of them I can use for my online article."

He said yes, and they ended the call.

"Who was that?" Christine asked

"Someone who wants to interview me for a newspaper."

"Ooh," Christine said teasingly. "So famous now."

"Not really," Dawson said, laughing.

"Is that Akua Helmsley, by any chance?" Mercy asked.

"Yes," Dawson said.

"Who is she?" Christine asked.

"She writes for *The Guardian* online," Mercy answered. "I've been reading her work. Very interesting. People say she's just a pretty face, but I think they are being sexist. Her reporting is solid."

"Oh, really, she's attractive?" Christine asked with interest.

Dawson wished Mercy hadn't said that.

"You always used to avoid the press," Christine said slyly to him. "No wonder you're so eager to cooperate this time."

He felt his face getting warm. "Don't be silly," he said with studied nonchalance.

Christine burst out laughing. "I'm only teasing you, Dark. Don't get so flustered."

COMMANDER LONGDON OKAYED Dawson's interview with Akua Helmsley. In another time, the answer might have been no, but the GPS was trying to launch a new era of good relations with the press, including the construction of the brand-new and Internet-ready GPS press relations building in Accra. The only proviso Longdon had for Dawson was that he couldn't go into detailed descriptions of police procedure or inside politics, and that he take no longer than two hours for the whole meeting.

EARLY ON TUESDAY morning Dawson met Helmsley in a meeting room at the Golden Tulip Hotel conference center. She had invited him to have breakfast, but he had declined. He did not want to have to tell Christine that he had had breakfast with the attractive Akua Helmsley, or lie about it.

She used a small digital device to record their conversation, asking about his childhood and what life had been like for him. He was evasive about his relationship with his father and told her that he preferred not to discuss it, but he did tell Helmsley about the disappearance of his mother when he was a child, how that had shaped his desire to become a detective, and how Daniel Armah had inspired him.

In talking about the Bao Liu case, Dawson gave light details only and emphasized Yaw Okoh's presumed innocence until he went to trial in several months and was proven guilty.

"Here are some of the pictures we have," Helmsley said, opening up her laptop after the interview was over. "Some are of the crime scene and I want you to feel comfortable about my putting them up on *The Guardian* website."

As she clicked through them, Dawson realized with shock that Helmsley had not a few, but dozens of pictures showing the progress of the unearthing of Bao Liu's body, from when his head was first revealed through to his complete removal from the soil.

"How did you get these photos?" he asked. "I didn't see you at the scene so early on. I thought you arrived after I did."

"This is the way it happened," Helmsley said, turning slightly in her chair toward him. "We were out early that morning to take pictures of workers coming to their respective mines. We do this with their permission. However, on this occasion, we heard that something was going on at Mr. Liu's site.

"So we rushed over there to find that a body was being dug up, and at that point, we decided we would retreat to the cover of the surrounding fringe of trees and take some shots with a long telephoto lens."

"Why?"

"Because we thought onlookers or Wei Liu would take offense at our presence. People are skittish about cameras. We stayed there for a couple of hours until you showed up and asked everyone to leave. That's when we came down and you met us."

Dawson was angry. "This could all be evidence in the case, Akua. How could you keep these from me?"

"Well, actually, Chief Inspector," she said rather coolly, "I'm not journalistically obligated to hand over material to the police unless it's by court order."

"Obligation is not the point," Dawson snapped. "It's what is *right* to do."

"Okay, *okay*," she said, flushing. "I agree it would have been helpful to do so in this case. Anyway, here you are. Full access. Better late than never."

Dawson felt awkward as he cooled off. "Sorry," he muttered. "I think I flew off the handle a little bit."

"No worries," she said, now looking unperturbed, but Dawson suspected she was hiding her emotions well. She slid the laptop over. "Here you go. Take a look through them. I need to get something from my room."

He continued to look through them from where they had left off. As he clicked through quickly, the images became a time-lapse movie. At the beginning, the *galamsey* boys and their Chinese boss crowded around the site where Bao's head had been first spotted. There was Kudzo Gablah, and then the workers Dawson had never met. They were digging, along with Wei Liu, and quickly a crowd of onlookers began to gather. Urban area or rural outpost, bystanders at a murder scene were universal.

Little by little, Bao's head was unearthed—becoming his neck, then chest and back—as others joined the dig. Dawson noticed that one or two people abandoned the area quickly, probably not able to stomach the sight. Gradually, Bao's impossibly arched body emerged, and the crowd looked on in fascination, drawing even closer.

Dawson made out that now Wei Liu was frantically trying to drive people away and that gradually, some of them complied while others loitered. As the space between them cleared, Dawson saw something—someone—that made him sit up straight. Yaw Okoh was among the observers.

He came back to the scene of the crime, Dawson realized with a jolt. Yaw had not mentioned that. And then Dawson's blood turned to ice, and he erupted into a cold sweat as he realized he had made a terrible mistake.

CHAPTER THIRTY-SIX

IF YAW HAD MURDERED Bao, it meant he had returned to the scene of the crime, as the photos showed. If he had *not* murdered him, however, might he have been able to "confess" to the murder by mentally reconstructing it at the scene? In several of Samuels's photos on Akua's laptop, Yaw was staring at Bao's dead body, apparently engrossed by it. Dawson cast his mind back to which questions Yaw might have been able to correctly answer by his having been at the crime scene. Certainly, *How many pieces of rope did you use to tie Bao?* And, *In which direction was Mr. Bao's head facing when you buried him with the excavator?*

But some other aspects he *couldn't* know from merely observing the scene. For instance, that after arriving at the mining site to help fix the excavator, Bao had called Someone—or tried to—at some time after four. Yaw had to have been there to witness that. And what about the fact that Bao wasn't strangled? How could Yaw know that without being present at the crime?

As Dawson examined the photographs, his mind swung back and forth. One moment he thought, *Of course Yaw is the murderer,* but in the next, a panicky feeling seized him as he questioned himself, *Are you sure?* Now he was seeing something else in the images that nagged at him like an itch he could not scratch. Kudzo was standing next to Yaw, and in one photo, he seemed to be addressing Yaw, and although Yaw did not seem to be responding verbally, he did appear to be *listening*. Had the two young men known each other before this occasion?

He stared again at another picture in which Kudzo was talking to Yaw and pointing to his own face as if demonstrating something, but *what*?

Akua returned. "Everything okay?"

Dawson looked up. "Did you film any of the activity at the crime scene?"

"Actually I did a couple of two-minute videos on my phone while Samuels was taking photos," she said. "Why do you ask?"

He pointed at the image in which Kudzo was gesturing toward his face. "I want to get an idea of what he's saying here. A video might help."

She located the two videos and played the first. It showed the final minutes of Bao's body being removed from its burial place by Wei, Kudzo, and one of the other *galamsey* boys. At one point, Akua had panned to show the entire body of onlookers, and it appeared that Yaw had not arrived by then.

The second video was taken about ten minutes later. Wei was kneeling over his brother, hysterically crying and pawing pathetically at Bao's dead body, while Kudzo stood by in shock. Dawson held his breath, praying that this was the moment he was looking for.

He saw it. "*There*. Pause it, please. Run it back a little and then replay."

She did that and Dawson watched.

Kudzo was standing about a meter away from the body. He looked shocked. At one point, he circled around the body and peered at Bao's face. He pulled back with revulsion. From within the cluster of onlookers, Yaw appeared at Kudzo's side. He nodded to Kudzo, but didn't speak. Kudzo pointed at Bao's face and replicated Bao's widely gaping mouth. Kudzo took a few deep breaths while making a scooping gesture with his right hand close to his mouth. Then, as quickly as Yaw had arrived, he disappeared as if he had melted away.

"What does Kudzo's gesture mean?" Dawson muttered.

"Looks like a scooping action."

"Play it back one more time, please?"

He watched again, and then he nodded. "I get it now."

"What do you get?" Akua asked him.

Dawson stood up to leave. "I can't say yet until it's confirmed."

HE CALLED KUDZO, who didn't answer at first, but Dawson tried again and got a response. Kudzo sounded tentative, probably worried that he was once more in trouble, but Dawson hastened to reassure him.

"But I need to ask you a question," he said. "Do you know a certain Yaw Okoh?"

Dawson heard a hesitation before Kudzo answered. "No, please."

But his voice set Dawson's left palm tingling.

"Kudzo," he said quietly. "I know you know him."

"Did you say Yaw or Kwao?" Kudzo said quickly.

"Yaw."

"Oh, sorry—I thought you said 'Kwao.' Yes, I know Yaw."

Beautiful recovery. "From where?"

Kudzo cleared his throat, and Dawson could feel his nervousness over the phone. "One day when Mr. Bao was still alive," Kudzo said, "Yaw came to the site looking for work. He say he can operate excavator, but Mr. Bao say he don't need someone like that at that time. Then Yaw also went to Mr. Chuck's place and look for work, but they too, they didn't have. I took Yaw's phone number in case I hear of some excavator job, and he also took my number."

Dawson realized they were both speaking English, and he switched to Ewe to avoid Kudzo misunderstanding a question. "When you found Mr. Bao dead, after some time, Yaw came around and you were talking to him, is that correct?"

"Yes, please."

"Did he talk to you?"

"No, please," Kudzo replied. "He didn't say anything at all to me."

Dawson described to him the short video of the crime scene

that included Kudzo communicating with Yaw. "Were you trying to show him something?"

"Please, you mean?"

"You tell me if I'm right," Dawson said, deciding to phrase it differently. "You were showing Yaw how there was a lot of soil inside Mr. Bao's nose and mouth."

"Yes, please. I told him maybe it went inside his mouth and nose when he was trying to breathe, because one time when I was working at a mine, the wall of one of the pits slid down and buried two guys. One of them died, and when we pulled him out, his mouth was open, full of mud, like Mr. Bao's."

Dawson remembered: when he had asked Yaw if he had strangled Bao, his response was, "Please, for what? He will try to breathe inside the soil and die like that."

Is this how he knew? Did Kudzo inadvertently supply Yaw useful information that he could later use?

"Tell me the truth, and you will not get into any trouble," Dawson said to Kudzo. "Did you tell Yaw that Mr. Bao's excavator was not operating and that he was going to fix it on that Friday morning?"

"No, please. I never told him that."

"Do you think he killed Mr. Bao?"

"No, please. I don't think so."

"Then why did he say he did?"

"Because he loves his father."

And Dawson had the feeling that Kudzo, who had a kind of wisdom beyond his years, was right.

CHAPTER THIRTY-SEVEN

DAWSON FELT HE NEEDED to talk to Daniel Armah, the best person to explore ideas with while on a case. He was at home when Dawson called.

"Of course," Armah said. "Come by and let's discuss it."

Dawson set out immediately, and for the entire journey from Obuasi to Kumasi, he wrestled with the questions: *Do I have the right man? Did Yaw really kill Bao Liu? If not, who did?*

Armah welcomed Dawson and invited him to the backyard for refreshments—Star beer for himself, and Guinness Malta for Dawson. They wasted little time getting down to business, and Dawson laid out the present theory about Bao's murder and Yaw's key involvement.

One: Bao allegedly killed Amos, Yaw's beloved older brother.

Two: Yaw, grief stricken, becomes mute from a "conversion reaction."

Three: His anger growing, he decides to avenge Amos's death.

Four: By a mechanism yet unknown, Yaw learns on the day before Bao's murder that the site excavator is not working and that Bao intends to repair it sometime on Friday morning.

Five: Yaw lies in wait until Bao arrives, attacks him, and ties him up in a torturous posture.

Six: Having stolen the keys to one of Chuck Granger's excavators, Yaw drives the machine over to Bao's site and dumps loads of moist, heavy soil and gravel on top of the Chinese man, ultimately causing his painful death by asphyxiation.

Seven: As a means of evading the police Yaw continues the charade of muteness.

Eight: Yaw is arrested but still refuses to talk.

Nine: Yaw talks and confesses to the crime after his father attempts to take the blame for the murder in an apparent attempt to protect Yaw.

"But now we have an alternative possibility," Dawson told Armah. "What if Yaw is protecting his *father* to atone for the hurt he feels he has caused Mr. Okoh? Yaw has witnessed and observed the crime scene and taken mental note of Kudzo's astute observation that Bao might have been suffocated while gasping for air and inhaling soil. Yaw also learns from Kudzo what time Bao tried to call Wei, since Wei mentioned it to Kudzo the morning Bao was found. So Yaw can use these facts to 'confess.'"

"The only missing piece, then," Armah said, "is that we don't know how Yaw could have found out that Bao was expected at the site that Friday morning."

Dawson agreed. "That is bothersome, yes."

"Let's go back and look at the other possibilities to be sure we haven't omitted something."

"All right," Dawson said. "First there's Lian, Bao's wife. I don't have any reason to believe she had a motive to have her husband killed. As I said to Chikata, Bao was her rock and her financial support. No, she isn't a suspect from my point of view."

"But I sense a gap in what you know about her," Armah countered. "You've met her only once, and we don't know a lot about her relationship with her husband. Was it a loving one? Did they argue? In your story, you said Bao was flirtatious with Amos's girlfriend. Could it be that he was a womanizer and that Lian knew about it and had him killed?"

Dawson was doubtful. "Anything is possible, but . . ."

"I can see that isn't going down very well with you," Armah said with a chuckle.

Dawson grinned. "But you're right. I should follow that up. I have an idea whom I could ask." He was thinking of Mr. Huang.

"Good. Who else? What about the victim's brother—what's his name?"

"Wei. He has an alibi—he stayed overnight with his friend Feng."

"I see. And outside the family circle? The young man—Kudzo?"

"His alibi is solid. But there's Chuck Granger, the American whose mining site is adjacent to Wei's. Granger had motive. He hated Bao and saw him as a threat. But he was down in Accra on business with Tommy Thompson, director of PMMC, on Thursday and he came back on Friday."

"That's confirmed beyond a doubt?"

"Not exactly," Dawson confessed. "I tried to contact Thompson once without success, and then the business of Yaw came along and I got sidetracked. I'll ask Chikata to look for the man and talk to him in person."

"Good," Armah said. "I concur."

"So I have a couple of possible leads, at least," Dawson said, feeling better.

"Yes. By the way, this journalist, Helmsley, has she told you anything useful?"

"She's working on conspiracy-type things," Dawson said. "For example, she claims that a whistle-blower has told her that the PMMC actually buys illegal gold and uses that to inflate figures about the amount of gold produced in Ghana."

"Actually, I've heard that before too," Armah said, leaning back and unconsciously cracking his knuckles one by one. "Who is her source?"

"She declined to say. Supposedly she went down to PMMC in Accra and was kicked out for asking Tommy Thompson snooping questions. She says her source also tells her that PMMC buys the gold from Chinese or at below market price and they don't like galamsey who don't play the game."

"In other words," Armah said, "what if Bao was resisting the

PMMC? They would not have taken kindly to that. They might either react by teaching him a lesson or killing him—without getting their hands dirty, of course."

"But would the PMMC worry about one Chinese individual not playing by the rules?"

"Why not?" Armah asked. "One here and one there can add up. It's reported that a rich Chinese miner can pay off a police task force with as much as ten thousand dollars."

Dawson's eyebrows shot up. "You said ten thousand dollars?"

"Dollars. Green."

Dawson shook his head in astonishment. "I had no idea they deal in those kinds of sums."

"Yes, indeed. So some of the special police or military forces that conduct these raids on the Chinese mining sites are in reality taking money to ignore the owners and in fact allow some of the workers they arrest to return to the mining site after a photo opportunity is held for the benefit of the press. From time to time, we see these headlines in the papers about illegal miners being rounded up for deportation or imprisonment, along with a picture of a group of sullen Chinese guys. It's all for show. It's a cynical move designed to give the public the impression that their government is actually doing something."

These types of shenanigans bothered Dawson tremendously.

"So now you have all your pieces scattered all over the table like a jigsaw puzzle," Armah said. "Granger, Thompson and the PMMC, Bao, Wei Liu, Mrs. Liu, Yaw. The question is how they fit together."

CHIKATA HAD BEEN called back to Accra. It had been too much to hope that he could be transferred to Obuasi for the long term. Commander Longdon had now assigned Detective Constable Asase to be Dawson's junior partner.

Still, Dawson needed Chikata, and he called him to explain the mission. "We need to know if Thompson was with Chuck Granger that Thursday to Friday."

"Yes, boss."

"One other thing. You have to be careful with this one—it will test your questioning skills. Akua Helmsley is planning to write an article accusing the PMMC of falsifying gold production figures by including illegally mined gold. Ask him if that's true, but don't say anything about Helmsley's article. Watch his reaction, the way his eyes move, his posture, and so on."

"I see. All right, boss."

Dawson ended the call and sat thinking for a moment about who was up next for questioning.

DAWSON DROVE TO Sofo Line, where Mr. Huang owned a hardware supply store. Sofo Line, an area of Kumasi favored by the Chinese, was once on the "outskirts" of the city. Only two years ago, free and wild vegetation had grown on the tough red soil, but as a traffic interchange that claimed to be the largest in West Africa was constructed, residential and commercial buildings had followed. Sofo Line would inevitably become densely populated.

Up on the hill stood Prempeh College with its lush grounds nourished by the Ashanti Region's generous rainfall. Prestigious as it was as a boys' boarding school, it would have been Dawson's choice for his boys if the family were to live in Kumasi permanently. But although the city was growing on Dawson, he probably would always want to return to Accra.

Several hundred meters along, Dawson spotted the store, logically named Huang's Hardware, next to a Samsung outlet, and pulled up in front of it. Opening the shop door, Dawson received a welcome blast of air-conditioned coolness. Dawson looked around. It was larger than he had expected and quite busy with both Chinese and Ghanaian customers searching the packed shelves for shovels, pickaxes, machetes, tools, pans, buckets, and all kinds of equipment, much of it mining related. *Huang must be doing quite well for himself*, Dawson speculated.

He asked one of the store workers where Huang was and was

directed out of the store and around to the back, where Dawson
found Huang watching as young workers unloaded supplies from
a large truck. When he saw Dawson, he walked over. "Good
afternoon, Inspector." He seemed neither overjoyed nor dis-
pleased to see him—merely courteous.

"Good afternoon, Mr. Huang."

"Can I help you?"

"Maybe we can go where it's a little quieter?"

Huang unlocked one of the back doors, and it opened up into
a short corridor, at the end of which was an employee entrance
to the store. Huang grabbed a couple of chairs and brought them
closer together.

"Please," he said, gesturing to the chairs.

Dawson chose one and sat. "Sorry to disturb you, sir. I know
you're busy."

"Oh, no problem," he said, waving it away. "I saw you arrest the
young man from the village for killing Mr. Bao."

"Allegedly," Dawson corrected him gently. "I came here to ask
you something about Bao and his wife."

"Yes?"

"Did they get along well with each other?"

Huang looked worried. "Why, something wrong?"

"Nothing is wrong. I just wanted to know."

"I think everything fine," Huang said cautiously, "but I didn't
spend so much time with them, even though I knew them. You
know, we Chinese in Kumasi, we keep to ourselves. We don't like
to get into each other business."

"I understand," Dawson said, thinking, *Then he's going to dislike
my next question.* "I apologize for asking this, but there was a rumor
that Mr. Bao was very fond of young Ghanaian women. Do you
know anything about that?"

Huang appeared mortified. "No, oh no, sir," he stammered,
shaking his head.

"No, what? No, it's not true, or no, you don't know anything
about that?"

"I don't know anything, Inspector. Please. Sorry. I don't know, sir."

"But you heard the rumor before?" Dawson pressed.

Huang shook his head firmly. "No, sir. Inspector, please, I have to go now. Thank you, sir." He stood up and Dawson followed his lead. Huang hurriedly guided him to the entrance to the store.

"I need a bucket," Dawson said, breaking the awkward tension. "Can you show me where to find one in your shop?"

Huang was visibly relieved to move to matters of commerce. "Oh, sure," he said, a smile bursting upon his face. "I can show you."

He took Dawson to a section of the shop where buckets—plastic, metal, big and small—were stacked, and Dawson chose one.

"Thank you, Mr. Huang. Thank you very much."

As Dawson completed his purchase and left the store, he considered the way Huang had responded to his questions and concluded that the Chinese man knew something, or had heard something, about Bao's philandering. He was just too embarrassed to admit it, or he simply did not want to involve himself in that way. The question remained whether Lian had known about it and if it had had anything to do with Bao's murder. Perhaps Dawson was wrong, perhaps he was stereotyping Lian, but his instincts were that even if she had known, she would have kept quiet about it and never taken any action against him.

But Dawson had been surprised before. This could be one of those occasions.

CHAPTER THIRTY-EIGHT

IN THE MORNING, COMMANDER Longdon held a staff meeting, which Dawson and Asase attended. When Dawson's case came up, he summarized his misgivings over the foregone conclusion that Yaw Okoh had killed Bao Liu. As he did so, Dawson sensed Longdon's growing impatience.

"I don't understand where this sudden change of mind over Yaw's confession is coming from," the commander said irritably. "I've read your full report, and in fact, it's watertight. The culprit has now been remanded into prison custody, so the next step is waiting for trial. You know it is almost impossible to get back to a suspect once they are out of police custody and under the prisons' jurisdiction. Why are you going back on this?"

"I suspect it's a false confession," Dawson said. "Yaw may be protecting his father."

"Protecting his father," Longdon repeated, as though carefully considering the validity of each word. "All this psychological talk for *what*? Drop it now, Dawson. Right now, we have open cases that I want you to begin working on."

"Yes, sir," Dawson said, obediently.

But he had no plans to obey.

SERGEANT OBENG LIVED in Obuasi Central, the oldest part of town. Constable Asase knew, more or less, where his house was. Dawson walked with him down Nkansa Drive, a busy paved street crammed with customers and shops on either side. *If I ever need a backpack, mattress, propane tank, gas cooker, new mobile phone, boxer briefs, Nike running shoes, or a soccer ball,* he thought, *I'll be in the right place.*

Asase turned off the main street into the marketplace thick with the odor of dried fish, snails, and fresh meat. A cage held squawking chickens for purchase. They passed next to the fruits and vegetables where a pickup truck loaded with green plantains blocked their path and forced them to make a detour. Beyond that, the clothing and textiles part of the market was quieter, with sounds noticeably muffled by the fabrics. Asase made a left on Central Station Road, and then a sharp right into a narrow, nameless alley along which a trash-laden gutter ran. He stopped in front of the battered doors of two small dwellings, their torn mosquito nettings dangling like a man hanged.

"I don't quite remember which is Obeng's," Asase said. "Let's try this one."

He knocked on the khaki-brown door on the right. They waited a couple of minutes, and then Asase tried the other door, with the same result. Dawson peered in through the narrow opening in the top. It was dark inside, but he was sure he could see a hand on the floor.

"We have to get in," he said, stepping back. He planted his foot on the door and pushed. It opened with a crack. Dawson and Asase entered and saw in the gloom Obeng crumpled on the floor like a sack of *cocoyams.*

Dawson's heart plunged. *Dead,* he thought, but when he stooped down and touched the body, it was warm, and now he saw Obeng was breathing. A tenacious stream of drool trailed from one corner of his mouth, and he reeked of alcohol as if he had bathed in it. Drunk, not dead.

Asase tried the light switch on the wall. It clicked without a response. No power.

Dawson slapped Obeng's cheek—the one without the drool. "Wake up."

The sergeant's eyes fluttered open and then drifted closed again.

"Get me some water," Dawson said to Asase, who went out and returned minutes later with a cup of water from a neighbor. Dawson took it and splashed Obeng's face twice. He startled awake and shakily propped himself up on his elbow, looking at the other two men in bewilderment.

"Oh, massa," he said thickly. "*Mepa wo kyew*, good morning."

"It's afternoon," Dawson said. "Sit up."

Obeng sat with his back against the bed, which was a set of boards placed on top of cement blocks. The room was as chaotic as if it had experienced its own self-contained whirlwind, and it smelled of urine, alcohol, and everything unwashed, including Obeng. He was in a bad way. He rubbed his hand over his face, trying to focus.

"What happened to you?" Dawson asked.

"Please, they sacked me yesterday."

Longdon gave him a chance, but Obeng couldn't deliver. "And you've been drinking all night?" Dawson asked.

Obeng, staring at the floor dazed, didn't respond. The answer did not need stating. Dawson gave Asase a couple of *cedis* and the constable went out to buy a bottle of water. When he returned, Dawson removed the seal and unscrewed the cap. "Drink," he said, holding the bottle to Obeng's lips. The maneuver was poorly coordinated and water spilled.

"Please, I can do it," Obeng said. "Thank you." He drank gingerly first, then more thirstily.

"Give us a moment, please," Dawson said to Asase, who seemed grateful to leave. "How long since your last drink?" Dawson asked Obeng.

"Please, it was last night," he said weakly, "but I don't remember the time."

His speech was not slurring, and the cadence of his speech was normal. Dawson judged that Obeng had slept off the intoxication. He helped him up so that he could sit on the bed. Dawson sat opposite him on an old wooden crate.

"How did this happen to you?" he asked the sergeant. "The drinking."

"Please, when my wife left me. Three years ago now."

When Dawson had first met Obeng, he had had the feeling that something about the man's life was disturbed. Now he knew the origin of that turmoil.

"Where are your children?" he asked.

"In Kumasi," Obeng said. "With the mother."

"If you don't stop drinking," Dawson said quietly, "they might lose their father."

Obeng nodded sadly, as if he knew it, but could do little or nothing about it.

"I am still on the Chinese man's case," Dawson said.

Obeng nodded. "Yes, please."

"I need to know something. How far did you get in the investigation of the death of Amos Okoh?"

"Please, the death was an accident, so the case was closed."

"How did the accident happen?" Dawson asked.

"Amos was walking on the bridge, and he slipped and fell inside the pit."

Too easy. "Did something happen between him and Bao Liu before he fell in the pit?" Dawson asked.

Obeng hesitated, his bloodshot eyes shifting. "No, sir."

"People say Bao Liu said something bad to Amos and his girl-friend, and so Amos became very angry and tried to attack Bao from the bridge. Bao shook the bridge and tipped Amos into the water in the pit below."

"Please, it's not true," Obeng said dully. "It was just an accident."

Dawson stared at him, and the sergeant began to wither. "Obeng, why are you protecting the Chinese man?" Dawson asked softly. "What is going on? He's not even alive anymore."

Obeng covered his face. "Please, I'm afraid."

"Of what?"

"My family . . ."

Dawson understood now. *It's not Bao Liu he's shielding; it's some-one else.* "Has someone threatened to hurt you or your family if you tell the truth about what Bao Liu did?"

"*Mepa wo kyew,* I beg you, please," Obeng said, appealing to Dawson not to press him any further. Obeng was terrified of something and or someone, and Dawson decided he would with-draw—but only for now. He would be back for another try sometime very soon.

Dawson stood up. "Come to me if you want to tell me some-thing," he said. He fished in his pocket and gave the sergeant five *cedis.* "You have to get something to eat now, but don't drink any more beer."

"Yessah," Obeng said getting up himself, unsteadily.

DAWSON GOT BACK home at a little past five in the afternoon and found Christine behind the house preparing *fufuo* with a young girl who was related in some distant way to Christine, although Dawson couldn't remember how. The long pestle in both hands, the girl was doing the rhythmic pounding of the *cassava* and plantain in the mortar while Christine turned the glutinous mass in alternation with each strike. Dawson might have pounded *fufuo* no more than twice in his life. Traditionally, girls and women did it.

"Hi, love," Christine said, looking up. She didn't have to watch the pestle to keep the rhythm. "How was the day?"

"So-so," Dawson said, eager to forget it for a while. "Where are the boys?"

"Sly went to play football with his friends," she replied. She looked distressed. "But I've given Hosiah extra homework and told him he can't go out to play until he learns to behave himself. You need to talk to him."

Dawson frowned. "What's happened?"

"He got into another fight at school. They were at midmorning break. The headmistress punished him by making him fetch five buckets of water for the toilets. Talk to him. I don't know what else to tell the child."

"All right," Dawson said.

He found Hosiah sitting at the kitchen table staring with furrowed brow at the arithmetic problems on the sheet of paper in front of him as he sucked on his pencil in calculation confusion. He looked up at his dad apprehensively, expecting a scolding.

"Two-thirds plus three-quarters," Dawson read from off the paper Hosiah had been studying. "Is that what is puzzling you?"

Hosiah dropped the pencil in frustration. "I don't understand how to do it, Daddy."

Dawson sat next to his son, picked up the pencil, and connected the two denominators with a curved line. "Remember how I told you that the two numbers on the bottom have to agree on one number? How do we get that?"

"Add them?"

"No. What else could we do?"

Hosiah thought for a minute. "Oh. Multiply them."

"Good. So what do we get?"

"Um . . . twelve."

"Right." Dawson gave the pencil back to his son. "Draw a line and put twelve underneath. Now, what do we do with the top numbers—the numerators?"

He guided Hosiah through the steps until they got the correct answer.

"Not so bad, right?" Dawson asked, rubbing his son's head.

Hosiah smiled. "Can I do the next one by myself, Daddy?"

"Of course. Go ahead."

With only a couple missteps, Hosiah arrived at the correct solution. Dawson helped him with the remaining thirteen calculations.

"You've done a good job," he said to Hosiah. "I'll talk to Mama and see if you can go out and play now. First, you have to explain why you got into a fight today at school."

He listened as his son stumbled through his account of what had happened. Abraham, one of the bigger boys at school, had cut in front of Hosiah as he waited in line for the midmorning snack. Hosiah had reacted by trying to push Abraham away, and a shoving match had escalated quickly into a full-blown fight on the ground.

This was tricky. While Hosiah should be able to stand up for himself, Dawson wanted to steer him away from fighting. "Did you say to Abraham, 'I don't like it that you got in front of me?'"

"No," Hosiah said sulkily. "If I said that, then he would just hit me."

"And that's when you defend yourself. Remember some of the techniques I showed you?"

"Yes, Daddy."

"But instead what happened is that you started a fight."

"*He* started it because he got in front of me!" Hosiah whined.

In some ways, he's right. "Don't raise your voice," Dawson said quietly.

"Sorry, Daddy."

"You always defend yourself, but you should never be the first one to hit, push, or kick another person. That's not the way the Dawsons behave. Okay?"

"Yes, Daddy."

"In the end you didn't get your snack. You and Abraham had to carry buckets of water, and Mama has now given you extra homework as more punishment, and you can't go to play football with Sly. So you see what you ended up doing? You only hurt yourself."

"Yes, Daddy."

Dawson pulled him over to his lap, holding him close. "Remember when your heart was sick and you were so good and smart at the hospital?"

Hosiah nodded.

"Mama and I were very proud of you, because you handled your heart condition so well, and all the doctors and the nurses admired you. I even had doctors who weren't taking care of you stopping me in the hospital to tell me how amazing my son is. And then they left me standing there thinking, 'I don't even know who that doctor was.'"

Hosiah giggled.

"But fighting isn't something that will make Mama and me proud of you," Dawson said, "and nobody else will respect you for it. Okay?"

He nodded.

"Good," Dawson said. "You want to go with me to the park and play some football together? Just you and me?"

Hosiah looked up at his dad, eyes shining. "*Yes!*"

LATER ON, BEFORE bed, Christine asked Dawson what had happened with Hosiah.

"Actually," Dawson said, "I've figured it out. Punishment is not what he needs more of."

"Oh, really?" she asked, smoothing cocoa butter into her gorgeous skin. "Tell me."

"Put yourself in his little shoes. It's been about a year since your heart operation and you're doing well. Now you play football, and you're good at it, and you have new friends and popularity. Now your father comes along; uproots you from your environment, your school, and your friends; and takes you to a strange school, and a strange home in a strange city. Now you need even more support, especially from your father, but he's so busy with work that he almost seems to be ignoring you. You're angry, but you can't take it out on your father, so you take it out on others."

Christine tilted her head, considering. "Maybe. So what now?"

"I'll try to get home earlier from now on," Dawson said. "I'll check both of their homework and talk to them about school, and then go with them to the football park."

"Wow," Christine said admiringly. "I like that! I'm assuming you've got the Obuasi office more organized now."

"It's much better," Dawson said, pulling his T-shirt off and getting ready for a shower.

"And the case?" Christine asked, putting her hair up for the night. "All settled, or still having doubts?"

"Still having doubts, but I'm stuck. Don't know where to turn."

"Something will come up," Christine said confidently. "It always does."

CHAPTER THIRTY-NINE

IT WAS ONLY THE following afternoon that Christine's prediction proved accurate. Dawson was at the office digging up more reports of armed robberies of victims who were carrying gold or cash for gold, when he received a call from Chikata. He had visited Tommy Thompson at the corporate offices of PMMC in Accra.

"Something strange is going on, boss," Chikata said. "Akua Helmsley said she talked to Thompson, right?"

"Correct."

"I had a solid conversation with him. He was very cordial and open with me. You know what he told me? He said not only has Akua Helmsley never spoken to him, she has never visited PMMC."

"What? *Never?*"

"He called each of his underlings separately into his office and all of them said exactly the same thing: they have never seen the woman set foot on the premises."

Dawson frowned. "That can't be, surely. You say Thompson didn't seem evasive in any way?"

"Not at all," Chikata said. "You know, when I asked him why Helmsley would have claimed to have spoken to him, he looked at me as if I had just come from another planet and said, 'So you don't know about Miss Helmsley's MO?' 'What MO?' I asked. 'Miss Helmsley either deliberately makes up her facts or gets them wrong,' he said."

"Can he prove that?"

"The network was down for the moment," Chikata said, "so he couldn't get access to her articles, but he said several of the figures she cited in her article were wildly inaccurate, and on occasions when he's tried to call her to object, she hasn't taken his calls."

At first, Dawson had been certain Helmsley would not do something like this, but now he was wavering. Could he have over-idealized her? What if her zeal for the truth had slipped down a slope of fabrication?

"So then I asked him about Helmsley's claim about the PMMC and the Ministry of Lands, Forestry, and Mines," Chikata continued, helping Dawson to focus, "that they use illegal gold earnings to inflate the official revenue figures, and he began to laugh. He said the idea is so ridiculous that if Helmsley publishes that she'll be laughed out of town."

Dawson remembered that he himself had been skeptical when Akua had stated the accusation to him, and he began to feel uncomfortable, experiencing doubts about her.

Chikata continued. "And then Thompson made another comment that he was almost certain that if Helmsley really has a so-called inside source, it's probably one of the three disgruntled employees they've sacked in the last year or so."

"Who are they?"

"Thompson gave me the names and contact phones, so I'll get onto that and see if I can interview them."

"Good work, Chikata. Thanks."

"Welcome, boss."

Dawson was lost in thought for a moment. What Chikata had just told him was bothersome. "How are things with the new boss?" he asked, perhaps just to get away from the pondering for a moment.

"Hm. I wish my uncle was back."

"That bad?"

"Not terrible," he said, "but not great either."

"You were spoiled by your uncle, don't forget."

"You always say that," Chikata grumbled.

"Because it's true," Dawson said, laughing.

A moment after he had ended the call to Chikata, he received one from Commander Longdon. "You are summoned to Kumasi Regional Headquarters for a meeting," he said.

He sounded grave, and Dawson had a plunging feeling in his stomach that he was in trouble. Again. "Summoned, sir?"

"Yes. So as not to waste time, I have sent my driver to pick you up. Please go with him as soon as he arrives."

"Yes. Yes, sir."

THE VEHICLE WAS an SUV manufactured in India. Dawson sat in the front next to the constable driver and chatted casually all the way to Kumasi Regional Headquarters, belying his anxiety over what was going on. His stomach fluttered nervously. Was he in trouble, or was it something else? He searched his mind for some breach he might have committed. Was it the way he had engineered Chikata's temporary transfer to Obuasi? No, that was unlikely, because Chikata's uncle had played some part in that, and as Assistant Commissioner of Police, Lartey was highly placed. Dawson gave a mental shrug. Nothing could be done except to wait and see.

THE MEETING ROOM was on the second floor of the sprawling Kumasi Regional Headquarters building. At the top of the flight of steps, Dawson faced the door marked REGIONAL COMMANDER.

He took a breath and knocked. When he entered, he saw Longdon sitting at the conference table with three other people, one of whom was Deputy Commissioner of Police Deborah Manu, one of the very few female regional commanders. She was sharp featured and thin. The second was the rarely seen Commissioner Fortune Dzamesi, Director General of CID. Dawson did not recognize the third person, however. Dressed in a camouflage uniform studded with medals, he was obviously military.

Dawson's forehead became clammy with a light sheen of sweat.

This is even worse than I thought. What have I done? He was fearful, not of them, but of his imminent fate. He had fleeting visions of his family's marginal assets dwindling to a trickle or nothing at all as he endured unpaid leave, and struggles to take care of the boys' schooling, food, and health.

Stopping about a meter away from the table, Dawson braced in salute of his superiors, stiffening with closed hands to his sides, knuckles forward.

"Please," Longdon said deferentially to Commissioner Dzamesi and DCOP Manu, "this is Chief Inspector Dawson, our new chief crime officer at the Obuasi Division."

"At ease, Dawson," Dzamesi said with flick of the hand. "Have a seat." He indicated the only empty chair, and Dawson took it, looking from one solemn face to the other. They each had important-looking three-ring binders in front of them.

"I have to warn you, Chief Inspector," Dzamesi said, "that this is a top secret meeting. Everything we discuss here must stay in this room. Is that clear?"

"Yes, sir."

"Those you see around this table, including myself," Dzamesi continued, "are members of the Task Force on Chinese Illegal Mining. The president has given us the challenge of bringing these *galamsey* activities to a stop. In order to do this, we must apprehend these illegal Chinese nationals so that they may be deported immediately. And that is what we have pledged to do."

Lofty words. Dawson had his doubts. "Yes, sir."

The military man turned out to be Brigadier-General Frank Bediako, who was in charge of the Ghana Armed Forces Northern Command based in Kumasi. His eyes were narrow, and his jaw looked as hard as a coconut shell. "Perhaps I have missed something," he said in a voice as raspy as sandpaper, "but remind me what the chief inspector is supposed to be contributing to this meeting—or to the task force for that matter?"

"Sir," Manu said, shifting in her chair to look at him, "we do like to have the input of our officers who are in the trenches, so to speak, so I asked Commander Longdon to invite Chief Inspector Dawson. Perhaps you can explain a little more, Commander."

"Thank you, madam," Longdon said, and to Bediako, "Since his arrival, I have directed Chief Inspector Dawson in the investigation of the death of an illegal Chinese miner. Along the way he has collected a lot of information that could be helpful to the task force."

"Ah." The brigadier-general nodded without much passion. "Very well. Carry on."

"There is something I want to ask you, Chief Inspector," Manu said, turning to Dawson. "At times, when our officers have visited these *galamsey* sites, they have met only the absence of the Chinese men. Have you located any hiding places to which they commonly disappear?"

"No, madam," Dawson said. "No specific hiding spots. But more importantly, if the police are meeting their absence, then could it be there are informants within the police service?"

Dzamesi stiffened. "What are you talking about?"

Longdon was angry. "This is ignorance," he snapped at Dawson. "You have no idea what you are saying. How dare you speak out of turn? Have I ever discussed any issue of police informants with you?"

"No, sir," Dawson admitted.

Longdon glared at him for a moment before turning to Dzamesi. "I apologize, Commissioner. Mr. Dawson wasn't authorized to make that nonsensical statement. Kindly disregard."

"But wait just a moment," Manu said, leaning forward and looking at Dawson intensely. "I would like us to talk about this a little more because a similar thought has occurred to me now and again. Chief Inspector, what exactly do you mean by informants?"

"Madam, if the Chinese are escaping just before a raid, I fear that someone within the force is feeding them information about the date and time such raids are to occur."

Manu was fingering her chin. "Do you know of any informants specifically?" she asked him. "Is that why you've brought this up?"

"I can't name any," Dawson said. "Not yet."

Dawson stole a glance at Longdon. His face had turned to stone.

"We will take note of what you have said, Chief Inspector," Dzamesi said self-importantly, jotting something down on his pad. "For now, let us discuss some of the operations that we will be carrying out."

Manu, still not satisfied, cut in yet again. "Commissioner Dzamesi, I'm sorry to interrupt, but I don't believe we've quite settled the matter. If informants exist, they pose a significant obstacle to our getting the Chinese *galamsey* activities under control, and we need to pursue the issue."

"'We,' meaning the task force?" the commissioner asked impatiently.

"Why not?" Manu said with a shrug. "I suggest that it should be incorporated into the mission statement of the task force—with the president's endorsement, of course."

"I understand your concern, Manu," Dzamesi said quietly, "but such probes generate ill feeling in the force and have a detrimental effect on morale. I will bring it up with the inspector general of police, but I don't think it should be the business of this task force."

Worthless lip service, Dawson thought. *He will never take up the matter with the IG.*

"Very good, sir," Manu said respectfully, but Dawson knew she was not pleased by Dzamesi's response.

"So," the commissioner continued, "our main task at hand is uprooting these illegal Chinese miners. We will be concentrating first on the mines in a wide area around Dunkwa. Within the next few days, officers with the police SWAT Bravo Strike Force here in Kumasi will join the brigadier-general's forces and conduct a raid at those sites. On an almost weekly basis, we plan to move farther north to areas like Obuasi, Aniamoa, Ntoburoso, and so on."

Dzamesi looked up for responses, and a short discussion followed. When a space opened up in the chatter, Dawson said, "Please, sir, what will be my role during these raids?"

Dzamesi was taken by surprise. He looked at DCOP Manu, who

in turn looked at Longdon. "Do you usually send your detectives on such raids?" she asked.

The commander shook his head. "For safety reasons, we do not."

"That seems sensible," the commissioner commented.

"Is this not a special case, though?" Manu came in. "The chief inspector has been investigating the death of a Chinese man at one of the illegal mining sites that will be included in the upcoming raids. I would say that, in fact, it's *imperative* that he be in attendance."

"Why?" the brigadier-general demanded, frowning.

Let's see how she handles this, Dawson thought, with growing admiration.

"Not only must Mr. Dawson witness this raid in order to make his final investigatory report complete," Manu said confidently, "he has gathered some very useful and specialized knowledge about these miners and the *galamsey* sites. For example, the chief inspector knows how many workers were at the mine where the Chinese man died, and he knows their names. This is important because we might have to question some of the people we round up, and Mr. Dawson can assist with this. Correct me if I'm wrong, but the goal of these raids is not just to uproot and terrify people. Are we not also seeking information?"

"That is true," Dzamesi conceded with hesitation.

"Right," Manu said. "In addition, the chief inspector has familiarized himself with the workers in the *adjacent* mine, which belongs to the American, Chuck Granger. This is detailed information that we don't have, and I suggest that it would be valuable at the time of the raids."

Some muttering and throat clearing took place. Dzamesi finally answered heavily, "All right. Chief Inspector Dawson can be involved in the raid in observation status only." He looked at Dawson sternly. "I want to make that clear. You will not play *any* active role."

"Yes, sir," Dawson said. "Please, if you don't object, will you allow Constable Kobby to accompany me? Apart from this being a learning experience for him, he was the first policeman on the scene of the murder, and I believe he deserves it."

Dzamesi flipped his palms upward, looking at Longdon. "That's up to you, Commander."

Longdon opened his mouth.

"It's a good idea," Manu said, putting the words into it. "Thank you, Commander."

And now, Manu and Dzamesi were even, Longdon was squashed, and Dawson held the DCOP's negotiation skills in very high regard. She had argued successfully for Dawson's inclusion, and he made a mental note to thank her later in private. As for Longdon, he sat rigid with his mouth shut and his jaw tightly clamped.

The rest of the meeting was tying loose ends, and at the close, Dawson wondered, *Are we finally doing something about the illegal Chinese miners? Or was this just window dressing for the benefit of Ghana's president?* An even more cynical thought struck Dawson. Maybe even the *president* was merely putting on a show, and this national inquiry would end up buried in the same lifeless cemetery with all the other worthless presidential task forces, blue ribbon commissions, and parliamentary subcommittees.

CHAPTER FORTY

WHEN DAWSON REACHED AKUA Helmsley by phone, evening was approaching.

"I need to talk to you," he told her.

"I'm on my way to The View," she said. "I'm meeting someone but I'm early, so I have a little time. Can you come there?"

"I can be there in about an hour," Dawson said. "I'm coming up from Obuasi."

On the way, he called Christine to let her know he would be making a stop before getting home.

"Okay," she said, "but remember you promised to help the boys with their homework?"

"Yes. I'll try to be as quick as possible."

AS HE ENTERED The View on the top floor of the building, Dawson's suspicions were confirmed: a Ghana Police chief inspector couldn't afford to eat or drink here. The room was large and airy. Floor-to-ceiling windows provided the view for which the place was so famously named. The floors were solid wood, as were the impeccably laid tables at which customers, most of them expatriates, sat and talked, ate and drank. Business was light at this early hour, so a couple of the black-and-white uniformed waiters were attending to just three tables, while the others hovered around the bar.

Dawson saw Helmsley sitting alone at bar on the other side of the room, and he walked across.

"Nice to see you, Chief Inspector," she said, as he sat down.

"Thank you," he said. "I'm on my way home, so I'll have to make this quick." He wanted to establish the strictly business nature of the meeting at the outset.

"Of course," she said. She wore a sheer white top and tight black slacks. Her hair was elegantly swept back. She smelled like heaven must smell, and he was beset by guilt. He should be treating Christine to a place like this, rather than meeting another woman here.

"I'm having wine," she said. "Would you like something?"

"I'm fine, thank you."

She ignored him and lifted a finger to the bartender. "One Malta, please."

"Thank you," Dawson said. "You didn't have to."

"I know." She took a sip of her wine. "So. What's on your mind, Chief Inspector?"

He waited for the bartender to finish pouring. "It's about Tommy Thompson."

"Ah, yes?"

"You said you went to see him at the Accra office?"

"I did."

"My partner Philip Chikata—you remember him—went to PMMC to talk to him. He claims you've never stepped foot on the premises."

She chortled. "I'm not surprised."

Dawson could tell she genuinely wasn't, as if he had told her it rained in Kumasi. For *his* part, he was taken aback by the mildness of her reaction.

"Tommy Thompson is a liar," Helmsley said coolly. "Furthermore, he is trying to discredit my name. I'm sure he said some really unpleasant things about me."

Dawson said nothing in response, but yes, she was right.

"Whether you believe him or not," she continued as he watched her facial expression, "I know I don't need to tell you there are some very nasty men out there who cannot stand having a woman snooping around the way I do."

"And the whistle-blower?" he asked her. "Is he or she one of the disgruntled employees fired over the last year or so?"

She shook her head decisively. "No. The person is working at PMMC right now."

"I see."

"Contrary to popular gossip," Helmsley said, "I don't sensationalize my reports, nor did I sleep my way to my position, Chief Inspector."

"I never thought that," Dawson said, a little hurt.

"I appreciate your saying so. Anyway," she said with a backward flap of the hand, "that's neither here nor there. I'm glad you're here, because there is something I want to ask you."

"I'm listening."

"Speaking of whistle-blowers," she said, "would you be willing to be one, should the occasion arise?"

Dawson's Malta arrived. "You'll have to be more specific," he said, as the bartender poured. "In what regard?"

Helmsley paused, waiting for the bartender to leave, and gave a quick glance around. "I want to look into *galamsey* corruption at the highest levels of the police force."

"Why do you want to do that?"

"That's like asking you why you want to solve crime," she objected, but she was smiling.

"True, but that's when the crime has been committed. Do you know of *galamsey* corruption in the police?"

"Come on. It's a foregone conclusion. How is it that during these raids, some of the Chinese bosses are nowhere to be found? It's because someone tips them off."

She amazed him. It was as if she were echoing exactly the discussion with DCOP Deborah Manu.

"I know of no one," he said. "At least not yet."

"If you come across it," she said, "will you let me know?"

"It depends," he said, taking a sip of Malta.

"On what?" she asked, angling her head. Lit by the recessed ceiling lamps, she was stunning.

"On whether it's too dangerous to tell you," he said.

"Not this again, Dawson," she said. "You're going to have to stop trying to protect me. I'm a big girl. I can take care of myself."

"No doubt about it," he agreed. "But everyone needs someone else to watch their back. I'm going to watch yours."

"I accept graciously," she said, smiling and dipping her head slightly. "Now, something else I'm working on."

"Is there anything you are not?"

"Funny." She laughed, but quickly grew serious. "This one is all about staged armed robberies perpetrated on gold buyers or poten-tial investors from abroad who—" She broke off and changed the direction of her gaze. "Ah, here he is."

Her date had arrived. Probably of Lebanese-Ghanaian mix, he was on the chubby side and decidedly shorter than Akua. *He must be really rich*, Dawson thought unkindly, and then regretted it. Helmsley introduced the two men, and Dawson wasted no time in excusing himself.

"We'll catch up later," Helmsley said to him as he took his leave.

"Sure." Before he left the room, he took a quick look back and saw Akua sitting very close to the gentleman, with her hand rest-ing on his thigh.

DAWSON ARRIVED HOME at seven thirty, and immediately sensed as he came through the door that the evening was going to be a bit bumpy. Christine was ironing clothes in the kitchen, and that she was unhappy was obvious with one glance at her expression.

"I'm sorry, I'm sorry," he said, coming beside her and putting his arm around her waist.

"It's okay," she said, pressing her lips together. "I'm sure your meeting, wherever that was, was very important."

He didn't like the sarcastic treatment, but he was determined not to allow it to rattle him.

"Tell me how I can help, love," he said. "I'm all yours."

"Check the boys' homework," she said. "I haven't had time to

do it. Hosiah needs to finish his bath so Sly can get in. The water
is running slow. And I'm not sure if Sly has his uniform laid out
for tomorrow. If he doesn't, he can use the one I'm ironing now. I
don't understand what he does with his shirts."

"I'll check it all out, don't worry." He kissed her neck. "I'm
really sorry."

"I'm fine," she said. "Go and attend to them."

Just as he was leaving, she asked, "Anyway, where were you?"

"I was just late leaving Obuasi."

"But you said you had a stop."

"Yes, I had some questions for that journalist, Helmsley."

"Oh," Christine said, head studiously down as she ran the iron
back and forth. "Nothing you couldn't handle on the phone?"

"No," he said, frowning.

"And where did you meet this wonderful journalist Helmsley?"
she asked.

Her tone ruffled his composure. "Please, Christine. There's
nothing personal with the woman. It's all business."

"Okay. Sorry."

He turned, shaking his head, which was aching as if a vicious
little man were kicking his skull from the inside. He hurried to
the bathroom when he heard Hosiah let out a yell. Eyes clenched
shut, the boy was standing in the shower stall covered in soapsuds
crying out, "Ow! Ow!"

"Hosiah, what are you doing?"

"The water's stopped," he gasped. "And there's soap in my eyes."

Dawson scooped up a bowl of clean water from the standby
emergency bucket. One never knew when the water would be cut
off. "Here," he said, pouring it over his son's head. "Wash the soap
out. Hosiah, I told you, the water tank is not as big as the one we
have at home in Accra, so you have to keep your showers short.
You're not the only one living here, are you?"

"Yes, I know, Daddy," Hosiah said, rinsing his eyes out until he
was able to fully open them. "But I didn't really take a long time."
He continued with a meandering explanation.

"Yes, okay, I get it," Dawson said, cutting him short and handing him another bowlful of water. "Wash off quickly because Sly needs to come in for his bath too. Here's your towel."

"I don't use one, remember?" Hosiah reminded him.

"Oh, that's right—you don't," Dawson said. "Well, whatever it is you do."

Since probably the first day his son had been able to take his own shower or bucket bath, he had had the odd habit of not toweling off. He swept off the excess water from his body with his hands, and that was it. Neither Dawson nor Christine knew where the idiosyncrasy came from, but Hosiah was Hosiah.

"Finished!" Hosiah exclaimed, jumping out of the stall in birthday-suit glory. He did a fair imitation of a rapper while executing a small dance. "Look at me, Dad."

"Very nice," Dawson said, rumpling his son's head. "Now hurry up and get ready for bed. Sly? *Sly!* Where does the boy disappear to?"

CHAPTER FORTY-ONE

BY NINE ON FRIDAY morning, the sun was promising a sweltering day. Dawson sat in the front passenger seat of the Tata SUV as the driver took it over rough, undulating terrain. In the seat behind him, Constable Kobby was quiet.

Following the dark blue SWAT Bravo police vehicle ahead, the SUV pitched and swayed. This was the tough part of the journey toward the Lius' mining site that Dawson's little Corolla had never been able to make.

They came around the corner and stopped at a meeting point east of Dunkwa and south of the point where the Ofin River makes a U-turn from south to north, but because the trailing edge of Dunkwa Forest blocked their view, the river wasn't visible from where they stood. Illegal miners had not yet ravaged this spot, but loggers had, and the forest had been severely thinned out over just a matter of a few years.

Some fifty soldiers from the 4th Infantry Battalion had assembled, dressed in green-and-brown camouflage outfits and armed with automatic weapons. They were a hard, lean bunch, good to befriend, bad to antagonize. They listened as a compact staff sergeant briefed them. Some sported sleek dark glasses to reduce the sun's glare, or perhaps just to add to their mystique.

The SWAT officers, in black-and-gray camouflage, were

fewer in number than their military counterparts. They piled out of their vehicle, came to order, and the unit leader, a deputy superintendent of police, addressed them. With Kobby nearby, Dawson leaned against the vehicle and watched the DSP giving instructions and cautions. When he was done, he approached the detectives. The name badge on his right chest read FRIMPONG. Dawson was junior to him in rank, so he briefly braced in salute, as did Kobby.

"You will hold back from the scene until it has been secured by the soldiers and Bravo," Frimpong instructed them. "Some of these *galamsey* guys are very dangerous, and you are not to engage with them in any way. We don't want any injuries or fatalities. Understood?"

"Yes, sir," Dawson replied. "Please, what is the specific strategy for the raid?"

"We have at least two groups of illegal miners working inside this part of Dunkwa Forest," Frimpong said. "In fact, if you listen carefully, you can hear the sound of their excavators from here. We're splitting up to carry out dual operations as simultaneously as possible. If we do only the forest first, some of the illegals might escape under foliage cover and go to warn the others."

Dawson nodded. Frimpong took a folded sheet of paper from his top pocket and smoothed it over the hood of the SUV.

"So, we are here," he said, pointing to the diagram. "We will go through the tip of the forest, here. At the other side, we will come to the American man's site first, and then the first of the Chinese illegals at this site." He circled it.

The Lius' site, Dawson thought.

"Now," Frimpong said, "I understand you are familiar with these two spots through your investigations of the murder of the Chinese man. What do you know that might help us?"

Dawson produced his own sketch from his pocket and went through it with the DSP.

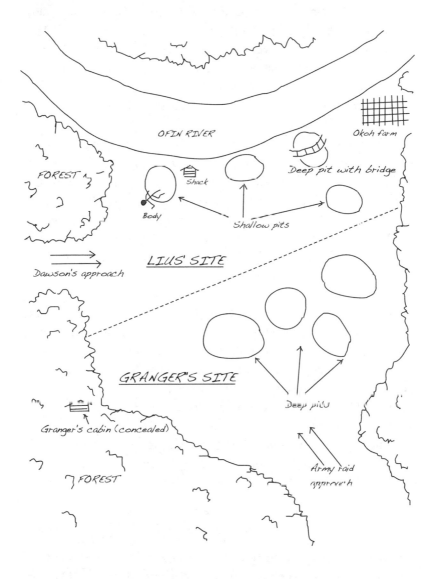

OFIN RIVER

Okoh farm

FOREST

Deep pit with bridge

Shack

Body

Shallow pits

LIUS' SITE

Dawson's approach

GRANGER'S SITE

Deep pits

Granger's cabin (concealed)

Army raid approach

FOREST

"We will first arrive at Chuck Granger's mining area, sir," Dawson said, circling his finger around the spot. "He has a cabin concealed by the trees over here to the left as we approach. It's a potential hiding place, and a sniper could shoot at us from there and then disappear into the forest."

"I appreciate that piece of information," Frimpong said. "I wasn't aware."

"The mining pits on Granger's property are very deep," Dawson continued, tapping each one, "and the tops and sides are muddy and slippery. In other words, we should proceed with caution, sir."

Frimpong nodded and pointed to the second set of pits on the diagram. "And these shallow pits are on the Chinese man's site?"

"Yes, the Chinese guys never had as much machine power as Mr. Granger," Dawson explained, "so their pits are shallower to enable the workers to get in and out."

"Got it."

"However, sir," Dawson said emphatically, "Mr. Liu does have one pit that is deep. That's this one with the bridge over here to the right. It's off this bridge that Amos Okoh fell—or was made to—and drowned. Again, sir, the men must tread with caution. Now, the shack you see over here on the Liu's site, sir, is on higher ground than the pits; therefore, our men running up to it could be subject to gunfire."

"Thank you, Dawson," Frimpong said, sincerely. "This is really good work. I will put in a good word about you to your superiors."

"Thank you, sir."

DAWSON AND KOBBY followed the military and police units, the 4th Battalion taking the lead through the dappled shade of neat rows of cocoa trees fringing the southern portion of Dunkwa Forest. *All this could disappear and give way to mining grounds,* Dawson thought. All it would take was a bulldozer—with or without the permission of the cocoa farmer.

As the forest ended, the cocoa farm trailed off and gave way to banana trees, oil palms, and shrubbery. The procession stopped for a moment. They could hear the drone of excavators in the distance. Dawson and Kobby were in the back of the pack, so they never saw the sergeant's signal to begin the raid. The units exploded out of the trees with a swiftness and ferocity that startled even Dawson, and he burst into a run himself to keep up, Kobby right at his side.

Dawson saw Chuck Granger's site ahead. It was deserted. *Tipped off by someone,* Dawson thought. *Who?* Approaching the ridge between two of Granger's huge pits, the men fell back to single file, slowing their pace slightly because of the risk of falling. Now the Liu site was coming up, but Dawson couldn't see all the way to the front until the men spread out and charged into the area, separating off into sections. One group charged up to the shed, kicking the door open and entering. But they came out empty-handed. Other soldiers went on to the bridged pit, as Dawson had suggested to Frimpong, but they found no one.

Dawson turned in a circle, searching for some sign of life. The rusty sluice boxes were still there, sad and lonely, and so was the excavator. But no illegal miners were in sight anywhere. Frimpong and the sergeant gave instructions and the units dispersed into the surrounding forest. A lot of thrashing around and yelling followed, but minutes later, the men came back reporting that nothing and no one could be found. Dawson beckoned to his constable to follow him as he went into the shed. Apart from a few mud-caked rags, it was empty. No machetes, firearms, or spent shells.

"Nothing here, boss," Kobby said, standing arms akimbo. "Do you think the miners have abandoned the area and gone to another site?"

Dawson shook his head. "No, they would not have left the excavator here." Clearly, someone had tipped off Wei and his crew as well, but Dawson kept that to himself. They left the shed and went back to the units where Frimpong and the sergeant were conferring and making phone calls. The guys stood around waiting for orders, many of them looking disappointed at how this so-called operation had come to nothing, ending as quickly as it had begun.

Dawson joined the two leaders in discussion.

"We're moving on to the next mining site," the sergeant said. "It's over that hill."

Dawson followed his pointing finger across the ravaged landscape.

The men fell into formation and the procession went at a steady trot up the rough incline. The drone of the excavators, now an all too familiar sound to Dawson, became louder. Just over the hill, he saw a site below them that was severalfold larger than the Lius'. It sprawled within a valley up to the Ofin River, which they could see now. Four excavators were at work scooping up enormous heaps of earth from the edges of the pits and swinging around to drop the payloads into the washing trommel, which processed a thousand times what manual washing with a sluice box could handle.

Ghanaians were working the excavators, while seven Chinese men supervised. One of them spotted the invading troops above them as the ambush commenced. He shouted out and began running in the opposite direction. The other six Chinese men scattered, and the Ghanaians leapt out of the excavator cabs. One of them lost his footing and slid down the side of a pit, clawing at the wet mud as he tried to stop himself plunging into the milky water below. He stopped barely a foot before the water's edge.

With Kobby next to him, Dawson followed the military and police part of the way as they swarmed in and chaos erupted. Two Chinese men slipped and fell and were set upon by the men of Bravo. One tried to run to the forest but was intercepted by a soldier who clubbed him on the side of the head. He went down like an axed odum tree.

Breaking up into smaller groups, the men of the 4th attacked the four shacks dotted around the property, pulling out bewildered

Chinese men and one woman, all of whom were made to lie prostrate. But some of them didn't understand the shouted orders, causing more confusion and resulting in their being shoved to the ground.

Dawson never saw anyone setting the shacks alight, but they were ablaze in short order, and Dawson felt the heat from the closest one. DSP Frimpong appeared from the other side of the blaze. "You and Kobby should retreat a bit," he warned. "You are too close."

"Yes, sir." Dawson beckoned to Kobby to pull back with him.

As he turned, his blood turned to ice as he saw a Chinese man appear from the forest with a pump shotgun held at waist level. He brought it up, and Dawson heard the crisp metal click of the fore-end as the man pulled it back and forward again.

"*Gun!*" Dawson screamed, and dived.

He heard the initial crack of the shot, brief and sharp, followed by the reverberation swelling and ricocheting as light as air throughout the valley. Two meters away, Kobby went to the ground, and at first Dawson thought that he was scrambling for cover. But the way he collapsed and flipped over said everything: he had been hit.

Dawson scuttled across the ground toward the constable like a crab. *Kobby.*

He heard the shotgun fore-end slide harshly back and forward again and thought, *He's going to kill me*, but perhaps the Chinese man jammed his weapon or had an unexpectedly empty chamber. No report came. Instead, automatic fire from a Battalion soldier's weapon rang out like a tongue rolling its Rs, and the Chinese gunman crumpled dead as dry twigs.

Dawson was at the constable's side. "Kobby, Kobby, look at me."

His eyes were open, staring unfocused. Dawson's heart leapt as they shifted and looked at him. Blood was expanding on the right side of Kobby's chest. Dawson lifted the constable's shirt and singlet underneath. "Kobby, breathe. You're hit, but you're going to live. Believe me, okay?"

Dawson was trying to see where the wound was and realized Kobby had several. He had been peppered with shots. Dawson shouted for a medic. *Is there a medic?* He didn't even know.

"Massa, I'm sorry," Kobby whispered.

"Sorry for what?" Dawson said sharply. "Stop it. You haven't done anything wrong."

Kobby was staring vacantly at the sky but Dawson forced the constable to redirect his gaze. "Look at me. You tell yourself you're going to live and not die, you hear me? You don't ever give up. You keep your eyes open, and you keep breathing, okay?"

Kobby seemed to be hanging on Dawson's every word. "Yes, sir. I will do that, sir."

A soldier was running up the incline to them. "What happened?"

"Shotgun blast. Are you a medic?"

His ID plate read ESSIEN. "No, sir," he said. "There is no medic here."

Dawson removed his shirt and bunched it up, giving it to Essien. "Press on his bleeding areas hard as possible," he said, and then got on his phone to call their driver. Kobby would need to be transported out as soon as possible. Members of the 4th and Bravo were coming over as they began to realize that one of their own had been hit. On the floor of the mining valley, a dozen or so Chinese men were kneeling or lying on the ground handcuffed and subdued. The Ghanaians had fled, but then they had never been targets in the first place.

Dawson was shocked when he saw the men of Bravo setting the excavators alight under orders from the sergeant. Why not simply confiscate them for use elsewhere? Then, as word spread from one man to the next about what had happened to Kobby, what Dawson feared was going to happen did indeed begin. The men of Bravo and the 4th began to take it out on the Chinese, slapping, clubbing, and punching them. It wasn't right, but then Dawson was in no mood to be a hero for the Chinese. He just wished they would go away and leave his country alone.

CHAPTER FORTY-TWO

AT KATH, DAWSON SAT in the packed waiting area quietly praying for good news. Kobby had been taken into surgery almost immediately. If he died, Dawson would never live it down. Yes, he took the blame. A chief inspector looks after his men. He and Kobby had been standing too close to the mayhem. He should have pulled back to behind the cover of trees and taken the constable with him. That way, they would not have been in the Chinese madman's line of fire.

Over and over, Dawson kept hearing the *click-clack* of the shotgun's fore-end, the snap of the report, and its echo through the valley. Nor could he forget the way Kobby had dropped to the ground like a sack of bricks.

His phone rang. It was Commander Longdon.

"Good afternoon, sir."

"I heard about the incident. What happened?"

"Kobby and I were standing at the perimeter of the property as the raid was being conducted," Dawson explained. "From behind us and a little to the side, a Chinese guy came out with a shotgun and began shooting."

"No, you and Constable Kobby were not standing at the perimeter of the property," Longdon said, raising his voice angrily. "You were standing right in the middle of the action, which you had been specifically instructed *not* to do. You were sent as an observer, but as usual, you overstepped your bounds. You see, *this* is the reason I do not send detectives on such raids. Did I not say so at the meeting?"

He's enjoying this. "Yes, sir. You did, sir."

"Yet you chose to disregard me, and as a result, a man may lose his life. Do you realize that?"

"I do, sir."

Longdon heaved a sigh. "You will write a full and complete account of the event and have it for me Monday morning, eight o'clock sharp. Thereafter, I will decide if you will be disciplined or not. Consider yourself lucky if I don't take you off the case."

"Yes, sir."

Empty threats, Dawson thought with a grim smile. Longdon couldn't take him off the case and he knew it. He would get into more trouble than it was worth when DCOP Manu summoned him to account for his actions. Nonetheless, Dawson felt no better about the way the day had turned out. After the call ended, he sat dejected and brooded until he heard his name called and looked up to see Christine coming toward him. He had texted her briefly about the affair, and she had replied she would come down to the hospital to sit with him.

She forced herself into the tight space beside him. "Any news?"

Dawson shook his head. "Not yet. It's been almost two hours now. I don't know if that's good or bad."

"We can only hope for the best," she said.

"I appreciate your coming," he said, putting his hand over hers. "Mama took the kids?"

"Yes, she did, and gladly. You know her. Any excuse to look after them."

Dawson smiled, realizing that despite his reservations about his mother-in-law, she was often a godsend. He gave a detailed account of the raid and the shooting to Christine, who nodded at intervals as she listened carefully.

"I know you're blaming yourself, because that's your nature," she said, when he was done, "but if you had been farther back from the scene, it might not have made any difference. He was still

going to come up behind you. In fact, it might have been worse if
he had shot at you and Kobby from close range."

Dawson cocked his head and conceded her point. Christine
really knew how to make him feel better.

A nurse came to the corner of the waiting area and beckoned
to Dawson. He stood up and followed her to the operating suite
anteroom.

"Doctor will be with you," she said. "Please, have a seat."

Dawson sat, his stomach churning. He felt sick with anxiety
and suspense.

The surgeon emerged, surgical mask dangling from around his
neck. Dawson tried to read his face, but it was neutral.

He sat beside Dawson, looking tired. "Good news, Chief
Inspector."

Dawson felt some of the tension leave him, like a stretched rubber band returning to normal length.

"Mr. Kobby suffered a collapsed lung," the surgeon continued,
"but we have now expanded it with a chest tube. Other than that,
the shot penetrated soft tissue and shattered some ribs, but nothing life threatening."

Dawson found himself hyperventilating with relief. "Thank
you, Doctor. From the bottom of my heart."

He smiled. "You are welcome. He will be in recovery for about
an hour, and then return to the ward for further treatment."

"But you think he'll be okay?" Dawson asked, needing the certainty.

"Barring the unforeseen," the doctor said.

"I'm very grateful to you for all you have done. If I had lost
him . . ."

The surgeon smiled as he stood up. "Yes, I know."

DAWSON WAS AT Kobby's bedside when he woke up. He
looked around, puzzled.

"You're in the hospital," Dawson told him. "Do you remember
what happened?"

Kobby shook his head, looking down at his bandaged chest. "No, sir." He winced at the large-bore tube in his right side.

"You were shot," Dawson said.

Kobby searched his mind. "I remember the mission, boss—going to get the Chinese guys, but what happened after that is completely blank."

"It's okay," Dawson said reassuringly. "It doesn't matter."

"Were you all right, sir?" Kobby asked him, turning his baby face to look at him.

"Fortunately, yes."

"What about the guy . . ."

"Dead," Dawson said. "One of the soldiers took him down."

Kobby reflected on that for a moment. "So, apart from what happened to me, the mission was completed successfully?"

"Yes," Dawson said. "Well, except that you were injured. You and I were standing too close to the raid, and that's my fault."

"Oh no, sir . . ." He trailed off, appearing saddened that Dawson felt that way.

Dawson stood up. "You should rest, Kobby. I will come back to see you tomorrow."

CHRISTINE WAS STILL in the waiting area and texting a friend when Dawson emerged. "How is he?" she asked, standing up.

"He's holding up well," Dawson said. "He's a good man. Come on, let's go home. I'm tired."

It was now dusk, and the street outside KATH was lit with roadside vendors cooking up goat or chicken kebab, or *waakye*, or *banku* and *okro* stew. Dawson and Christine walked side by side. He was despondent and wished he could start the day over.

"You came by cab?" he asked Christine.

"No," she said airily. "I came in the four-by-four."

"What four-by-four?" Dawson asked, looking at her in puzzlement.

"Over there," she said, pointing to a huge black Toyota Land Cruiser gleaming under the streetlamps.

Dawson laughed. "You're funny."

"Don't believe me?" she asked, taking keys out of her purse. The Cruiser's lights flashed twice, as if winking at them.

Dawson stopped in amazement. "Wait a minute. Whose vehicle is that?"

"It's mine," she said simply. "Come along."

Eyes wide, Dawson opened the passenger front door and got into the seat next to his wife. Not more than a few weeks old, the SUV's tan leather was still fragrant. When she turned on the ignition, the dashboard lit up with blue and amber lights, and the TV/GPS screen welcomed them aboard.

"Oh, my God," Dawson whispered.

"Nice, huh?" Christine said, smiling blissfully.

"Yes," he replied, "but if you've stolen it, you know I'm going to have to arrest you, right?"

She laughed as she pulled her seat belt across her chest. "Okay, I'll tell the truth. It actually belongs to Uncle Joe. When I told him I was going down to see you, he said he was expecting company, so he couldn't take me, but he said I could borrow it."

"Wow," Dawson said, somewhat awed as she pulled out into traffic. Who would have thought coming to Kumasi would have his wife driving the vehicle of choice for ministers of Parliament?

"I think I'd like to get one of these," Christine said. "I feel so powerful in it."

"Feeling powerful isn't enough," Dawson said dryly. "You have to be rich too."

She giggled and gave the monster some gas.

"Er, Christine, take it easy," Dawson said nervously. "You're not used to driving anything this big."

"Okay, okay," she said happily.

A little taste of luxury, Dawson thought ruefully. *That's all it takes to spark the craving for more.*

"What's on your agenda tomorrow?" she asked him.

"I have to write a full report of the incident to present it to the commander on Monday morning."

"I'm assuming none of that will be fun," Christine said, gunning the SUV and overtaking several vehicles.

"No, it won't," Dawson said, fumbling for the grab handle near his window. Christine's driving in a small sedan was ferocious. In an SUV, it was positively terrifying.

EVEN SO, KUMASI'S crawling evening traffic eventually got the better of Christine. As they sat trapped in a sea of vehicles, Dawson put his head back and closed his eyes for a moment as his mind roamed over the day's events. He wondered who had tipped off Chuck Granger and Wei Liu that the police and military forces were about to stage a raid on his camp. The best person to ask was Wei himself. He tried calling Mr. Huang to ask if he could translate for Dawson while he questioned Liu, but Huang didn't pick up. Dawson suspected that after the awkward questions he had asked Mr. Huang at his store, the poor man would never answer another call from Dawson.

He looked at Christine. "Do you know any Chinese? I need a translator."

"No, I don't," she said, swerving around a stalled taxi.

"Thought so. I was just checking."

"What do you need a Chinese interpreter for?" she asked.

"I'm going to interview Wei Liu."

"Right now? We're not going home?"

"Not yet," Dawson said. "Take the next right. Mr. Liu is going to understand and speak English tonight whether he likes it or not."

CHAPTER FORTY-THREE

A LITTLE PAST EIGHT, Christine and Dawson pulled up at Wei's house. Power to most of Kwadaso Estates was out, and the streets were very dark. The monotonous chorus of generators up and down the block was now the soundscape of practically every Ghanaian town and city.

At the sound of the horn, David, Wei's watchman, came out to peer at the visitors by the reflected light of the SUV head lamps. Once he'd recognized Dawson from his first visit, he opened up the gate and Christine drove in.

The lights in Wei's house looked bright, a testament to the power of the generator droning from somewhere in the back. Wei's pickup was parked in along one wall, but what caught Dawson's attention was the black Kia SUV positioned close to the front door. It looked like Lian's vehicle, and Dawson wondered if she was here—or perhaps Wei had simply borrowed the Kia.

"I'll wait here," Christine said, whipping out her phone to call her mother.

Dawson was glad she was in a secure area with David in attendance.

Wei opened the door to Dawson's knock and was clearly surprised.

"*Nǐ hǎo*, Mr. Liu," Dawson said, not quite sure if the greeting was right for late evening.

"*Nǐ hǎo*," Wei replied uncertainly.

"May I come in?" Dawson asked, with a gesture that he hoped conveyed his meaning.

Wei hesitated, and then opened the door wider and stepped aside to let his visitor into the air-conditioned sitting room, which smelled heavily of cigarettes. Looking around, Dawson felt like this was a downsized version of Lian's home, with the same kind of taste. The outsize sofa and matching chairs were made with shiny golden imitation leather and bold, strikingly colored wood. The center table was chrome and black lacquer. The wall-mounted HDTV, sixty inches at least, was playing a Chinese video featuring a beautiful but anguished young singer who, Dawson assumed, had lost her lover. In Dawson's estimation, some of the furniture was new. *Reaping some of his dead brother's money*, he thought, and then checked himself. He was making a prejudicial judgment.

Resting on one of the side tables next to an ashtray piled high with butts was Wei's laptop. Lying around were two kinds of TV remotes, three different brands of mobile phones, a Samsung tablet, and an iPad. Evidently, Wei loved gadgets and electronic devices.

"I need to talk to you," Dawson said. "No Mr. Huang today."

"Mr. Huang?" Wei said, with a perplexed frown.

"Did you go to the mine today?"

"Eh?"

"The mine—did you work there today?"

Wei shook his head. "Not understand."

Dawson was tired of the charade. He grasped Wei's shirt with both hands and pulled him so close that the Chinese man's soft belly bumped up against Dawson's taut one. Wei's eyes widened and his cigarette breath came harshly.

"Listen," Dawson said quietly. "Don't pretend you don't understand English, because I know you do. If you don't answer my questions, I will take you down to the station again and lock you up for two days. Am I clear?"

Wei nodded apprehensively. "Yes, sir," he whispered.

"Good," Dawson said, releasing him. "Take a seat over there, please."

Wei obeyed, sitting down in one of the armchairs, and Dawson took his seat opposite him.

"Is Lian here?"

"Lian?" He was puzzled.

"The Kia outside is not hers?" Dawson asked.

"Ah," Wei said with an uneasy laugh. "She give me the Kia; she say she like to drive Bao Mercedes."

"I see," Dawson said. "I was at your mining site today. It was deserted. Where were you and your workers?"

Wei looked bitter. "Those boys, they run away because my brother die there and they 'fraid *juju*. Anyway, now, no more gold there. Have to find other place."

So that's the real reason Liu's site was abandoned, Dawson thought. It still didn't disprove his theory of the existence of police informants, though.

"When Bao was still alive," Dawson said, "and all the boys were working at your site, did the police or military ever come to ask questions or arrest you?"

Wei turned the corners of his lips down and shook his head. "No."

"Did anyone ever come to tell you that the police were planning to raid your camp?"

"Raid? No. Never raid me and Bao."

"What about other miners at other sites? Did they know when the police were coming because someone informed them in advance?"

"I hear something like that before," Wei said with a dispirited shrug, "but never happen to us."

Dawson could see that his line of questioning was fruitless. The Chinese man was listless and distracted, and Dawson watched him as he seemed to slump further and further into his chair—a chubby, broken man who had lost so much. *Not everything, though*, Dawson reflected, looking at the HDTV.

He got up to look at a picture on the wall of Bao and Wei together. They could not be more different.

Dawson turned to look at Wei closely. "You miss your brother?"

Wei didn't answer. He stared at the wall photograph for several seconds, and his face began to crumple as his eyes moistened. "Why I don't wake up that morning?" he asked, his voice cracking. "Why I no hear alarm?"

He put his head in his hands and suppressed his weeping so that his body heaved as he wheezed and gasped.

"I'm sorry," Dawson said. He understood the man's anguish. After a few minutes, there wasn't much for Dawson to do but take his leave. The visit had been quite anticlimactic. As he got to the door, Dawson noticed a bunch of keys in a porcelain bowl on the sideboard to the left, including a car key with that famous logo. *Seems like Wei has driving rights to the Benz, as well,* Dawson observed. The death of Bao Liu was a mixed blessing for Wei: grief and financial gain both.

CHAPTER FORTY-FOUR

IN HIS CHILLED OFFICE Monday morning, Commander Long-don carefully read through Dawson's account of the shooting incident at the illegal mine on Friday. Spectacles half down his nose, he flipped back and forth between the three printed pages, and Dawson waited tensely.

The commander finally looked up over his glasses. "So you see the folly of your ways."

Dawson swallowed. "Yes, sir. And I apologize."

"Do you have anything to say in your defense?"

"All I can say is that I committed an error of judgment."

Longdon leaned back thoughtfully for a moment and rocked gently in his executive recliner for a few minutes. Finally, he sighed. "Chief Inspector Dawson, your excellent performance as a detective *per se* is not disputed."

But, Dawson thought. *There's always a but.*

"But what has happened in this situation," Longdon contin-ued, "is a demonstration of your persistent issue, which is your arrogance and disregard for authority. Many of your superiors have commented on this."

"It's something I have to work on," Dawson acknowledged.

"A word to the wise," Longdon said. "If we are to work well together, I expect you to heed my instructions, advice, and warn-ings. Is that understood?"

"Of course, sir," Dawson said. "And one other thing I wanted to mention is that I found out that Wei Liu's mining site was deserted because he is relocating, not because of informants forewarning him about our raid."

Longdon nodded with satisfaction. "Just as I said."

Dawson dipped his head contritely. "You were right; I was wrong, sir."

"We must move on to other items," the Commander said. "Now that you've had enough time to reorganize the office downstairs, I would like a detailed written report on the changes you have made. I go for the regional meeting next week, and I want to report the progress."

"Yes, sir, I can have that for you." Dawson hesitated on his next point. "Sir, that reminds me. I found three cases in the office that were started by my predecessor and Sergeant Obeng and remain open. They are incompletely written, and I wonder if you know about them."

"Do you have the files?"

"I'll get them, sir." Dawson excused himself, ran downstairs, and returned with the documents.

"Two of the files concern armed robberies," Dawson said, opening one of the three folders. "The first is a British national by name of Colin Wilshire who was allegedly attacked at gunpoint in Santase, Kumasi, and robbed of up to seven thousand dollars' worth of gold when he was returning to his house after a buying deal. Do you recall that case, sir?"

"No," Longdon said, looking puzzled. "What is the date on the file?"

"It happened in March of this year, sir."

"That's when Chief Inspector Addae was very sick and work became disrupted," Longdon said. "Some of the reports were not passed on. We have to look at reopening the investigation. What is the other one?"

"It's an American ex-basketball player called Beko Tanbry. He too had some dealings in gold. His SUV was ambushed between

Obuasi and Kumasi around Pakyi. He made a report, but there is no follow-up."

Longdon looked regretful. "I put Sergeant Obeng temporarily in charge when DCI Addae was ill, but little did I know that the alcoholism was impairing his abilities."

He takes no responsibility whatsoever for any of these investigation lapses, Dawson thought. Pitiful. *This man is not a leader; he's a worthless figurehead.* No wonder the morale of the place was in the toilet.

"And the third case?" Longdon asked.

"It concerns the death of Amos Okoh."

Longdon nodded. "An unfortunate accident."

"Please, there are two versions," Dawson said gently. "One is that it was an accident, the other that it was deliberate, but no real attempt at closing the case was made. I would like to do that, sir."

Longdon nodded. "Good. I think we should get that completed."

"I can begin work on all of these," Dawson said.

The commander frowned. "That might make your plate too full."

"If you would spare Constable Asase to assist me," Dawson said, "I can take it on, sir.

"Because the cases are a lapse on our part, I want Regional to handle them," the commander said abruptly.

"I don't quite understand, sir. Since it's Obuasi's lapse, shouldn't we be the ones to fix it?"

The veins in Longdon's bulky neck swelled as he lost his temper. "Did you hear what I said?" he shouted. "The cases are going to Regional. Again you challenge me? Get out of my office! *Get out!*"

Dawson's eyes narrowed. *This man is crazy.* As he rose from his seat, Dawson locked his gaze with Longdon's. *I am not afraid of you, Commander.*

THAT NIGHT, DAWSON dreamt he had fallen into a mining pit full of blue water. Each time he tried to surface, Commander

Longdon, standing above on a bridge crossing, shoved Dawson back into the water with a long bamboo pole sharpened at the tip. Akua Helmsley came running along the bridge to fight Longdon off, but as she got closer, he turned and drove the pointed end of the pole through her neck, almost decapitating her.

Dawson sat up in bed with a gasp. Sweat had soaked his T-shirt. He looked at his phone. The time was 4:20. He also saw that Akua Helmsley had sent him a link the day before via Whatsapp. He tapped it and it took him to *The Guardian*'s website, where she had a new post. GHANAIAN AUTHORITIES SHOW FORCE: BUT CHALLENGES STILL LIE AHEAD.

She had written about the raid and the shooting. She even had a picture of the deserted mining camp with the incinerating excavators. Without qualification, Dawson admired Helmsley for her work. She was on the ball, and now he dismissed any doubts he had entertained about the veracity of her story that she had confronted Tommy Thompson at PMMC. The question was now, why was *he* lying?

He saw that she had texted him again about forty-five minutes later, asking him to call her. In the dark, Dawson admitted to himself that he had deliberately avoided contact with her ever since Christine had thrown out that hint of jealousy. He didn't feel good about avoiding Akua, but he didn't want marital problems either, especially over nothing. His personal and professional worlds had collided somewhat.

Why was he now filled with a foreboding that something awful had happened? It must have been the nightmare. Dawson rose to remove his damp T-shirt. Trying to sleep anymore was fruitless, so he took his shower and got dressed quietly while Christine slept blissfully with a light snore. Overnight, she had gradually hogged most of the bed, as usual. *Wish I could sleep like my wife*, he thought, peeping into the boys' bedroom, *or my children, for that matter*.

Dawson went outside to think in the cool of predawn, taking a seat on the cheap plastic chair under the avocado tree for a moment. But he felt restless and uncomfortable, so he rose and went outside the front gate to watch Kumasi stirring awake.

His phone rang and his stomach dropped when he saw it was Commander Longdon. A call this early could only mean trouble.

"Good morning, sir."

"Morning, Dawson. You need to travel to Pakyi as soon as possible. I'm on the way there myself. There has been a fatal shooting. This one is high profile."

Dawson swallowed and closed his eyes tight. He felt faint. "Who is it, sir?"

"The journalist. Akua Helmsley."

CHAPTER FORTY-FIVE

DAWSON NEEDED A TOUGHER vehicle than the Corolla to go out into the bush, so he called Uncle Joe, who sent one of his drivers over with a jeep that Dawson could have for the day. He drove fast, reaching the turnoff just before Pakyi in under forty-five minutes. The directions were simple: just keep going into the deep bush, and then keep going some more. The unpaved, dusty road was barely wide enough for two vehicles side by side. It was rough in some sections and waterlogged in others, but the jeep, which had four-wheel drive, handled all of it without a problem.

After thirty minutes of travel, Dawson saw the vehicles in a cluster ahead: two black police Tatas off to the side, and a silver-gray Toyota Prado in the middle that Dawson recognized as Akua's. He pulled over and jumped out, his heart beating hard and heavy at what he was about to see. Commander Longdon was with two uniformed low-ranked officers.

Longdon turned as Dawson came up. "It must have been an ambush," he said. "It looks like both of them were forced out of the vehicle at gunpoint and then shot."

The Prado was facing them. The door on the passenger side was ajar, and just below it, Akua lay on the ground crumpled like a broken doll. She had a single wound in front of her right ear, dried blood fanning out from it like a river delta. It was a professional job.

Stunned, Dawson recoiled. *Oh. God.* He felt numb, with a sense of utter defeat.

"The man's body is here," Longdon said, moving to the driver's side of the Prado. But Dawson barely heard him, and he stayed where he was, staring at Akua's body.

"Dawson?" Longdon was looking at him with the expression that said, *Are you okay?*

"Yes," Dawson said, coming around the left-hand side, feeling as if he were floating in an unreal world. He couldn't feel his feet touching the ground.

"His identification says he's Joshua Samuels," Longdon said.

Two biblical names, Dawson thought irrelevantly. "That's Helmsley's cameraman."

"Oh, you know him?" Longdon asked in some surprise.

"I met him and Helmsley at Bao Liu's mining area the day he was found dead. They were trespassing and I warned them off. She asked me if she could keep in touch in order to get updates on the investigation."

"Ah, I see," the commander said. He introduced Dawson to the two officers, a corporal and lance corporal and from the Pakyi station.

For the moment, Dawson put away any antipathy he had felt for Longdon. There was time for that, and it wasn't now. "Who found them, sir?" he asked.

"Some hunters," Longdon said. "Around three o'clock this morning. But they weren't able to report it until about six, when they reached Pakyi. It's a long walk back. " He put his hands on his hips and shook his head slowly. "Cold-blooded brutality. It's a terrible shame."

"But what could be the motive for such an attack?" Dawson asked, bewildered.

"If I had to guess," the commander said, "I would say it was a robbery gone bad."

But why had Akua and Samuels been in such a remote area in the first place? Dawson frowned as he noticed something that had not struck him till now, and he turned to the commander. "This is the direction the Prado was facing when it was found?"

"Yes, of course," London replied. "Why?"

"It's pointed toward the main road," Dawson said. "So she was coming *back* from somewhere."

"I should say so, yes," Longdon agreed.

Dawson thought of something and took out his phone, going straight to Whatsapp. "Akua Helmsley texted me at three seventeen yesterday afternoon," he said.

"Oh," the commander said with interest. "Texted you about what?"

"She wanted me to call her back," Dawson said, "but she didn't say more than that. I didn't call."

"Ah," Longdon said. "That's useful information. So, we know she was killed sometime between yesterday midafternoon and early this morning."

Dawson was imagining the worst. What if Akua had wanted advice about what she was investigating, or to let Dawson know where she was going next? Perhaps she had waited for his return call as long as possible, and then started out on her mission. If Dawson had phoned her, could he have stopped her from going on a dangerous expedition and getting killed?

What have I done? Dawson felt sick. "Do you have CSU coming, sir?" The more businesslike he was, the less emotional he felt.

"Yes," the commander said. "I want the entire unit here so this is handled correctly."

CSU ARRIVED NEAR ten. The sky was gray, and thick clouds were moving in, promising rain in the afternoon. It was mercifully rainy-season cool, which would help retard decomposition of the dead bodies, but certainly wouldn't stop it.

The technicians took photos, got some serviceable fingerprints, and searched the vehicle and surrounding areas. They found nothing more of importance, and neither had Dawson.

No laptop, briefcase, purse, handbag, backpack, or any other personal belongings, so once the bodies had been collected and the SUV driven away to the Motor Traffic Unit at Kumasi Regional HQ, there was nothing left but the task of solving a new murder.

CHAPTER FORTY-SIX

FROM PAKYI, DAWSON HEADED immediately to the Golden Tulip Hotel in Kumasi. He was functioning, but life seemed surreal, slow, and thick, as if he were moving through soup. *How can Akua be dead?* He repeatedly saw her in his mind, collapsed and lifeless beside the Prado, and the blood on her face—so much blood.

He realized as he arrived in Kumasi that he had been navigating large portions of his journey without being aware of his surroundings—like sleep driving. He shook his head and blinked several times to wake himself up, refocus, and bring back reality to its baseline.

He turned off Victoria Opoku-Ware Road, onto Rain Tree Road near the Royal Golf Course, and into the Tulip's car park. Inside the hotel lobby, he went to reception and asked to see the manager.

"Please have a seat," the desk attendant said. "I'll call him."

But Dawson didn't take a seat in any of the comfortable chairs in the gleaming lobby with its twinkling recessed lights. He stared at their reflection in the polished tile floor, lost in thought. He jumped when he heard a voice to his side saying, "Good afternoon, sir."

He looked up and found the manager in front of him. His badge said SARPONG. He was small in stature and dressed in a navy suit, white shirt, and Adinkra tie.

"Good afternoon, Mr. Sarpong. My name is Dawson—chief inspector with CID. May I speak to you in private?"

"But of course. This way, please."

Dawson followed him to his office at the side of reception, which Sarpong unlocked with a swipe card. It shut behind them with a solid click. It was a quiet room with a thick carpet.

Before Sarpong offered him a seat, Dawson spoke. "I have some bad news. One of your guests, Akua Helmsley, was found murdered this morning."

"Oh!" Sarpong took a step back—staggered really—and held on to the back of one of the armchairs as if he might otherwise fall. "Oh, no."

His eyes were wide, his mouth open.

"I'm sorry," Dawson said, and instantly he felt himself return to normal, because now it was Sarpong in shock and Dawson who had to take charge.

Sarpong sat down weakly. "So that's why," he murmured.

"That's why what?"

"That's why the policemen were here yesterday."

"What policemen?" Dawson asked sharply.

"This morning when I came on shift," Sarpong said, "Mr. Brooks, the night manager, told me that around nine o'clock, two detectives from CID came to the hotel saying that Miss Helmsley had been reported missing and that they needed to search her room."

"Did the manager give you a description of the two men?"

"No, sir."

"Did they take items away?"

"Yes. They asked him to open the safe, and they removed documents from it."

What documents? Dawson frowned. None of this made sense. Commander Longdon had not mentioned this. He would have been aware, wouldn't he? Dawson thought about it for a moment. It was possible someone reported Akua missing to one of the larger Kumasi police stations like Manhyia Divisional Headquarters. They might have forwarded the report to Regional, which might have then sent two detectives down to investigate. Sometimes the left didn't know what the right was doing.

Something was still wrong, though. By nine at night, it would have been barely twelve hours or so since Akua had been seen last. That didn't constitute a disappearance. *Unless* . . . Unless whoever came to look through Akua's room already knew she was dead. Dawson's blood chilled. "May I see her room?"

"Of course you may."

They took the lift to her room on the third floor. The *Guardian treats its reporters well*, Dawson reflected, *unless it's Akua's own money that paid for this.* It was an executive room with a king bed, minibar, a sprawling bathroom, two armchairs with matching footrests, and a polished rosewood floor.

The desk was clear except the lamp on top of it—nothing in the drawers. The wardrobe had Akua's clothing both in drawer space and on hangers, with shoes on the floor of the wardrobe. The safe was indeed wide open and empty.

Neither of her two suitcases contained any items. Obviously she had not been planning on any travel. Dawson looked around. In fact, except for her clothing, this room had been emptied out, and anything else that Akua might have had in her possession on her excursion into the hinterland was now in someone else's hands.

"Thank you, Mr. Sarpong," Dawson said finally.

The manager cleared his throat. "Please, do you know whom I should contact regarding her belongings?"

"The Regional Headquarters will take care of it. I think they will inform the British High Commission as well as the family. I'm sure someone will be in touch with you very soon."

"Thank you, sir."

"Oh, one more thing," Dawson said. "Please give me the number of the manager who was here last night—Mr. Brooks, you said? I'd like to get a description of the men who were here."

WHEN DAWSON GOT back to the jeep, he perched on the side of the driver's seat with the door open and one leg out as he called manager Brooks. He tried the number twice before getting through. He introduced himself to Brooks, who confirmed the story of the visit by the so-called CID detectives.

"They were both dressed in black suits and black ties," Brooks said, "and they were wearing sunglasses."

Dawson almost laughed. It sounded more like that movie *Men in Black* than anything CID detectives would wear in real life. But it certainly appeared to have impressed Brooks.

"What else?" Dawson asked. "Age, height, body type?"

"They were both average height, one a little fatter than the other, with the belly sticking out. One had a mustache; the other did not. I would say they were in their thirties."

"What names did they give you?"

"Only one of them, the fatter one, showed his ID, and he said his name was Hammond."

"Did you stay with them while they searched the room?"

"Yes, sir. They were there for about ten minutes—that's all. They took some papers from the safe."

Dawson thanked Brooks and put in a call to Commander Longdon. He didn't pick up, so Dawson began heading back to the Obuasi office. His phone rang about thirty minutes later.

"Yes, Dawson?" Longdon said. "You called me."

"Good afternoon, sir. Please, were you made aware of any search of Akua Helmsley's hotel room conducted by two detectives from CID?"

After a pause, Longdon said, "I don't get you. You say what about Miss Helmsley?"

"Two men claiming to be from CID went to the Golden Tulip last night and ransacked her room. They took some documents from her safe."

"Impossible," the commander said at once. "No one in CID was authorized or asked to do that."

"Perhaps from Regional?"

"No, no," Longdon said firmly. "Someone else is behind this. I don't know who, but it is not CID."

"Then the only entity that comes to mind is the BNI," Dawson said.

"The BNI are the last people on earth to impersonate the CID," Longdon pointed out.

He's right, Dawson thought. He didn't have a high opinion of the Bureau of National Investigations, and had indirectly tangled with it before. If he had to write anything about it, he would describe the BNI as *Ghana's controversial internal intelligence agency whose authority overlaps with and sometimes unlawfully exceeds that of the police service.* Not an auspicious designation.

"What do you suggest, sir?" he asked Longdon.

The commander didn't speak for several seconds. "I will be meeting with DCOP Manu first thing in the morning, and we will come up with a plan, because this could potentially spark a political row between Ghana and the UK."

What he was saying in essence was that this had to be kicked to a higher level, and in fact, it might end up, ironically, in the hands of the BNI in the end. In the next thirty-six to forty-eight hours, Dawson might well be officially removed from any investigation into Akua's death. But Dawson didn't care. He was going ahead with it regardless. Whether it was fair or not, he felt culpable for Akua's death. He would not let the matter rest.

CHAPTER FORTY-SEVEN

EMOTIONALLY WRECKED AND TIRED after waking up so early, Dawson had no interest in returning to Obuasi Headquarters. He simply wanted to go home. So early was it in the afternoon, the house was empty on his arrival, a rare experience for him. Sly and Hosiah had football practice until about five thirty, and it was Christine's turn to pick them up.

First, Dawson called Armah.

"Oh, my Lord," he said, when Dawson had told him the news of Akua's murder. "I'm so sorry."

Dawson described the precision of the execution-style shootings, and then the mysterious men who went to her hotel room.

"The whole scenario is sinister," Armah said. "It sounds like she had a secret that someone didn't want to get out. She has such a wide Internet audience."

"*Who is that someone?* is the question."

"Yes, that is it," Armah agreed. "During your conversations with her, did she hint at anything sensitive?"

"The one thing I know she was working on was the story that the PMMC fabricates mining statistics and buys illegal gold, but days ago when I met her at The View restaurant, she started to tell me about what she believed were armed robbery scams in the Kumasi-Obuasi area—well, anywhere that gold is mined and/ or traded. She talked about investigating corruption surrounding gold dealings at the highest levels of authority."

"I see," Armah said. "Not good. People don't like that."

"I know. Which means they won't like me either, because I intend to continue on the path Akua was headed down."

"Be careful, Darko."

COMMANDER LONGDON HAD kept the dockets on the armed robberies, but as was Dawson's habit, he had taken a snapshot of the important pages with his smartphone. He had not done a transfer of pictures from his phone to a flash drive in a while, so he spent time doing that before deleting the images from the phone. No, he wasn't supposed to do any of this, but yes, he did it anyway because of the way records tended to disappear in the impenetrable recesses of police exhibit rooms.

He turned to the docket of the American ex-basketball player, Beko Tanbry. The events had transpired about six months before. The first image was the front of the docket.

DOCKET
GHANA POLICE FORCE

Date of offense: 12 March

Complainant: Tanbry, Beko

Principal Witness(es): Beko Tanbry; Kwadwo Yeboah (driver)

Accused: Unknown

Offense: Armed robbery

Victim(s): Beko Tanbry; Kwadwo Yeboah

Next was the report itself.

Police Report
Obuasi Divisional Headquarters Police Station

Date of Report: <u>12 March</u>
Time of Report: <u>1823h</u>
Date of Incident: <u>12 March</u>
Time of Incident: <u>1500 (approx.)</u>
Reporting Officer: <u>Detective Sergeant Augustus Obeng</u>

At 1815h on Friday 12 March, complainant and victim Mr. Beko Tanbry reported that he and his driver Mr. Kwadwo Yeboah went to a certain place several miles off the main road at the turnoff before Pakyi to purchase gold in the amount of 100,000.00 (one hundred thousand) US dollars from a certain man whose name was given as Mr. Michael. The purchase was executed and Mr. Tanbry and Mr. Yeboah were returning to the main road when they were forced to stop by a Mitsubishi SUV that was on the road across their path.

At that point, two gunmen with their faces completely covered by masks jumped out of the Mitsubishi and approached Mr. Tanbry's vehicle, demanding that Mr. Tanbry and Mr. Yeboah alight with hands raised. They demanded the gold that had been purchased, and when Mr. Tanbry stated that he was not in possession of said gold, he was assaulted by one of the robbers and threatened with death by the other. Mr. Tanbry then showed them where the gold was hidden in a compartment in the ceiling of the vehicle, and the robbers removed all the gold. They tied the two victims up and then escaped in the Mitsubishi. Neither Mr. Tanbry nor Mr. Yeboah was able to see a license plate on the vehicle.

Mr. Tanbry is a retired American professional basketball player in the US, age 42. He resides in Atlanta.

Were Mr. Tanbry's route and destination the same as Akua's? As far as Dawson knew, there was only one turnoff road just before Pakyi.

He went to the next page. It was a short entry from May 6:

> Mr. Beko Tanbry stated his wish to return to the USA. He is available by phone and email. Mr. Kwadwo Yeboah is also available by phone.

Dawson saw the phone number and hoped it was both correct and still valid. He dialed it. It was around noon in Atlanta, so the timing was right. He got voice mail and left a message, wondering if people in the US checked their voice mail. In Ghana, one seldom did.

Meanwhile, Dawson tried to do a search on this Beko Tanbry, but the URL got stuck and would not budge because of the all too common network congestion. Dawson sighed. It was so tiresome.

He thought he might as well take a look at the other armed robbery case—that of the Englishman, Charles Wilshire—but just as he was about to start, his phone rang and he saw it was a US number.

"Hello," Dawson said. "Please, are you Mr. Tanbry?"

"Yeah," he said, sounding wary. "Who's this?"

Dawson introduced himself and told Tanbry he was investigating a series of armed robberies in the Ashanti Region in which gold or its proceeds were stolen.

"Yeah, well if you think you're going to investigate *me*, mister," Tanbry said, "you're dead wrong."

"No, not that at all, sir," Dawson said evenly. "I'm making this call because I'm the new crime officer in Obuasi and I need to close some cases. I'm just asking for your help."

"I hope you're better than the crime officer who was there before," Tanbry said.

"He died of a stroke," Dawson said. "He had been sick for some time."

"Oh, damn. Sorry. Is that guy Longdon still there?"

"The commander? Yes, he is. Did you have contact with him concerning the robbery you experienced near Pakyi?"

"Yeah. After weeks of the crime officer at the time doing practically nothing—I guess he was sick, like you say—I went upstairs to see the commander to ask what gives with the investigation. 'Oh, we're working on it,' he says. 'We have several leads,' blah blah. Lyin' through his teeth."

"Please, can you describe the robbery incident in your own words, sir? It would help me a lot."

"Okay, but I gotta give you some background first, okay?"

"Thank you."

"So here's the deal," Tanbry said. "I have a clothing line and retail business in Atlanta. The last four years or so have been really tough. Last year, a Ghanaian friend of mine—I won't name him—started telling me about some scheme he had to make a lot of money buying and selling gold via an American contact there in Ghana named Granger."

"Chuck Granger?"

"Yeah. You know the guy?"

"Yes, sir—if it's the same one. I met him while investigating the murder of the Chinese miner who had a site adjacent to Granger's."

"Oh, right. I saw the Chinese guy a couple times when I went to talk to Granger—didn't know he got killed. What happened?"

"He was buried alive in the dirt."

"Shit. That's messed up. It's like the Wild West out there. Anyway, Granger is the one who was in that crappy reality show in Ghana about small-scale mining. The government kicked him and the crew out after a while."

"That's him."

"Yeah, so, my Ghanaian friend is talking about this gold scheme and I'm like, whatever, whatever. Then, back in January, he invites me to a meeting in a hotel with some other guys I didn't know, and he's put together this fancy PowerPoint presentation about how this Granger dude has at least half a million dollars worth of gold available for purchase. Get that out of the country and sell it in the right market, I could make a profit of a cool million."

"Where can you sell gold for that kind of profit?" Dawson asked. It seemed too good to be true.

"Dubai," Tanbry said at once. "The UAE government doesn't keep track of gold coming in or leaving the country. On the PowerPoint, my friend showed how the gold would be purified in Dubai from about seventy-five percent to ninety-nine point five, and sold for a massive profit."

"What about Mr. Granger? Was he included in the scheme?"

"After the purification, he was supposed to get a kickback, yeah, for sure. My Ghanaian friend explained that if you get a good supplier, you gotta give them a reason to be loyal and keep supplying the stuff."

"At this point, are you convinced by the presentation?" Dawson asked.

"I gotta say, it looked solid at the time, but I was still cautious and wanted to invest only ten thousand and not half a million— just to see how it went. But there's this Houston oil guy who's at the meeting as well, and he gets up and says he's providing the private jet to Ghana and arranging all the customs and immigration stuff, and he's not putting in those kind of resources for a measly ten thousand. 'You gotta think big, Beko,' he says, 'or don't think at all.'"

Dawson's image of the Houstonian was straight out of the movies: a blustering, stout man in a cowboy hat with a cigar.

"So they all piled up on me, arguing, persuading me, until I agreed," Tanbry went on, "but I had to see this gold for myself. Was I gonna trust just any dude with that kind of money? Hell, no. So it meant coming to Ghana. It wouldn't be my first time. Five years ago I was in Accra looking into real estate, so it's not like the place was completely strange.

"Took about six weeks to get everything in place. So I get out to Accra on the private jet, and then to Kumasi, then to Obuasi and Dunkwa and all that, and I meet Granger and I'm thinking I'm gonna buy the gold from him, but no, Granger only wants to do local stuff. He's got a Ghanaian middleman who does the international. This guy's name is Mr. Michael."

Mr. Michael again, Dawson thought. *Who is he?*

"So, I ask Granger how the hell I'ma contact this Michael dude. 'You don't,' Granger says. 'He's gonna call you.' Okay, so I wait a couple hours, and Mr. Michael calls me. Weird voice— creepy as hell. He tells me to head out toward Pakyi, make a left onto an unpaved road just before I get to the village itself, and just keep going till I come to his place. 'How far out?' I ask him. 'Not too far,' he says, which don't mean shit in Ghana, sorry to say, Inspector."

"Okay, go on," Dawson urged, ignoring the candid observation.

"I asked if I could bring an Obuasi gold expert with me to examine the goods, and Michael said okay. When we get there, it's this big-ass building in the middle of nowhere that looks like a fortress. The dude must be making a ton of money—got a giant generator that runs everything including the AC. He had two armed guards outside who frisked us for weapons, and then one of them took us down a bunch of corridors deep into this mansion till we get to this den. All the furniture there is shiny glass and chrome, floor looks like marble. There's an armed thug standing guard in the room, and this one little nerdy-looking guy sitting at the desk. So, of course, I think he must be Mr. Michael. I was wrong."

"Who was he?" Dawson asked, curious himself.

"Some damn assistant!" Tanbry exclaimed with a snort. "'Where's Michael?' I ask. Hell, I didn't come all this way to meet some assistant. But the assistant, who looks like he's got ice in his veins instead of blood, says Michael isn't available, but all the gold is set up and waiting for me according to his instructions.

"At first I was kinda doubtful, but when they brought out that gold for me to see, damn, it was beautiful, man. The gold expert with me told me it was top-notch and gave it the thumbs-up. So it's all weighed out and stuff, and the machine counts the cash I brought, and I get my gold.

"Couldn't believe how easy it was, man. I had a secret compartment in the ceiling of my SUV, so we put it all in there, but I was nervous. We'd driven about thirty minutes when we came around the corner and an SUV was blocking our way, and these two masked gunmen come out shooting, and I thought, this is it, I'ma get smoked. They make us lie facedown and tied us up, and they start ripping up the SUV looking for gold. Finally they find it and bolt, and I'm half a million dollars poorer, and I don't have any gold. That pisses me off."

"At any time, did you think that the attackers might have been in league with Mr. Michael?" Dawson asked, thinking that it was surely obvious.

"Are you kidding me?" Tanbry exclaimed. "That's not even all I thought. I began to suspect the police were in on it as well."

Dawson sat up. "Why do you say that?"

"Look, man, Longdon wasn't not investigating any of this shit because he was lazy or incompetent. It was because he was in with this Mr. Michael dude. And the little sergeant guy down there who supposedly took the report was probably taking orders from the commander. For all I know, once I'd left, they put my case in the round file."

"But do you have any *solid* proof that Commander Longdon was in league with Mr. Michael?" Dawson asked.

"I don't, but maybe someone else does. You ever hear of a journalist called Akua Helmsley?"

Dawson was startled. "Yes, I have." He hesitated to tell Tanbry she was dead. "How do you know her?"

"When I flew out of Ghana, she was in the seat next to me. We struck up a convo, and I told her pretty much everything that had happened to me. She said she'd like to do a story on it, and so we exchanged numbers. Months passed and I figured she'd forgotten about the whole thing when out of the blue she calls me."

"When was that?"

"Three days ago. She said she'd gone to see the commander about the gold scam."

Dawson frowned. Longdon hadn't mentioned Akua's visiting him three days ago.

"And then she said she planned to go out to see this Mr. Michael. I'm beggin' her please, Akua, this is too damn dangerous. I was worried as hell, and I'm praying she's okay."

I have to tell him. "Mr. Tanbry, sir. I'm very sorry to tell you that Akua Helmsley was found dead this morning."

He gasped. "No way. No fuckin' way. Goddammit. Shot, right?"

"Why do you say that?"

"Am I right, or not?"

"Yes, you are sadly correct. Seems like she was returning on the same route that you were when you were robbed."

"Ah, sweet Jesus," Tanbry whispered. "They killed her straight up, man. They fuckin' killed her."

"Who?"

"Mr. Michael, man. Him and his goons. Go get 'em, Inspector. They fuckin' killed her."

CHAPTER FORTY-EIGHT

OLD DEVILS WERE CREEPING back and burrowing under his skin like determined earthworms in the soil after a rain shower. His head knew he was blaming himself too much, but his heart begged to differ.

He left a note on the desk for Christine and the boys saying he would be back soon. Loathing himself more every passing minute, he got into the jeep and traveled from Melcom Road north to the Asafo Interchange. From there, he made a right, found a spot to park at the edge of Asafo Market, and went in and bought a cap with the Manchester United Football Club logo, and a pair of shades even though it was now dusk. Then, reasonably disguised, he took a walk toward the Neoplan bus station. Just before he got there, he made a sharp left down a narrow lane.

How did he know this place? He had heard of it, and then it was just a matter of following his nose. No, not the stink of urine in the alley—the other smell, sharp and distinctive and, yes, so familiar. Guys were languishing against the walls of the passageway, which opened up into a covered patio filled with smoke. A least a dozen men were sitting around casually puffing on joints, and fat ones too. A lot bigger than what one generally gets in Accra.

A guy with a clean-shaven head and built like a fort gave Dawson an up flick of the head, which identified him as the go-to. Dawson asked him about prices and found that *wee* was cheaper here than in Accra. Darko stood and smoked, daydreaming and floating, his stresses melting away. No good reason to give this herb up, really. Nothing wrong with indulging from time to time.

He had random thoughts, some of them making him laugh to himself. Like an undecided hummingbird, his mind flitted through a brightly lit field of characters: Bao Liu; his brother, Wei; the American man Chuck, who looked like a school-yard bully; Liu's wife, delicate Lian; Yaw Okoh and his morose father; Obeng and Commander Longdon . . . Dawson drifted back to Wei and something he had said. What was it? Something that didn't quite fit. He lost it. It was gone.

Dawson looked at the joint. Still quite a bit left. It was wonderful, yet he felt sick. He looked to his right and offered the rest of it to a guy who had finished his own but was looking wistful for more. He took it with a mellow smile. *"Medaase."*

HE DIDN'T WANT to go home smelling of smoke, so Dawson bought a new T-shirt on the way out of Asafo Market and exchanged it for the one he had on, which he handed to a random youngster sitting idly watching the world go by.

Dawson walked around the streets to clear his head, absorbing the noise of market sellers and blasting loudspeakers, the sight of merchandise in all its unrelated and colorful glory, and the smell of food cooking. He was ravenous, that much he knew. As for the *wee* smoking, he was neither angry nor pleased with himself. *Small wonder,* he thought sarcastically. *You're still high.* Later, he would be disappointed with himself, and it could mean he would not shake his despondent mood for a few days. *You don't have a few days.* He bought some Orbit peppermint gum, went back to the car chewing, got in, and headed back home.

THAT EVENING, AFTER Sly and Hosiah had gone to bed, Christine and Dawson sat together on the sofa. He had refrained from talking about the bad news until now.

"By the way," she said, as if reading his mind, "I heard about Miss Helmsley. I'm sorry, Dawson. I know you admired her."

He nodded. "Thank you. Yes, I did."

She leaned against him, and he put his arm around her. "And I owe you an apology for the other night—insinuating that you and her had anything more than a professional relationship. It was foolish talk."

"It's okay," he said, gently running his fingers through her elaborate weave. "It's nice to know you still get jealous."

She chortled softly. "Yes, but I could do better. What happened, Dark? To Helmsley, I mean."

"It was an ambush," he said. "She and her driver were shot in cold blood at close range."

"Oh my goodness. Awful." She shuddered.

"If only I had found out where she was going," he said, "I might have saved her."

She nodded. "Yes, I know you want to save everyone, but you can't."

"Yeah, so you claim."

She raised her head to look at him, and he was grinning. They laughed.

"Come on," he said, reaching for the TV remote, "let's find a movie to watch."

PREDICTABLY, CHRISTINE FELL asleep leaning against Dawson about halfway through the action movie, which starred a bunch of actors he had never heard of.

"Come on, sleep machine," he said, switching off the TV at the conclusion and shifting her off his shoulder. "Time for bed."

He shifted her and she groaned in protest, staggered up, and went sleepily to the bedroom.

WEDNESDAY MORNING CAME and went, and it wasn't until half past twelve that Commander Longdon called Dawson in for a meeting.

"The shooting of Miss Helmsley is having widespread reper-cussions," he said, folding his fingers together on his desk. "Her father is well-known and quite wealthy, and the Helmsley family are well connected with the British diplomatic corps. As you can imagine, it's important to handle this at the highest level. I had a meeting with DCOP Manu this morning, and she informed me that she will assign three detectives from Regional Headquarters to the case. In other words, they will be in charge of the inves-tigation from this point on. Our role will be supportive only. Is that clear?"

"Yes, sir," he said insincerely. He wasn't going to passively wait around for these three detectives to get to work.

"Do you have anything new I should know about?" Longdon asked.

"Yes, I do, sir," Dawson said, aware that he had to handle this delicately. "Akua Helmsley mentioned to me that she was writ-ing a story about the rash of armed robberies in the Obuasi area involving gold that foreigners had bought. Did she contact you about the matter at all?"

"No," Longdon said, shaking his head. "I have never spoken to the woman."

Dawson jumped slightly as he received an electric jolt to his left palm. Why was the commander lying?

"She didn't come to see you about four days ago?"

"Not at all. Why?"

"I believe that she was ambushed as she was returning from a visit to Mr. Michael, the gold dealer mentioned in Sergeant Obeng's report," Dawson said. "What do you know about this man, Michael, sir? Is his business legitimate?"

"As far as I know, yes. What is your interest in him?"

"I think he should be questioned in relation to the murder of Helmsley and Samuels. Sir, I know you want Regional to handle everything, but it will take them some time to get up to speed in this case, and time is of the essence. I want to go to Mr. Michael's place to question him."

"When?"

"Today. Now."

The commander looked uncertain. "I will have to clear it with DCOP Manu, and I will let you know shortly."

"Yes, sir. Thank you, sir. May I check back with you in about an hour?"

Longdon sighed wearily. "Yes, Dawson. You may."

CHAPTER FORTY-NINE

CONSTABLE ASASE HAD DONE almost a month of driving duty in the past, so he was fit to be at the wheel of the Tata jeep when he and Dawson started out from Obuasi to Pakyi. They got to the now infamous left turnoff and continued on the dusty laterite road. Asase handled the rough ride with ease, dodging cavernous holes and skillfully navigating treacherous muddy patches.

With more efficiency than Dawson had anticipated, the commander had provided a police jeep for the expedition within three hours, apparently with DCOP Manu's blessing.

"Boss, do you know exactly how far it is?" Asase asked.

"To be honest, I'm not sure," Dawson replied. "What I do know is that when we see the place, we'll know it."

But the farther they went, the more Dawson was plagued with an unsettling anxiety over the excursion. He shifted restlessly in his seat as they rounded a sharp corner.

Asase suddenly slowed down. "Sir—"

A black Toyota 4x4 was parked diagonally across the road.

Dawson knew at once what was happening. "*Shit*. It's a trap. Back up, *back up!*"

Asase slammed the jeep into reverse and raced backward. A man in dark clothes and a black mask got out of the Toyota with a pump-action shotgun and began running toward them. He brought the weapon to chest level.

"Get down, get down!" Dawson said.

Asase hit the brakes, and they ducked behind the dash as they heard the shotgun go off. But nothing hit their vehicle and no second blast followed. Dawson popped his head up. "He's running," he said. "Drive! *Get him!*"

Asase gunned the jeep. At first the would-be assassin tried to reach his vehicle, but he looked behind him and saw Dawson and Asase coming too quickly for him to make it. He swerved left and headed for the bush. At the verge, he stumbled and dropped his weapon. As Asase hit the brakes, Dawson swung open his door and jumped out, followed by Asase a second later, both running after the man. Dawson had been a little closer to him to start with, and began to gain on him. Tough shrubbery covered a depression at the side of the road. The man leapt across it, but he had misjudged both its width and depth, and he fell. Dawson put in a burst of speed and jumped into the depression, landing solidly on the guy as he started to scramble up. Dawson pulled him down. They wrestled briefly until Asase leapt in, and he and Dawson immobilized the man facedown.

Dawson fumbled for his cuffs, but Asase had his out already. Together they brought the man's hands together behind his back and cuffed him.

"Don't move," Dawson said to the man, gasping. He needed a second to catch his breath. He looked at Asase, who was pouring sweat. "Okay, we turn him over on three."

He counted and they flipped the man over. Dawson put his fingers at the base of the mask and ripped it off the man's face.

"Oh, my God," Dawson said, flabbergasted. "Obeng. Obeng, *why?*"

CHAPTER FIFTY

OBENG BEGAN TO WEEP. *"Mepa wo kyew.* I'm sorry. Please, I'm sorry."

"How could you do this?" Dawson was stunned. "Is someone else with you? Are you alone?"

"Yes, yes, I'm by myself," Obeng said.

"Are you lying to me?"

"No, please. I swear I'm alone."

"Let's take him to the jeep," Dawson said to Asase.

They pulled Obeng up to his feet and supported him as they climbed out of the depression, which was awkward and took some effort. The sun was ruthless and all three men were soaked with sweat. Asase went back to retrieve the shotgun.

Desperate to understand what was going on, Dawson sat in the back seat with Obeng. "Now, start talking," Dawson snapped. "Who sent you?"

The sergeant bowed his head. "Please, I need protection," he said weakly. "If you guarantee that me and my family will not be victimized for telling the truth, I know I can trust you, and I will talk."

"I will do my best," Dawson said, not wanting to overcommit himself, "but I'm losing patience now. Who sent you, Obeng? Who ordered you to kill us?"

The sergeant looked down at his hands. He seemed paralyzed.

"Mr. Michael sent you?" Dawson asked.

Obeng shook his head. "No, sir."

"Then it can be only one other person," Dawson said. "Commander Longdon."

Almost imperceptibly, Obeng nodded his affirmation.

In the driver's seat, Asase recoiled and looked away. "No," he said firmly. "That cannot be. Not the commander. Excuse me to say it, boss Dawson, but this is a lie. Why the sergeant is accusing ACP Longdon of this, I don't know, but it has to be this Mr. Michael."

Obeng grunted, bitter amusement in his expression. "Constable, what you are saying is funny because Mr. Michael and the commander are the same person."

Asase's head whipped around and Dawson jerked upright. "*What?*"

"Yes," Obeng said, nodding. "One and the same."

"How is that possible?" Dawson asked skeptically.

"When, for example, a businessman wants to trade in gold," Obeng began explaining, "a middleman like Mr. Granger will tell the businessman that Mr. Michael will call him about the deal. You can never call Mr. Michael. Granger will inform the people at the mansion—they are all Longdon's family members—and they will take the number of the businessman, pass it on to the commander, and tell the businessman to wait for Mr. Michael's call. The commander will call the businessman and arrange the deal. He disguises his voice and tells the guy what time he should go to the mansion. Anytime someone arrives at the mansion expecting to see Mr. Michael, they are told that he is not available but that he has left all necessary instructions to complete the deal."

"So no one has ever seen the Mr. Michael they *think* they are speaking to," Dawson said, "because he doesn't exist."

"Yes, sir," the sergeant said. "Commander Longdon gives the orders for the robberies after the person has left the mansion. Whether they sold or bought gold, whatever they have on them is stolen and goes back to the mansion. The victim loses twice. When the victim reports the crime, the case goes to the Obuasi

Division. What happens with such case is the same thing Mr. Tanbry experienced."

"In other words, the investigation goes nowhere," Dawson said grimly.

"The commander will tell the victim about the increase in this kind of crime over the past year," Obeng continued, "and how the department will do its very best to get to the bottom of it. Some people like Mr. Tanbry are suspicious, and the lady, Akua Helmsley, was getting close to understanding how the scam worked. She was dangerous to Commander Longdon. He wanted to destroy even the slightest threat."

It was worse than Dawson ever could have imagined. "He had her and Samuels killed?" he asked.

Obeng nodded. Dawson thought bitterly back to the day before when Longdon had called him about Akua's murder. At the scene, the commander had expressed his outrage. *Cold-blooded brutality. It's a terrible shame.* Dawson recalled his words clearly. And all along it was Longdon himself who was responsible?

Could Obeng be lying? Dawson didn't think so. "Who carried out the ambush on Miss Helmsley and Samuels?"

Obeng looked up wearily. "Two guards at the mansion—the *machomen.* They did it early in the evening the day before Miss Helmsley and Samuels were found."

"Where were you?" Dawson asked.

"I was on duty in the charge office that day," Obeng said.

That would be easy enough to check, Dawson thought.

"You see," Obeng continued, "the first time I was caught drinking on the job, the commander told me he would spare me from being sacked if I could help him with some simple services, and I'd also get some money out of it. I started being a guard at the mansion one or two times when I was not on duty, and then one day Commander Longdon's cousin asked me to substitute for one of the guards in a certain kind of operation. I didn't know what it was until almost the time of the ambush, when the guy I was with said all I had to do was help him get the two men in the vehicle out at gunpoint and then stand guard while he got cash out of the vehicle."

"And you were paid for the job?" Dawson asked.

"Yes, please. I got my share of the cash."

Dawson could deduce what had happened over the last few hours. "Early this afternoon, Commander Longdon called you to say he had an emergency job?"

"Yes, please. He told me two people would be traveling in a jeep and that I should shoot to kill, but he didn't tell me who would be in the vehicle. When I saw it was you, I couldn't do it. I just fired the shotgun and hoped it would scare you away." Obeng looked at Dawson. "You don't know how much the commander hates and fears you."

The "fear" part surprised Dawson at first, but what Obeng really meant was Longdon feared that the truth would be found out.

"One more question, Obeng," Dawson said. "Was it you who told some of the Chinese miners when a raid was coming?"

"Yes, sir," he said.

"Did the commander tell you to do it?"

"No," Obeng said, head down. "I did it for the money. The Chinese people gave me a small dash for the information. This is Ghana. You do whatever you can to get money."

How very true that is, Dawson reflected.

KUMASI

NOVEMBER

CHAPTER FIFTY-ONE

DAWSON SIPPED HIS MALTA while Daniel Armah had beer on a late Saturday afternoon as they sat on the back porch and reminisced. The older man had about five stories for every one of Dawson's. They came around to the topic of Commander Longdon.

"Tell me again how you took him into custody," Armah said, settling comfortably back in his chair. "I never get tired of hearing about it."

"This is how it went," Dawson began. "When we went to the commander's house, he was in the sitting room having drinks with friends. He was surprised to see us. 'What are you doing here?' I went up to him and touched him on the shoulder. I told him he was under arrest as an accessory to murder, armed robbery, and all the rest of it."

"His reaction?" Armah asked.

"Surprisingly calm. He told me that as a junior officer, I could not arrest him and that I should get out. And at that point, in walks DCOP Manu, who says coolly, 'I am your senior officer, so I'll do the arresting.' Commander looked confused, as if he didn't really know what was happening to him. DCOP Manu cautioned him, and told him, 'Come along, it's time to go.' And the best part is she turned to his guests and said, '"Excuse the interruption. Please carry on."'

Armah laughed. "What a wonderful woman she is."

"She will oversee the Obuasi Division until they find Commander Longdon's replacement," Dawson said.

"She will do more than a capable job," Armah said. "But listen, there's one other person I'm curious about. The American guy—Chuck Granger? How does he fit in, if at all?"

"I think he's in the clear," Dawson replied. "He has an alibi provided by Tommy Thompson, and even though Thompson could have cooperated with him to provide a fake one—meaning Granger really came back to Kumasi from Accra earlier than he said he did—I don't think Granger had the slightest interest in Bao Liu."

"I see. Well done, Darko."

"Thank you, Daniel," Dawson said warmly. He hesitated before speaking again.

"I sense something is bothering you, isn't it?" Armah said, smiling gently.

Dawson sighed and leaned forward, rubbing his forehead as if it hurt. "I'm just not one hundred percent sure that Yaw Okoh really killed Bao Liu. I lose sleep over it every night."

Armah nodded. "That little voice of intuition of yours always speaks the truth. If this is bothering you, you must go back again over the same territory and look for something you missed."

CHAPTER FIFTY-TWO

IN SUNDAY'S SWELTERING NOON heat, Dawson found Mr. and Mrs. Okoh working on their *cassava* farm. Both were hoeing and turning the dry soil, but she had the additional burden of carrying a small child on her back.

"*Ayekoo!*" Dawson called out, recognizing their hard work.

They responded in kind, mopping their brows of sweat as he came up to them, and, exchanged greetings. They invited him over to the shade at the edge of the plot, and they sat on a fallen log.

"How are you?" Dawson asked them.

Mr. Okoh turned the corners of his mouth down and turned his palms up briefly. "By His Grace, we are managing."

Dawson nodded. "And who is this little one?" he asked, gently passing his fingers over the soft hair of the infant strapped to Mrs. Okoh's back.

"That is Ama," she said with a smile, glancing over her shoulder. "Amos's child."

"She is sweet." Dawson said. He looked up at them. "Have you seen Yaw?"

"Yes, please," Okoh said, looking sad. "We went to visit him last week at Kumasi Central Prison. All the life has left his body."

"I'm sorry," Dawson said.

Mrs. Okoh cast her eyes down. "He is suffering," she said. "He won't eat. He has become very thin."

Dawson couldn't imagine a thin Yaw. "Mr. and Mrs. Okoh, deep in my heart, I no longer feel your son killed the Chinese man," he said. "He wanted to save his father from going to prison."

"Yes, please." Okoh said, and his wife murmured agreement. "God bless you, *Owura* Dawson."

Dawson sat a little forward. "Is there nobody else that you know who might have wanted to kill the Chinese man?"

Okoh looked at him with weary eyes. "Please, I can accuse someone just to get my son out of prison, but that won't bring me any peace either, will it?"

Dawson didn't need to answer that. "I will do my best to free your son." And he added, importantly, "By His Grace."

IN THE EVENING, while Christine and the boys played a noisy board game, Dawson sat at the table in the sitting room and went back over his notes page by page. This is exactly why he jotted things down. Once something was said, done, or observed, it was over forever. One might think one has a good memory, but the mind always distorts, regardless.

Dawson read through Wei Liu's interrogation after the man had almost assaulted Kobby. He could understand *why* the Chinese man, in his distraught state, had done that, but it was absolutely not an acceptable excuse. Again, he wondered how these Chinese illegals viewed Ghanaians. With disdain?

Some of Dawson's notes were short—like those about his chat with Danquah at Ofin Trading. Not that they weren't important, just that Dawson didn't think their content was as crucial as that of others. He read over what he had quickly written down after he had visited Wei at his home.

misses Bao
grief stricken, if only heard alarm and Bao trying to call
denies he knew about police raids b4hand

Dawson went back to his interview with Wei at the police station and frowned. He skipped forward again. And then back.

Discrepancy. His heart began to thump in his chest. Was he mistaken? He looked again. No, there *was* a discrepancy. He leaned back and for several minutes watched Christine, Hosiah, and Sly as they moved pieces and counted out spaces on their board game. Christine groaned as she was returned right back to the start. "Oh, goodness," she said. "Why can't I ever win this silly game?"

Dawson got up and went to the bedroom to lie down for a while and stare at the ceiling as he tried to tie everything up. He must have dozed off for a while, because the next thing he knew it was 10:25. The boys were already asleep, and Christine was watching the news in the sitting room. Dawson came around to her and kissed her on the cheek. "I have to go out," he told her. "Something has come up in the case, and I might not be home tonight."

She looked a trifle anxious, but it wasn't as if she weren't accustomed to Dawson's episodic late-night police operations. "Please be safe, Dark," she said.

CHAPTER FIFTY-THREE

AS HE DROVE TO Kwadaso Estates, Dawson thought about the questions he had for Wei Liu, questions that could be crucial to solving the case. As he approached the house, a glistening silver Mercedes pulled up in front of the gate from the opposite direction. Was that Bao's car that Lian was now driving? Dawson stopped the Corolla and watched as a woman got out. Yes, it was Lian.

She unlocked the door to the side of the gate and entered. Seconds later, she pulled open the gate with some effort, and Dawson deduced that David the watchman had Sunday off. Dawson parked quickly as Lian got back in the Mercedes. He jumped out, stayed low, and trotted up behind the car at an angle as Lian drove through. The motion sensor lights in the yard lit up as the Mercedes parked next to the Kia.

Dawson scuttled right to hide behind the wooden shed in the corner of the yard. Lian returned to the gate to close and padlock it, then went to the front door of the house. Wei opened it, greeted her, and she entered. The door shut firmly behind them, and Dawson heard the turn of two locks.

What is she doing visiting her brother-in-law at this hour? The sensor light turned off, but Dawson had spotted more along the side of the house underneath the eaves. He hoped he was right that the sensors were probably set so it would not be triggered by something moving close to the ground, like a dog or cat. Still, approaching the building was risky, and he hesitated to do it.

Try it. He got down on his belly and slowly pulled himself along the ground like a crab until he reached the house. From his previous visit, Dawson figured out that the window above him belonged to the sitting room. An external AC compressor was on full blast a few feet to his left. The window was heavily curtained, and Dawson could see nothing inside, but he could hear Lian and Wei chatting and laughing with the TV on in the background. *A pleasurable visit for both of them, obviously,* he thought. He soon heard the clink of bottles and glasses. Bao's wife and brother seemed to be extraordinary happy so soon after Bao's death. Or perhaps they were drinking in his honor—some kind of Chinese custom. Not that Ghanaians were any better—drinking to oblivion at funerals.

After twenty-five minutes of crouching by the wall and hearing no change in the pattern of conversation and drinking, Dawson was getting stiff and began to wonder if this move had been wise. He'd learned nothing all that special, and worst of all, he was trapped inside the compound. The wall and gate were topped by an electric fence, so he could not get out that way.

Then, the TV went off, and the voices faded. *They must be leaving the room.* Dawson reversed his position, crept back in the direction he had come, made a right-angled turn along the next wall, and traveled laboriously at a crawl to the other end. It was exhausting and he was breathing heavily. A bulky generator stood at the rear of the house. This time he saw no sensor lights mounted along the wall, but the darkness was more pronounced than at the front of the house, so he wanted to be sure. Fumbling for his miniature Maglite, he realized he had forgotten it.

No matter. Skirting another droning compressor mounted on the wall, Dawson ran low along the ground until he reached a lit, tightly shut window. He could hear muffled music from within, and Chinese dialogue that he guessed was a TV movie. He stood up slowly, off to the side of the window.

Just as he was to take a peek, an electric power cut plunged the house and the yard into darkness, and the compressor went silent. *Shit.* An alert went off in Dawson's mind. If the generator wasn't wired for an automatic switchover from the grid, Lian or Wei—or both—would come outside to turn it on. That meant Dawson had to be ready to bolt in whichever direction would keep him hidden.

He waited, counting out fifteen seconds, which was the usual interval for a switch from the grid, and to his relief, the generator wheezed, and the engine started up and roared into action. The light in the room came on again, and the AC started up. *Good,* Dawson thought with relief, bringing one eye level with the window frame.

Curtains partially blocked his view, but Dawson saw enough. Intently watching their briefly interrupted TV movie, Lian and Wei lay in bed in each other's arms. At intervals, he pulled her close and gave her a kiss on the lips. Dawson had begun to suspect something was going on as Lian arrived at the house, but actually witnessing the event was still startling. Wei and Lian were seriously involved with each other. *For how long?* If they were adulterers before Bao's death, it changed everything.

Dawson took photos of the couple's tender embraces, as well a short video segment, stopping as Wei began to get more aroused and the TV movie faded from their attention. Dawson felt a little perverted, but business was business.

The light in the room went off, and Dawson heard the couple murmuring and moaning. He called Manhyia Station for assistance. The Lius' lovemaking was about to be rudely interrupted.

CHAPTER FIFTY-FOUR

DAWSON SAT UP AND squinted at the dawn creeping in the window and wondered for a second where he was. He had slept only a couple of hours, resting his head on his arms folded across one of the tables in the CID room at the Manhyia Division. Had last night been a dream? No, it hadn't.

At first, Wei had resisted arrest, and a small struggle between him and two officers had ensued. Lian became oddly limp and almost as difficult to handle. On the way to the station, both were quiet, their heads bowed.

It was twelve after six now. Dawson went to the washroom to freshen up. When he returned, he acknowledged the two CID detectives who had come in and were sitting complaining about the increasing frequency of electricity cuts.

Dawson called Christine. She had obviously been waiting for his call and answered before the second ring. "You're okay?"

He chuckled. "Yes, love. Everything's fine. Sorry—I should have texted you earlier."

"It's all right. When will you be home?"

He sighed. "It will be a long day, for sure. Early evening, I hope."

"Okay, I'll let the kids know."

At times like this, the clash between a "normal" life and dedication to his job hit home hard.

•　•　•

IN THE MALE cell, a sea of black prisoners, the bulk of them between eighteen and twenty-four years old, swamped one little Chinese island—Wei Liu. He looked both resentful and scared as Dawson called him to the front. "Good morning, Mr. Liu."

He didn't return the greeting. He appeared dispassionate, perhaps too tired to show much emotion.

"I will be interviewing you very soon," Dawson said.

Wei drooped, and turned his face away.

At the female cell, though, Lian was not taking things as calmly. She was distraught, weeping at intervals. Her Ghanaian counterparts stared at her, and some of them began to giggle. Furious, Lian turned to yell at them in Chinese. *Poor woman*, Dawson thought. Her husband dead, she and her lover in jail with people she didn't like in a country she hated.

ASASE BROUGHT WEI to the CID room and sat beside him. Dawson took a seat on the opposite side of the table. Wei fidgeted and did not make eye contact.

"How do you feel this morning, Wei?" Dawson asked.

He didn't answer.

"We're going to have a talk," Dawson continued. "No more lies. Just the truth. Okay?"

Wei's jaw contracted rhythmically, but still he said nothing.

"When you and I first met," Dawson said, "Mr. Huang told me that your brother Bao came to Ghana about three years ago, correct?"

Wei, resting his forehead in one palm, nodded.

"Mr. Liu, I need you to answer my questions so that we can hear you." Dawson said. "After Bao was here for two years, he wanted Lian to join him, and he asked you to accompany her, am I right?"

"Yes."

"You and Lian love each other, not so?"

Wei shifted his weight. "Yes," he said sullenly.

"When did you fall in love with each other? In China, before Bao and Lian got married?"

Wei shook his head. "No. After they marry." He sighed. "Sometimes, Bao go away to do mining for one month, two month—leave Lian alone."

"So you used to keep her company," Dawson prompted, thankful Wei seemed to be emerging from his cold, hard shell. "And that's how it happened that you fell in love."

"Yes."

"And Bao never knew about it?"

Wei sneered slightly. "No." He shrugged. "And he don't love her either."

"I see," Dawson said, pausing. "Then when Bao left China for Ghana, you and Lian were left together for two years?"

"We were happy," Wei said, with sudden enthusiasm. "Very happy."

"I understand. How did you feel when Bao asked Lian to come to Ghana?"

Wei shook his head. "Lian not want to leave China, but she have to obey her husband. Only thing, she happy I go with her."

"And while you were here," Dawson said, "you continued to be with her whenever you had a chance and Bao was away."

"Yes, sir."

"You said Bao didn't love Lian. Why do you say that?"

"He don't love her like *I* love her," Wei said fiercely, pointing at his heart.

"Did Lian hate Bao?"

Wei nodded. "Yes."

"And you hated Bao too?"

The Chinese man shook his head. "I never hate Bao. Only love Lian."

"Did Lian ask you to kill Bao?"

"*No!*" Wei exclaimed in alarm, perhaps realizing that his words were being misconstrued. "She never do that."

"But *you* wanted to kill Bao," Dawson said, "so that you could have Lian to yourself. Just like you had her to yourself for two years in China."

"No," Wei said flatly.

"I know you killed your brother, Wei," Dawson said evenly.

"No." He gestured simply by turning his palms up. "How I kill him? I sleep Feng house by that time, but you wan' me say I kill Bao because you Ghanaian guy and you no like the Chinese people. You know is that guy Yaw who kill Bao, but you wan' me take blame."

And there, Dawson conceded, Wei had him in a corner that was going to be difficult to get out of.

TIRED, DAWSON SET off for home. The afternoon had worn on and worn him down. He would try again with Wei in the morning. The man was bound to confess. But a small voice nagged at Dawson. *Are you sure Yaw Okoh is not the killer?* Was Dawson hunting for something that simply wasn't there? Was he really biased against Wei because he was Chinese? It was the first time an accusation like that had come up in Dawson's career.

When Dawson got into the house, he heard the boys in hysterics and found them watching a DVD on the laptop while Christine was cooking. He glanced at the screen, saw they were watching a cartoon, and then went to his wife's side to put an arm around her waist.

"Mm, smells delicious," he said, lifting the pot lid and getting a whiff of heavenly groundnut stew. "I'm famished."

She smiled at him. "We'll eat in a few minutes. Just boiling the yam."

"What's so funny, guys?" Dawson asked, sitting down at the table.

Hosiah and Sly looked at each other conspiratorially and started to giggle.

Dawson sent an inquiring glance at Christine.

"I'll tell you exactly what they're laughing at," she said, appearing miffed. "They're watching a cartoon called *The Sleepy Hippo* or something like that, and they say when the hippopotamus starts to snore, it sounds like me."

This sent the two boys into stitches again, with Hosiah almost falling out of his chair. "Look, Daddy," he said. "I'll show you."

Dawson waited while Hosiah found the right spot on the DVD where the hippo sank to the ground and began to snore. Sly and Hosiah looked at Dawson for his reaction, and as much as he tried to keep his face straight, he could not hold his snort in. Seconds later, he was stifling laughter as the boys went weak with hilarity.

"Oh, you too?" Christine said, shooting Dawson a daggered look. "Look, I don't snore. You guys are crazy."

Through the boys' giggles, Dawson told them to put the laptop away and get washed up for dinner, both because the joke had outstayed its welcome and because he was hungry.

But as the family ate and talked, Dawson gave more thought to the sleepy hippo, and then he began to understand who murdered Bao Liu and how.

CHAPTER FIFTY-FIVE

EN ROUTE TO KUMASI Headquarters, Dawson heard the doubt in DCOP Manu's voice as he spoke to her on the phone and tried to explain why he needed an emergency search warrant, which a senior officer was authorized to sign.

"It can't wait for a magistrate's approval, madam," Dawson said. That tedious process could take a day or more. "By that time, we may have to release the suspects."

She sighed. "I'm in a meeting right now. We are about to interview Commander Longdon. I will call you as soon as I'm done."

"Um, madam, if it wouldn't be too much trouble to do it immediately," Dawson said in his best suppliant voice, "I would appreciate it, because actually I'm on the way to you now and will be there in about fifteen minutes."

Manu said something under her breath that Dawson didn't quite hear. "All right," she said, defeated. "Hurry up."

ASASE DROVE THE police jeep, Dawson sat in the front next to him, and the Lius sat in the backseat. They arrived at Wei's house, and David let the vehicle into the front yard of the house, watching with curiosity as the group alighted, including the Lius in handcuffs.

The warrant was for the entire premises, both inside and outside the house, but they would start with inside. Asase and Dawson guided the prisoners to the sofa in the sitting room and they sat down.

"We are examining all pieces of electronic equipment," Dawson told Asase. "Search the bedroom for any computer, laptop, tablet, phone, and bring them out here if you find any. I will start on these."

Asase disappeared into the bedroom. The sitting room center table held Wei's Samsung tablet, an iPad, two Xiaomi phones, and a laptop, which Dawson asked Wei to turn on and access with his password. Dawson looked at the browser history, which showed sites selling mining equipment, from large machines like excavators to smaller items such as sluice boxes.

On the Samsung, Dawson found Chinese news sites and a few for downloading Chinese movies, but the history was otherwise uninteresting. One of the phones was inoperable, and the other had an insignificant browsing history. The iPad was pretty new and had little on it besides the software that came with it.

Asase came out of the bedroom with another mobile phone and put it on the table. It looked newer and sleeker than the other two.

"Which of these phones do you use?" Dawson asked Wei.

He pointed at the newest one, and Dawson asked him to open up to messages. But Wei had the phone set to Chinese, and Dawson had no idea what the messages said.

Dawson hadn't found what he wanted. He and Asase looked through the kitchen as well, to no avail.

"Let's go outside," Dawson said. "We'll take the suspects with us."

The small wooden shed behind which Dawson had hidden after following Lian into the yard seemed inconsequential, but it was all that was left to search.

The door was padlocked, but the latch was flimsy, coming apart with Dawson's firm tug. The shed's interior was musty and damp. Barely enough to fit one person, the space was filled with electronic waste: two old TVs, circuit boards, a couple of discarded laptops and desktop computers, keyboards, and the skeletons of three vintage flip phones—nothing like what Dawson had imagined when he first saw the shed.

Leaving the others clustered around the door, he stepped in and moved some of the clutter aside, stirring up a puff of dust. He sneezed twice as he sifted through the piles of discarded equipment on the floor. Nothing of any use there. He transferred his gaze upward to a listing shelf containing a ball of tangled copper wires, which he took down. Behind it was a padlocked, grayish-blue lockbox. It stood out because it was much newer than anything else in the shed and nowhere near as dusty.

Dawson took it down and tried the lid without success. "Whose is this?" he asked Wei. "Where is the key?"

Wei shrugged. "I don' know."

Dawson didn't believe him. He examined the box, which had a simple lock on the top. The question was where the key was. A locksmith down the street could probably have this open in seconds, but there might be an even quicker way. Where had Dawson seen a bunch of keys? He remembered now.

"Go back inside the house," he told Asase. "At the side of the door is a bowl with keys in it. Bring them all."

While the constable was gone, Dawson stood and stared at Wei, who looked studiously away with his jaw clenching. Asase came back with the bowl, which contained five keys. One of them looked like the right size, and Dawson inserted it into the lock, which turned easily. He opened the box. On the top, he found Chinese and American currency, a large wad of *cedi* bills, and some receipts for purchases made at a warehouse.

At the very bottom, the box held two objects. The first was another key, this one bearing the CAT logo. Dawson held it up to Wei. "The spare key to one of Chuck Granger's excavators. Am I right?"

Wei didn't answer, but Dawson was perfectly sure that it was the one missing from the four hooks in Granger's office.

The second object in the box was an electronic device of about four by one and a half inches, with a small screen at the top. Dawson picked it up at its edges and rested it on the lid. "Olympus digital voice recorder," he read out. "Made in China, naturally."

Dawson used the corner of his voter ID card to turn it on, and then alternated between the FWD and PLAY buttons. No sound came forth, and Dawson could tell from the screen, that the recorder had had three erased recordings. The fourth, however, was still there. He glanced up at Wei and smiled. The Chinese man looked away. Dawson pressed PLAY, turned up the volume, left the recorder where it was, came out of the shed, and shut the door behind him. From within came the sound of someone snoring.

"That's what you left playing in your room at Mr. Feng's house when you went to kill your brother," Dawson said to Wei. "Feng heard it in the middle of the night and thought you were in the room sleeping, but by that time, you had already left the house through the window early enough to give yourself enough time to wait for your brother at the mining site and then to murder him."

Wei stayed motionless and kept his gaze down.

"Chuck Granger gave you the key to the CAT excavator," Dawson said. "He tied up your brother and you operated the excavator to bury him alive. Because you and Granger worked together, you had enough time to return to your room in Feng's house before six o'clock when he came to wake you."

No one actually saw Lian move. She did so with the swiftness of a cobra strike. Her hands cuffed in front of her, she came at Wei and hit him in the face with a double fist. He fell over with a grunt. She went down with him, screaming in Chinese while striking Wei repeatedly. Dawson and Asase pulled her off. Now, so weak from her emotions and physical exertions, she could only crumple to the ground weeping.

Asase helped Wei sit up. Blood was streaming down his face from a deep cut in his forehead where Lian had hit him. He turned to her, calling her name several times, trying to get her to look at him, and then saying something in Chinese in a tone that Dawson thought sounded anguished and pleading. But what exactly was

Wei telling her? He grabbed the voice recorder from the shed, switched it on, and came close to Wei so that he got it all.

As Wei continued to address Lian, he broke down completely and sobbed.

"Bring something to stop the bleeding," Dawson said to Asase, who ran to the jeep and returned with a not-so-clean rag, but it would have to do. Asase pressed it to his forehead and told him to hold it there.

Dawson knelt down beside Wei. "Why is she so angry with you?" he asked, rubbing his back gently. "What was she saying to you? Eh? Come on now, Wei. It's time to tell me."

"She never tell me to kill Bao," Wei said, looking up at Dawson imploringly, "but I do it for *her*. I thought make her happy now she only have me, but now she say she like Bao for husband, make her feel safe. She like me too, but for lover only. She want us *both*. Why she say that, Inspector? She love me, she hate Bao, but now I kill him, she say want him back. Why she say that?"

Wei fell back, looked to the sky, and bellowed in the purest agony.

CHAPTER FIFTY-SIX

THE DAWSONS WERE DRESSING up for a Sunday afternoon outing.

"What I don't understand," Christine said, adjusting her earrings in the mirror, "is what you were looking for on Wei's computers and all that."

Dawson pulled on his socks. "You remember when Sly and Hosiah were joking around about the snoring hippo?"

"How could I forget?" Christine said dryly.

"It got me thinking how you can get almost any sound effect online, including someone snoring. I was searching for evidence in Wei Liu's browser history that could show that's what he did, but nothing was there. It never occurred to me that he could simply record himself snoring with a device and play it back. He tried three different times to get the recording just right and he erased them all. The fourth one was the best, and that's the one he forgot to erase."

"You say Wei claimed he killed Bao all for Lian," Christine said. "He was lying, wasn't he?"

"Maybe not a conscious lie," Dawson said. "I think that's how he rationalizes it to make it more acceptable to both himself and Lian. In the final analysis, though, Wei killed his brother for selfish reasons alone."

Dawson called out to see if the kids were ready. They said yes, although Hosiah hesitated in his reply, meaning he probably was not.

"And Chuck Granger?" Christine said, stepping into her flats. "What about him?"

"He was Wei's accomplice," Dawson said, buttoning up his shirt. "He tied Bao up while Wei brought over the excavator to bury him. You see, Chuck wanted to annex Bao's mine, but Bao was having nothing of that. Wei, on the other hand, wanted to join forces with Chuck and offered that in return for Chuck helping to kill Bao. But the *real* reason Wei wanted to kill Bao was that he wanted to have Lian all to himself. He loved her and felt he deserved her more than Bao did."

"What about Commander Longdon?" Christine asked. "What's going to happen to him?"

"DCOP Manu got a full confession from him," Dawson answered. "He, Granger, and Tommy Thompson at PMMC were in league with each other. Thompson covered for Granger's fake alibi. Granger sold illegal gold to Thompson. Thompson lied when he said Akua never came to PMMC to talk to him, and he also alerted Longdon that Akua was hot on the trail. When she went to see Longdon, that confirmed what Thompson had said, so Longdon had her killed."

"And he tried to get *you* killed as well," Christine said, shaking her head.

"What really bothers me about that," Dawson said, "is he didn't care if Asase got shot as well in the process."

"Ruthless," Christine said. "Okay, enough of that. Are you ready?"

"Yes."

Hosiah and Sly were outside kicking a soccer ball back and forth.

"Boys!" Dawson thundered. "Not in your good clothes. *Please!* You should know that by now."

He and Christine ushered the kids to the car.

"Where are we going, Daddy?" Hosiah asked, settling into the rear with Sly.

"We're going to see the Okohs," Dawson said, starting up the

Corolla. "They're a nice family I met while I was doing my investigation."

"Where?"

"In Dunkwa. It's south of here. You'll see."

"What's in Dunkwa?" Sly asked.

"Gold," Dawson said.

"Ooh," Hosiah said, brightening. "Can we get some?"

"No," Dawson replied flatly. "Stay away from the stuff. It's a lot more trouble than it's worth."

GLOSSARY

Adinkra *(ah-din-KRA)***:** symbols carrying particular meanings or that are proverb based.

Agya *(eh-JA)***:** father. (Twi)

Akwaaba *(ah-KWAH-ba)***:** welcome.

Akan *(ah-CAN)***:** largest ethnic group in Ghana, residing primarily in southern regions of Ghana. Also: Akan languages.

Ampa *(am-PA)***:** that's true.

Anaa?: or? (Twi) Often said at the end of a question.

Ayekoo *(ah-yay-Kohh)***:** well done, congratulations (acknowledgment of someone's hard work, especially physical).

Banku *(ban-KU)***:** cooked, fermented corn dough.

Bolgatanga: capital of the Upper East Region of northern Ghana. (*Bolga*, abbreviated)

Cedi *(SEE-dee)***:** Ghana's monetary unit.

Chaley (cha-LAY): bro, pal, dude (colloquial). May be affection-ate and/or tinged with playful disdain.

Cocoyam: edible tuber; known elsewhere as *taro.*

Cutlass: machete, probably the most common murder weapon in Ghana.

Dabi (deh-BEE): no. (Twi)

Ewe (EH-way): ethnic group of the Volta Region of Ghana, as well as Togo and Benin.

Ewurade (ay-wu-rah-DAY): God, often an exclamation.

Fufuo (fu-fu-aw): dense, glutinous carbohydrate made from pounding boiled yam, *cassava,* or plantain, and eaten with differ-ent varieties of soup.

Galamsey: small-scale miners or mining, often illegal (corrupted from, "gather and sell").

Grass cutter: large rodent common in sub-Saharan Africa, captured and bred for food. The meat is high in protein, low in fat.

Guinness Malta: lightly carbonated, non-alcoholic malt beverage, brewed from barley, hops.

Head porter: a person who carries large, commercial loads on the head.

Hip-life: hip-hop infused with Ghanaian styles.

Inshallah: God willing. (Arabic)

Juju: referring to the occult, belief in curses, talismans, and fetish objects.

Kenkey (KEN-kay): balls of fermented corn dough; a favorite among Ga people.

Kente (ken-TAY): a silk and cotton fabric made of interwoven cloth strips; indigenous to the Akan, but all ethnic groups wear it.

Keta (KAY-tah): coastal town in the Volta Region of Ghana.

Kwasea (kwa-see-ah): foolishness, stupidity.

Maadwo (mah-JO): good evening/night.

Maakye (mah-CHIH): good morning.

Maaha (mah-HAH): good afternoon.

Machoman: thug.

Medaase (mih-dah-sih): thank you. (Twi)

Memu mo aha: good afternoon (to two people or more).

Mepa wo kyew (mih-pa-wu-CHEW): please. (Twi) Literally, "I take off my hat to you."

Mmofra (MOH-fra): children. (Twi)

Mo!: well done! Congrats.

Ní hăo (nee-how): hello. (Chinese)

Oburoni (oh-bu-ro-NEE): foreigner, white person.

Onyina (oh-nyee-NA): variety of tree/wood in Ghana.

Oware (oh-wa-RAY): board game played with pebbles and shallow wells carved in wood.

Owura (oh-WU-rah): mister.

Palava: unnecessary fuss or trouble (from *palaver*: prolonged, idle talk).

Red-red: black-eyed peas with fried ripe plantain cooked with palm oil and spices.

Tro-tro: passenger minivans, usually holding fifteen to twenty people.

Truck pushers: young men, usually in pairs, who move around town pushing four-wheeled carts bearing scrap metal and other loads.

Twi (chwee): one of the Akan languages.

Waakye (wah-chih): rice and beans.

Wee: marijuana.

Whatsapp: a popular instant messaging app used by millions in Africa and other regions of the world (almost unknown in the USA).

Yaa nua (yeah-nwa): reply to a formal greeting, e.g., *Maakye*, to someone of equivalent age.

Xièxiè (shieh-shieh): thank you. (Chinese)

ACKNOWLEDGMENTS

My sincere thanks to the following:

Lance Corporal Frank Antwi Boasiako, for his friendship and assistance with CID procedural details.

Daniel Osei Owusu, for information on Chinese miners in the Ashanti Region.

Kwame Obeng, for extensive tours of alluvial and deep mining sites in the Ashanti Region.

Chris, Charity, and Frank Scott, for their hospitality at Four Villages Inn, Kumasi.

Esi and Amowi Sutherland, for introduction to and tour of the lovely and inspirational Mmofra Park in Accra.

Sammy Mensah, for his unparalleled driving skills on treacherous rural roads.

Lukas Jones-Quartey, for inspiring one of Hosiah Dawson's charming eccentricities.

Many thanks also to the two investigative reporters who shared invaluable information with me but wished to remain anonymous.